THEY WERE LOOKING FOR ANSWERS IN ALL THE WRONG PLACES.

DR. PHYL FORSTER—At thirty-seven she was at the top of her form, secure, successful—and lonely. Until Bea led her into the past—and desire blinded her to danger . . .

DETECTIVE FRANCO MAHONEY—He was the perfect macho cop, with the soul of a poet and the palate of a chef. Nothing could divert him from the trail of a killer—until he met Dr. Phyl . . .

BEA FRENCH—It was the name she gave herself when she could remember no other. Amnesia—and Dr. Phyl—were her only shelter, until a letter from beyond the grave awakened the terror again . . .

NICK LASCELLES—He was the answer to Bea's dreams, a writer researching a book on crime on the Riviera, a man to protect her—even as he dug up skeletons from her past . . .

BRAD KANE—Tall, blond, and gorgeous, the Hawaii tycoon was looking for the perfect wife. Until he saw Phyl and knew she was destined to be his . . .

D1044625

By Elizabeth Adler

ELIZABETH ADLER

The SECRET of the VILLA MIMOSA

A DELL BOOK

Published by
Dell Publishing
a division of
Bantam Doubleday Dell Publishing Group, Inc.
1540 Broadway
New York, New York 10036

The trademark Dell® is registered in the U.S. Patent and Trademark Office.

ISBN: 0-440-21748-2

Printed in the United States of America

Published simultaneously in Canada

December 1995

10 9 8 7 6 5 4

OPM

For my sisters
Dorothy and Irene

and my brother-in-law
Peter

and for my father and Ken
with love

Heaven from all creatures hides the book of fate.
—ALEXANDER POPE, *An Essay on Man*

Surely there are in everyone's life certain connections, twists and turns which pass awhile under the category of Chance, but at the last, well examined, prove to be the very Hand of God.
—SIR THOMAS BROWNE, *Religio Medici*

The SECRET of the VILLA MIMOSA

~ *Prologue* ~

*T*he man was blond, tall, and definitely handsome, with the kind of well-muscled body that looked as good in clothes as you knew it would out of them. He parked the rented automobile—a white Lincoln Town Car, not the Ferrari or even the sporty Jeep Cherokee that you might have expected from one with his cool, slightly arrogant attitude—at the arrivals area of the San Francisco airport, then glanced impatiently at his watch. The evening flight from Honolulu was late, and parking for more than a few minutes was risky. He might be noticed, moved on by the traffic cop, given a ticket. He strode quickly into the arrivals building and checked the flight information screen. The plane had landed five minutes earlier.

Outside again, he leaned against the car, hands thrust into his pockets, watching the doors. He smiled when at last he saw her. Her soft dark copper hair swished around her shoulders as she headed for the taxi line. She didn't even notice him, didn't hear his footsteps as he came up from behind. He heard her gasp as she felt the quick prick of the needle in her arm. Her terrified brown eyes recognized him, and he smiled at her. With scarcely a sound she slumped into his arms and was bundled easily into the backseat of the waiting automobile.

He quickly flung a blanket over her, slipped into the driver's seat, and pulled into the line of traffic crawling toward the city. He shrugged and lit a cigarette. What the hell, he had plenty of time. In fact he had time to kill.

Forty minutes later he parked the car on Battery, stepped out, opened the back door, and looked at the girl. He checked her pulse and lifted her eyelids. She was out for the count. No trouble from her. He pushed her onto the floor, covered her with the blanket, and locked the car. Then he lit a cigarette and strolled casually around the corner to Il Fornaio.

The brasserie was crowded. The noise bounced from the walls as he pushed his way through to a seat at the counter, ordered a Carta Blanca and a small pizza with mozzarella, anchovies, olives, and capers. While he waited he checked the basketball scores in the *Examiner*. He had another beer with the pizza. Then, because he never could deny his sweet tooth, he ordered a tiramisu.

"That's about as close to heaven as a dessert can get." The young woman sitting next to him smiled. "I can never resist it myself," she admitted.

She took a sip of her margarita. Her hair was red and shoulder length, and she was about the same age as the girl he had just left, drugged and unconscious, in his automobile. He shrugged and called for his check. "Once in a while is okay."

She had given him an opening, and he could sense her waiting, but he turned away, heading for the cash register by the door. He felt her curious eyes on him, heard her laugh, sensing the so-who-cares shrug of the shoulders that accompanied it. She was pretty and she wasn't used to rejection. It was just that tonight she had picked on the wrong guy.

He unlocked the car, lifted the blanket covering the girl, and checked her again. She was still out, so he climbed into the driver's seat and eased the car into the traffic on Embarcadero. He knew exactly the spot he was heading for, but it was still too early—too much traffic, too many people, too many lights.

He cruised slowly through town, looping back on himself several times, finally heading north through subdivisions, past an area of elegant estates, past a golf course, up to where the road ran along the edge of a steep, wooded ravine.

He stopped the car and pulled the girl off the floor. She lolled against him and he cursed her dead weight as he half carried, half dragged her through the trees until he stood in a small clearing on the edge of the ravine. The fog had disappeared. A three-quarter moon illuminated the rocks and scrubby trees and, far below, the tumbling stream that wound its way along the bottom. He hesitated, thinking longingly of the gun in his pocket. But it had to look like an accident. This was the only way.

He lifted the girl to her feet. He held her in his arms for a second until he got his balance. Then, with all his weight, he thrust her over the edge into the abyss.

She made no sound. She didn't even know what happened.

The moon went behind the clouds and the fog rolled back, winding ghostly tendrils around him as he strained to hear the sound of her fall. With a pleased whoosh of expelled breath he turned and felt his way through the trees to the car, then drove slowly through the dense fog, back to the sumptuous anonymity of his suite in one of the city's finest hotels.

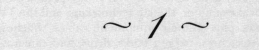

~ 1 ~

*H*omicide Detective Franco Mahoney of the San
Francisco Police Department watched impassively as
the men from the Fire Department Rescue Services
clambered down Mitchell's Ravine toward the girl's
body. Not that you could see much of her, just her foot
in a red sandal and her arm sticking up through the
underbrush that had stopped her fall but failed to save
her life. Now she would be just another statistic on the
unsolved homicide list. He had seen it all before, but
now he had a job to do. He had to find her killer.

He glanced at his watch. It was 8:00 A.M. His shift was
just finishing, and he thought longingly of the other,
luckier guys, heading wearily for home or for breakfast
at the diner on Brannan, talking over the night's mayhem or maybe just talking dirty, letting off steam. It
had been a long night: the usual drug killing in an
alley; a stabbing in a squalid tenement room with more
blood from the tiny Chinese victim than he had ever
seen in a butcher's shop; and a body of a man tossed
out onto the highway and run over several times before
he was discovered and found to have been shot. The
call about the girl in Mitchell's Ravine had come at

7:34. It was his turn, his bad luck at the tail end of the shift. Some nights he wondered if he had done the right thing, becoming a cop.

He sighed as he surveyed the clearing at the edge of the ravine. It was crowded with guys from the Fire and Public Health departments as well as the paramedics, the medical examiner, the lab technicians, and the TV news crews, plus all their equipment: cables, winches, ladders, stretchers, oxygen tanks, drips, and cameras. The damp grassy clearing was now a sea of mud.

There had been just enough time to look around and assess that there was no sign of a struggle before the rescue services arrived, and by now any vital clues had disappeared, churned into the mud.

Several uniformed cops, their eyes fixed on the ground, were sifting through the undergrowth, but Mahoney knew in his gut they were not going to find anything. There would be no torn-off buttons today, no threads caught on a branch, no spent bullet casings, no perfect clue.

As a murder crime scene it was a dead loss. He grinned, excusing himself the pun. *Agatha Christie would have had just one perfect footprint,* he thought longingly. *Me, I'm left with just a body.*

And once the rescue services had arrived, that body had taken precedence. Everything must wait until it had been retrieved, even if it meant trampling on the evidence. The woman in the ravine still had her rights as a person, though probably for the last time. Then she would become just another toe-tagged Jane Doe in the chilly steel drawer in the city morgue until the public medical examiner finally got around to carving her up in search of physical evidence. Or until some distraught parent or grieving—though maybe not—relative recalled that Aunty Flo or sister Joleen or Cousin Peggy Sue hadn't been seen around in a while and came inquiring.

Mahoney turned reluctantly to face the TV news cameras and told them briefly what he knew: that the body of a woman had been discovered early that morning by a man out walking his dogs. No, the man was not a suspect. And no, he had no other suspect as of that minute. Thank you and good-bye.

Franco Mahoney had been a cop for fourteen years, seven of them as a detective on the Homicide Squad. He was said to be one of the best, a meticulous sifter of information and a finisher. He was known as a cop who never let go of a case. Years might pass, but Mahoney never forgot an unsolved murder. The facts and evidence rerolled themselves in his head in bed at night, and sometimes something clicked. He'd gotten convictions on a number of homicides that had been pushed to the back of the filing cabinet, labeled "unsolved," by sheer persistence, hard work, and intuition.

He had a "nose" for a killer. "It's like I can smell them. They are like bad meat, guys. That's all there is to it," he would tell the news reporters whose favorite he was because he always kept his sense of humor and always gave them a good story, and besides, he looked good on TV. The perfect macho cop.

"She's coming up," the chief of the rescue squad yelled.

Franco watched as the sling stretcher was winched carefully upward. He had seen more murder victims than he cared to remember. Like any cop, he knew the only way to keep his sanity was to keep a mental distance between him and the victim. When that victim was a child, it was humanly impossible, and when it was a young woman, like this one, it was tough.

She was maybe twenty-four; her face was grotesquely swollen, a mass of purple bruises with livid red patches where the skin had been scraped away. There was dried blood on her nose and ears, indicating a fractured skull, and her copper hair was matted with dark, congealed blood. Maybe she had been pretty, he thought bitterly. Fun-loving, free. Until last night, when some cheap bastard decided not to let her live.

He stepped back to let the paramedics take over as she was winched over the edge. Clearing his throat, he began to take notes: "Female Caucasian. Probable age 24. Estimated height 5'7". Weight 115. Hair red—"

"Jesus, man, there's a pulse. She's still alive!"

The paramedics were kneeling over the stretcher, frantically inserting a drip into her arm, feeding her oxygen through a mask, wedging her broken skull with sandbags. They quickly eased pressure pants over her legs, inflating them to constrict the blood flow, forcing the blood pressure into her upper torso and head, then enveloped her in shiny aluminum shock foil.

"Wait a minute." Franco stared at the double row of puncture wounds along her right forearm. "What's that?"

The paramedic looked closely at the punctures. "Damn me, Mahoney, those are teeth marks. A dog bite, I'd say. And a biggie."

Mahoney followed them back through the woods as they rushed the young woman back to the waiting ambulance and loaded her quickly in. "Think she'll make it?" he asked.

The paramedic shrugged. "I don't even know if we can stabilize her to get her as far as Trauma."

Mahoney sighed as he assigned a uniformed cop to the San Francisco General Trauma Unit. "Stay outside the operating room," he ordered. "Let me know if she wakes up." It was no longer his business to care. He was a homicide detective. He needed a body before he could do his job.

"No need for us yet, Mahoney," said the medical examiner, Pete Preston, climbing into his car. His job also came after death.

"Not yet, Pete," Mahoney said. "But I have a feeling in my bones this one's gonna be murder." He sighed, shrugging off the early morning's events. "How about I buy you a cup of coffee?"

In the Pacific Heights apartment where she lived alone, Phyl Forster awakened, as usual at 7:30 A.M. There was no need to turn off an alarm because she didn't need one. It was part of her medical training. She had learned to catnap when she had a spare ten minutes and to wake up routinely.

Thirty-seven today, she thought, striding toward the bathroom. *Surprising how it creeps up, and funny that I still feel only thirty-six.* She paused and looked around her glamorous apartment. She glanced at the huge windows with their view of San Francisco Bay, at the shelves of books, the interesting paintings and pieces of sculpture by young American artists. She admired the old silk rugs that were scattered on the pale wooden floors, and the hi-tech bathrooms and kitchen, all steel and halogen, white, gray, and black.

Some people considered her home, with its deliberate lack of color, soulless, but Phyl thought the rugs and artworks and books were what gave it life. All the rest was just background, the accoutrements of living: there to serve and not for show. "Plain but good," as somebody's grandmother would surely have said approvingly. And all bought and paid for by herself.

She dressed in the same spare style: monochromatic understated chic by Japanese designers. With her shiny black hair sleeked into a chignon, her pale skin, her red lipstick, and her startled-looking deep blue eyes, she was a familiar figure on television and at book signings across the country. As well as having a successful psychiatric practice, she also wrote popular psychology books that sold in the millions. *Dr. Phyl Focuses on: Matrimony. Dr. Phyl Focuses on: Menopause. Sibling Rivalry. Divorce. Drugs, Alcohol, Domestic Violence.* Any trauma you could name Dr. Phyl could explain in simple terms and tell you how to cope or how to overcome it. Oprah loved her.

She showered, thinking of the day ahead: a morning clinic at the San Francisco General Hospital, where she gave her services free, the afternoon at the University of California Medical Center, where she was a consultant, then private patients from four-thirty to seventhirty. Try to beat the traffic on her way home. Shower, then a glass of red wine.

Afterward, wrapped in a white terry robe, with her black hair tumbling free from its tight chignon, her face clean of makeup and artifice, she would have supper. Alone. Again.

But now she was toweling her hair dry as she watched the early-morning newscast on TV. Political scandals; traffic; weather . . . plus some news just in. Another homicide. A macho-looking detective told her that the victim was a young woman discovered in a ravine by a man out walking his dogs.

Phyl watched, fascinated as the cameras zoomed in on the rescue services clambering down the ravine to the woman's body, half hidden among the foliage of a large bush. They got her into a sling and began to haul her up. She caught a glimpse of coppery red hair, an outflung pale arm, a foot with a red leather sandal still dangling from the toe.

She shuddered and pushed the off button, horrified at her own voyeurism. She had surely seen enough dead bodies in her years as a hospital intern and resident, but this was obscene. The girl looked so vulnerable, her final moments exploited by prying TV cameras. Last night she had been alive, perhaps out with her friends, walking, talking, maybe having dinner, dancing. Poor thing. Phyl knew she had to be somebody's "little girl." And no doubt today that mother would be told the dreadful final truth.

"Goddamn," Phyl said savagely. She switched on the hair dryer and glared at herself in the bathroom mirror. Life could be rotten, as many of her patients could testify, but it was better than what had happened to that poor girl.

She dried her hair, swept it back so tightly her scalp hurt, then twisted it into a knot at the nape of her neck. She dressed quickly. She wore minimalist silk underwear: She was lean, and her curves had no need of underwires and Lycra, and besides, the silk was her touch of luxury, her secret beneath the facade of severe black and white she presented to the world. Sometimes she shared that secret, but not often these days. She shrugged as she buttoned the jacket of her black pantsuit. What the hell, work ruled. Besides, celibacy was fashionable.

Leaning into the mirror, she applied the Paloma red lipstick carefully. Without the bright lipstick her mouth looked soft and vulnerable. Colored a vivid velvety red, it made a statement. She was a woman to be reckoned with. A woman at the top of her profession. A woman who knew what she was doing every minute of her day. Even if sometimes, she thought with a pang, her nights seemed a bit lonely.

She clipped gold and onyx studs in her ears, no other jewelry, just a man-size watch, big enough for her to tell the time without lifting her arm, big enough so her patients wouldn't think that she was keeping her eye on the clock.

She picked up her black suede purse, felt for her keys, and checked her working uniform one last time.

After grabbing the big black bag containing the files she needed for the day, she took the elevator down, got her car, a compact black Lexus, as understated as she was. Then she drove to the real world: the San Francisco General Hospital on Potrero Hill.

It was only 8:20 A.M., and her first appointment wasn't until 9:00, so she headed for the cafeteria and the cup of coffee she hadn't been able to stomach earlier, after seeing the dead woman on television. Halfway along the corridor she changed her mind. The Italian deli down the street made more powerful coffee —and a wickeder Danish.

Outside, she heard the scream of an ambulance. She turned to watch. The paramedics were out in a flash, and a second later they had the stretcher on a gurney and were running with it, one holding the drip leading into the patient's arm, toward the waiting group of doctors and nurses. The patient's body was swathed in shiny aluminum shock foil. Her head was strapped to the stretcher and supported by sandbags on either side. Phyl caught just a glimpse of a bruised ashen face, tightly shut eyes, blood-matted copper hair. *The girl from the ravine.*

She's not dead after all, she thought, surprised. Then, remembering the waxen color, she added grimly, *Not yet.*

Somehow the Danish didn't seem as enticing as it had a moment ago. She turned on her heel and walked back into the hospital, her head down, thinking about the young woman; about the parents who would be summoned to her bedside, about her chances of survival. It was clear she had serious head injuries, and

Lord knew what other damage, internal as well as external.

Poor, poor girl, she thought sadly.

Shaking her head to clear it, she grabbed a cup of coffee from the machine and headed down the shiny corridors to her office to begin her day.

By twelve-thirty she had seen eight patients, and she was starving. Gathering together her notes and her files and putting them in the black bag, she thought hungrily of tomato, chicken, and fresh basil on focaccia. Halfway to the door she hesitated, glancing undecidedly at the telephone. She still hadn't been able to get the sight of the young woman from the ravine out of her mind. Right through all her interviews this morning she had kept superimposing herself on her thoughts: the foot with the jaunty red sandal dangling from its toe; the battered face as colorless as moonstones; the bloody head. A shudder ran through her, and she strode quickly out the door and down the hall to the Trauma Unit.

Recognizing her, the nurse on duty smiled. "You mean the Jane Doe who was brought in at eight twenty-two this morning," she said briskly in response to Phyl's inquiry. "They assumed she was dead when they saw her down there in the ravine, but when they got her up, she still had a pulse. And broken ribs, possible internal bleeding, and a couple of holes in her skull, left temporal area. They rushed her right into OR, and she's not out yet." She glanced up from her notes. "I guess they're doing their damnedest for her," she said encouragingly. Then suddenly alert: "You know her then?"

Phyl shook her head. "I saw the rescue on the morning news. Somehow she just stuck in my mind."

"I can imagine," the nurse said feelingly. "It's a pity you don't know her, though, because we have no identification. The cops are searching the ravine for her purse or any other clues, I guess. But as far as I know, she's still just plain Jane Doe."

"Maybe they'll run her picture in the newspapers," Phyl suggested, still thinking of the mother, not knowing her child was so near death. Surely a mother's touch, the sound of her voice, just her presence in the same room would help. Suddenly it seemed terribly important to find her, to bring her here.

"There won't be any pictures," the nurse said. "Not the way she looks. Even her own mother wouldn't recognize her."

Phyl sighed regretfully as she thanked her and turned away. It was foolish to become so involved; she didn't even know the young woman. Still, she hoped she made it through. Forgetting all about the focaccia sandwich, she drove slowly through the traffic to the Medical Center at UCSF.

Later she saw her private patients, and for once she found herself losing her concentration. She was relieved when her last patient failed to show at seven, and it wasn't until she was driving home that she remembered she hadn't eaten a thing all day.

No wonder you were losing it, she admonished herself, because she felt guilty that she hadn't given her all to her patients. She swung the car onto Sansome, turned again on Embarcadero, and found a parking spot right in front of Il Fornaio.

As usual, the restaurant was jammed. "I could seat you at the bar, Doc," the hostess said. Phyl often dropped in after work when she was too tired to think of fixing supper at home, and everyone there knew her well. "There's a quiet corner where no one will bother you."

The hostess showed her to a seat at the far end of the bar and handed her a menu. Phyl ordered a glass of red wine. A copy of the *Chronicle* was lying on the counter. It ran a picture of the rescue scene at Mitchell's Ravine on the front page. WOMAN'S BODY FOUND IN

RAVINE, was the headline. She read it, surprised, but then remembered that at first everyone had thought the girl was dead. Probably tomorrow, unless something more important took over the news, the paper would reinstate her in the land of the living. Unless, by then, she *was* dead.

She toyed with her pasta, thinking about going home to her empty apartment, remembering it was her thirty-seventh birthday. On an impulse she ordered a glass of champagne and then almost instantly regretted it. A birthday celebrated alone was not a real birthday.

She flicked through the newspaper, stopping at an enticing travel article about Paris. "Paris." The very word sounded full of promise: springtime and chestnuts in blossom, café tables under the trees, and walks by the Seine. A handsome man in your bed, sharing cups of hot, strong coffee the next morning . . . The stuff of dreams on a rainy San Francisco night.

She sighed wistfully again. She recalled vaguely there was to be a psychiatric conference in Paris later in the year. Maybe she would find time to attend. Feeling better, she called for her check, powdered her nose, and added a flash of Paloma red to her lips.

The woman sitting next to her turned and smiled as she got up to leave. Her red hair swung around her shoulders, and Phyl thought with a pang of sorrow of the girl hovering between life and death in intensive care at the San Francisco General.

She called the hospital from the car. The neurosurgery had been successful, but the girl was in a coma. The doctors were still not sure about brain damage. It might be a while before they knew, one way or the other.

Tears spilled down Phyl's cheeks as she drove slowly home. She was remembering things she did not want to remember, things that as a good psychiatrist she had tried to put behind her: the fear and the guilt and the grief . . . And now, because of a brutalized red-headed girl lying in a hospital, they had all come flooding back again.

Fool, she told herself severely. *You're a damn fool, Phyl Forster.*

~ 3 ~

The girl was hurtling through a dark tunnel, faster, faster toward a speck of light. She needed that light, needed it urgently, yet no matter how fast she catapulted toward it, it was always the same distance away. But she knew she must not let it go; she had to catch up with it: it was where she belonged. Faster, she told herself, faster, fly toward it . . . and then she was falling, oh, God, she was falling, drifting down, arms outstretched. The sound of the wind was in her ears as she fell into an abyss from which she knew she would never return.

"No," she screamed. "No, no, no . . ."

"It's all right, honey, you're okay. Just don't worry about a thing."

She tried to open her eyes, but her lids seemed to have weights on them. And she couldn't move, couldn't feel. There was no use flying down the tunnel toward the spot of light. She was dead after all. "I don't want to be dead," she cried, anguished. "I don't want to be—"

"You're not dead, honey," the nurse said soothingly. "You're right here in the hospital. You had an accident, but you're going to be okay. Don't worry about a thing."

The girl did not trust her. She knew the abyss was

waiting. "Then why can't I open my eyes?" she whispered hoarsely.

"You will, honey. You will. Just give yourself time. Lie quietly now. Rest. The doctor is on his way."

She lay still, taking in the sounds around her: the low hum of machinery and electronic bleeps, the rustle of starched cotton, and the pad of rubber-soled feet across the room. She could smell things, too: hospital smells of disinfectant and soap. And something sweet, a gentle floral scent that was hauntingly familiar. So delicate, so pretty, so . . . familiar. But she just couldn't recall exactly what it was.

She tossed her head in frustration on the pillow, then gasped as a pain like a hot knife shot from the base of her skull and exploded somewhere in her brain.

"Lie still, honey." The nurse pressed her back against the pillows. "Here comes the doctor now," she added, sounding relieved.

There was the sound of brisk footsteps, then a cool hand on hers and gentle fingers on her pulse. "Well, young lady, we're certainly glad to have you back with us again." The doctor's voice was crisp, deliberately cheerful, encouraging.

"Why?" she asked in her new, strangely hoarse voice. "Did you think I was going to die?"

He laughed, a nice easy sound, and she felt her own mouth stretch into a smile. "We try hard not to let the pretty patients die on us," he joked.

"Sexist," she whispered, and heard him laugh again.

"The truth," she begged. "Please. Tell me the truth."

She could feel him hesitate. Then: "There was an accident. You were injured. Broken ribs, damage to the spleen—we had to remove that—"

"My head," she insisted. "What happened to my head?"

"Depressed fractures of the skull, in two places. We operated, fixed you up. Good as new."

"Then why," she asked plaintively, "can't I open my eyes?"

He lifted her left lid and shone a light into it. It bounced somewhere in the back of her brain, triggering memories of daylight and sunshine. Maybe she had come out of the dark tunnel after all. "Are you real?" she whispered, still not believing.

He took her hands in both his. They felt strong, comforting, human. "You are in the San Francisco General Hospital. You've been in a coma for almost three weeks. You're alive all right. Now all you have to do is get better. And don't worry about opening your eyes. Soon enough they will open, and then you can check us out for yourself. Meanwhile, get some rest. Maybe later we can talk again. Then you can tell us who you are."

"Who I am?"

"Later," he said. "Don't worry about it now."

She heard his departing footsteps on the floor, a whispered conversation with the nurse, the closing of the door. From the deepening silence she knew she was alone.

An accident, he had said. Three weeks in a coma. In San Francisco. Was San Francisco her home then? She thought about it for a minute. Vague images of Telegraph Hill, the Transamerica building, the Golden Gate Bridge flipped through her mind. She told herself triumphantly, *You do know it.* But she did not know this hospital; she didn't know where it was or what had happened that had put her here.

An accident. She pondered the word, visualizing a car crash, the harsh screech of metal against metal, the sharp crescendo of breaking glass, the burn of brakes and rubber, but it was like a film without characters; it meant nothing to her. She did not remember it. She shivered. *Maybe it was better she didn't.*

The doctor had said head injuries, a brain operation. . . . The pain zigzagged upward again as she turned her head restlessly, and she moaned. And then it came to her. She couldn't open her eyes because her face was smashed. They were keeping her sedated so she couldn't see the terrible faceless mess she was. . . .

She tried to lift her hand, she wanted to feel it, trace the damage with her fingers, but her arm was anchored by needles and tapes and drip bottles and machinery.

Tears of despair trickled from her closed eyelids, coursing a hot, salty path down her cheeks, into her ears. Like a child, she thought; in bed, crying in the dark, calling for her mommy—except there was no mommy.

"Mom?" she said tentatively, out loud. But she knew her mother was not there. She tried to bring a picture of her into her mind, but nothing came. *That's odd,* she thought, puzzled. *I can remember how the Transam building looks, and the Golden Gate Bridge, but I can't remember my own mother's face. I can't even remember her name.*

My *name.* She searched the blackness inside her head for an answer. There was none. There was just nothingness, and the tunnel threatening to drag her back again, away from the light, away from remembering. Away from life.

"You're going to be fine now, honey." The nurse's voice had a smile in it. "Maybe tomorrow we can unhitch you from some of these drips and machines. And maybe, if you're good, you can have a little ice cream for your supper."

"I don't like ice cream," she replied automatically.

"Well, frozen yogurt then. You like that, don't you?"

Did she? She couldn't remember, yet she had just remembered she didn't like ice cream.

Panic forced her eyelids open. They lifted slowly, like a theater curtain on a dim set, but still it dazzled her.

Gradually the room swam into focus. Someone was bending over her; the light behind her head was like a halo.

It was a madonna's face. Pale skin, dark hair, red lips parted in a welcoming smile. She felt a cool hand on her brow as the madonna said, "Hi there. Glad to see you're finally awake. I'm Phyl Forster."

The girl gripped her hand as though it were a lifeline. "Phyl," she whispered, "you must know me. *Tell me who I am.*"

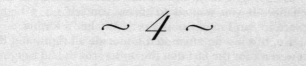

~ 4 ~

Mahoney leaned back in his swivel chair in the squad room on the fourth floor of the precinct station, concentrating on what he had just read about the Jane Doe found in Mitchell's Ravine. It wasn't much, that was for sure. Multiple injuries, in particular two depressed skull fractures that might have been caused by a blunt instrument. On the other hand, they might have been sustained when she bounced from the rocks.

Then there were the dog bites. Obviously she had raised her right arm to protect herself from an attack. The dog was big, no doubt about it. "We're talking your Rottweiler, Doberman-type dog," the experts had told him. "Not your pit bull, though. They have a different grip. And a pit bull would never have let go."

Had a stray Rottweiler attacked her? Chased her to the edge of the ravine? Maybe she had stepped back, unthinkingly, into the abyss. He shook his head; he didn't think so. Where there was a dog like that, there was a man. Had he set the dog on her? Had he planned to rape, then kill her? He shrugged wearily. The world was full of crazies. Anything was possible.

He went over the details yet again. There was still no

identification. There was an around-the-clock uniformed cop waiting at the hospital, and since he hadn't heard anything from him today, he guessed the girl was still in a coma. It was still a "will she or won't she make it" situation.

He thought about suicide and decided there was no chance. If you wanted to throw yourself off a high place in San Francisco, it wasn't Mitchell's Ravine.

No, this was an attempted homicide all right, and if it weren't for the fact that the undergrowth had caught and held her, and for the marvel of modern neurosurgery, then it would have been "homicide," not just "attempted." And God knows there was nothing harder to prove than "attempted" murder; he knew only too well that it was likely to be downgraded to "aggravated assault." Either way the poor girl was the loser. She either lost her life or lost the satisfaction of sending her assailant away for a lot of years.

He pushed back his chair and strode to the coffee machine. He took his coffee black with no sugar. Tasting it, he wished it were stronger, then decided that with the amount he drank on any given day he'd probably be a shaking caffeine wreck if it were.

Mahoney was a big man, thirty-nine years old, a fitness fanatic who spent what spare time he had working out at the Y or running in the hills. A two-time San Francisco Marathon runner, he had plans for the New York event. Maybe he would do it next year, if he could make enough time to train up to it—and get off the coffee habit. Still, the caffeine addiction was better than the addiction of the Italians on his mother's side of the family, who drank more grappa than anyone he knew and still stayed standing. And the Irish half, his father's side, who could put away the Paddy's with the best and still sing "Galway Bay" at the end of a long night without tripping over the words.

He leaned his bulk against the wall, sipping the coffee, watching the early Friday evening turmoil: a dozen phones ringing; an early drunk yelling obscenities in the holding tank; a blank-eyed man being interviewed; a desperate-looking couple demanding help finding their teenage son; an arson suspect; a youth accused of a stabbing. He thought you needed the patience of a saint to be a cop, and that was something you weren't told at cop school. That, and never to assume anything. He couldn't say how many times he'd proved that one right. Because, folks, he thought, wending his way back to his desk to pick up his ringing phone, in the real world virtually nothing was the way it seemed.

"Yeah?" He leaned back, his feet on his desk, the phone clamped between his shoulder and his ear, sipping his coffee. "Doctor who d'ya say? She's here now? Okay, tell her I'll be right with her."

He checked his notes again. A Dr. Forster had been appointed by the neurosurgeon to help in the rehabilitation of Jane Doe. He hadn't known she was a woman doctor, though. He sighed, suddenly realizing who she was. Female and famous. Great. Just what he needed on a busy Friday night with a virtually clueless attempted homicide. He guessed he was one of the few who had never seen her on TV or read one of her books. And he didn't see how she was going to be of much help now. He knew if the girl came out of the coma, Dr. Phyl Forster would want to protect her from his questioning. And he knew he had a job to do. He would want to question her as soon as possible, before she forgot what she remembered.

He decided to let Dr. Forster wait awhile. Give the lady psychiatrist a little character test. See if she could keep her cool or whether she would play Miss High and Mighty Famous doctor with the poor dumb cop.

Phyl had driven straight from the hospital to the precinct house. The neurosurgeon had told her that Mahoney was anxious to interview the girl as soon as she came out of her coma, and she wanted to explain personally that he must not. At least not yet. She paced the

corridors, peering impatiently through the glass doors
at the organized chaos inside. She thought it was a bit
like the hospital: a sudden slice of real life that jolted
her out of the safety of her own carefully planned and
controlled environment.

She glanced impatiently at her watch. Goddammit,
where was the man! She had been waiting ten minutes,
and she was exhausted. Maybe it was reaction to seeing
the girl come back to life, like a swimmer surfacing
from deep water. God, the relief. Then the flutter of
apprehension when she realized the girl didn't even
remember her name. Anyhow, she just thanked the
Lord she was alive, that her motor senses were functioning properly, and that she was rational, if under-
standably distressed.

"Ms. Forster?"

She swung around and met Franco Mahoney's Irish
blue eyes. *Unsmiling* eyes, she noticed. She offered her
hand. "I hope I'm not interrupting, but I wanted to
talk to you about your Jane Doe. The woman in the
ravine."

His eyes hardened. "Is she awake? I asked to be told
the moment she came out of it—"

"And I came here to tell you exactly that, Mr. Mahoney."

"Detective," he corrected her.

"*Detective* Mahoney." She sighed. She could tell he
was going to be difficult. He was handsome, too, if you
liked big and brawny with half a day's growth of beard.
Six-four or thereabouts, broad in the shoulders, narrow at the hips, and with that macho gun in his holster.
He had thick black hair with a wave in it, worn combed
straight back, a strong nose, a firm jaw, a wide, easygo-
ing mouth, and his sea blue eyes had crinkles at the
corners, as though he smiled a lot. Though you'd
never believe it now. If this wasn't a head-to-head con-
frontation, then she had never seen one.

"She regained consciousness just over an hour ago.

I've spoken to the neurosurgeon, and he agrees that it is too soon yet to start asking her questions. She is still very ill. And she is distressed."

Mahoney heaved an exasperated sigh. "Miss For-ster—"

"*Dr.* Forster."

His blue eyes grinned mockingly at her. "*Dr.* Forster. You understand we have an attempted homicide here. My job is to catch the perpetrator of the crime. The assassin."

"The girl is not dead."

"Would-be assassin," he amended impatiently.

"And *my* job is to help return her to health. *Mental* health, Detective Mahoney. Apart from her consider-able physical injuries, she has suffered severe mental trauma. If, as you suggest, it wasn't an accident after all, and someone really did try to kill her, you can only imagine what she is going through. Trying to remem-ber."

"*Trying* to remember?"

"Right now, Detective, your Jane Doe cannot even remember her own name."

"Jesus."

He slumped back in his chair, ignoring her. She stared at him stonily.

Leaning across the desk, she gave him her most fem-inine pleading smile. "I'm sorry, Detective Mahoney, but it's for the girl's own good. Imagine if she were *your* wife or *your* daughter. You wouldn't want her to be forced to confront the facts about what happened, be-fore she was well enough to withstand the shock." She shrugged sadly. "This young woman is suffering from retrograde amnesia, a loss of memory for events pre-ceding the trauma. Caused obviously by the injuries to the skull, but I feel certain also by the mental trauma of the assault. Often in these cases the memory returns involuntarily. Maybe by tomorrow she will have remem-bered; maybe she'll be eager to talk about it, anxious to get to the truth, finally. If not, then I shall try to help her. Meanwhile, bear with us. Please.''

He sighed. "Okay. If you say so.''

Times might change, she thought exasperatedly, *but not men. At least not all of them.*

"I guess you're right," he admitted grudgingly. "But you'll understand I'm just as concerned as you are, Dr. Forster. Somebody tried to kill her. If she dies, then it's my job to bring that person to justice, and in order to do it, I'm gonna need her help.''

"So what do you know about her? Besides her probable age and what she looks like?''

"I can tell you in two words. Not much. When she was found, she was wearing Levi's and a white Gap T-shirt. A blue cashmere sweater was found nearby. And sandals.''

Phyl remembered the red sandal dangling forlornly from the girl's toe. She shivered. "No jewelry? A watch, a wedding ring?''

"Only pearl earrings.''

"Good pearls.''

He nodded. "Small but good, they tell me. Still, she could have bought them anywhere. Same with the jeans and the T-shirt. The cashmere sweater had no label, and the sandals were French. Expensive, like the earrings and the sweater, but you can purchase them in good stores across the country. Or even in France, I guess. No purse. We searched that ravine thoroughly. There was nothing else. There's no missing person matching her description. No fingerprints on record. No one has come forward claiming to know her.''

"So tell me, Mahoney, what makes you think someone tried to kill her?''

He gave her a long, exasperated look and then said slowly and deliberately, as though he were explaining to a child, "The ravine is far enough out to need a car to get there. No car was found near the scene. She did not live in the area, so she wasn't just out walking her dogs. She had to have been taken there and then dumped. Or, more likely, pushed over the edge."

"She wasn't raped." Phyl knew that from the medical reports.

He shrugged. "Maybe she wouldn't come across and the guy got mad. It happens. More often than you think," he added grimly.

"So there are no clues?"

"None, other than the dog bite. And what she herself can tell us."

"And that brings us back to the reason I'm here." She gave him the smile again and a little feminine shrug of the shoulders.

"So it does," he said abruptly, standing up, dismissing her. "You've got forty-eight hours. Then we'll have to reassess."

He walked her to the door. "Thanks," she said sarcastically as he opened it, "for your cooperation."

He watched her walk down the corridor, noting her long, slender legs and the swing of the hips under the black suit. "Hey, Forster," he called after her. She hesitated, then turned slowly around.

"It's *Doctor,*" she said icily.

"Yeah. *Doc.* There's a nice little Italian restaurant around the corner from the hospital. Maybe after I've interviewed the girl, you and I could go there. Have a bite? Compare notes?"

She laughed at his chauvinist cheek. "Why, thank you for the invitation, Detective Mahoney," she retorted sweetly. "I'll have to think about it, and 'reassess.'"

Phyl was back at the hospital, bearing flowers, at nine the next morning. She had puzzled all night over what might have happened to the girl and about who she might be, worrying why no one had come forward to claim her. No mother had come in search of her lost daughter; no lover; no husband. Not a co-worker or a girlfriend. She was like the invisible woman—there, but no one could really see her.

She was there all right this Saturday morning, though. In person, sitting up and taking nourishment. It was a shock, seeing her shaved head with the livid scars running across the scalp, and the still-bruised and swollen but undeniably pretty face.

"Well, well," Phyl said, smiling with genuine pleasure. "Aren't you the lively one today." She leaned forward and kissed her on the cheek, depositing the big bunch of flowers on her lap. "For you."

The girl's eyes widened with pleasure. She picked them up and buried her nose in them. "Mimosa," she whispered. "Such a heavenly scent. I smelled them when I first woke up. It must have been you who brought them?"

Phyl noted that she recognized the flowers, but she made no comment. She took a seat next to the bed and accepted the offer of a cup of tea from the nurse. "How's your patient doing?" she asked, smiling her thanks.

"Better than we expected last night, Doctor. You can see for yourself, she's on the mend."

"Last night I was in a tunnel." The girl looked at Phyl despairingly. "I thought maybe I was dead. It was so dark, terrifying. I couldn't escape. And then I was falling, just falling and falling into an abyss, and I knew I would never come back—"

"Well, now you are back, so you see, it was all just a bad dream."

"Phyl?" The girl met her eyes. "What happened to me?"

Phyl hesitated, but she knew she had to deliver the truth. "It wasn't just a dream. You did fall. Down a rocky ravine. Fortunately your fall was halted by the undergrowth. There were a lot of bushes. They saved you."

The girl looked down, puzzled. "Maybe that's what I

remember then, the falling. . . . I've been thinking about things, trying to remember. And I can. I mean, I can remember things about San Francisco—buildings and the bridge. But I don't remember where I live. I remember the taste of frozen yogurt and that I don't like ice cream. I remember I like the color red, but not whether I have a red dress. I remember the scent of mimosa, but not where I've smelled it before. I remember you, from last night, and the nurses and the doctors, but I cannot recall a single person from my past." She lifted huge frightened brown eyes to her and said, "What am I going to do?"

Phyl patted her hand encouragingly. "Okay, now you listen to me. You are just a few hours out of a coma, only three weeks away from a major trauma and surgery. There's no need for you to remember one damn thing right now, so stop worrying about it. Soon enough you'll remember. Until then concentrate on smaller things. Think about books you might have read, music you enjoy, favorite paintings, the kinds of clothes you like to wear."

"I like what you are wearing."

Phyl laughed. It was Saturday, and she was in her off-duty uniform: black jeans, black suede loafers, white shirt, and black leather jacket.

"Especially the belt. Is it from Tucson?"

Phyl stared at her. The belt was Native American, black leather with a silver and turquoise buckle. "Santa Fe," she said, pleased. "You recognized it."

"I suppose I did." The girl looked surprised, and she laughed.

"See, your memory is coming back already," Phyl said comfortingly.

"It just seems to be there," the girl said. "Things pop out. Like the mimosa and the belt."

"That's the way it goes. And speaking of going, I must be on my way. I don't want to tire you out and undo all the good work."

"Phyl?"

Phyl glanced inquiringly at her.

"Why did you come to see me? If you don't know me?"

Phyl hesitated. She didn't want to tell her about seeing her on television. But there was also another reason, one she didn't choose to talk about to anyone. She said, "I was at the hospital when they brought you in. I was concerned about you. I'm a psychiatrist, and I work here, at the General, three days a week."

The girl smiled wryly. "A psychiatrist. Then I guess I'm in the right hands. You've got yourself another nutcase to straighten out, Doctor." Her eyes widened in astonishment. "Dr. Phyl Forster," she said. "It's you. You're famous."

"Well, look at that. You remembered."

"I did, too," she replied, pleased with herself. "And there's something else I'm sure I'll never forget: the sight of your lovely face, smiling at me when I came out of that tunnel of despair."

Gratitude shone from her copper brown eyes and Phyl gulped back her emotion. "Glad I was there," she said quietly. "See you later, young lady."

"Phyl?" The girl called her back as she was halfway out of the door. "Just one thing. Do you have a mirror? I want to see what I look like. I still can't get out of bed, and nobody seems to own a hand mirror in this hospital."

Phyl hesitated; she knew it was dangerous. First, because the girl was only a few hours out of the coma. Second, because she was bruised and battered, and with her swollen face and shaved head she looked like hell. And third, because she might suddenly recognize herself and remember what had happened. And it was too soon. It would be too much of a shock.

"Maybe tomorrow," she promised, waving good-bye. "I'll bring a mirror."

"*Y*ou're young," Dr. Niedman told the girl later the next morning. "Strong as a horse. It would take more than a broken skull to kill you."

"But they *shoot* horses to kill them, don't they?" she wailed irrationally. "And I got pushed over the cliff."

Niedman sighed. Detective Mahoney had called him and insisted on interviewing the girl earlier that morning. That was why she was so upset.

"Don't believe everything you hear from the cops," he said with a cheerful grin. "Maybe you were just out walking and fell. After all, who would want to harm a nice girl like you?"

"I don't know," she said simply. "But then I don't know who I am either. If I did, maybe I would know why someone wanted to kill me."

There was a knock at the door, and Phyl Forster came in. Her blazing blue eyes met Niedman's. "I heard Mahoney was here," she said angrily. "Did he ask your permission to interview the patient?"

"Unfortunately he did. He said that you had given him forty-eight hours and that every hour that passed made his job more difficult. Now that the patient was awake and sitting up and taking notice, he suggested we might be thought to be obstructing the course of justice. I had to agree, though I didn't approve.''

Phyl snorted angrily. She thrust a Saks bag at the girl and deposited a kiss on her cheek. "For you," she said. "To perk you up for the unveiling." She turned back to Niedman. "Today's the day she gets to see your handiwork."

Niedman laughed as he stood up to go. "Sorry about the haircut," he said to his patient, "but I'm the best stapler in the business. A few months and you won't even remember you had to be patched up."

"Oh, I hope I will," she said, looking alarmed, and they laughed.

"First, though, we have to get you out of that hospital nightshirt and into something a bit more flattering," Phyl said. "The nurse will help you change, and I'll be back in a minute."

The girl stared wonderingly after her. Then she opened the bag and unwrapped the layers of white tissue paper. She smiled with pleasure as she saw the pale pink silk and lace. "How pretty," she said, running her hand across its cool smoothness. "How lovely."

Phyl was on the pay phone in the hall, calling the precinct, tapping her foot impatiently as she waited for Franco Mahoney to pick up the call. "You jumped the gun, Mahoney," she said when he finally responded. "By seven hours, not to mention the period of 'reassessment' we talked about."

"I talked it over with the surgeon in charge," he replied coolly. "He gave me the go-ahead. Naturally, if he hadn't, I wouldn't have done it."

Phyl gritted her teeth. He was an arrogant, interfering bastard, and he might have done untold harm to her patient. "Goddammit, man, what did you ask her? Why didn't you let me be there at least?"

"Hey, hey, I'm no ogre. I was gentle. I didn't insist, for God's sake. I asked her what she knew and she said,

'Nothing.' I asked her her name, and she said she didn't know. I couldn't decide whether she was telling the truth or just stalling. You're the expert, you tell me?"

"Of course she's not stalling, you idiot! The girl's been traumatized. She can't remember because sub-consciously she doesn't want to remember. She has pushed it all back to some recess in her mind with a Do Not Disturb sign on it. And it's my belief she's not going to remember voluntarily. Not until something happens that stirs her memory."

"And what then?"

"What then?" Phyl thought about it. "Why, some-one had better be there to pick up the pieces, that's all." And as she said it, she knew that she would be the one.

She hung up the phone and walked slowly back to the patient's room.

She was sitting up, smiling, wearing the new pink nightdress. She searched Phyl's face for a reaction.

"Now you look better," Phyl said approvingly. "I thought this might be the only time in your life you could wear pink." She grinned. "When your hair grows in, you'll be back in blue."

"It's beautiful. Thank you. But you didn't have to . . . I mean, I'm nothing to you."

"Sure you are. You're something to all of us here. You came to us broken, and we put you back together again. And speaking of that, are you ready for the un-veiling?"

The girl's apprehensive eyes met hers. "Is it really bad?" she whispered, suddenly afraid.

"It's not wonderful," Phyl admitted. "The truth is, your face is swollen and badly bruised, but it's not seri-ously damaged. You still have the same nose you were born with; your eyes are in the same place; you didn't lose any teeth. In other words, there's nothing that time, and a new crop of hair, won't fix. Just prepare yourself for the sight of the scars on your scalp. And the—the *nakedness* of it.''

Phyl held the mirror. The girl took a long look at herself. Tears spurted from her eyes.

"Take it easy,'' Phyl said gently.

"But I don't know her,'' she whispered, anguished. "I don't know that girl.''

Phyl took a Kleenex and mopped the tears. "You will, one day soon. I'll help you to find yourself again. I promise. And anyhow, you don't look exactly like you right now.'' It was like talking to a child, she thought. And then she suddenly wanted to cry, too.

"Why are you so good to me?'' the girl said, pressing her head against Phyl's cool hand. "I'm no one. Nothing. A meaningless nonperson. You don't have to be nice to me; you're busy, successful, famous. Why are you bothering with me?''

"It's my heart of gold,'' Phyl said lightly.

"No, it's not. It's more than that, isn't it?''

Phyl nodded.

"Won't you tell me?''

The girl was holding *her* hand now, reversing their roles. Phyl's chest felt tight, and the muscles at the back of her neck were rigid with tension.

Her voice shook as she said, "Perhaps one day. When you are better.'' She pulled herself together and said briskly, "I'm forgetting the rules. You are the patient. And I'm the analyst, here to help you. Not the other way around.''

They looked at each other. Phyl sniffed back her tears and reached for the Kleenex. "If you are still prepared to let me be your doctor, I think maybe you are crazy after all.''

"Your mascara is running,'' the girl said gently.

"So much for tearproof!''

They grinned at each other, and then Phyl reached

out and hugged her. "I just felt you needed someone around," she said. "Why not me?"

"I can't think of anyone better."

Their eyes met again. "Except maybe my mom," the girl added wistfully.

~ 6 ~

It was strange being anonymous, the girl thought, staring at her face in the mirror a week later. Strange but somehow peaceful. After all, if no one knew who she was, then no one would try to kill her. And why would anyone want to kill her anyway? What had she done to create such anger, such violence in a person?

She stared down at the row of red scars on her arm where the doctors said a dog had bitten her. Surely she should remember that. It was a big dog, Detective Mahoney had told her. A Rottweiler or a Doberman. Did she know anybody with such a dog? he had asked. All she could do was shake her head, and then she had gasped with pain and put up her hands.

"I'm sorry," Mahoney had said, and she could read the sympathy in his warm blue eyes. "I really don't want to hurt you. But between us, the doc and I have to sort you out. I have to figure out your past, and she's working on your future. All we need is a little input from you."

"I'm trying," she said, desperately casting around in the blank that was her mind for any stray memories.

"All I can think is that you don't look a bit like I imagined a detective should look."

His eyes crinkled at the corners as he grinned at her. "The leather jacket's just a disguise to fool the felons, make them think I'm one of them."

"They'll never believe it." She smiled back. "You look too nice to be a criminal."

"You'd be surprised how 'nice' a lot of criminals can seem. That's how they persuade lovely girls, like you for instance, into letting them take them home. Or out on a date."

She knew he was angling for a response, and she only wished she could give it to him.

"Maybe I wasn't the sort of girl who got picked up in a bar and let a guy take her home," she said doubtfully. "Do you really think I was that dumb?"

"No, I don't. But you sure as hell are pretty. Who knows, somebody might have followed you."

He was getting nowhere, and she heard him sigh as he looked down at the yellow pad with only a few brief notes scribbled on it.

"I'm sorry," she said. "I really want to help. I want to know who I am. Maybe I'm not remembering because I feel safer. If nobody knows who I am, nobody will want to kill me."

He shrugged as he stood up to go. "Run that one by Dr. Phyl," he said. "It's more her line of work than mine. One more thing, though. When we found you, you were wearing light clothing—too light for San Francisco in early March. And the rest of the country was under ice, apart from a couple of hot spots. Maybe you had just arrived from a warmer climate. Mexico? Florida maybe? Or Hawaii? The Far East? I've checked the airlines, but you'd never believe how many women travel alone to these vacation resorts and how many flights there are each day. We're checking them all, individually, but if you happen to dream you are on a flight tonight, just let me know which one it is. It'll save a hell of a lot of time."

He winked cheerily as he went out the door, and she laughed even though it made her head hurt.

But she still did not recognize her face in the mirror. And she could not recall getting on a plane. And she had not recognized her clothes when he showed them to her.

She had flinched in horror from the bloodstained T-shirt and sweater, but she had touched the red leather sandal and read the label inside: "Stéphane Kelian, Paris." She felt Mahoney's eyes riveted on her as she hesitated, running her finger along the label.

"Paris?" she said, searching her brain to explain the tingle of emotion she was feeling. But there was nothing, and she burst into tears.

Phyl had arrived then and practically shoved Mahoney out of the room.

"Brute," she called after him down the shiny hospital corridor.

"Give me a break, Doc," he cried, backing away, arms outstretched pleadingly. "I'm just a guy doing his job."

"Ohhh!" Phyl was all but speechless, and the girl's tears had turned to laughter at her outraged face. That was when Phyl had suggested hypnotizing her.

"We've taken every test, tried everything," Phyl said, "and frankly, we're getting nowhere. Retrograde amnesia such as yours often responds to hypnosis. But do you think you are ready for it?"

"Ready to know the truth, you mean? For better, for worse?"

Phyl nodded sympathetically. "For better, for worse. Either way I want you to know you can count on me for support. Whatever happens."

"I know." The bond between them had grown into friendship over the brief time they had known each other. One woman looking to absolve her past; the other seeking it.

Phyl breezed through the door, carrying a huge bunch of mimosas. Today was the day of the experiment. "It's the first thing that really triggered a memory," she said, setting the flowers on the table. "Maybe it will help."

She drew the curtains and sat opposite the bed in the darkened room. "Are you nervous?" she asked, patting her hand comfortingly. The girl nodded. "No need to be. Just relax. Empty your mind and listen to my voice."

She did as she was asked. Phyl's voice was low, soothing, rhythmic. The girl's eyes closed on command, and she was taken back in time, such a long way, such a long time ago. . . .

"Where are you now?" Phyl asked gently.

The girl drew in an amazed breath. "Oh, it's a lovely place, so beautiful. It's the place I love most in all the world." Her voice was light, childlike.

"And where is that?"

"A long, long way. Oh, yes, it's a long way away. It's so peaceful. . . ."

"Do you know where it is?"

Her voice faltered. "Where, I don't—I'm not sure. . . ."

Phyl saw she was disoriented and said quickly, "Tell me what you see in this lovely place."

"I see a child, sitting on the steps of a wonderful pink villa. I hear the sound of a hundred songbirds. I feel the coolness of the marble against my legs and the warmth of the sun on my face. And oh . . . I can smell the mimosa. . . . There's just the sound of the birds and the rustle of the tall trees in the breeze . . . and—and something else."

Phyl leaned closer. The girl's expression had changed from innocent happiness to frozen fear.

"What is it?" Phyl said urgently. "You can tell me, you can trust me with your secret. . . ."

"Footsteps on the gravel. Someone is coming up the driveway. Getting closer, closer. . . . A great dark cloud is looming over me, stifling me, shutting out the lovely pink villa and the light. . . . There's only the scent of the mimosa. . . ."

Tears flowed down her cheeks, and Phyl watched her quietly for a moment. "Poor child," she whispered. "Do you know who it is coming up the drive?"

The girl shook her head, crying silently.

"Is the child you?"

She shook her head again. "I don't know. I just don't know who it is."

"Do you know how old the child is?"

"Non, je ne connaît pas."

Phyl blinked in surprise. "You answered me in French. Do you speak that language fluently?"

"Oui. C'est le même pour moi, français ou anglais."

"And can you tell me where you learned to speak French so well?"

"I—I don't know."

She was distressed again, and Phyl asked one last question: "Do you have a French name?"

"My name? I have no name. . . . I don't know . . ."

"It's all right. Don't distress yourself. But I want you to remember everything you have told me about the pink villa. You can wake up now. Come, open your eyes. Look at me."

The girl's eyes flew open. She put up her hand to touch the wetness on her cheeks. "Tears?" she said wonderingly. "Why was I crying?"

"Peut-être vos mémoires sont triste?"

"Triste?" She stared in astonishment at Phyl. Then she said, "My God, I spoke to you in French. *What does* it mean, Phyl?" She stared pleadingly at her. "Please tell me."

Phyl went over what she had recalled about the villa. "Do you remember anything like that happening to you?"

The girl shook her head angrily. "Oh, God, I wish I did."

"Don't be upset. It's progress. Quite a breakthrough, I'd say."

"Really? You mean that?" She looked pathetically pleased at the small ray of hope Phyl offered. "Did I tell you my name?"

Phyl laughed. "No, not yet. But we can't go on calling you Jane Doe forever. Why don't you just go ahead and choose a name? Any name you please. Think of all the famous redheads throughout history."

"Beatrice," the young woman said thoughtfully after a while. "You know, Dante and Beatrice. She's famous enough. Besides, I don't feel like a Rita Hayworth or a Queen Elizabeth the First."

"Mmm, Beatrice . . . Bea. Sounds good. And how about French, since it's the first thing you have remembered?"

"Bea French. It sounds great." She laughed, pleased, pushing her terror of not knowing who she was temporarily away from her. "Now maybe I'll be a somebody again, instead of an anonymous nobody."

$\mathcal{I}$t was 7:00 P.M. two weeks later, and Mahoney had just finished his shift. Three hours late as usual.

"You know you only do it just to make the rest of us guys look bad," Detective Valentino Benedetti complained. "Why can't you finish on time like the rest of us?"

He was a tall man with a red face, a beer belly, and flat feet that were the bane of his life and the butt of every cop joke in the squad room. He was also known for working the fewest hours. Somehow he got away with it. Unless it was legitimate paid overtime, of course.

They were sitting at the bar in Hanran's, attempting to solve the day's problems over a beer.

"Why d'ya only drink that light crap instead of real beer, like Bud? What kinda cop are you anyways, Mahoney?"

"A tired cop, Benedetti, that's what I am. I've just spent four hours hanging around court, trying to get an ignorant felon put away for robbing his grandmother and then tying her to the bedpost with her stockings. Surprise, surprise, she died. He pleaded not guilty. He only meant to tie her up for a joke, he said. The fact that the stockings were tied around her neck and that she choked to death in front of his eyes meant nothing. He put on the performance of his life. Said he's only nineteen, he loved the old lady, she had been a mother to him. It was just spur-of-the-moment kid stuff; he was a good boy really. And he had a stack of witnesses to prove it. As shameless a bunch of liars as you're ever likely to meet. He got two years' suspended sentence and fifty hours' community work. Jesus, Benedetti! D'ya ever wonder why you're a cop?''

They downed their beers in silence, contemplating the inequities of the American judicial system. Benedetti ordered two more, and the barman slid them down the counter, along with a bowl of pretzels.

"Y'ever hear what happened to the girl in Mitchell's Ravine?" Benedetti asked, taking a deep swallow of Budweiser. "I mean, I know she didn't die, and technically it's not your problem. I just wondered if the assailant ever surfaced. Y'know, if he'd come back to try again in case she remembered who he was and told the cops?''

Mahoney shook his head. "I've been tied up for the last couple of weeks. We got nowhere on the airlines check, nowhere on missing persons, and nowhere on fingerprints. Nobody came forward looking for her, and as far as I know, she's still in the hospital recovering from the head wounds. The interesting thing, though, was the dog bite.

"There are a lot of big houses in that area, and most of them have guard dogs. I had them checked, but suddenly they are all sweet family pets. All of them were in their nice homes being fed Alpo and steak and affection the night of the attack. At least that's what their owners claim, and there's no way to prove otherwise. And they all are solid citizens, families of wealth and standing, pillars of society.''

He grinned mockingly. "But you and I know all

about pillars of society, don't we, Benedetti? We know never to trust a man by the cut of his clothes and the amount of money in his bank account. Because underneath he's just a man."

"Like you and me," Benedetti replied gloomily, ordering another couple of beers. "Only without the big bank account."

Mahoney put up his hand. "No more for me, pal. I'm going to call the hospital and see if I can pay my young Jane Doe a visit before they close for the night. Thanks for the beer."

He strode through the crowded bar to the pay phone, dialed the hospital, identified himself, and asked to be put through to the nurses' station on the girl's floor.

"The patient is sleeping, Detective Mahoney," the nurse told him. "But Dr. Niedman has just finished his rounds. Would you care to speak with him?"

"Sure. And thanks."

Niedman came on the phone, sounding harassed.

"I won't keep you, sir," Mahoney said quickly. "I just wondered if you could bring me up-to-date on the progress of the Jane Doe from Mitchell's Ravine."

"Ah, you mean Bea French," Niedman said tiredly.

"Excuse me? *Bea French?*" Mahoney almost yelled at Niedman. Nobody had bothered to contact him and tell him she had remembered who she was. "Is that her name then?"

"Not exactly. She and Phyl Forster invented it. After Dr. Forster hypnotized her and found she spoke fluent French, they seemed to think it appropriate."

Mahoney felt his blood pressure rising like sap in his veins. Goddammit, good old Doc Forster had gone ahead and hypnotized the girl without so much as telling him. God knew what else she had revealed besides the fact that she spoke French. He was exploding with anger. It was the first real clue they had, and he was the last to know.

He thanked Niedman, hung up the phone, and checked his watch. It was almost eight-thirty.

He stalked to the parking lot, automatically eyeballing the kids loitering on the sidewalk. They quickly melted into the night. He knew a couple of the faces, and he guessed they were up to no good, hanging around in the rain, but he was off duty and in a hurry. Tonight they had gotten a break.

His '69 black Mustang convertible started at the first touch, and he took a couple of seconds to enjoy its finely tuned growl before taking off in a shriek of rubber and adrenaline.

Phyl Forster lived on a very smart street in a very smart building in Pacific Heights. Mahoney parked on the double yellow and surveyed the canopied entrance, the uniformed doorman, the immaculately maintained facade. He whistled. Doc Forster was doing all right.

Sticking his hands in the pockets of his jeans, he sauntered toward the entrance. The doorman stared suspiciously at him until he flashed his badge, then hurriedly let him in. Mahoney took in the marble lobby covered in about an acre of oriental rug, the huge gilt-framed mirrors reflecting crystal vases filled with fresh flowers, and the antique consoles and deeply cushioned chairs. He wondered what the doctor's monthly maintenance bill was.

He waited while the doorman telephoned to see if Dr. Forster would see him. "You can go on up," he finally told Mahoney reluctantly. He wasn't used to police in his quiet, affluent building. "Apartment Ten B."

Mahoney strode carefully across the oriental rug into the wood-paneled elevator. He checked his appearance in the mirror as the elevator zoomed noiselessly upward. He smoothed back his hair, brushed the rain off his leather jacket, and thought about what he wanted to say to the doc about Bea French. He was still simmering with anger.

The door to apartment 10B stood open, and he walked in. Phyl was wearing an oversize white terry robe, no makeup, and her black hair hung loosely around her shoulders. She was curled up on a black couch, and she looked drained and exhausted. She stared at him but didn't get up.

"To what do I owe the honor, Mahoney?" she asked wearily. "Isn't it a bit late for the cops to come calling?"

Unsmiling, bristling with anger, he stared back at her. "Why the hell didn't you tell me you were going to hypnotize the girl? Why didn't you let me know the result? How the hell is it that I'm the last person to get to know what's going on with Bea French?"

Her sapphire eyes darkened to jet with sudden anger. "How dare you shout at me!" she yelled back. "Didn't you tell me she was no longer your concern? Unless she died, of course. Then you could have had a field day. The clever, macho cop, the darling of the media, solving yet another homicide. Well, I'm sorry to disappoint you, Mahoney, but she didn't die. She's very much alive, and now she's in my charge. Not yours."

He stood over her, his hands in his pockets. His eyes met hers as he said quietly, "And what do you think our murderer will do when he finds out Bea is still alive? That he didn't kill her after all? You're the clever one, Doc. You tell me. Whoever he is, he wanted her dead. How does the old saying go? 'If at first you don't succeed, try, try again'? Take it from me, Doc, he will."

Shocked into silence, she stared back at him. He thought she looked suddenly vulnerable, her face pinched and drained of color.

He turned away, glancing around the sumptuously simple, immaculate apartment. Everything gleaming, everything carefully arranged, everything in its place. He took off his black leather jacket and flung it onto the Eames chair that looked as though no one had ever sat on it, and walked through to the pristine steel and granite kitchen.

He opened the refrigerator, checked the contents, and then began taking things out of the cupboards.

"What the hell do you think you're doing?" Her voice shook with indignation and fatigue.

"What does it look like I'm doing? I'm cooking dinner, since you don't look as though you have the energy."

"You're cooking dinner! I didn't ask you to dinner. I didn't even ask you over for a drink!"

He threw her a mocking grin. "Y'know what's wrong with you, Forster? You sit on your butt all day. Or maybe it's all that lying on the couch that does it. You should be working out, training, running. Getting all those endorphins working for you. Sharpening up your brain cells."

"Like yours, I suppose." She flung herself from the sofa and leaned threateningly across the expanse of black granite counter that separated her from the kitchen.

He glanced up from chopping tomatoes. "You think I'm just an ignorant backstreet boy, don't you? A guy who made it up to detective the hard way? Y'know what? You're right. And it was tough." He shrugged his wide shoulders expressively. "A scholarship to Berkeley, working every job I could get so I could eat as well. Graduated magna with an honors degree in English literature. My thesis was on the effect of the European Romantic poets on the American approach to human relationships today. I was in my second year as a grad student at Stanford when I decided I wanted to be a cop instead of a professor." His eyes met hers coolly. "Just so you know who I am, Doc."

She stared at him silently. His shirtsleeves were rolled up as he chopped tomatoes and softly whistled an aria from *La Traviata* whose title she couldn't re-

member. She sank into a chair and put her head in her
hands, ashamed.

"I'm sorry," she said. "I'm just so goddamn tired.
It's been a long day. A long week, month, year . . .
And anyhow, you're wrong. I'm the one up from the
streets."

He flung the vegetables into a pan with a slug of
olive oil, then folded his arms, leaning against the
counter, waiting gravely for her to tell her story. But
her pale face suddenly looked closed and tight with a
remembered pain she was not going to reveal to him.
Not yet, anyway.

"I'm so busy taking care of everyone else's problems
there's just no time left," she said finally, shaking her
head in bewilderment. "No time for myself. I bring my
work home with me."

He glanced around the cool, perfect, beautiful
room. "Yeah. I can see that. It looks as though you
forgot to live here."

He took a bottle of red wine from the rack and
checked the label. "Good stuff," he said approvingly,
pouring her a hefty glass. "My Italian mama used to
tell me a glass of red wine brought a blush of color to a
girl's cheeks and a glow to her heart. I've always hoped
it was true."

She smiled as she took a sip, staring tiredly into her
glass.

He walked across the room and studied her CD col-
lection. Soon the pure sound of Callas singing an aria
from *Norma* wafted through the lofty silent rooms like a
refreshing breeze.

Fifteen minutes later she was sitting opposite him at
the kitchen table with a fragrant bowl of pasta and
fresh tomato sauce in front of her.

"Sorry, I couldn't find any bread," he said, pouring
wine into their glasses. "Except for a wizened crust that
must have been there for about a week. I guess you're

not much of a bread eater. Always thinking about your weight, huh?"

"I am not," she retorted indignantly. "I love focaccia, *and* olive bread, *and* sourdough. And I'm not always thinking about my figure. Thank God I don't have to. Yet."

He grinned at her as she wound a forkful of pasta and tasted it. She realized too late that he was baiting her.

"It's just that I don't eat at home that often," she said, needing to explain. "It's usually late and I just grab a bite on my way home."

"So why didn't you do that tonight?"

"I was too tired even to care," she said honestly.

"Or too lonely," he said, sipping his wine and watching her eat.

She glanced at him for a moment but said nothing. She watched him walk across the room as he went to change the CD. She thought he walked on the balls of his feet like an athlete. Lithe, like a panther. Only this panther stalked the jungle of the city streets. Then she remembered what he had said about the killer, and she was suddenly afraid for Bea.

He came back and sat opposite her, his elbows on the table, sipping wine, watching her eat.

She finished the pasta and sighed with satisfaction. "That was wonderful. It's also the first home-cooked food I've eaten in about a year."

She sat back, and they looked at each other. "What do you want from life, Mahoney?" she asked, suddenly curious.

He laughed off her question. "Oh, to be police commissioner one day. Or maybe run for mayor. Just like any other red-blooded cop. And?"

"And what?"

"And what do you want from life, Doc?"

She flung her arms wide, indicating the beautiful apartment, the priceless rugs, the artworks. "What more can any woman want?'' she said defensively. "I've got it all."

"It sure looks like it, Doc," he said, standing up abruptly and putting on his jacket.

She glared at him. He didn't say it, but she knew what he was thinking. Maybe she wanted a man who loved her; children; a happy, bustling home; maybe a dog or two. . . .

Dammit, what was she doing, letting this macho, chauvinist, poetic, opera-loving, fitness-freak cop put her life on the line? She had it all organized, everything in its place. Didn't she?

"You're tired," he said, offering his hand. "Thanks for the dinner. And the company. Let me know what happens with Bea."

It seemed odd to hear the girl's new name on Mahoney's lips, as though his saying it brought her to life again.

A resurrection, she thought as she closed the door behind him.

Dr. Niedman was waiting for her the next morning. "Our patient is doing well, Dr. Forster," he said. "In fact, well enough to be dismissed." He glanced up from his notes. "The question is, of course, dismissed to where? I understand from Detective Mahoney that his investigations have led nowhere, and as you, too, seem to have drawn a blank, I'm at a loss to know what to do about her. I can't see putting her into a psychiatric ward since there is nothing mentally wrong with her other than the loss of memory. On the other hand, how can she cope if we simply turn her over to welfare?"

Phyl thought about Bea with her shorn head and her terrible scars, knowing nothing about herself, not even what had happened to her. She thought of her out on her own, out on the street, and she remembered what Mahoney had said the previous night: that if the killer knew she was alive, he might try again. Perhaps he already knew it from the newspapers. Maybe he was just waiting for her to get out of the hospital. . . .

"Bea can stay with me," she said quickly. "After all, I'm the one responsible for her rehabilitation."

Niedman's bushy eyebrows raised over his eyeglasses in surprise. "Isn't that a bit over and above the call of duty, Dr. Forster?"

"I like her," Phyl said defensively. "We have become friends as well as doctor and patient."

"I see. Well, she is a nice young woman, and I for one am glad of your offer. It certainly helps resolve my dilemma. I figure next weekend, if that's all right with you?"

Phyl went to tell Bea the good news. "It's been six weeks," she said. "You must be sick and tired of gazing at these four walls, so you can come and gaze at mine for a change. At least the view is better, though I can't guarantee the food." She thought of Mahoney's delicious pasta and smiled.

Bea laughed delightedly. "Believe me, *anything* is better than hospital food. But are you sure, Phyl? I mean, it's a terrible imposition, taking in a perfect stranger—"

"Hey, hey, what do you mean? A perfect stranger? Let's not forget that right now I know you better than anyone else. Besides, I like you. And it'll be fun having a roommate. I haven't had that pleasure since college." She laughed, looking around the bare hospital room. "At least we won't be fighting over closet space."

That night Mahoney came by again, surprising Phyl. And this time he arrived with a gift: a charming cream and chocolate Siamese kitten. It looked minute in his big hands, purring confidently, quite certain it would be loved.

"I thought the apartment was too lonely," he explained. "A cat will keep you busy, keep you from getting introverted. Think of her as therapy. And make no mistake, this kind of cat thinks it's human. You do as she tells you. She wants to play, you play. She wants to eat, you serve her food. She wants to hug, baby, you get hugs. So tell me right now, Doc, if you're not prepared for all that, and I'll take her back to the breeder."

"Who is the breeder?" The tiny cat's wide blue eyes stared into her own.

"My aunt Sophia, in Sacramento."

"You drove all the way to Sacramento to get this kitten for me?"

He looked nonchalant. "I thought you needed something to care for. It takes you out of yourself, y'know, having to think of someone besides yourself. Even a little cat."

She looked accusingly at him. "You wanted to make me more 'human.' "

He grinned. "I guess you could say that. Anyhow, her name's Coco. Kinda chic, I thought. Like you."

"This is a very personal gift, Mahoney," Phyl said warily. The kitten was crawling up her shoulder, burying its soft damp nose in her neck, tangling its paws in her hair. She laughed. "But your aunt Sophia certainly knows what she's doing."

"Then you want to keep her?" He looked anxious. "Remember, she needs love and affection."

She glanced skeptically at him. "I guess I have enough of that to give, despite what you think. And what can I give you in return?"

"Buy me dinner sometime?"

She laughed, hugging the kitten to her breast. "You drive a hard bargain, Detective Mahoney. By the way, I'm getting a roommate."

"I know. I spoke with Niedman. When?"

"On the weekend. I thought maybe if she were here with me, I could work with her. I also remembered what you said about the killer, and I thought she would be safe. Until she remembers who she is, that is. Besides, she has no money, though for all we know she might be an heiress."

"A chance in several million, but I learned the hard way a long time ago never to discount *any* possibility. That little cat needs a litter tray, if you don't mind my speaking frankly, Doc. Better fix it real fast so she knows where to go. Then you'll never have any problem with her."

"Spoken like an expert."

"Yeah, well, I have three of my own. That and opera and cooking keep me from being too introspective. Well, I'd better go. I'm due in court in half an hour. See ya, Doc." He paused at the door. "By the way, I'm following up the French connection with the passport and immigration authorities. If Bea is French, we'll soon know who she is."

~ 8 ~

*B*ea felt like an amateur in the game of life. She knew how to do everyday things, even what music she liked, and how to cook. Nothing fancy, but she was capable enough, and she remembered recipes, many of them French. She remembered the familiar faces of TV personalities, the names of authors whose books she enjoyed, movies she had liked. But she didn't know where she had seen those faces before or where she had read those books or in what movie houses in what towns she had seen the films.

"Don't worry about it," Phyl told her. "It will come to you bit by bit. Remember you are on R and R leave here, rest and recuperation. I just want you to get strong again and enjoy life."

But even though Phyl sounded confident, Bea wasn't at all sure that her memory would return, because every time she tried to cast her thoughts back she came up against the same blankness. It was as though her mind were covered by the same black cloud as the child on the steps of the pink villa she had dreamed about. Because she was convinced it was only a dream. If that villa had ever existed, she would have remembered it. And if she were the child, she would have known who she was.

She had not told Phyl that. Phyl still thought it was a breakthrough. And certainly the fact that she spoke French as easily as she spoke English was a remarkable discovery. And it was good Parisian French, the experts had deduced from her accent, though she didn't recall ever being in Paris. It was the only definite thing from her past. Unless it was not a true memory but just a second-nature reaction, something locked into the computer part of her brain that never disappeared, like knowing how to cook.

Phyl had said that it might be an asset that would prove useful later, though she refused to say why. Anyhow, Bea did not want to think about later. She didn't want to think beyond the moment.

She had been at Phyl's a month and had rarely left the apartment, but this evening Phyl said she was taking her shopping. Bea didn't know whether she was looking forward to it or not. The idea of the crowded stores and people staring at her cropped head, of making choices, walking in the street, eating in a restaurant terrified her. *Real life terrified her.* She liked it here, in Phyl's beautiful apartment. It was big, light, uncluttered. *Safe.*

Mahoney rang from downstairs to announce his arrival. He had gotten into the habit of dropping by from time to time. "To check on the cat," he said.

"To visit *Phyl*, you mean," Bea said, teasing him. She laughed at his embarrassment. "Come on, Detective Mahoney, admit it. I can't blame you, she is gorgeous. And wonderful. And generous."

"And an occasional pain in the ass." Mahoney grinned, letting the kitten clamber up his leg, claws clinging to his jeans. He scooped it up and sat it in the palm of his big hand, and it stared arrogantly around, claiming its victory.

"And anyway, how do you know I'm not working

undercover, pretending I'm here to see Coco when in reality I'm checking on you? Seeing if you're holding out on me and have remembered everything?"

"I'm not holding out," Bea said seriously. "I really can't remember a single thing about the past. Not even"—she hesitated, and a flash of fear crossed her face—"not even who tried to kill me."

The door slammed as Phyl breezed in, home early to take Bea shopping. Since Bea had moved in, Phyl's whole life had changed. Here she was, the dedicated loner who kept her emotions to herself and valued her privacy and independence above all, sharing her home with the victim of a murder attempt and a Siamese cat. Furthermore, she liked it. She liked having someone yell hello when she came home and the appetizing smells of cooking coming from the kitchen and Coco scampering eagerly to greet her, claws skittering on the polished boards. She didn't even mind the cat hairs on her black jacket.

Somehow in these weeks together they had helped each other. Phyl, the smart psychiatrist who locked away her own emotions and her past by burying herself in her work, and Bea, the girl with no past and a threat hanging over her future.

Phyl yelled hi as she flung her raincoat onto the sofa instead of hanging it neatly in the closet, as she would certainly have done a few weeks ago. Today she was going to begin Bea's rehabilitation. She had plans for her. And over dinner, after the shopping expedition, she was going to reveal what those plans were.

She sighed when she saw Mahoney with Bea.

"Not you again, Mahoney," she said scathingly. "How are they ever managing at the police department without you? Or are you just on your way to solving the crime of the century?"

Mahoney sighed exaggeratedly, and Bea grinned, watching them spar. He folded his arms wide and quoted in a melodious voice:

Or if thy mistress some rich anger shows,
Emprison her soft hand and let her rave,
And feed deep, deep upon her peerless eyes. . . .

Then he said solemnly, "Doc, someone should tell
you that aggression does not suit you. Seems to me
Swinburne had the right answer."

"I'm not your 'mistress,' so don't quote European
poets to me, Mahoney. And if you're here to collect on
that dinner I owe you, I'm sorry but I already have a
date."

Mahoney grinned. "Yeah. Bea told me. Shopping
and dinner. Sorry I can't join you. I just came by to
make sure you're treating Coco right. And to tell you
that we've drawn a blank at passport and immigration.
Every Frenchwoman in Bea's age-group entering the
country prior to her—to the incident has been accounted for. Meanwhile, I'm still working on the thousands of names on the airline manifests of women traveling to San Francisco in the week prior to that. Every
name is being checked against its real-life owner. We've
also inquired about private aircraft. There were plenty
that night. From Mexico, Baja, Palm Desert, and
Hawaii. All were piloted by their owners, and none was
carrying a female passenger."

Bea looked downcast; she'd had high hopes that he
would find her name on the airline lists.

Mahoney patted Bea's shoulder comfortingly and
said, "I have to go, or I'll be late solving that crime of
the century and miss my chance at being mayor!"

Phyl was holding the kitten, and he stopped to tickle
it behind the ears. "You're looking good, Doc," he
said with an approving grin.

"Oh, thanks, Mahoney," she said sarcastically again.
"But I'm not sure I need your backhanded compliments."

He laughed as he walked to the door. She turned
her head as she felt his eyes on her.

"I don't know, though," he said consideringly. "Maybe it's all that sitting I warned you about, or maybe it's the home-cooked food, but I'd say your butt looks bigger."

"Oaf," she yelled after him as he slammed the door, laughing. "Beast. Asshole."

The door opened again, and he poked his head around, looking shocked. "Doc, Doc, really. Resorting to bad language. You must ask yourself what that means. . . ."

"Oh, you—you cop," she yelled as he disappeared again, still laughing.

Bea was laughing, too, and despite herself, Phyl joined in. "Why do I like him?" she asked half to herself. "The man is a conceited chauvinist."

But he had made Bea laugh, and she liked that. Her protégée was ready for her first outing, and she inspected her. She was pleased with what she saw.

Bea's soft copper hair was growing in, finally hiding the hideous scars. Now it feathered softly around her face, making her look like a young Audrey Hepburn. Her velvety copper brown eyes were two shades lighter than her hair, and her skin was no longer the color of moonstones but of fresh cream. She was still too thin, of course. The bones were too close to the surface, showing every bump in her spine, the sinews of her long neck, her wrist and ankle bones prominent. But compared with only a month ago, she looked wonderful.

She was wearing jeans and a shirt Phyl had bought for her, and Phyl knew she would be a joy to dress. And she was right. Everything looked good on Bea's tall, slender frame.

They covered the designer departments in the stores and the younger boutiques, and despite Bea's protests, Phyl insisted on equipping her for every possible occasion, from casual to cocktail.

"But where am I going to wear all these lovely

clothes?'' Bea demanded as they struggled back to the car burdened with yet more shopping bags.

"That's what I'm going to tell you over dinner," Phyl said briskly. "And if ever two women deserved a good dinner, we do. We have battled the stores bravely, particularly you, and emerged with the trophies of victory. Now let's celebrate."

She had booked a table at Stars, and Bea slipped the supple new bronze suede jacket over her T-shirt and jeans. She put on the dangling amber earrings Phyl had insisted on buying and a touch of the Prescriptives Havana lipstick the saleswoman had recommended.

"Well, look at you," Phyl marveled as they took their seats in the restaurant. "You're turning every head in the place."

"I thought they were staring at you." Bea glanced cautiously around. "This is wonderful," she said, pleased. "But I wish you hadn't spent all that money on me, Phyl. I promise I'll pay you back, though. One day. When I get a job."

"Speaking of a job, that's what I wanted to talk to you about."

Bea stared at Phyl with astonishment, as she ordered a bottle of wine and studied the menu.

"Here's to you, darling Bea," Phyl said, raising her glass. "To your recovery, to your health, and to our friendship."

"It's I who must thank you. For everything. For giving me a roof over my head, for the lovely clothes." She looked gratefully at Phyl and added softly, "For my sanity."

"It's time for phase two of the recovery," Phyl said. "You may find this idea a little frightening, but it will achieve two things. Both of which are important to you."

Bea stared anxiously at her. She didn't want anything to change; she just wanted life to go on as it was now.

Phyl said, "I have a friend, Millie Renwick. She's as rich as a Rockefeller and mad as a hatter, and she's the most upbeat person I know. She lives in New York, and she's looking for a social secretary—someone to keep up with her appointments, make calls for her, and act as a traveling companion." She laughed, remembering. "A general gofer is more like it, if I know Millie. She's an old dragon, but it's all on the surface. Anyhow, she's planning a trip to Paris. And since you speak French and Millie cannot utter a word to save her life, who better for the job than you?"

Bea's stomach clenched in sudden fear at the thought. She didn't want to go to New York; she was afraid to go to Paris.

"I know Millie well," Phyl said. "I've helped her through a couple of personal traumas and have tried to overcome her guilt at having so much money and indulging herself. Though you can take it from me, she gives away as much as she spends. There's no more generous and charitable woman on earth than Millie Renwick. But I'm warning you. She's an original. They don't make them like Millie anymore.

"I want you to go alone to New York to meet her. Make the quantum leap all by yourself. If you're ever going to get back into the world again, then this is the time to go for it." She looked eagerly at Bea. "So? What do you say?"

Despite her fears, Bea knew Phyl was right. She smiled, a little sadly. "So that's what all the smart clothes were for?"

"Millie is a clotheshorse, and she frequents only the best places: the best restaurants, the best hotels, and the best resorts. It can't be bad now, Bea, can it?"

They laughed together, and then Bea said, "You mentioned there were two reasons my working for Millie was a good idea. What's the other?"

Their eyes met across the table. "I want you out of San Francisco. Away from the danger."

Bea's eyes darkened with fear. "You mean, you think he might come back for me? He might try again?" It was a thought that had gone through her own mind many times.

"You'll be safe with Millie," Phyl reassured her. "No one will know you or what happened. Soon you'll be in Paris. And that's another thing. I thought maybe in France you might start to remember."

"And what then?" Bea whispered, terrified. "What if I remember who I am? And who tried to kill me?"

"All you have to do is call and I'll be there," Phyl promised. "You can count on me. Anyway, I've been invited to attend a medical conference in Paris next month. That's not too long to wait. And it gives me something to look forward to. Seeing Paris and you and Millie."

She told Bea she had booked her on a flight to New York on Thursday. Only two days away. "So there's no time to change our minds," she said firmly because she knew Bea didn't want to go. And she knew, too, how empty her apartment would seem without her. She hated to lose her, even though she knew she was doing the right thing.

She took a photograph of Bea before she left, looking tall and elegant in her new mint green pantsuit, clutching the kitten under her chin with both hands, like a little girl. She was smiling tentatively, and there was a worried look in her eyes, but Phyl thought she looked dazzlingly pretty. She bought a silver frame and placed the picture on the table by her bed. As though it were a picture of her own daughter.

"Don't take Millie on face value or you'll never last a day," were her final words as she put Bea on the plane to New York. Bea soon found out why.

$\sim 9 \sim$

$\mathcal{M}$anhattan had ground to a halt in a torrential downpour aggravated by hurricane-force winds. Buses and cars stacked up at the broken traffic lights, and taxis were an impossibility. Bea was forced to walk ten blocks to her future employer's Fifth Avenue apartment building opposite Central Park. Nevertheless, soaked and windblown, she managed to arrive exactly on time.

The Renwick apartment took up an entire floor, and as Bea stepped from the elevator, Millie herself flung open the door.

"What kept you?" she demanded, sweeping impatiently from the lofty gilded hall into a gold-brocaded drawing room. She waved an imperious arm for Bea to follow. "You're late. I hope this isn't a regular occurrence with you? The blasted butler just quit and the housekeeper ran off last week with some of my best jewelry and there's a new Filipina in the kitchen who can barely understand English. I declare, I'm just about to go out of my mind."

Small and plump with girlish golden curls, she was dressed in an elaborately ruffled cerise dress and high heels. Her wide mouth was generously lipsticked, her mascara was lavishly applied, and her arthritic hands glistened with large rings in gemstones of every color. She was a cloudburst of color, and the style was entirely her own.

Phyl had warned Bea that Millie Renwick was a rich, spoiled woman of uncertain years. She said the only thing certain in her life story was that there were more years than she owned up to. The details of her past varied to suit the moment and her audience—from orphaned heiress of a grand old family to shrewd businesswoman; from lucky gambler to poor little rich girl.

Millie's shrewd blue eyes took in Bea's face for the space of a minute. "Well," she said in her gravelly voice, "if ever I saw anyone who needed a job, it's you. You look as though you could use a good meal." She shook a Marlboro from a crumpled pack. Ignoring the elaborate gold lighter on the table next to her, she took a book of dime store matches from her pocket and lit it. She waved out the match, inhaling with the ardor of a true nicotine addict.

She examined the soaked young woman dripping onto her Chinese silk rug. After a flurry of coughing, she said sarcastically, "What's Phyl into these days besides psychiatry? The Animal Rescue Service?"

Sticking her chin in the air, Bea turned and squished indignantly back to the door. "I think I had better go."

"Oh, for God's sake!" Millie flicked ash exasperatedly into a large crystal ashtray already overflowing with lipstick-rimmed butts smoked down to the filter. "You can't live with me and be touchy. Take off your coat and those ghastly wet shoes, and sit down. Here. By the fire. Come, tell me about yourself."

She flung Bea a smile of such genuine warmth and roguish charm, half apologetic, half mischievous, that Bea found herself doing as she was told. Millicent Renwick was that kind of person she was soon to discover.

One minute you adored her; the next you couldn't stand her. One minute she was good; the next she was horrid. Just like the litle girl with the curl in the middle of her forehead in the children's poem.

Bea obediently slipped off her soggy shoes and her wet coat and put them on the marble hall floor, where they wouldn't ruin anything. Then she returned to the library and sat cautiously on the edge of a gold brocade sofa.

Millicent's curious eyes, dark as black currants, met hers. "Well?" she said expectantly. "Phyl told me the bare bones of the story, but not all of it."

"There's not much to tell. There was an accident. Although the police think maybe it wasn't. They think someone tried to kill me." Bea lifted her wet hair from her brow to show the scar running into her scalp as she told Millie the story.

"I'm fine now," she said reassuringly, anxious for the job. "The only thing is . . . I don't remember any of it. And I don't remember who I am."

"And the police didn't help?"

"No one of my description has been reported missing. No one came looking for me. No one seemed to care whether I lived or died. Except Phyl. And Detective Mahoney, of course."

Millie dragged thoughtfully on the last of her cigarette, then stubbed it out amid the heap of butts in the crystal ashtray. "Well, well, a woman with no past." She stared at Bea and then smiled and said cryptically, "The perfect companion for the woman with no future.

"You can start immediately by fetching me another pack of ciggies from my room. And then we shall have some tea. Tell the Filipina in the kitchen, Earl Grey for two. And not too strong this time or I'll kill her. And sandwiches. Smoked salmon and egg salad. Finger sandwiches, no crusts; she knows the way I like them.

And then get on the phone and order me up a new butler. I don't like answering my own doorbell."

She glanced at her enormous diamond-studded watch. "And after that it'll almost be time for the first glass of champagne." She rolled her eyes heavenward and grimaced. "God, why at my age do I think a glass of bubbly taken before the sun is over the yardarm is the first step on the path to decadence? When I don't give a damn about decadence. And anyway, it's not alcohol that'll kill me; it's these blasted ciggies. . . ."

Bea moved into the grand fourteen-room apartment overlooking Central Park. Her pretty blue and white room was next to Millie's palatial suite. "Near enough to yell if I need you," Millie told her cheerfully. She was sitting on Bea's bed, watching her unpack, passing critical comments on each garment as she hung it in her closet.

"Mmm, not one for color, are you, dear girl?" she said witheringly, eyeing yet another neutral-toned linen dress. "How do you ever hope to get yourself noticed in beige? I can see Phyl's influence at work. You know I've never seen that women in anything but black and white. I can tell you it would drive me nuts."

She smiled, wafting away cigarette smoke and added smugly, "I've always found the best way to catch a man's eye is to wear a bright color. Pink preferably. And a few good diamonds, of course. But then, I guess after what you've just been through, you don't want to be noticed right now." She patted Bea's hand sympatheticaly. "Don't worry, dear girl. You'll be safe with Millie."

Bea smiled gratefully. She could see that life with Millie was going to be a series of ups and downs, but she knew Millie really was kind under that bullying facade.

"Who needs men anyway?" Millie demanded, holding up a copper-colored sweater that almost matched Bea's hair and shaking her head disapprovingly. "I've been married three times, dear girl. First to a polo player. Then, in my racing phase, to a jockey. And last to an international playboy. And let me tell you there is nobody less *fun* than *a playboy*. After him I figured three times was enough. Marriage was not for me. Not that I haven't had the odd little flutter''—her dark eyes twinkled with mischief—"but at least I didn't marry them.''

Bea laughed with her, and then Millie said impatiently, "Hurry and get changed, dear girl. We're off to lunch at Le Cirque. Put on the smartest of those ghastly beige suits and a big smile, and prepare to enjoy some of the best food in New York. And make sure you order all the most fattening dishes; you could use a bit of flesh on your bones. And then tonight there's a fund-raising dinner at the Waldorf. Our President is speaking, you know. I thought it might be interesting, and I bought a table so there will be lots of people to introduce you to.''

Bea's heart sank at the thought, and Millie caught her apprehensive glance. She said briskly, "Of course you'll cope. I'll just tell them all that you had an accident and that your memory is a bit hazy.'' She yelped with laughter as she added, "Other than that you are a perfectly normal young woman.''

Bea found herself whirled into two frantic weeks of lunches, fund-raising dinners, and charity balls. She even got used to Millie complaining all the time about her simple taste in clothes, her minimal use of makeup, and her unwillingness to eat a good breakfast.

"You're as bad as my mother,'' Bea retorted one day as she turned down dessert at yet another smart lunch.

"Even your mother would not have turned down dessert at Lutèce.'' Millie glanced at her overcasually as she added, "By the way, what was your mother like?''

Panic fizzed up Bea's spine. She stared blankly at Millie. "I just said that, didn't I? About my mother. And yet now, when I'm trying to visualize her, trying to think of her voice saying, 'Eat your breakfast or you won't grow up big and strong,' all I get is that same blank wall in my mind. There's just nothing there.''

Her voice had risen in panic, and Millie patted her hand soothingly. Phyl had asked her to watch out for any signs of returning memory, but she hadn't realized quite how upset Bea would get.

"Poor child," she said in a quiet voice, unlike her usual boisterous high-pitched chatter. "You must feel desperately lonely. And I can tell you I know a thing or two about loneliness myself. We shall just have to cheer each other up, won't we? After all, we're off to Paris next week, and there's nothing like France to put a glow in a girl's heart."

Bea surely hoped she was right.

~ 10 ~

Mahoney telephoned Phyl a few days later. "I'm calling in my marker," he said confidently. "Remember? You promised me dinner?"

"In exchange for Coco. I remember. And since I'm a woman who always pays her debts, Mahoney, you can name your time and place."

He could sense she was smiling. "Tomorrow," he said. "And anywhere as long as it's not McDonald's."

She laughed. "Tomorrow," she agreed. "Pick me up at seven-thirty."

"Seven-thirty," he said, uncrossing his fingers, marveling at his good luck because he hadn't really believed she would say yes.

"And, Mahoney . . . it won't be McDonald's, so try to look decent for once, will you?"

He laughed out loud as he put down the phone.

He rang her doorbell promptly at seven-thirty the next evening. She opened it and stood silently, taking in his smart dark suit, white shirt, and flamboyant red-flowered silk tie. His dark hair was still wet from the shower and showed track marks from the comb. If she'd wanted, she could have seen her face in the shine of his shoes. He was clutching a bunch of flowers in one hand and a small brown paper bag in the other.

"You look like a cop pretending to be a solid citizen," she said, amused.

"Yeah. Well, you're softening up a little yourself," he replied, grinning as he saw her blush. Her dark hair was loose tonight instead of in its usual tight knot. She was wearing black as always, but this time it was a gauzy low-cut dress with a slinky skirt, and she smelled of lilies and gardenias.

His eyes admired her as he handed her the bouquet. "You smell better than nature's roses," he said.

"It's Bellodgia," she replied coolly. "A bit old-fashioned, but it suited my mood tonight. And thank you for the beautiful roses."

They were pink with a hint of cream, and their velvet petals were just beginning to unfurl.

"They're called Oceana," he said. "I thought they were like garden roses, a bit old-fashioned. Like your perfume. Seems I got the mood right for the night."

He gave the paper bag to the cat, who was wrapping itself around his legs, purring. "And this is for young Coco. To keep her busy while the doc is out."

They laughed as the kitten swiftly tore out the catnip mouse and tossed it into the air, pouncing after it.

Phyl offered him a glass of champagne.

"A wonderful choice," he said, tasting it appreciatively. "And not obvious. Laurent Perrier is a fine old house, and its Grand Siècle ranks with the best."

Phyl stared at him with astonishment. "Is there no end to your surprises, Mahoney?" she demanded. "I would not have recognized Grand Siècle in a blind tasting. How on earth did you?"

He shrugged nonchalantly. "Just one of those things they teach you at cop school." He grinned teasingly. "No, I didn't mean that. I spent a year in France after college, part of it in Épernay picking grapes. Every bar and café sells champagne as a matter of course, so I got to taste all the small growers. I liked it so much I made a point of visiting all the grand houses. I have a reasonable palate and I knew what I liked, and this happened to be one of them." He shrugged again. "So you see. No mystery. Just a lucky shot on your part that you picked my favorite."

"I almost wish you were doing the cooking," she said wistfully. "You're hard to beat."

"Anytime you say, Doc. Just whistle and I'll be there, trying out my Italian specialties on you. Marcella Hazan's wild mushroom risotto, Roger Vergé's Petites Niçoise farcis and pistou soup, my mama's old-fashioned vegetarian lasagna. And the best desserts this side of Rome."

"Tiramisu?" she asked jokingly. It was one of her favorites.

"Hate the stuff, but if you like it, Doc, you shall have it."

"Not tonight," she said, collecting her jacket. "And it's getting late."

Mahoney's eyebrows rose when he saw the long black limousine waiting at the curb. She threw him a mocking grin as the driver held the door open. "You didn't think I was going to let you drink and drive, did you? After all, I wouldn't want to be responsible for your not becoming mayor."

He glanced apprehensively over his shoulder before getting in next to her. "At least it's black," he said nervously. "If any of the guys spot me, I hope they'll think I'm on my way back from a funeral and not that I have a sideline as a pimp. Doc, limos were not in the deal. A simple dinner was all I asked."

"And that's what you'll get," she replied serenely. "The best simple dinner you've had in a while, I'll bet. Though maybe not," she added, remembering his spaghetti. "And would you mind, just for this evening, calling me Phyl instead of Doc? Somehow it suits the occasion better."

He nodded solemnly as they drove north out of the city into Marin County. "You've got it, Phyl." He shook her hand. "Meet Franco. And you know what? A guy could get very used to this kind of life. Beautiful women, limos, great meals . . . Maybe I've died and gone to paradise."

"Don't bet on it, Franco," she warned.

It was an unusually warm May evening, and the windows of the Lark Creek Inn stood open to the balmy air. The candles on the table flickered in the soft breeze as they sipped a bountiful California merlot. "Edgy but beautiful," Mahoney said. "Like you."

"Thanks, Franco. Tell me why there is always something backhanded in your compliments."

He sighed exaggeratedly. "I don't know, Phyl. I guess you'll just have to analyze me to find out what's wrong with my psyche."

"There's nothing wrong with your psyche," she retorted. "It's your head that's the problem. It's swollen from all that media attention." She leaned closer, interested. "Tell me, how do you do it? Solve all those unsolvable crimes?"

"Hard work. Intuition. Painstaking searches through the facts. Good eyesight—you need it for inspecting the crime scenes. And a bad memory for the daily horrors of it all." He grimaced. "There's no glamour about being a homicide cop, Doc. Except that created by the media."

"Then why did you choose it? Instead of academia?"

"My Irish great-grandfather was a cop, and so was my Italian grandfather and my father. Seems I couldn't beat the genes."

"Or you wanted to do some good," she suggested softly. "To help your fellowmen."

He laughed. "Sure. I'll accept that. Saint Franco. That'll go down well in the squad room. Phyl, the truth is I'm just a hardworking cop who, for some reason I've yet to figure out, finds it satisfying to catch murderers and crazies who feel they can play God and kill other guys just for a fix. Or for five bucks. Or for merely looking at them the wrong way. And rapists who shoot their victims so they can't tell on them. And kids who tie their grandmothers' stockings around their throats and watch them choke to death, in return for their meager life savings. A hundred and fifty bucks hidden under an ancient mattress. And what does a kid like that want it for? A pair of Nike airs and a cheap leather jacket so he can impress his friend's girl, maybe buy her some coke and then maybe she'll fuck him.''

Franco's handsome face was grim, and Phyl stared in horror at him. "I'm sorry," he said quietly, "but you asked.''

"I understand.''

He looked admiringly at her. The breeze fluttered the candles, casting the light upward onto her face. Her shoulders and the swell of her breasts looked like fresh cream against the soft black chiffon. "You should wear red," he said lightly, changing the conversation and the mood. "It would look great with your coloring.''

She looked down, embarrassed; the conversation was becoming suddenly personal. "Red is for Las Vegas hookers," she said coolly. "Or overdressed old ladies on cruise ships.''

"Is that so?" His eyes mocked her. "Some of us think it is the color of roses and valentines. Now, I wonder what a good psychiatrist would make of that?''

"She would probably say that at your age you are still a foolish romantic, Franco Mahoney.''

They both laughed, and he thought how much he liked her cool independence. They talked, striking sparks off each other, as they ate simple roast chicken that he swore must have been bred by a chicken connoisseur and cooked by a real grandmother who knew her stuff.

"I couldn't have done better myself," he said, with a

satisfied sigh. "This was a very wise choice, Dr. Phyl. You know me better than I thought."

"That's my job," she said with a mischievous smile. "But I insist you taste the bread and butter pudding. It's simply the best."

"If you say so, ma'am. You see, I'm just putty in your hands." He laughed, enjoying himself hugely. "I could get used to this boy toy role: limos, wine, dinners, a beautiful companion who is paying for it all. Though it does seem a tad extravagant in return for a kitten."

"Not just any kitten." She took his hand across the table, and he looked at her in surprise. "You were right, of course, that night. You analyzed my silly, selfish, compartmentalized life accurately. I would never have dared be so truthful with myself. I might never have stopped thinking about the past and got on with the present. But because of you, and Coco and Bea, my whole life has changed."

He looked searchingly at her. "You want to tell me about that past?"

She glanced down, tracing the pattern on her knife with her finger. Her voice was so low he had to lean closer as she said hesitantly, "I was married, once. We were too young, of course. We were both doing our internships at Chicago General. It may be the busiest hospital in the country, especially weekends. The Saturday Night Special, they called it, though Friday was just as bad. People out drinking, fighting, slaughtering each other. We met there, in the emergency room over a multiple stab wound. He was Stanford, and I was Yale. We hated each other on sight, and so of course, we fell in love."

She smiled sadly, remembering the sweetness of youth and love. "He was the old-fashioned type; he wanted marriage. And children. And a wife who stayed home to look after her family. The child came along almost immediately. A girl. So pretty, so sweet." She glanced up at him, her face suddenly alight with love for her child. "Oh, Franco, you know how most babies always seem to be crying? Well, not this one. She was a dream baby, right from day one.

"My husband's family were well-to-do; they were financing their son through med school. It was different for me. I was abandoned when I was just a kid. I never really knew my own mother, and there wasn't any father around. When she took off, I was taken into court and then put in foster care. I had seven different sets of foster parents between the ages of three and seventeen. And boy, how I missed my mother all those years. Even now . . . it's hard to adjust to not being wanted.

"So you see, I was determined that wouldn't happen to my little girl. I gave up my ambitions and settled down to become a full-time mom in a pretty little house in Dearborn. My husband worked eighteen-hour days; he was exhausted. I understood; after all, I had been there. I said we must go on vacation. Just the two of us." There was an endless pause as Phyl silently stared down at the table. Franco waited, afraid to speak.

Finally in an emotion-choked voice she whispered, "We dropped the baby off with the grandparents in San Diego and kissed her good-bye. She waved her plump little arm at us and blew kisses as we went off to Mexico. Blue skies, the sea, perfect peace, just for a week or two."

Franco saw the raw wound in her soul as she looked up at him with blank blue eyes. He reached out to her to take her hands in his. He wanted to enfold her in his arms, to tell her it was okay. . . .

"We had been there two days when we got the phone call. She was sick. They suspected meningitis. There was no flight out until the next morning. There was no charter available for hours—"

"Don't tell me," Franco said, gripping her cold hands. "It's too painful. I understand."

Phyl didn't seem to hear him. Her eyes were brilliant

with unshed tears. "She died before we could get there. She was just two years old. And all I could think of was that she must have been calling for me, Mommy Mommy. . . . And I wasn't there. *Her mommy wasn't there.*"

"Oh, God," Franco said, sharing her anguish.

He could see her fighting for control. "It took years for me to be able to cope with it. Sometimes I wonder if it made me better at my job. Going through the pain? I try not to think about it, but somehow, when I saw Bea on television and they thought she was dead, it brought it all back again. And I thought about her mother, not being there, about her being told . . . her daughter was dead. . . ."

"Thank you for telling me," Franco said simply.

Phyl nodded. "It was just as bad for my husband. He thought we should have another child right away, but I couldn't bear it. I went back to med school, back to the hospital grind. . . . We divorced a couple of years later. He's a successful internist now, in San Diego. Married with four kids. And I am Dr. Phyl, focusing on almost anything but myself."

"And maybe now that's just what you should be doing. Thinking more about yourself as well as Bea. Life is for living, Phyl, and you are a woman with a lot to give. Give yourself a break, love yourself more."

"And then maybe someone else can love me?" She managed a grin. "Remember me? The ice maiden? Oh, I don't think so, Franco. I've chosen my course."

He stared at her, seeing how beautiful she was with the tears still glistening on her long black lashes and her soft mouth tremulous with the pain of her love and the guilt she could not give up. He thought that beneath that invincible facade, Phyl Forster was the most vulnerable woman he knew. And one of the bravest and most lonely. He knew that one day she had to crack.

He gripped her hands more tightly and bent to kiss

her fingers. Somehow he hoped he would be around when that happened.

"Well, now you know the real me, and that's enough of the past," she said, blinking away her tears and giving him a brilliant smile. "Let's talk about Bea."

She took her hand from his and smoothed back her hair. "Let's order that bread and butter pudding," she said brightly, and again he admired her courage and deplored her foolishness.

She told him that Millie demanded all Bea's time, and that suited Bea just fine because she still wasn't sure who, or what, she was.

"There's such an enormous gap in her life, you see," Phyl said, "and that's what terrifies her. The background to her existence just isn't there. All those details that go to make up a person: the parents, the sisters, brothers, cousins. The schools and college, cheerleaders and football games. She doesn't know what her life was like. She says it's driving her crazy, and so mostly I think she is pushing it away and living for the moment. And tomorrow they are off to Paris."

"Sounds good to me. Better than moping around your apartment waiting for her memory to return. Or the murderer to try again."

Phyl's eyes widened. She sounded frightened as she said, "You don't really think he will?"

"What can I tell you?" Mahoney lifted his hands, palms up, helplessly. "Except we've drawn a blank on all our inquiries and the case is now officially on hold. Stashed in the unsolved mystery file. The consensus is that it was a random killer on the loose. They figure anyone could have been a potential victim. It just happened to be Bea."

"And is that what you think?"

Phyl looked so scared Mahoney wanted to put his arm around her, to tell her it was all right, that he would find the killer; he would work it all out, and she need never be afraid again. But he couldn't promise any of those things.

He said, "No, I don't agree. I think this was a purposeful and knowing murder attempt. The guy knew Bea, and for some reason he wanted her out of the way. What I have to find out is why. And unless Bea regains her memory, I'm afraid there's not much hope.

"Detective work is fifty percent slog and fifty percent intuition," he added bitterly. "You get so you can feel who the villains are, even when they are cloaked in normality. Straight, decent-seeming folks, just like you and me. But the famous Dr. Forster must know better than anyone what goes on in people's minds. In those deep, dark recesses. Things that are hidden behind good looks and charm and expensive clothes. The wife beaters, the child abusers, the murderers. They are all just folks, like you and me."

"Speak for yourself," she retorted. "And let me know what nice, good-looking, charming young man tried to kill Bea. And why!"

"I'm not giving up," he said. "I can promise you that."

Mist was wreathing ghostly tendrils down the road as they drove home. Phyl closed her eyes, leaning tiredly back against the cushions. "Now tell me the limo wasn't a good idea, Mahoney," she murmured.

"It wasn't a good idea, Doc," he obliged, and she groaned.

"I'm still waiting for it," she added.

"What's that?"

She rested her head against his shoulder, and he smiled tenderly, staring straight ahead at the lighted towers of the city.

"The poetry quote, of course. I've never known you to miss an opportunity. Or to be lost for words."

"You're right." He thought for a minute and then said, "How about this?"

She walks in beauty, like the night
Of cloudless climes and starry skies;
And all that's best of dark and bright
Meet in her aspect and her eyes. . . .

"Byron," he said.

"I know." She had opened her eyes and was looking at him.

"Corny, maybe, but appropriate. It was meant as a compliment to my hostess, who is as beautiful as the night."

Her eyes were smiling at him in the dark. "Thank you, Mahoney," she whispered.

"Franco, please." He read the meaning in her eyes, and he patted her hand tenderly.

The limo drew up in front of her apartment building, and Mahoney jumped out and raced around to open the door for her before the chauffeur had a chance. He looked at her, lying back against the cushions. There were violet smudges under her eyes, and her lipstick had worn off. He thought she looked like a tired young girl. He took her hand and walked her up the steps to the door. "Go get some sleep."

He bent his head and kissed her lightly on the cheek, breathing in the scent of her. "Thanks, Doc, for a memorable evening. It was fun."

She nodded. "You make me laugh, Mahoney. I like that."

He grinned. "It goes with the job, ma'am. We are only here to serve."

"Then you can serve me dinner. Next time."

"Yes, ma'am. You've got it, Doc. Anytime you say."

She watched him walk to the car. He turned and looked back at her, and she said quietly, "And thank you, Mahoney, for listening to me. And for all you have done for Bea. I know if anyone can find the murderer, you can."

He made a mock salute as he quoted:

And therefore, since I cannot prove a lover
To entertain these fair well-spoken days,
I am determined to prove a villain
And hate the idle pleasures of these days.

"Shakespeare, *Richard the Third.*"

She rolled her eyes heavenward in mock despair as
she waved good-bye, but he saw she was smiling again
as he closed the door.

The limo driver flinched when Mahoney told him to
drop him at the old City Jail.

"Just wanted to see if you were awake," Mahoney
said, grinning. "Make it the Police Department."

"Same building, isn't it?"

"It might even be the same place!"

He just wanted to check Bea's file one more time.
He was sure there must be something in there that
held a clue to the secret.

~ 11 ~

Millie and Bea were staying in the Chanel suite at the Paris Ritz and had spent the previous days at the couturiers on the Avenue Montaigne, ordering Millie's fall wardrobe, as well as in the Left Bank antiques shops, generally buying up a storm. Millie simply bought anything she fancied on the spur of the moment and usually regretted it later.

"The truth is, dear girl, that my father manufactured plumbing fixtures in Pittsburgh, as his father did before him," she said. They were sitting in the Ritz bar a few nights later, enjoying a drink before dinner while Millie checked out the patrons to see whom she knew.

"That's how I can afford all this," Millie confessed. "Daddy made himself a tidy fortune, before the accident at the plant that killed him. He was still a young man, and he left my mother an even younger widow, with a four-year-old daughter and a great deal of money. Mama was a shy woman, without many friends, and it was a solitary life for a child." She sighed, reflectively, sipping her Campari and soda. "Maybe you're better off not recalling your childhood, Bea. It might turn out to have been as disappointing as mine."

"I don't think so," Bea said. "I don't get bad feelings about the past." She had become used to Millie's sudden clumsy, probing questions. She knew she was only following Phyl's instructions and trying to help, but so far without any luck. Except Bea felt completely at home in Paris. The language was her own, just as much as English, and she spoke it so fluently the Parisians paid her the biggest compliment of all by assuming that she was one of them.

Millie waved at an acquaintance across the room. She seemed to know people everywhere they went. She said, "Perhaps it's because of my provincial Victorian-style upbringing that I've always craved change and excitement. I always adored people and parties and clothes and jewelry. You know how I like tinsel and flash. Well, when I was a girl, I yearned for red silk instead of burgundy plush, I wanted rubies instead of garnets, diamonds instead of opals. I liked the grand hotels where my mama occasionally took me for holidays, with their sparkling chandeliers and sparkling wines fizzing in saucer-shaped glasses. Even when I was very young, I wanted orchids, not tea roses, shiny gold bracelets instead of demure ivory bangles.

"I still remember Mama saying, 'You must eat up all your potatoes and vegetables, Millicent, before you can have dessert.' " Millie snorted disparagingly. "Is it any wonder I was plump as a pumpkin, as well as short? And you know what, Bea"—she leaned closer and said in a loud, confidential whisper—"I never wore silk next to my skin until I was eighteen years old. After my mother died.

"I had no family, except for a remote cousin in Ohio who never contacted me again after writing to express his regrets, so there was no one to consider except myself." She signaled the waiter for the check and signed it with a flourish. "But I wasn't afraid to take the reins of life and gallop the horses myself. No, sir. Not Millie Renwick.

"I inherited the lot, y'know," she continued in the chauffeured car on the way to Robuchon. "The big house in Pittsburgh that I hated, and all its ghastly Turkey-carpeted, silver-candelabraed splendor. Plus the fifty million dollars that went with it. And let me tell you, Bea, fifty million was a lot of money in the 1930s. Especially for a young girl. I was an heiress. A catch."

She yelped with laughter at the thought. "I moved out of the house, out of Pittsburgh into Manhattan. Took a suite at the Plaza, hired someone who knew about these things to take me shopping, and bought myself an entire new wardrobe. Head to toe. Everything from the skin out." She sighed luxuriously, remembering. "And it had to be silk, though satin was nice, too. And I wanted everything in bright colors.

"I had Mama's old diamonds reset at Buccelatti and bought myself a whole slew of shiny new stones in every color: earrings, necklaces, bracelets, rings, watches. Then I took myself off to the hairdresser and emerged four hours later a platinum blonde, like Jean Harlow. She was all the rage then, dear girl."

She patted Bea's knee affectionately. "For years I never told anyone this, you know. Except Phyl. She said it was good for me to talk it out, so now I tell anyone who's foolish enough to listen to the truth about me." She tilted her bright blond head consideringly to one side. "Well, approximately the truth anyway," she amended.

"But then, dear girl, I began to look around for companionship. And I found it among the polo playing set in Palm Beach. I bought myself a wonderful Addison Mizner gem of a Moorish castle and married a handsome man twice my age, the captain of the visiting Argentinian team. Of course, I didn't need Phyl to tell me I must have been looking for my daddy. Anyway, he didn't last long. *No good in bed, dear girl,*" she said in another loud, confidential whisper, making Bea giggle. "Not that I was any good myself, being a novice filly at the time, but I knew it had to be better than that. Or why were so many people doing it?"

They had arrived at the restaurant, and she wafted confidently inside, shaking hands with the maître d' and greeting waiters by name.

"I didn't realize you came to Paris so often," Bea said, astonished. "Every place we go, they know you."

"It's not just my baby blues, dear girl. I'm also a phenomenal tipper," Millie replied shrewdly. "I can afford it, and it smooths life's path and makes other people happy, so why not?"

"Money really means nothing to you, does it?" Bea said with amazement.

"Don't you believe it, dear girl. Money means everything to me. It has bought me a lot of pleasure, and I like to think I've been able to share it."

"Phyl said you were a champion of good causes."

"Did she now? Then she was talking out of turn. Everyone knows I'm just a frivolous, rich old biddy who fritters her time and money on selfish pursuits. And that's why we are here tonight," she said, ordering for both of them because she knew best.

Bea laughed as she looked around the exclusive restaurant. Millie had told her it was one of the best in Paris, and as she tasted each dish, she knew Millie was right. Though how Millie managed to eat and talk nonstop at the same time amazed her.

"After Palm Beach, I moved on to Saratoga and the horse-racing set," Millie continued. "I was very partial to a flutter on the races. Still am. And that's where the second husband came from."

She chewed the stuffed sea bass, remembering. "He was a small man, of course. Had to be in his profession. Though he wasn't small in the department that mattered. He certainly taught me a thing or two in bed, I can tell you, dear girl. Even if he did treat me a bit like a horse. I always felt he wanted to tack me up—y'know, the saddle and stirrups and the whip—and then after-

ward take me out into the stableyard and hose me
down: the curry comb and a sack of oats, that sort of
thing. Of course it couldn't last, but then I never expected it to. I wasn't into 'lasting.' After all, I was only
twenty-two, and I was still learning my way around life
and men.

"Next came the playboy. He had a title; it was *almost*
phony but not quite. He was the third son, and his
eldest brother was actually the count. But he was the
best-looking man I'd ever seen. And he was the perfect
party animal; he had been to every major event in the
previous twenty years. I thought he was the perfect
match for me because at that time I was determined to
be known as the party girl of the decade. Very Scott
Fitzgerald, you know. And speaking of Fitzgerald, of
course, I met him, down at the Cap, with that crazy
wife, and Chanel. And Picasso, that naughty man, and
Cocteau."

She sighed, recalling gay times on the Côte d'Azur.
"It was all just tiny fishing villages then, dear girl, and
endless sunny days, and the Hôtel du Cap was small but
still the chicest place on the coast.

"Anyway, surprise, surprise, the aging playboy lost
his playboy ways when he married the young heiress.
Suddenly he didn't want to party anymore. He wanted
to be the country squire in a huge château with liver-
ied servants. He even started thinking about entering
politics. I was out of there so fast he never even saw my
dust."

She exploded into laughter at the memory. "Then I
went back to the States and bought the Fifth Avenue
apartment. I kept the Palm Beach place, though I
rarely used it. I could never stay in just one place; the
grass was always greener somewhere else, and I was
always traveling, crossing the oceans on liners and
cruise ships and the skies in flying boats and Pan Am
Clippers. Those were the days," she said reminiscently,
over dessert and coffee. "Now it's boring old seven-

forty-sevens and Concordes and private Gulfstream
jets. So now you see, Bea, why everyone knows me at all
the great hotels around the world.

"They greet me with open arms and, I hope, genuine affection, because I've known some of them since
we were all young, forty years or so. I'm always generous, and they seem to find me amusing, and they put
up with my eccentricities and my demanding ways.
Like you, dear girl," she added, giving Bea's cheek an
affectionate pat.

Bea beamed happily at her. "Of course they do,"
she said loyally. "And thank you for telling me your life
story."

"There's a catch to it," Millie warned, lighting up a
Marlboro. "I expect to hear yours in return, one day
soon."

Bea promised, smiling, to do her best to remember
it. She thought Millie Renwick was okay. And she understood that her millions had bought her fleeting
happiness and a great deal of loneliness, wandering
the grand hotels of the world, hoping the warm
welcomes of the hotel managers and staff occurred not
just because she spent a fortune and tipped well, but
because they were genuinely glad to see her.

"It's probably all due to my father getting killed like
that when I was nothing but a kid," Millie said, suddenly moist-eyed. "I guess I've been missing him all my
life.

"And talking about the Côte d'Azur has made me
nostalgic for the place." She wiped away her tears and
looked at Bea, her eyes sparkling with a sudden idea.
"Why not let's go there tomorrow?"

"But Phyl is coming to Paris in a couple of weeks,"
Bea protested.

"And no doubt she'll be tied up all day and half the
night with the shrinks' conference. She can fly down
and join us afterward, at the Hôtel du Cap. They know

me there. They'll look after me like the prodigal daughter.''

Bea knew by now there was no use arguing. When Millie made up her mind, it stayed made up. The Hôtel du Cap it was. And tomorrow.

~ 12 ~

It was early June, and the Côte d'Azur was living up to its name: all blue skies, calm azure sea, and brilliant sunshine. As Millie had forecast, the staff at the Hôtel du Cap welcomed her like an old friend. She filled her afternoons contentedly playing bridge with a host of new acquaintances, while Bea lazed by the pool overlooking the Mediterranean and acquired a light golden tan.

Inspecting herself in the mirror a week later, Bea thought she looked different: *like a new woman.* She shook her head to fluff out her hair until it resembled a shaggy copper chrysanthemum. It was long enough now to flop into her eyes and form a little ducktail at the nape of her neck, but she decided she wasn't going to cut it yet. She laughed, admiring it. She was so glad to have hair she might never cut it again.

While Millie still slumbered in her lavish suite, Bea spent the early mornings wandering through the street markets of Antibes and Nice, admiring the stalls, heady with the scent of roses and lilies and gleaming with morning-fresh peaches and apricots, eggplants, and ol-ives. She joined the chic women browsing through the bargain-priced linen jackets and skirts with Paris labels and the inexpensive jewelry and strings of brilliantly colored glass beads.

Then she sat on a café terrace, shedding her worries like dust motes in the sunshine, happily watching the world go by over a *café crème* and a buttery croissant. The hospital and the broken skull and the man who wanted to murder her seemed a million miles away. Only the dark terror of not knowing the past remained to haunt her, the nightmare of falling endlessly down the black tunnel, falling and falling. . . .

Some nights she would leap, shaking, from the bed and run to the open window, to look out at the midnight blue sky, and feel the cool air on her fevered skin, waiting for her heart to stop pounding and to feel normal again. Or as normal as it could be for a young woman who did not know who she was. But there were still many nights when the beauty and stillness did not soothe her. Those were the nights when despair overtook her, and she sobbed until dawn, when exhausted, she finally slept. She never spoke to Millie about those awful nights. She did not want to burden her with her problems. And if Millie noticed her pallor and swollen eyes, she made no comment.

Bea was also reluctant to worry Phyl. She decided her new friends had done enough for her. It was up to her to manage her own life now.

Millie had hired a white Mercedes convertible, and with Bea at the wheel, they explored the coast and the hills behind. Millie was full of memories of the way it used to be, "in the old days," when she was just a girl, kicking over the traces, dining and dancing and flirting and gambling.

"It was still unspoiled, dear girl," she said, filled with nostalgia. "You should have seen it then, Bea, when this string of towns and high rises along the coast were just tiny fishing villages. There are some compensations to getting old, I suppose. The things one has seen and done, the memories. You never lose them, you know."

Millie flung herself into the hectic social life of the Riviera, looking up old acquaintances and making new ones, attending openings and galas and dinners and concerts, and enjoying herself thoroughly. And being a woman who could afford to indulge her whims and fancies, she suddenly announced that she intended to buy a house somewhere along the coast that she loved best.

Bea did her best to talk her out of it, saying it was just another whim that she would live to regret, but Millie was adamant. She had made up her mind she wanted to spend her summers on the Riviera. "Just like the old days."

They were going house hunting that very morning, and Millie had dressed for the occasion. She looked like a plump tropical bird in a floating lime green and pink dress with her blond curls hidden under a shady pink straw hat.

She threw a critical glance at Bea, cool in navy silk shorts and white T-shirt.

"You should always wear a hat, Bea," she told her severely. "Believe me, if you don't, you'll regret it when you're forty. You'll have skin like a piece of old leather." She laughed as Bea obligingly pulled on a Yankees baseball cap. "That's not quite what I meant, dear girl. But on you it looks good."

Bea drove to the smart real estate office in Cannes, and Millie told the smooth buttoned-down agent she wanted "something with a touch of class."

"Don't bother showing me any of those white plaster boxes all tricked up with marble and sliding glass doors on lots the size of a postage stamp," she warned him. "I want terraces and balustrades and proper French doors and arches and columns. And a view of the Mediterranean. *Class,* my dear man. That is what I want."

And the agent raised a supercilious eyebrow and informed her that the firm dealt only in the best.

But a few days and several dozen houses later both she and the agent were exhausted and beginning to lose their patience. "I'll leave it to you," she told Bea, retreating to the comforts of the hotel and the bridge table. "You know exactly what I want, dear girl. Find us something nice."

Bea spent the next few days happily zigzagging along the coast, inspecting properties, but still found nothing that was quite right. She was up in the hills near Vence when she noticed the thunderclouds stacking ominously over the mountains. The temperature and humidity were soaring, so she decided to stop for a cool drink at a café.

The small village square was deserted, and the only other customer on the café terrace was a young man who was busy writing.

She sipped her cold drink, watching him, wondering what he was writing that kept him so absorbed. He was *almost* good-looking, she conceded. Not too tall, with rumpled curly brown hair that looked as though he had run his hands through it once too often. And he had an interesting bony face and a generous-looking mouth that she thought would have been described in romantic novels as "finely chiseled." She guessed he was in his early thirties and decided he must be a writer, wondering if he was famous and if she should know him.

She jumped as lightning suddenly forked through the blackened sky, followed by a peal of thunder and the spatter of raindrops. A wind gusted from nowhere, scattering the man's papers, and she ran to help pick them up before they were soaked. He thanked her in French, but she could tell from his accent he was English.

There was another flash, and the rain began to come down in torrents as they ran together into the café.

"Better sit out the storm in here," he said, smiling at her. "Let me buy you a drink to thank you for saving my priceless manuscript."

They sat at the small scarred wooden bar, sipping a glass of rosé wine, and he told her his name was Nick Lascelles. Then he asked where she was from.

Bea stared at him blankly. It was such a casual question, so easy. For anyone else. "San Francisco, I guess," she said finally.

He looked quizzically at her. "You don't sound too sure."

"Oh, I am," she said quickly, embarrassed. "Of course I am."

"You're on holiday, I suppose."

"Sort of. I'm supposed to be working, but it seems more like a holiday." She told him about Millie, playing endless games of bridge at the Hôtel du Cap and said that Millie wanted to buy a villa and she was supposed to be out looking for one to satisfy her requirements.

"And what are you doing here?" she asked finally.

"I'm researching my book. About crime on the Riviera, from the turn of the century to the present day. Crimes of passion, violence, grand theft, and murder. Solved and unsolved." He grinned. "You'd be surprised how many there are."

Thunder rumbled ominously around the hills, and he glanced at his watch, then looked hopefully at her. "The storm will be around for a while. Won't you join me for lunch?"

The café had filled up, and they squeezed into a little table by the window. Bea watched the rain bouncing from the cobblestones in the square and realized suddenly that she was enjoying herself. Nick Lascelles was nice, he was young and attractive, and he talked nonstop throughout the generous seventy-five-franc meal of the day.

Over the soup he told her that his mother was

French and his father English. "From one of those 'good' families with an old name and not much money," he said with a grin. "I was the poorest boy at the 'rich boys' school they sent me to in Switzerland. No helicopters whisking me off for weekends on the yacht like most of the other boys; no private planes sent to take me home for the holidays."

As he ate his omelet, he told her that all that was left of the once-vast family fortunes was the old manor house and a few acres in Gloucestershire that his brother had inherited. And an old run-down vineyard near Bordeaux with the prettiest little château that had been left to him and that he was attempting to update into the twentieth century.

"But what I really am is a writer," he said finally, over the steak frites. "I began on a local paper and after years of slaving, writing up village flower shows and the church fetes, I graduated to one of the national dailies. Then I branched out and wrote my first book about wine; then a guidebook to France; articles about European life for the American glossies. That sort of thing."

There was so much food Bea couldn't manage the cheese and salad, and she watched, astonished, as he wolfed his down and told her that he would make a decent living if only he didn't keep funding it all to the Charity—that was what he called his vineyard—for new roofs and modern steel fermenting vats and new equipment.

"Then why do you do it?" Bea asked curiously. "Why bother trying to save an old vineyard when you'd be much better off financially without it?"

His nice gray eyes met hers seriously. "I feel an obligation. After all, it's been in the family for almost two hundred years. I've got to get it into shape for the next generation, so there will be something for them to inherit." He grinned as he added, "Of course, the roof is collapsing and the floorboards are rotting and for all I know there's deathwatch beetle in the beams as well. And the thirty hectares of vines have been neglected for a couple of decades. But it's my ambition to restore it to its former glory. I want to produce a Grand Cru wine with an *appellation contrôlée* and then live out my remaining years in serious splendor."

He grinned as he added, "I expect it to keep me broke for the next twenty years or so. That's why I call it Château Charity—because I give it all my money."

Bea laughed along with him. He was so cheerful and positive about what he wanted, and something in her yearned for that kind of strength.

They had finished their coffee, and it was getting late, but she invited him to come by the hotel that evening for a drink. "Come meet Millie," she said. "I think you'll like each other."

She was waiting for him promptly at seven-thirty, wearing her prettiest dress, a short amber linen sheath whose color blended with her golden-tanned skin. Her soft copper hair hung in soft bangs, and her anxious brown eyes lit up when she saw him striding confidently toward her.

Nick's curly hair was neatly combed for the occasion, and he wore a rumpled cream linen jacket, a white shirt, and jeans. Bea thought he looked great, though she noticed Millie eyeing him critically as she ordered him to tell her all about himself.

"Nick didn't bring his résumé, Millie," Bea protested. "He only came for a drink. Can't we talk about the weather or something?"

"I never talk about the weather," Millie said impatiently. "The weather is either good or bad, and then the conversation is finished. It's *people* I'm interested in. Bea told me about your book, dear boy. And I have a terrible feeling you might be writing about some of my old friends. They were all rogues, you know. There's something so fascinating about crime," she added with a delighted shiver, "though poor darling Bea doesn't think so."

Bea shot her a warning glance; she didn't want Nick Lascelles to know what had happened to her. At least not yet.

But Millie seemed to find Nick so entertaining she decided he was staying for dinner. "It's so nice for Bea to have a young friend," she said, making Bea roll her eyes in embarrassment.

But Millie meant it. She watched them approvingly, thinking how animated and pretty Bea looked tonight, in the simple amber linen with the string of green and silver beads, picked up, she knew, for a few francs in the Antibes market. A girl like Bea didn't need flamboyant clothes; she gave anything she wore an instinctive touch of elegance.

"Invite Nick again, dear girl," she boomed as she said good night to him later. "I like having him around."

Bea made a wry face at Nick. "I'm afraid you've got your orders," she told him mischievously as she walked him to his car.

"Suits me," he said, pleased. They stopped and looked uncertainly at each other. Then he leaned forward and kissed her lightly on each cheek. "Same time tomorrow night?"

She nodded, waving, as he climbed into his little red Alfa convertible and drove away. It had been a good day, she thought, the best since her accident.

The next day the real estate agent told her of another villa, old and run-down, and unlived in for years. "But it has everything Madame Renwick wants," he said. "It has character, elegance—and a view of the sea. It has been owned by one family since it was built around 1920. No one has lived there for decades, but they've only just put it on the market. It's a gem, off on its own on a hillside. But I warn you it will need work." He glanced superciliously at her and added, "Naturally, the price will reflect that. You can tell Madame Renwick the villa is a bargain."

He showed Bea on the map how to get there and told her there was a *gardien* on the property who would show her around.

The morning air felt fresh and sweet after the previous day's storms. Bea put down the top of the Mercedes and drove along the coast road, then up into the hills, enjoying herself, thinking more about Nick Lascelles than the house she was going to see. No doubt it would be another wild-goose chase. She just didn't understand why Millie was so insistent on buying a villa anyway, and she almost wished it wouldn't be suitable so they could call it a day. It was just another whim Millie would be sure to regret later.

She drove along the dusty white lane to the top of the hill, past a peeling pink stucco wall tumbling with roses and bougainvillea. She stopped the car at the big iron gates and pulled the old bronze bell set in a stone niche. She listened to it ring and stared up the drive curving into the distance between the trees.

No one came, so she pulled the bell again, waiting in the hot silence. There was no one around, no human noises of cars and machines. As she waited, she leaned against the pink stucco wall. It felt warm against her back, and she closed her eyes, listening to the chirrup of the crickets and the sigh of the wind in the tops of the tall old cedars and the endless drone of bees in the blossoms. The sun was hot on her bare arms, and the scent of wild rosemary hovered in her nostrils. . . . It was so wild and quiet, so secret. . . . She felt like the last person on this beautiful earth—

"Mademoiselle, I was told to expect you."

Her eyes shot open, and she stared at the *gardien*. He was old and frail, in bright blue work overalls. The sleeves of his blue shirt were rolled back, revealing sinewy arms and hands gnarled from decades of physical labor. His face was deeply lined, and the blue eyes looking back at her had the faded innocence of another, more peaceful era. He removed his battered straw hat and bowed politely.

"It is a pleasure to see a visitor here again, mam'selle," he told her as they walked up the drive together. He looked pleased when she answered him in French. "It has been a long time since anyone came here. Too long." He sighed deeply. "A lifetime, it seems."

Their footsteps crunched on the gravel as they turned the curve in the drive, and then the house came into sight.

Bea stopped dead in her tracks. Her legs refused to walk, and her eyes to believe what she was seeing, and her heart suddenly pounded so hard it hurt. She stared at the beautiful pink villa. At the tall windows with their faded green shutters, at the big double doors standing open with a glimpse of the shadowy hall beyond, and at the columned portico with wide marble steps.

The sunny day receded, and she felt herself tremble.

The ghostly scent of mimosa was in her nostrils, though it was the wrong season and none was in bloom. The sound of songbirds filled her ears, though none were there. Was it just déjà vu? A combination of all the villas she had seen over the past weeks and her own imagination and longing? Or was she really looking at the house of her dreams?

"*Et voilà*. The Villa Mimosa," the old man told her proudly. He glanced, concerned at her. "Are you ill, mam'selle? Please, please, come inside. The sun is hotter than you think. It is unwise to be without a hat. . . ." He hurried off to fetch a glass of water.

She was alone in the hall. The hair at the nape of her neck prickled, and goose bumps rose on her arms.

She knew this house. She knew exactly how the rooms were arranged: dining room to the left, grand salon to the right, and at the back of the house the long room with its many windows leading onto the arched terrace overlooking the sea.

The floors were a cool pink-veined marble, and in front of her rose a graceful, curving staircase, leading up to a wide gallery.

"The staircase banister is made from a very rare wood," the *gardien* said, handing her a glass of water. "From the tropics somewhere. It was built specially." He was eager for her to like it. "Everything is of the best, mam'selle, as you can see."

Bea walked slowly through the villa, feeling as though she had stepped into her dream. Even though the plaster was flaking and the old wallpapers were stained and peeling, it was just as beautiful as she had known it would be. She shivered, asking herself *why* she should know. What trick of fate had brought her here? Could it have been the *future* she had seen in her dream?

"I have worked here since I was just a boy, a gardener's lad," the old *gardien* said. "For Madame Leconte. She married the Foreigner soon after, and then they went to live abroad." He hesitated, trying to recall, but he was old, and his memories were vague. "When Madame returned," he said finally, "she was pregnant. She wanted the child to be born here, in France, in this house that she loved so much. And that was her undoing."

He sighed deeply, remembering. "Her husband doted on her. I never saw a man behave like that. He treated her like a precious piece of Limoges porcelain. And all for nothing. Two weeks after the baby was born, she was dead."

A thrill of horror ran down Bea's spine. "Dead? How?"

"She fell, mam'selle. Down the precious staircase that he had built specially to please her. Her husband, the Foreigner, left immediately after the funeral. He never lived here again."

Bea shuddered, looking at the fatal staircase. She

imagined the woman crashing down it onto the marble floor below.

Yet despite its tragic history, she did not find the house frightening. It was like an enchanted villa in a fairy story, protected by its high walls and tall cedars and pines, its thickets of thorny damask roses and the mimosas that gave it its name. She thought that it was like a sleeping castle, waiting to be discovered by the prince who would bring it back to life.

She walked outside and sat on the marble steps, closing her eyes, trying to recapture her dream, imagining she was that child again. . . .

The marble steps were cool against her bare legs. . . . The sky darkened ominously, and she held her breath, waiting for the sinister sound of footsteps on the gravel.

But when she opened her eyes, it was just to see that the sun had gone behind a cloud as another storm approached. She glanced up, startled, as a flock of mewling gulls flew overhead, and she then remembered the song of a hundred birds in her dream. She turned anxiously to the old caretaker. "M'sieur, where are the songbirds?"

He looked at her, astonished. "Why, mam'selle, how do you know about that? There have been no songbirds here since the 1930s, when the aviary was destroyed."

Bea's velvet brown eyes darkened with fear. "Then if there are no songbirds," she whispered anxiously, "how can I remember them?"

~ 13 ~

"Of course it's just coincidence," Millie said, peering anxiously at Bea. They were sitting in the gardens of the hotel, and Bea had just poured out the whole story of finding the Villa Mimosa, the villa in her dream.

"You've looked at so many houses, dear child, they've all blurred together in your mind. I sometimes get that déjà vu feeling myself and I will admit it's eerie to feel as though you know a place when you know you've never been there before."

Bea looked at her, scared. "Perhaps I have been there before, Millie. What if I lived there before—before my accident?"

"Don't be ridiculous, Bea. The agent told you no one has lived there for decades. And you saw the evidence for yourself, the neglect, the peeling wallpaper, the antique plumbing—" She shuddered, imagining it. "But yet you say it has charm," she added thoughtfully.

"It is the most beautiful villa I've ever seen," Bea said sincerely. "It's like a secret house, waiting to be discovered by someone who will love it and lavish time and care on it."

"And money," Millie added.

Bea nodded regretfully. "A lot of money, I'm afraid."

They fell silent, contemplating the Mediterranean, rippling like molten pewter under the newly gathering storm clouds.

"Maybe it was the future you were seeing and not the past," Millie said after a while. "Perhaps that was it, Bea. That's why you thought you recognized it. My astrologer—she's the famous one you read about in the newspapers, the one who counsels the movie stars and presidents—told me it can happen like that sometimes. And she's always right."

Bea glanced hopefully at her. Somehow Millie made it all sound logical. She decided to call Phyl and tell her what had happened. Phyl was flying to Paris tomorrow, and she would be in Nice a few days later. Then she would take her to the villa and tell her about her strange experience; she would ask her whether it was all just longing and wishful thinking on her part *or something more sinister.*

Nick picked Bea up that night just as the storm broke. They parked the car behind the old quay in Cannes and ran, laughing, hand in hand, into a deserted café. They sat at a table in the window, watching the rain bounce from the cobbles and the lightning flash. He grinned and said, "It's déjà vu. I have the feeling we have done this before."

Bea threw him a startled glance. "That's the second time today it's happened to me," she said. "Only this time I know it's real." She looked wistfully at him, thinking how different his life was from hers. Nick knew who he was and where he was going. He did not know that behind the carefree facade of the person called Bea French lay an unknown quantity: a young woman who faced the nightly terrors of the dark tunnel—and a faceless killer.

He seemed so sympathetic, so tuned in to the girl he

knew as Bea that she wished she could go on being that girl forever. But she knew she could not. One day the terror of the past would come to claim her; she just knew it. And she felt as if she were deceiving him.

Suddenly she was telling him about what had happened to her in San Francisco: how the police suspected someone had tried to kill her, about her loss of memory and the dream she had had under hypnosis, and how today that dream had seemed to come true when she had seen the Villa Mimosa.

"Millie thinks maybe I saw the future," she said tremulously, afraid he would think she was crazy. "But what about the songbirds? How else could I have known about them if I had never been there?"

"Poor Bea," Nick said, trying to console her. "What a dreadful time you've had. But don't worry, I'm sure it's all going to work out, and soon you'll remember everything."

She shook her head miserably. She didn't think so. "I'll call Phyl tonight," she said, a touch of hope creeping into her voice as she thought of Phyl's steadying presence. "Phyl will know what to do."

Nick was intrigued by the story the *gardien* had told her about Madame Leconte's fatal accident. "It's exactly up my alley," he said thoughtfully. "Tragic death in a grand Riviera villa. It must have made the headlines when it happened. Tell you what, Bea. I'll go through the newspaper archives tomorrow and see what I can come up with. If I find more information about the house, maybe it will help you remember."

Nick found what he was looking for the next morning, in the archives of the Nice *Matin*. The newspaper, dated October 5, 1926, carried the story of Madame Leconte's fatal fall on its front page. It said that she came from a well-known Marseilles family and had lived at the Villa Mimosa for several years. She had given birth only two weeks previously, and it was thought that a dizzy spell had caused her to fall from

the top of the stairs onto the marble floor of the hall
below. There was no mention of any inquest and no
mention of her husband. It merely stated that the funeral had taken place that afternoon.

At two-thirty Nick went to meet Millie and Bea in
Antibes. They were going to inspect the Villa Mimosa,
but then Millie suddenly said she felt "too tired" to go
with them.

"I would prefer a quiet game of bridge, dear girl,"
she said wearily to Bea. "But you must go. Show the
Villa Mimosa to Nick. If he likes it, too, tell them we'll
buy it."

Bea stared incredulously at her. "You can't do that,
Millie. You might hate the place. You must at least see
it first."

"I've learned to trust your taste by now," Millie said
carelessly. "And besides, there's all that good antique
furniture I bought in Paris, urgently awaiting a home.
Get a good decorator to put it in shape, dear girl. And
tell him I want it ready yesterday. Or else he's fired.
Understand?"

"You know you're just acting on impulse again, Millie," Bea warned. "You'll regret it later, just like always."

Millie shook her head, making her blond curls
bounce. "Oh, no, dear girl. I'll not regret this one,"
she said, with a secretive little smile, waving them off as
she headed serenely for the bridge table.

"Even for Millie, this is crazy," Bea said nervously to
Nick as they waited for the *gardien* to open the gate. "I
mean, I know she's really rich and can afford to indulge her every whim, but"—she shrugged—"not
even to take a look at it first!"

"This is some expensive whim." Nick marveled,
peering through the gates. "Do you have any idea how
much land this place must have? And what land
around here costs per hectare?"

"No. And nor does she. That's just it, Nick. Millie knows nothing about it. *Why* does she want to buy it?"

"Maybe because you're in love with it?"

Bea shook her head. "No chance. She's buying it because she's in love with the past. She's an old lady trying to recapture her youth."

Looking at Bea, so young and pretty with her fluff of sun-gilded hair, Nick thought she was wrong. He thought lonely old Millie Renwick had found in Bea the granddaughter she had never had. Maybe it was because of the terrible thing that had happened to Bea. The loss of memory had left her so alone in the world and made her so vulnerable he would bet that Millie was trying to please Bea and trying to help her get her memory back. And if it cost her the price of the villa, so what?

They followed the old *gardien* up the drive, and when Nick finally saw the Villa Mimosa, he gave a low whistle of appreciation. Bea had not exaggerated. It was a rose pink wedding cake of a house with colonnaded terraces and a pillared portico and marble balustraded balconies. But neglect was apparent everywhere: The faded green shutters hung askew, many windows were broken, and there were a thousand cracks in the marble terraces. The overgrown lawns stretched down the hillside toward the sea, and old rosebushes fought for their beautiful existence with the rampaging bougainvillea and honeysuckle, the tamarisks and the mimosas.

A small stream tumbled musically from a grotto on the hillside above the house, and an empty stone fountain adorned with crumbling naiads and dolphins peeked forlornly from the high grasses of what had once been a velvet lawn. And a grove of ancient silvery olive trees creaked and sighed eerily in the wind that sent lazy ripples across the azure sea beyond the peninsula.

Nick took Bea's hand as they stood looking at it, and the villa cast its spell over them. It was like love at first sight. He could see it in his mind's eye: the pink stucco walls glowing softly under a new coat of paint, the reglazed windows reflecting the sunset, and the old shutters flung wide to catch the breeze. He could almost smell the fresh-hay scent of newly mown grass and hear the tinkle of water in the fountains.

They walked hand in hand into the hall and stood looking up at the great curving staircase. Nick shook his head and said, with a puzzled frown, "Something's wrong. You see that broad landing halfway down. And then the other half landing, near the top. How could Madame Leconte possibly have fallen from the top to the bottom, the way the newspaper said? She would have been stopped by the curve of the landing."

"Maybe she fell from halfway and the newspapers got it wrong. You know how it is."

"I wonder," Nick said thoughtfully. "I have a feeling there is more to this than meets the eye. Let's see what the *gardien* can tell us."

The old man was waiting outside. He had cut a rose for Bea. It was big with dark velvet petals, and she smiled her thanks as she breathed its old-fashioned scent, of musk and incense. "They were Madame Leconte's favorite," he told her with a smile. "She loved their perfume."

But he knew little about the accident. "I did not see it, m'sieur," he said. "Remember, I was only a boy, still in school, living in the village with my family. We were poor, and I was working part-time as a gardener's lad to earn a little extra money." He thought hard. Then he added, "There was a journalist who came here. He was very young, not much older than myself. He wrote the story for the Nice *Matin*. But whether he is still alive, only *le bon Dieu* knows. . . ."

The secretary at the Nice *Matin* newspaper office was very helpful. She told them that, of course, she knew the journalist. Everybody knew Monsieur Marquand.

He had been one of the star reporters for years until his retirement. *Naturellement* he was still alive, very much so. And he could usually be found in the Café du Marin Bleu in Antibes, where he had spent his mornings every day for the past fifteen years.

They found Aristide Marquand sitting comfortably at his usual table on the terrace, sipping a glass of pastis. He sprang nimbly to his feet when they introduced themselves, throwing an appreciative Gallic glance at Bea. He might be old, but he was still handsome and spry and a bit of a dandy in his panama hat, sharply pressed white pants, and dark blue linen jacket. And a Frenchman was never too old to appreciate a pretty young woman.

"It's strange you should ask," he said to Nick, accepting another drink. "I was thinking about the Villa Mimosa the other day. Heard it was finally on the market."

"A friend of ours is thinking of buying it," Nick said, "but we heard there had been a tragedy there." He told Monsieur Marquand that he was also a journalist and was researching a book on crimes on the Riviera. "So any information you can give me would be appreciated," he said, looking hopefully at him.

"It is a strange story, what happened at the Villa Mimosa," Monsieur Marquand said. "Stranger than anyone knows. But enough time has gone by for it not to matter anymore, so I shall tell you."

They leaned forward, waiting impatiently for what he would say, as he slowly sipped his pastis, collecting his thoughts.

"Life was changing on the Riviera then," he said finally. "People were flocking down here, not just to the winter resorts of Nices and Cannes, as in the old days, but to the summer beaches. It was Chanel who started the craze, of course, when, brown as a sailor boy, she came here on the duke of Westminster's yacht, in 1922. Then the Americans came, Cole Porter and the Murphys and Fizgeralds, and the society people from Paris.

"It was a whole new era, of sunbathing and beach pajamas and floppy hats and potent drinks. There was the tiny Hôtel du Cap and the old villas here in Antibes, and then suddenly all the chic young couples brought their children and their nursemaids. They built extravagant villas and had them designed by smart people from Paris, white and blue and green with cool marble floors and black satin sofas. They put huge striped umbrellas by their new turquoise pools overlooking the sea. And they carved beautiful gardens from the rocky hillsides and planted fully grown palms and shade trees. Everything had to be instant, you see; there was no time to wait for plants and trees to grow. They wanted it all *now*.

"Ah, my dear young people," he said reminiscently, "you have no idea what it was like, how wild and almost pagan it was then. The sun seemed to shrivel their brains and relieve them of their inhibitions. It was an era of wild, naked parties at the beach, of dancing until dawn in newly sprung-up clubs. Of winning and losing heavily at the casinos, of drinking pale pink wine and lingering over lunch on the terrace of the Hôtel du Cap."

Aristide Marquand's faded blue eyes held a hint of regret as he regarded them. "Ah, m'sieur," he said softly, "it was about lovers. And about requited passion behind green-shuttered windows on long, hot summer afternoons.

"But this woman, Madame Leconte, was never part of it. Always she was on the outside. The lumpy woman of a certain age, dining alone at a table on the terrace, returning afterward, always alone, to her villa. Maybe standing under the stars on her balcony and gazing yearningly at the moon in the midnight velvet sky, longing for love. And though they called her *Madame* Leconte, it was merely an honorary title, in consideration of her age and her financial status. But everyone knew her simply as *la célibataire*. The spinster."

Bea gave a shocked gasp. "Oh, how cruel," she whispered.

The old man nodded. "It was. But these were superficial people living a glamorous, superficial life. To qualify for their charmed circle, you needed to possess looks or style or talent or an aristocratic name, to be a writer, an artist, or a composer, the latest musical comedy star, a prince or a duke. Mere money was not enough."

Nick ordered another pastis, and the old man sipped it while he told them that Madame Leconte was the daughter of a backstreet Marseilles lad who through his own ingenuity and enterprise had made himself a fortune dealing in armaments. He had married later in life, and when his daughter was born, he had named her Marie-Antoinette because she was his own little princess. He had kept her at home with governesses to educate her, and he was said to adore her so much he was always afraid of losing her to some other man. His wife had died early. Then later, when he died, Marie-Antoinette was already nearing forty years old, and she was left all alone.

"She was never pretty, you understand," Monsieur Marquand said. "She was a stocky woman with dark hair, the kind that has no luster. Her eyes were black with heavy brows, and her face was long and narrow with incongruous dimples that rude street urchins would say looked like pissholes in the snow. Of course, she didn't seem to know she wasn't pretty. She was protected, you see, and her father always told her how beautiful she was, until I swear she must have seen another face in her mirror. She knew the truth only later, after he was dead and she was alone in the Villa Mimosa."

Her father had built the house for her in 1922, because she loved the sunshine and fresh air and did not

like their grand apartment in Paris. And now she inherited everything. *La célibataire* was an heiress at forty.

"I remember the first time I saw her. She had sallow
coloring and a full-breasted, matronly figure, and she
wore 1920s flapper fashions that did not suit her." He
glanced at Nick and added with an expressive shrug,
"To tell you the truth, m'sieur, had you put her in the
peasants' black dress and shawl, she would have looked
just like them. You would never have known she was an
heiress.

"And then love walked into her life. He was American, blond, handsome, and much younger than she. 'A
fortune hunter,' everyone said, but if he was, then he
wasn't the usual sort. Either that, or he was a very
clever young man. When he was out with her, his eyes
never left her. Not even a glance toward the young
beauties flaunting themselves, flinging themselves at
him.

"They were seen everywhere together, at all the
smartest cafés and clubs. She bought a new boat, and
they would speed around the bay, stopping for a swim
or lunch at the little beach restaurants. He accompanied her to the salons to advise her on clothes; he had
her old-fashioned jewelry reset. He persuaded her to
buy a car, an open-top Bugatti, of course—that's what
everyone wanted then—red with a dove gray leather
interior, and she learned how to drive it. No one ever
saw him at the wheel; it was always she, so no one could
ever say she had bought *him* the car. He seemed to take
nothing. Except her heart.

"He returned with her to Paris, and they were married, and then he took her back to wherever it was he
came from. My memory fails me on that. Anyhow, a
year later she returned. Alone and obviously pregnant.
Remember, she was a woman in her forties, and she
was considered too old to begin a family.

"Naturally there was gossip. I remember the servants
said that she looked pale and ill, that something in her

eyes reminded them of a terrified animal, like the ones they had seen unloaded from the carts and herded into the abattoir in Marseilles. 'Those animals knew they were marked for death,' they said.

"I saw her once myself, coming from her doctor's office in Cannes, and it seemed to me then, being young and impressionable, that she knew it, too. It was there in her big, dark, empty eyes. *Death.*

"The handsome husband came back. The servants said he behaved like a saint, that he showered her with attention and kindnesses, with flowers, gifts, love. And she shunned him. She walked in the gardens alone. She took her meals alone in her room. She slept alone. But after all, she was a pregnant woman; it was normal to be tired, distracted, a little off-balance . . . especially at her age.

"The baby came. A boy. And a few weeks later she fell down the stairs. And I was proved right. Death had marked her."

Monsieur Marquand shrugged his thin shoulders resignedly again. "A sad tale, you say. Yes. A great sadness." He fell silent, thoughtfully sipping his drink.

Bea heaved a sigh, close to tears.

"There's something more, isn't there?" Nick said. "Something else happened."

Marquand nodded. "You have a journalist's instinct for a story. And it's all so long ago now, what harm can it do to tell you?

"I was very young then, the most junior reporter. It was late, and I was alone in the office, typing up my copy—births, deaths, marriages, small local events. I hadn't yet graduated to the grand society events and scandals, not to say the news. I was just someone the paper sent when there was no one else to go. A call came through from one of the servants at the Villa Mimosa. There had been an accident. *La célibataire* was dead.

"It was my big opportunity. I flung myself on my

bicycle and pedaled furiously through the sleeping town, along the coast road, up the hill to the villa. Light spilled from the downstairs windows, across the lawns and terraces. There might have been a party going on, it looked so festive. I rang the doorbell and waited. No one came. I found out later that the husband had sent all the servants to bed. The door opened under my touch. I stepped into the hall and found myself staring at the body of *la célibataire*.

"She was lying facedown on the marble floor. She was some distance from the foot of the stairs, and I remember thinking someone must have moved her after she fell. My heart jumped into my throat as I glimpsed the sticky mess that had been the back of her head. Then the husband appeared suddenly from the library.

"He was wearing a silk dressing gown, and he lit a big cigar and stood there, staring at the body, smoking coolly. I marveled at his strength because you never know how a man will react to shock and grief. He was a man in charge of his emotions, and I admired that.

"Then he saw me, and anger flared in his eyes. 'Who the hell are you?' he demanded. 'Get out of here. How dare you intrude? No one is allowed in here but the chief of police.' He rushed menacingly at me, and I ran out, shouting apologies. 'Don't you dare come back,' he yelled after me. But I was a cub reporter with a hot story, and I wasn't about to let go of it so quickly.

"I hid in the bushes outside the window and waited. The chief of police arrived. He was driving his own car, not the official one, and had obviously dressed in a hurry. He went inside, and the door shut. I peered through my window, straining to hear what was said.

"The husband welcomed the chief genially, smiling, shaking his hand. He poured brandy generously, telling him what had happened. He had not seen the accident. He couldn't sleep; he had been in the library, reading. But he had heard her cry out and then the sounds of her fall. The injuries did seem somewhat remarkable, the gaping wound in the back of her head, but obviously there was some explanation. 'Why don't you and I go into the library and discuss it, maybe have another drink, a cigar?' he said."

Aristide Marquand paused, and his shocked eyes met Nick's as he said, "And then, monsieur, he did something that made my blood run cold. I have seen many victims, and many murderers in the course of my journalistic career, but I never saw anything to match it for callousness.

"Marie-Antoinette's body was between him and the chief. She was lying there with her blood and brains splattered all over the white marble floor. And her husband stepped over her smashed head as though she were nothing but a tigerskin rug. Take it from me, monsieur, you watch anyone near a body, normally he will keep his distance, circle it, keep ten feet away from it. He never, *never* steps over it. *And this was his wife.*

"I peeked through the window at them talking, smoking their cigars, sipping good brandy. They had smiles on their faces, as though this were a social visit and his wife weren't lying dead in the hall after all. So I crept back inside and tiptoed over and looked at her again. And then I knew she had not fallen. There was a big hole in the back of her head. A big red hole made, I was certain, by a bullet.

"Well. The chief emerged an hour later. They shook hands on the steps. The body was whisked away to the mortuary and sealed in its coffin. There was no inquest, just the chief's story that it was an accident. She was buried the next day, and that was that. Except I knew she had been murdered. And I thought the man who had done it was her husband."

Marquand shrugged as he met their stunned eyes. "A young boy's wild imagination, you might say. Then tell me how was it that the chief, a local man who had never owned more than a modest apartment, suddenly took early retirement on the pretext of ill health? He bought himself a grand villa near Marseilles; he had a smart new automobile in his new garage and enough in the bank to allow him to live in luxury the rest of his life."

Nick was full of questions. He wanted to know who the husband was, where he came from, what had happened to him. And what about the baby?

The old man shook his head. "I never really knew. I told my chief what I'd seen, and he said I was nuts, and if I ever mentioned a word, he would fire me." He shrugged philosophically. "So that was that. I was young, I had my career in front of me. . . . Besides, there was nothing I could do. Nothing I could prove. And now it's just the ramblings of an old man. But I can tell you that the husband departed the day of the funeral. And he left his son, just a few weeks old, in charge of an English nursemaid. I can still recall her name, Nanny Beale.

"They lived alone in that ghostly villa, with just the servants. They were a familiar sight along the coast, driving along in Madame Leconte's big silver Rolls to the promenade in Nice or Cannes. I remember the nanny was very proper. She wore a gray flannel coat and black shoes in winter and one of those funny round English hats with a brim. In the summer she always wore a crisp white apron over a blue dress, with the same style hat, only in straw, and sensible, immaculately white shoes. She never smiled, just nodded a lofty 'good day' here and there. They were a bit of a mystery, though I guess the servants must have gossiped about them, as they always do.

"But what I can tell you is that Nanny Beale came back here years later. She had a cottage down the hill from the villa, and she lived out her last years there, tending her roses. And her memories, I guess. Anyhow, m'sieur, it is still there, her cottage. No one goes there. No one touches it. As far as I know, it is just as she left it. Maybe there you might find some of the answers you seek.''

~ 14 ~

*M*ahoney pounded wearily up and down the hills of Marin County. He was light on his feet for a big man, but he had been keeping up a steady pace for three hours now. Sweat soaked his running shirt, and his knees had turned to lumps of lead. He told himself angrily that he was out of shape; he had been too busy to keep up his training, and the New York Marathon was just pie in the sky.

He sighed as he slowed to a jog, keeping up the slower pace for ten more minutes before decelerating into a walk. He mopped his brow with a big red spotted handkerchief, finally allowing himself to sink onto a convenient boulder, breathing deeply and slowly. The gigantic redwood trees in Muir Woods loomed in the distance, and the hillside below him was dotted with pretty houses. Beyond that lay Sausalito and the wide sweep of the bay with the far-off orange gleam of the Golden Gate Bridge.

A plane was making its ascent over the horizon, leaving a faint white trail across the blue sky, and he thought of Phyl Forster, already on her way to Paris. He told himself San Francisco would be a lonelier place without her and then asked himself what the hell he meant by that. He hardly ever saw her.

The fact that she had called him at the precinct station last night and asked if he was free and if she could come by meant nothing. He had promised to look after the cat for her, and she wanted to drop it off, that was all. And then she had wanted to talk about Bea. Still, goddammit, he liked the woman. He *enjoyed* her. She brought out the best and the worst in him, with her verbal jousting and her undercurrent of vulnerability. She thought she was so goddamn tough, with her cool, uncluttered life. He heaved an exasperated sigh, thinking of last night; he'd just bet she would be a sucker for the wrong guy.

Mahoney lived in a seedy area near the waterfront, but his apartment had high ceilings and brick walls, wooden floors, and space. It was on the top floor and a walk-up, and when Phyl buzzed, he'd run down the stairs to meet her. "Just in case you were scared," he said with a mocking grin that showed off his good teeth.

"I'm perfectly capable of taking care of myself, Mahoney," Phyl retorted coolly.

"That's what they all say, ma'am," he countered, taking the cat basket from her and following her up the stairs.

"If you make any comments about the size of my butt, Mahoney," she said over her shoulder, "I shall have you arrested for sexual harassment."

"Now why would I make comments about your butt, Doc?" he asked plaintively. "It looks great to me."

"Mahoney!" Her eyes flashed as she swung around, and then they both laughed.

"You are a fool," she said, walking into his home.

"Yeah," he agreed. "Maybe you're right."

He poured her a glass of wine—Italian and red—as she wandered interestedly around the apartment. The windows were flung open to catch the last rays of the setting sun and the breeze coming from the ocean. A Wagner opera was blasting from the speakers, and three cats—two slender Siamese and a well-fed tabby that looked like a plumped-up cushion with yellow eyes —clustered on the kitchen counter, staring hostilely at the newcomer cat still in its carrying case.

The apartment was basically one room, cleverly divided by Japanese screens, and furnished with an eclectic mix of junk shop, Crate & Barrel, and Williams-Sonoma. There were some good secondhand oriental rugs and a few interesting antique pieces, and two of the walls were lined with bookshelves.

Phyl noticed that there were learned works on the psychology of the criminal mind, as well as bound scores of most of the operas. There was a huge section of poetry and dozens of cookbooks and old copies of *Gourmet,* a couple of shelves on cats and a stack of several years of *Cat Fancy Magazine.* There were also hundreds of detective novels.

"Everything for the well-rounded personality," she said, laughing, as she inspected the enormous cat playhouse that took up one entire corner of the room. She admired his stereo, the best Bang & Olufsen, and she told him she thought the paintings, most of which were just stacked against the walls, were intriguing.

"Yeah, they're all by unsuccessful young artists. Quite a few of them live around here, and they're all I can afford. Which doesn't mean to say they're not good," he added. "Anyway, I like them. I chose each one carefully for the pleasure it gave me."

She ran her hand over a piece of sculpture. It was carved from wood and was composed of subtle curves with a tactile smoothness that was irresistible.

"Ah, the wood sculptures," he said bashfully. "I confess to having created those myself."

"There really is no end to your talents, is there, Mahoney?" she said, sliding onto a stool at the kitchen counter.

"None," he agreed immodestly. "And to prove it, the kitchen you are looking at so critically was designed and built by me."

She stared at the steel restaurant stove, the butcher-block countertops, the copper-bottomed pans hanging from a rail behind it, and the battery of whisks and spatulas and lethal-looking knives and cleavers.

"What the hell are you doing, being a cop, Mahoney?" she demanded finally. "You could have been a great chef. Or a cat breeder. A sculptor. A poet. A professor. An opera star."

He looked at her and laughed. "Everything but the opera star. You haven't heard me sing! But *chef* maybe. Now this is a Roger Vergé recipe—fricassee of chicken with fresh herbs—and believe me, that man knows what he's cooking. I tell you, if I could, I'd swap places with him tomorrow."

He swept the cats off the table and set down their plates. "Vergé's restaurant is right there, where you're heading. In the south of France. You should try it. Tell me how my version compares."

"Maybe I'll do that." She hesitated, wishing for a minute he were coming with her. "Mahoney, Bea called me this afternoon. She said she had found the dream villa. The one she told me about when I hypnotized her."

He listened seriously while Phyl told him about the villa and about the woman who had died there. She told him that it had been uninhabited for decades and that Bea had remembered songbirds that were no longer there.

"How do you explain that, Mahoney?" she demanded finally.

"There are only two logical ways she might know the place: Either she *has* been there before or someone told her about it."

"That would have to be a remarkably vivid story-teller for her to remember all the details, the smell of mimosa, the songbirds." She looked at Mahoney. "I have no answers for her," she said honestly. "And poor Bea is relying on me to help her."

Mahoney shrugged sympathetically. "You can only do what you can do."

"Oh, dammit, mouthing platitudes isn't going to bring back her memory," she snapped angrily. Then she looked at him apologetically. "I'm sorry. I just thought if you could find her attacker, we would know who she is."

"Chicken or the egg," he said quietly.

He got up, put on another record, poured more wine. He said, "The National Center for the Analysis of Violent Crimes, the FBI's behavioral analysis unit, prepared a psychological profile of Bea's killer. Would-be killer, I mean. There wasn't much evidence for them to go on, just the method of the crime. The lack of use of a weapon indicated that he was a person who wanted to keep his hands clean, so to speak. It had to look like an accident, not for her sake but for his. This tells us that he is a person who cares what society thinks about him, a man with a public image. Perhaps even famous. Anyhow, he's your white-collar killer. They say he is probably in his late thirties or early forties, successful, charismatic, and attractive. And that people who know him probably think he's a nice, regular guy."

"But why would he want to kill her?"

Mahoney shrugged. "Personally, I believe she is a threat to him. He couldn't allow her to live."

"*Bea* is a threat?"

"She knows something about him that he couldn't allow anyone else to know. Something that threatens his existence."

"Then you don't think it was a random murder attempt that anyone might have done, but it just happened to be Bea?"

"No. I don't think that. I think our man knew exactly what he was doing. Did you ever think about those teethmarks on her right forearm? How about this scenario? Bea meets our man. His dog is trained to attack. He gives it the command. The dog goes for her throat and kills her. He shoots the dog, claims it turned wild. He is heartbroken about the accident."

Mahoney's blue eyes were suddenly implacable as they met Phyl's. "Homicide by canine. That would be a first, now, wouldn't it, Doc? No guns, no mess. And absolutely unprovable."

Phyl stared at him. "The person you are describing is a sociopath. He would rationalize his actions. He would feel no remorse. It would all seem logical and simple to him. Something that had to be done. *But why?*"

"That's what we still don't know, Doc. That—and who Bea really is."

Later Mahoney had driven Phyl home, and she had sat silently beside him, not even throwing a dig at him about the vintage Mustang. He could tell she was brooding over what he had told her, and when they arrived at her apartment building, he looked at her with compassion. Then he leaned across, put his hand under her chin, and tilted her troubled face up to him.

"Hey, hey," he chided. "This doesn't look like a woman on her way to Paris, glamour capital of Europe and culinary capital of the world. Look, forget what I told you. Just have a great time. And give Bea my love. Tell her I'm looking out for her. I'm not giving up."

Phyl leaned forward and kissed him lightly on the lips. "Thanks, Mahoney," she said, opening the door and sliding out of the seat. "I'll think of you in Paris."

"You do that, Doc," he said, smiling. "And don't forget. Vergé. The Moulin de Mougins. Think of me when you're eating that chicken."

"I'll try," she said with her mocking grin.

That had been last night, and Mahoney had spent the rest of it awake and prowling his apartment until it was time for his midnight shift, wondering what the hell he was going to do next on the Bea French case. Because there was sure as hell no evidence. Even her clothes had gone through the laser fingerprinting tests at the FBI and had come back negative. And there had been no stray fibers or hairs or scraps of any identifiable materials on them that could have been a clue.

Mahoney thought Bea French's would-be killer had got away with it. And his only chance to catch him would be if he tried again.

~ 15 ~

*P*hyl was almost never late. She sat in the back of the limo taking her to San Francisco International Airport, glancing nervously at her watch, fretting about the bumper-to-bumper traffic filtering slowly out to Candlestick Park. The sea of red taillights in front of her stretched into infinity, and she groaned. She should have left more time, but she had just had to see that last patient; he had been desperate, she couldn't leave him for a week without counseling. He needed her.

That was the trouble, she thought: They all needed her. It was one of the reasons she had decided on a career as a psychiatrist: she'd wanted desperately to be needed again. It could never replace the need of a mother for her child, but it satisfied some bleak, lost part in her own soul. Having gone through her own personal agony and mental turmoil, she empathized with her patients. It was only rarely that she let it get the best of her, only when she was particularly tired, like today.

Last night, when she finished packing, she had sat wearily on her bed, staring at the locked suitcases. If it had not been for the thought of Bea, with her pretty face and her anxious brown eyes, waiting for her in Nice, she might easily have picked up the telephone and canceled the whole trip. All she really wanted to do was crawl into bed and stay there for about a week.

But of course, she had not; even if Bea had not been the beloved friend she now was, she was still her patient, and that was where her duty lay.

She scowled, glaring at the traffic. "How are we doing?" she asked the driver, thinking worriedly of the time of her flight.

"We'll be okay once we're past the stadium," he said. "Don't worry, Doctor, I'll get you there in time."

She sank back and closed her eyes, thinking how many times she had told people there was no point in worrying about the inevitable. That the only answer was to deal with it. But that didn't apply to her and missed flights, she thought, feeling the stress in her spine. God, she hated to be late, she hated delays, and she had never missed a flight in her life.

The driver was right; at the Candlestick Park exit the traffic divided into a tributary of red lights, and the limo surged toward the airport. The driver summoned a porter and hastily unloaded her two bags while she ran to the first-class check-in. "I'm late," she said guiltily, handing over her ticket.

"The flight has already boarded, Dr. Forster," the man said, "I'll call ahead and tell them you're on your way. They won't close the gate till you get there." He handed her back her ticket with a smile. "But you'd better hurry."

"Thanks." She grabbed her hand luggage, turned quickly, and almost fell into the arms of the tall blond man standing behind her.

"Oh," she gasped, grabbing at him to keep from falling. When she looked up, the female in her noticed quickly that he was very attractive, even as she made her apologies. "I'm late," she called over her shoulder as she fled down the concourse to the gate. "I'll miss my flight."

She heard his laughter following her as she ran and thought with irritation it was all right for him to be so cool; his flight probably wasn't for another hour yet. An airline agent was waiting at the gate to escort her on board, and she glanced around the empty first-class cabin as she sank thankfully into her seat. *Good,* she thought, *I've got the place to myself. I'll just close my eyes and get some sleep. Then maybe I'll be up for this conference after all.* She shook her head, sighing impatiently at herself; a conference of international experts in her field was something she should have been looking forward to, not treating like a chore.

She glanced at her watch, surprised that the cabin doors were not yet closed; the plane was already ten minutes late. She asked the flight attendant what the delay was.

"We're waiting for one more passenger," he told her. "Meanwhile, may I offer you a glass of champagne?"

She shook her head, thinking irritably she need not have bothered nearly killing herself running all that way. She heard the flight attendants greeting the tardy passenger and then the captain requesting that the cabin doors be closed. She glared irately up at him as he walked by. It was the blond, good-looking guy whose arms she had fallen into at the check-in desk.

There was a twinkle in his eyes as he caught her glare. "Sorry," he said with an apologetic grimace. "I wanted to tell you there was no need to run, but you were too quick for me. You just took off—"

"Like a bat out of hell." She finished for him. She shook her head, laughing at herself. "I just hate to be late."

"I always thought that was a virtue," he said, handing his jacket to the flight attendant and stacking his hand baggage in the locker. "Anyhow, I'm the one who should be apologizing for delaying your flight. Especially now I know how much you hate to be late. Still, you don't have to worry, the tailwinds tonight will have us there on time."

He was smiling down at her, and she thought with a surge of interest that he really was attractive: tall and lean, with an angular face and light blue eyes behind gold-rimmed Armani eyeglasses. He had an easy, rangy body and thick, smooth dark blond hair, and he looked like a man very much at ease with himself. She wondered curiously what he did.

"How did you know that? About the tailwinds tonight?" she asked.

"I usually like to fly myself on these trips," he said with a deprecating little shrug of his shoulders. "Unfortunately tonight we had a spot of trouble in the electrical system at the last minute. And I have to be in Paris by tomorrow morning. So that's why I'm on this flight and why you were delayed." He laughed, a deep attractive sound as he said, "My apologies again," and went forward to take his seat as the plane began to taxi toward the runway.

Fatigue swept her curiosity about him away. She refused the meal, turned out her light, and closed her eyes, hoping for sleep, but she only managed a fretful doze. The flight was annoyingly bumpy, and the seat belt signs remained lit. She drank cups of hot tea and took Advil to sooth her pounding head and checked the time once more. They were five hours into the long flight, and an eternity of turbulent plane ride stretched in front of her.

She stood up to retrieve her black work bag from the overhead bin and noticed that her fellow passenger's light was on. Peering closer, she saw he was writing busily in a yellow legal pad. He was, she thought mockingly, a real little bundle of energy, making the most of every moment. Just the way she always told herself she should.

She took out the paper she had prepared for the conference and began to go through it once again. Dawn was breaking when she next glanced up, and orange juice and breakfast were being served. Thank God, she thought, putting away her papers, they were almost there.

Paris was obscured beneath a bank of carbon gray cloud when at last the plane began its descent. Phyl nodded good-bye to her handsome fellow passenger as she moved up the aisle. He was still gathering his papers together, and she thought he really was a cool customer. He acted as though the world would wait for him.

And maybe it would, she thought, surveying the usual chaos of Charles de Gaulle Airport. She had to wait ages for her bags, and by then all the taxis had disappeared and she was left alone on the sidewalk, staring at the bouncing rain.

Her knees trembled with tension and exhaustion as she glared at a waiting chauffeur-driven dark blue Bentley.

"Looks as though it's not your lucky day," an amused voice said, and she turned and looked into the laughing eyes of her handsome neighbor.

"It's my own fault. I should have had a car meet me." She shrugged. "I guess there'll be a taxi before too long."

"In Paris? In the rain?" He grinned. "No chance. But I'd be glad to offer you a lift."

She glanced at him and then at the enormous Bentley. "That yours?" she asked, nodding in its direction.

"It's a company car. My personal tastes run to more racy lines."

She laughed. "It looks wonderful to me right now. But I wouldn't want to take you out of your way. I'm at the Raphaël."

"The Raphaël first, please, Adams," he told the English driver. "Then home."

Phyl stepped into the car and sank gratefully back into its luxurious leather cushions. She looked across at him, smiling. There seemed to be about an acre of seat between them, but she was as aware of his masculine presence as though he were touching her. *It must be Paris,* she thought, amused.

"You look tired," he said sympathetically, and she groaned.

"You mean I look like a wreck. I certainly feel it. All I want right this minute is a hot bath, a cool drink, and a soft bed." Their eyes met as the car slid smoothly through the traffic. "Perhaps we should introduce ourselves," she said, holding her hand across the great divide between them. "I'm Phyl Forster."

"Brad Kane."

His hand was hard and unexpectedly cold. "I'm in Paris for a conference," she added. "Psychiatry."

"Of course. Dr. Phyl. Forgive me, I should have recognized you."

"Not necessarily. Besides, the way I feel now I'm sure I don't resemble the photo on the book jacket." She laughed, even though weariness was overtaking her. She liked her handsome good Samaritan.

The telephone rang and she closed her eyes as he answered it and had a quick conversation in French. "Please excuse me," he said to her, "but there are some important calls I must make."

She lay back, half dozing, listening to the soothing murmur of his voice in the background, wondering vaguely who he was, and what he did, and if it was a woman he was talking to in that soft, sexy French voice. Still, thinking longingly of the bed waiting for her, she was glad when they finally arrived at the hotel.

He took her arm as she stepped from the car and apologized again for having been on the phone. "I don't know what I would have done if you hadn't been there to rescue me from the rain," she said, smiling tiredly.

He held her gaze for a long moment. Then he took a card with his address and phone number from his pocket and gave it to her. "Call me, busy lady," he said lightly, "if you have a moment to spare in Paris." He took her hand and raised it to his lips, and then, with a quick wave and a smile, he climbed into the big car and was gone.

Like a man I met in a dream, she thought a short while later, sinking into a hot bath. The Raphaël was one of those smaller Paris hotels that pride themselves on luxury, service, and discretion. The water was hot, the soap smelled delicious, the Évian was iced, and the bed enveloped her in soft pillows, crisp sheets, and cozy blankets. She was asleep within minutes.

She awoke six hours later in a jet-lagged confusion of time and place, staring in puzzlement at the darkened room. Then it came back to her: She was in Paris.

The bedside clock said 6:30 P.M. She walked to the window and pulled back the curtains. The gray buildings across the street looked even grayer, and the sidewalks glistened. She sighed, watching the traffic surging past. It was her first night in Paris. She was alone, and it was raining.

She took a quick shower and put on her face and a little black dress. Then she added a splash of her favorite perfume and headed downstairs.

In the bar she ordered a glass of red wine, a Brouilly, and nibbled moodily on tart little green olives, thinking of the long evening ahead of her. A quick survey showed almost everyone in couples, and those still alone were obviously waiting for someone. Loneliness overwhelmed her, as gray and bleak as the clouds over Paris. She felt lost without her familiar busy routine when there was no time for such self-indulgences as "loneliness." For the first time in years she was not happy with her own company.

She crossed her long legs, trying to look nonchalantly as though she too were waiting for a friend. She was in the most beautiful city in the world, the bastion of great food, the citadel of culture, the haven of lovers. And she was alone.

The waiter brought her wine, properly lightly chilled, and she sipped it, thinking of the card tucked temptingly inside her purse with Brad Kane's telephone number and address. She told herself that, of course, she couldn't call him. He would surely be busy. A man like that must have a dozen girlfriends or probably just one special one. Anyway, she was sure he wasn't just sitting alone in his apartment contemplating a solitary dinner, the way she was.

She watched wistfully as the bar gradually filled up and people greeted one another with kisses on both cheeks, feeling even lonelier as she listened to the cheerful multilingual chatter. In desperation she fished the card from her purse and studied it.

Of course she couldn't call him. She put the card on the little table in front of her and stared at it. Then she stood up quickly, smoothed her skirt, and, before she could change her mind, hurried off in search of a phone.

She listened to it ring with the funny beeping sound of French phones, biting her lip, nervous as a schoolgirl hoping for a first date. She tapped the card impatiently on the marble counter. After ten rings, half exasperated, half relieved, she was about to replace the receiver when suddenly he answered.

"Mr. Kane?" she exclaimed. *Fool,* she groaned, blushing, *of course, it's him.*

"Who is this?"

Brad Kane's tone was cool, distant, as though he had other things on his mind. Or as though someone else were in the room.

"It's Phyl Forster." There was a long pause, and she bit her lip nervously. "We met on the plane." She knew she was stupid to have started this, but now she had to go through with it.

The pause seemed endless. At last he said, with a hint of a smile creeping into his voice, "It's very kind of you to call me. I didn't think you would."

"You didn't?" she said doubtfully. And with a surge of anger at herself: "Then why go to the trouble of giving me your card and asking me to telephone you?"

"Call me an optimist," he retorted, laughing. "Besides, I liked you. I thought you were beautiful and smart, and I wanted to see you again. Make that *want* to see you. If I apologize, would you consider having dinner with me tonight? Unless you have a business function, of course," he added smoothly, giving her an out if she wanted one.

Phyl smiled, suddenly elated. "Well," she said, playing the game, "I really should be meeting a colleague. . . . But it's my first night in Paris, and it's raining. Yes. I would like to have dinner with you."

"Great. Terrific. You want to go somewhere grand? Or real bistro French? The choice is yours."

"Oh, I'd love a real French bistro."

"There's a place right around the corner from me. It's a favorite of mine, and I think you'll enjoy it. I could pick you up at, say, eight-thirty."

She glanced at her watch. "The traffic is hell. Why don't I just get a taxi and meet you there?"

"In that case, why not come to my place first for a drink? You have the address?"

She nodded, smiling, relieved. "Yes."

"At eight-thirty then, Dr. Phyl Forster." He laughed. "And remind me to ask if the Phyl is for Phyllis? Or Philomena? Or Philodendron? Or philosophy . . ."

Or fool, she said to herself, smiling as she put down the receiver.

~ 16 ~

The traffic on the Champs-Élysées was backed up, and it was every man for himself. The cabdriver fluently cursed the weather, the other drivers, his fellowmen, and the French traffic laws as he edged a wheel onto the sidewalk, then sped past a dozen other trapped, horn-honking drivers. He made a quick right down a side street and a series of rapid zigzags and emerged onto the equally blocked Avenue McMahon. He surveyed the scene and shrugged resignedly.

"This will take at least twenty minutes. It's better if you walk."

Phyl glanced down at her elegant black suede shoes and the rain-slicked sidewalks. The downpour had subsided to a fine drizzle, like mist on the wind. She sighed resignedly. What the hell, they were only shoes, even if they had cost a small fortune.

The cabdriver told her how to get there, and she tightened the belt of her black silk raincoat, put up her umbrella, and strode to the corner of McMahon, praying she had translated his directions correctly.

The Avenue Foch was a wide, beautiful tree-lined street lined with elegant houses and apartments, but it was longer than she had thought. It was a stiff ten-minute walk, and she arrived at the smart apartment building breathless and damp and late. A uniformed concierge took her name, checked his list, and escorted her to the elevator. The brass cage whooshed her creakily upward, and then she stepped out into an enormous duplex penthouse.

Brad Kane was waiting for her. He looked even more handsome than she remembered: tall, lean, and blond. He was wearing an elegantly cut dark blue cashmere jacket, a blue shirt, open at the neck, well-pressed blue jeans, and expensive western boots. She thought with a smile he looked like a guy in a Ralph Lauren ad.

His light blue eyes were half hidden behind gold-rimmed eyeglasses as he walked toward her, his hands outstretched.

"Ma pauvre petite," he exclaimed, taking in her soaked appearance. "Paris has attempted to drown you. Come, we must take care of you."

She thought with astonishment, *He must be very rich.* The apartment was palatial; there seemed to be acres of polished parquet floors and enormous Aubusson rugs, massive pieces of gilded boulle furniture, beautiful Venetian mirrors, and sparkling chandeliers. As she followed him through the hall, Phyl caught a glimpse of a huge Rembrandt on one wall, and surely that was a Renoir, and wasn't that a Corot?

"Come with me," he said briskly, taking her hand as they walked through a sitting room, down another hallway—and into a bedroom.

Phyl froze at the doorway.

"Quickly, take off your shoes," he said. "And your stockings."

She stared numbly at him. He walked to the bedside table and pressed a bell. Then he turned to look at her and laughed. "It's all right. I'm not going to seduce you. I'll just ask my valet to dry them. After all, you can't sit all night with wet feet."

Phyl knew she was blushing and knew he was laughing at her. She thought angrily she hadn't felt this foolish since she was seventeen.

He pointed to the bathroom. "You'll find a pair of slippers and a towel in there."

She went to the bathroom and closed the door. She pulled off her tights, smoothed back her hair, and pressed a cool cloth to her burning cheeks. The terry slippers were too big for her, and she grinned wryly at her ridiculous image in the mirror, in sexy black Alaia and floppy slippers. She took a deep breath, took herself in hand, and shuffled back out to find him.

"Hi," she said, smiling hesitantly from the doorway. "Sorry I was late, but the traffic . . . and the rain—"

"No matter, now you are here." Their eyes met. "And just as beautiful as I recalled."

A young white-jacketed Asian hovered behind him in the doorway, clutching her wet shoes. "Give François your other things," Brad said. "He will dry them for you."

She did as she was told, and François disappeared. Brad led her to a chair and told her to sit down. Weakly she found herself obeying his every command. She was astonished by how compliant she was; she was always the one in control. She was surprised how easy it was for her to assume this new submissive role. And how subtly pleasant it was. She watched silently as Brad took a towel and knelt in front of her. He removed the slippers; then he took her right foot and began gently to dry it.

He glanced up at her and smiled. "You know it's a fact that not many women have pretty feet. Too many years of high heels and tight shoes. But yours are truly beautiful. Slender, smooth, beautiful bones. Delicate as a racehorse."

The sight of him on his knees in front of her holding her foot generated such a sudden erotic charge that Phyl felt herself tremble. *Fool*, she told herself severely again as she quickly put on the slippers and walked with him into the enormous salon. *You've been here only five minutes, and that's twice you've thought he was about to seduce you.*

"Sit here, my dear Dr. Phyl," he said, leading her to a sumptuous brocade sofa in front of a blazing fire. "Toast those beautiful toes while I attempt to redress the rain damage by pouring you a drink."

Champagne waited in a silver bucket on a side table. "To a happy coincidence," he said, raising his glass and looking deep into her eyes, "that you and I were on the Paris flight together. And that I get to see you again."

"You seem to spend a lot of time on planes," she said, remembering their conversation.

"My business causes me to travel a great deal."

She crossed her legs primly and took a cautious sip of the champagne. "And what exactly is your business?"

"You'll be surprised when I tell you." He grinned engagingly at her. "I own one of the largest cattle ranches in America."

Phyl gave an astonished laugh. "You don't look like my idea of a real cowboy."

"Maybe not now. But I was. Still am, when I need to be. When I was a kid, I loved all that: riding the range, rounding up the cattle. Now it's all numbers and percentages, taxes, and acreage, government subsidies and lobbies, and about a million problems. But I guess I still love it. Or at least I love the land. And the tradition. The Kanoi Ranch was started by my grandfather. When he died, my father inherited it, and now it's mine. Third generation may not make it the oldest in the United States, but it's one of the few still remaining in the same family."

"That's wonderful. To love what you do. What you are."

"And I really do love it. Passionately. You might call it my raison d'être."

His eyes hardened as he looked at her. "I would never part with Kanoi, though Lord knows I've had enough offers. Enormous offers. From the Japanese especially. But I'll never let Kanoi pass out of the family. Never. I'd die first."

"And when you do die, who will inherit?"

His look was enigmatic. "Why, my son, of course."

Phyl thought regretfully she might have guessed he was too good to be true; he was married. "And how old is your son?" she asked as nonchalantly as she could, taking a sip of her champagne.

He threw back his head and laughed. "He's no age yet. Zero. A figment of the future, yet to be born. And I have yet to find a wife. *The perfect wife.*" His eyes twinkled as he refilled her glass. His mood change from intense and serious to teasing and flirtatious was so sudden it took her by surprise.

"Tell me about yourself," he commanded.

She said uneasily, "I'm usually the one asking that question. Now I'm not sure I like it."

"But surely you have nothing to hide?"

"I have found that most people have something to hide. Maybe even you and I."

She began to tell him about her work and her busy life. "I'm constantly on the run," she admitted with a weary sigh, "from TV studio to hospital to patients to my writing to book tours. And I confess this Paris trip is an excuse to escape it all for a week." She laughed. "I feel like a kid playing hooky."

François reappeared with her shoes, miraculously dry and looking good as new. She put them on, and they walked around the corner to Chez Georges.

Brad put his arm around her shoulders as they walked, holding her close to him, sharing the umbrella. As she matched her stride to his long legs, Phyl was aware of the warmth of his body, his nearness, the touch of his hand. The gentle, intimate pressure of his arm on her shoulders sent a thrill of excitement through her, and she pulled away, afraid he might sense it. She told herself severely she was reacting like a high school teenager on her first visit to Paris, but then she smiled, suddenly not caring. She was enjoying herself in a way she had not in a long time, enjoying feeling young and carefree.

The bistro was crowded. Lamps cast pools of golden light over the white linen-clothed tables, and there was an aroma of good food and the soft murmur of conversations in French she could not understand. It added to her feeling of isolation, of separateness, alone with Brad Kane at their small corner table.

She was giddy from jet lag and wine, a different person from the calm, controlled, busy Dr. Forster. It was as though tonight she had left her real world and her cares behind. She felt feminine, sensual, alive to every nuance. And, she told herself nervously, less sure of herself. But Brad Kane was attentive and charming; he was handsome and sexy. And she was footloose and fancy-free in Paris. Life felt pretty good at Chez Georges that night.

Brad gave the waiter their order and then he began to tell her about his idyllic childhood on Hawaii. And about his parents: the good-looking father and the ravishingly beautiful mother. About running wild on their own private island retreat. And about the great house at Diamond Head and the thousands of acres of ranchland on the Big Island.

Phyl was enchanted by the ideal world he described; it was so different from the harrowing tales of family life she was so used to hearing, and she thought how lucky he was.

"It was my father who instilled in me my deep love of Kanoi," Brad said, and she thought, enthralled, that his voice was as deep and smooth as the red wine she was drinking. "He taught me the history of Hawaii, he told me how the Kane family had worked hard for almost a century to carve out our heritage. He told me about the sweat and toil and anguish that went into making the Kanoi Ranch what it is today.

"I adopted my father's wisdom like a sponge. He gave me my values. He told me that the Kane name and the Kanoi Ranch and fortune were paramount in our lives. Nothing else mattered."

He met Phyl's wide sapphire eyes frankly. "And that's why I travel so much. I divide my time between Europe, taking care of our business interests here, and the ranch in Hawaii."

"Tell me about your father?" Phyl asked, curious about every aspect of Brad's life. "He sounds like a dynamic character."

He laughed. "That he was. Jack Kane was a hard man. And a hard drinker. He never really counted any man his friend because he could never bring himself to trust anybody. But women found him exciting. He was tall, fit, good-looking. He could ride a horse better than any cowboy. I used to watch him when I was a kid, and I remember thinking he was the picture of grace, flowing with the animal as though they were one. And he lived for Kanoi."

"And your mother?"

Brad's eyes hardened. "My mother was spoiled and temperamental. But you cannot imagine any woman more beautiful. She had the kind of loveliness that strikes like a poisoned dart at men's hearts. My father hated other men to look at her. Yet he was never faithful to her."

"Did she know about it?"

"I guess she did," he said, staring moodily into his glass. He drank the wine in a quick gulp. Then, as if realizing he had revealed too much, he added lightly, "I mustn't forget that I'm with a psychiatrist." He gave her a quick sunny smile in another sudden mood swing that left her bewildered. "Next thing I know you'll have me on your couch, and I'll discover I'm full of complexes and phobias I never suspected I had."

Fatigue crawled subtly down Phyl's spine, her limbs were suddenly heavy, and her eyelids felt as though they had weights on them. She yawned, then apologized, and he said quickly it was his fault and they were both jet-lagged.

They strolled back to his apartment and picked up his car, a black Ferrari. *What else would a man like him have?* Phyl thought, leaning sleepily back against the soft leather as he drove her home.

At the hotel he stopped the car and turned to look at her. "I can't think when I've enjoyed an evening so much," he said softly. "Thank you, Dr. Phyl." Breathless with anticipation of his lips on hers, she gazed into his eyes. "We should do this again," he said, taking her hand and kissing it instead. "May I call you?"

Phyl said regretfully, "I'm busy with the conference. And I'm leaving for the Riviera on Tuesday."

"I'll remember that," he said. She waved as he sped away into the traffic.

The next evening, when she returned to the hotel from the conference, there were masses of white tulips and freesias and a note from him. "Dinner tonight? Please say yes."

She didn't think twice; she just canceled the conference reception and called him.

"I'll take you to one of Paris's oldest and finest restaurants," he promised.

She dithered for ages over what dress to wear, finally deciding on a feminine short black lace. She smiled as she remembered Mahoney's remark about red and tucked a red rose into her hair and rubies and diamonds in her ears. When she looked at herself in the mirror, she saw a different woman, a softer, tremulously alive woman. *A sexy woman,* she admitted with a long sigh that had nothing to do with fatigue or despair. And that was a woman she had not allowed to be seen for a long time.

In the bar downstairs Brad looked admiringly at her. "The American in me would say you look like a million dollars," he said, kissing her hand gallantly. "But tonight, the Frenchman in me must tell you, you look *ravissante.*"

He took her to Le Grand Véfour, and Phyl thought the rococo dining room with its gilt mirrors and enormous floral displays was divine; she thought the food was delicious and the wines were sublime. And Brad Kane looked after her as though she were some precious hothouse flower. She smiled as she felt herself blooming in the warmth of his subtle compliments, remembering herself telling Mahoney she was an ice maiden. Mahoney hadn't believed her, and she thought now he was being proved right. She could almost feel herself melting under Brad's warm gaze.

He was the perfect host and the most attentive escort. He recommended dishes he thought she would like, he ordered red wine because it was her favorite, and he pointed out all the celebrities dining there. He recounted the history of the grand old restaurant and told her stories of Paris life and gossip. He put himself out to entertain and amuse her, and he succeeded so well she was enchanted.

When the coffee came, he smiled and said quietly, "I seem to have done all the talking. Now what about you? Tell me about your life, Phyl Forster. About your fascinating work."

She came regretfully back to reality. "It *is* fascinating," she admitted, "finding out how people's minds work. You would be surprised at the apparently ordinary people who live outrageous fantasy lives. And the brilliantly successful people who tell me that their lives are full of despair and self-doubt. I treat manic depressives who can see no reason for living, and sociopaths who commit terrible sins and show no signs of remorse. I see abused children, disturbed teenagers, distraught new mothers who long to kill their babies.'' She shook her head, gazing sadly into her glass of wine. ''Sometimes I go home at night wondering if anyone in this world is sane. Including myself.''

''But you have taken on the burden of their problems,'' he said. ''Surely that's wrong?''

''Of course, it's wrong. And I try not to. At night I try to relax, to forget about it. I drink a glass of wine, I listen to music, read a book. There's only one case I've allowed myself to become personally involved with, and that's because of my own needs as much as hers. It's a case of lost memory.''

''But isn't it easy to reinstate someone's memory? Don't relatives come looking for them? A brother or husband, or mother?''

''Not this one. This girl lost her memory as a result of an accident, and so far no one has come forward to claim her.'' She smiled. ''I make her sound like lost property.''

''And in a way she is.''

''I suppose that's true. Still, I haven't yet been able to bring back her memory. Now I'm trying to rehabilitate her so that she can get on with her life. I found her a job with a friend of mine. That's why I'm going to Antibes next week. To see her.''

''Checking on the progress of your experiment?'' he asked, cynically, she thought.

''It's not quite that clinical,'' she replied, with a touch of her old assertiveness. ''My patient is just a young girl. It means a lot to me to be able to help her.''

''Touché, Doctor.'' He grinned apologetically. ''I guess I just don't have time for maladies of the head. A broken leg''—he shrugged expressively—''now that I can understand. But madness? Never.''

''My patients are not mad,'' she protested. ''They are disturbed.''

He laughed and took her hand. He turned it palm

up and kissed it tenderly. He said, looking at her, "I think you are a very kind lady, Dr. Phyl Forster, as well as a very beautiful one."

Desire lurked in his light blue gaze. In an instant she forgot all about work and murders and Bea. All she could see were his eyes; all she could feel was his touch. She was suddenly breathless with desire.

She wafted from the restaurant on his arm, barely aware of the polite good-byes from the staff. They drove back to Brad's apartment in silence, not touching, but alive to each other's nearness. He parked in the downstairs garage, and they walked hand in hand to the elevator.

He put his arms around her as they waited. He began kissing her. Gently. Small kisses, covering her face, her eyes, her throat. The elevator pinged, and a smart older couple got out. They glanced, amused, at them, wrapped in each other's arms, but Phyl didn't even notice.

Alone in the elevator Brad slid his hands under her jacket. He pulled her to him, holding her tight, as his mouth covered hers. Shivers of delight rippled through her; she did not want the kiss to end. When the elevator stopped at the penthouse, Brad swung her up in his arms and carried her into the apartment, his lips still on hers.

They sank together into the depths of the big brocade sofa, still lost in each other. Finally he stopped kissing her. He stroked back her tumbled hair and looked questioningly into her eyes. He read the answering message of desire in them. He tilted her chin and held her mouth up to his again, drinking her like wine. A charge shivered from Phyl's lips to her breasts, from the depths of her belly to her toes, and she moaned happily.

He took her by the hand and led her willingly to his bedroom. Dark-shaded lamps cast muted pools of light across the big four-poster bed, and a fire glowed in the ornate limestone grate. Silky soft rugs in muted pewter and rose covered the dark parquet floor, and tall shutters closed them off from the night. They were in a world of their own, a place Phyl had not been for a long time. Maybe never before.

He turned her around and unzipped the black lace dress. She wriggled her arms free and let it slide to the floor. In a minute both of them were naked.

They stood looking at each other. Then he held out his hand. She gave him hers, trustingly. He drew her toward him, and they stood, trembling naked body pressed against naked body. She threw back her head ecstatically as he began to kiss first her throat and then her breasts until they sank together onto the bed. He put his hands under her, lifting her body to his mouth, drinking her in until she trembled and moaned and gasped for mercy. And only then did he enter her.

He was a hard lover, demanding more from her than she had known she had to offer, and she wrapped her legs tightly around him, reaching for the almost unattainable peak of desire. Again and again.

A long time afterward, they finally lay silent and spent, tremors like aftershocks rippling through their bodies.

He lay back on the pillows, his hands behind his head. He glanced at her and said softly, "I haven't felt like that since I was fourteen."

Phyl smiled at him, still lost in a sweet, hot afterglow. She waited lazily for him to tell her about his first love, about some fresh high school girl and the first kiss that rocked him back on his teenage heels.

But Brad's voice was suddenly harsh as he said, "I was fourteen and brimming with sexual curiosity, though I had absolutely no practical knowledge. One afternoon I was out riding my bicycle when I got a flat. It happened just outside the house of a friend of my father's, so I pushed my bike up the driveway, thinking to get help.

"The door was open, and no one was around. I looked into the hall, but it was empty. I circled the house, expecting to find him at the tennis court or in the pool. The window of what he called his entertaining room stood open, and I heard a sound coming from there. I stopped to listen. It was a different kind of cry: strange, eerie. Something inspired me to caution, and I tiptoed closer and peered in the window.

"I saw a woman lying naked on the huge golden fur rug. It was she who was making those sounds. Her legs were wrapped around the man's neck; his hands were underneath her buttocks, holding her high. *And he was devouring her.* She was moaning and crying out. Her eyes were shut, and her face was contorted with passion."

Brad stared silently at the ceiling, and she waited, wondering what was coming next. After a moment he said, "It was my first introduction to sex, and the results were immediate. I hurried away, ashamed. But I've never forgotten that scene. It's indelibly imprinted on my memory, and I swear I've never made love once in my life without thinking of it."

"I can imagine," Phyl said understandingly. "Your first pornographic experience."

"More than that." Brad got up and walked naked to the window. He picked up a packet of Gitanes from the table, shook one out, and lit it. He drew deeply on it, then exhaled the pungent smoke, staring blindly out of the window into the lamplit leafy courtyard. His voice was chilling when he said finally, "The man was a friend I had known all my life. And the woman he was devouring so avidly was my mother."

Brad's eyes had a terrifying emptiness. Phyl knew she was looking into his soul, and she could think of no words to comfort him. There was nothing she could say to her lover. In her professional capacity, with the proper distance between patient and doctor, she would have been able to find the formula, the correct answers to lead him out of his bitter memories. But this was different. As she lay naked in his bed, with the imprint of his lovemaking still on her, all she could say was "I'm sorry."

He shrugged moodily. "That's just the way Rebecca was. How my father put up with it all those years, I'll never know. Nor why. My father was a good-looking man—rich and successful. But my mother was aristocratic, a socialite from way back. And he was just the son of a rancher." He shrugged. "I guess they must have suited each other. I never talked about it with him. And I have never told anyone else about what I saw." He came over and kissed her lightly on the cheek. "I shouldn't have told even you. Forgive me."

She forgave him, of course, but she was still shocked. Brad Kane's mood swings from somber to cheerful were disquieting.

But then once again, he shrugged off his dark passion and took her for breakfast at the Café Flore. Later they shopped on the Rue du Cherche-Midi and browsed among the book stalls on the banks of the Seine. Phyl forgot all about the conference she was in Paris to attend. Brad was handsome, he was charming, and he was amusing. And by now she was so sexually crazy for him and he for her that she thought people must be able to sense the heat coming from their bodies as they paused to kiss shamelessly in shop doorways or just to stare deeply into each other's eyes. They were in that flash heat of sexual attraction when they wanted nobody but each other. Phyl didn't think about Bea or Millie. Or Franco Mahoney. All she thought of was Brad.

They spent long sensual afternoons in her shuttered bedroom, and romantic evenings in dimly lit bistros, and wonderful nights in his apartment. They would shed their clothes as they walked through the doorway, touching, kissing, devouring each other. One night Brad couldn't even wait to undress, and he took her up against the wall, lifting her onto him, driving savagely into her. She cried out with pain, but he didn't stop until they slid, tangled together onto the floor, half sobbing, half laughing. They made love everywhere, in his bed, on the priceless Aubusson in front of the fire in the grand salon, and in the shower, slithering with soap and their own juices.

It was Monday night when Phyl finally came to her senses and remembered that she was supposed to fly to Nice the next morning. They were in Brad's apartment, and they had just made love. He was standing by the bedroom window, lazily smoking a Gitane, when she told him.

He stared silently at her, then turned and gazed out over the rooftops. "Cancel it," he said coldly.

"I can't do that. I promised."

"And your promise means more to you than I do?"

"Oh, please, Brad, you're being childish. And you know it's not true. I would much rather be here with you."

"Then why won't you cancel? Arrange to go some other time?"

Phyl shook her head, smiling at his foolishness, secretly pleased that he wanted her so much. She sat up in bed, pulling the sheet up to her chin, smoothing back her long dark hair, aware that her body was still damp with the heat and sweat of their lovemaking. "Brad, please," she said coaxingly. "We're talking about my patient. The one who has lost her memory. It is serious, and I simply can't break my promise to her."

"As you wish," he said abruptly. She watched, blank-eyed with shock, as he strode into the bathroom and closed the door.

She heard the shower and wondered why he could not accept the fact that there was something important she must do. He must know that she would rather be here with him. She sighed as she told herself that she had been acting irresponsibly. Surely Brad would resign himself to her absence when she told him she would be gone only a few days.

But he did not speak as they took the elevator down to the garage. "I'll be back Friday," she said when he dropped her at her hotel.

His blue eyes were remote. She stood on the sidewalk, smiling appeasingly at him, but he drove off without another word.

Tears stung her eyes as she walked forlornly into the hotel.

The telephone in her room was ringing. Her heart lifted as she ran to pick it up. Thinking it was Brad, she called a joyous "Yes?"

"Just checking in, Doc," Franco Mahoney said cheerfully. "Making sure you're keeping all those smart-ass Frenchmen in line. And to tell you that Coco is settling in nicely here, along with her kinfolk. I'm telling you, Doc, you'd better not stay away too long or she won't want to go home again."

Franco Mahoney's voice sounded strong and straightforward. Light-years away from Paris and Brad Kane's turbulent moods. "Thanks for looking after her for me, Franco," she replied wistfully.

"No problem, Doc." There was a long silence, and he said gently, "Say, are you all right? Don't tell me the frogs are getting you down?"

"French, not frogs." Phyl corrected him automatically. "No, no, I'm all right. Just tired, I guess. You know, jet lag and all that."

"I figured you'd be seeing Bea tomorrow. Just wanted you to give her my best regards and tell her I'm still working on her case. And I hope she is, too. Maybe if she thinks of something, I'll hop on a plane and come over there myself," he added half-jokingly.

"I'll call and let you know, Mahoney," she said wearily. "Meanwhile, it's late. I've got to get some sleep."

"Yeah, that's another thing I was going to ask you. What the hell are you doing out till four in the morning? Are they working you to death at that conference, or what?'' He had been calling every hour on the hour and had been worried.

"That's right, Mahoney," she replied. "Good night. Kiss Coco for me."

"I'll do that," he replied laconically.

~ 17 ~

The interior decorator who'd been summoned by
Millie from Cannes was going through the Villa Mimosa, assessing the work that was needed to make it
habitable. Bea was waiting on the front steps, staring
into space, lost in her own thoughts.

She recognized Nick's little red convertible as it
whizzed up the drive toward her. "Millie told me you
were here," he said cheerfully. "Hop in. We're off to
see Nanny Beale's cottage."

Her eyes widened. "Really? But how do you know
where it is?"

"I jogged old Monsieur Marquand's memory with
another round of pastis at the Café du Marin Bleu. He
remembered it wasn't too far from the villa. Just drive
down the lane, he said. There's a small turnoff near
the bottom; you'll see a few houses. He said we'll know
which is hers because it looks English."

They drove along a narrow winding road until they
spotted the cluster of houses tucked into a fold in the
hillside. The cottage was tiny with a picket fence and a
patch of garden filled with roses and delphiniums and
Michaelmas daisies.

"That's an English garden all right," Nick said with a laugh.

Even though the cottage was unoccupied, it did not look neglected. The garden was weeded, the paintwork looked fresh, and the roses had been well pruned. They peered through sparkling clean windows, and from the glimpse of the neat interior, they knew someone was caring for it.

Nick went off to ask a neighbor while Bea waited for him. She sat on a splintery wooden bench in the green shade of overhanging vines, imagining the old English lady tending her pretty garden, maybe sitting here in the evenings watching the changing light over the sea as the sun set. Perhaps thinking about the past and the little boy who had been left to her to bring up alone.

Nick came back with the information that someone came every week to do the garden and clean the house. The neighbor had given him the name of the agency involved, and if they hurried, they would just catch someone there before it closed for the two-hour French lunch.

They drove quickly to the next village, and Bea waited in the car for Nick. He was gone for ages, and she kept glancing impatiently at her watch. When he finally emerged, he was triumphantly waving a key.

"I used all my charm," he said, grinning. "But I practically had to guarantee my bank account, not to say my life, before the dragon of an agent would part with it. I also got her to tell me who pays the gardener for his labors. Something called the Flora Beale Trust, managed by a bank in London. It pays quarterly and promptly, and the dragon lady was not anxious for her arrangement to be disturbed. But when I told her I was a writer and that I might feature her in my book about life on the Riviera, she became putty in my hands. Handed the key over in a flash—and with a smile." He laughed as they drove off. "Ah, the awful lure of fame."

Still, they felt like trespassers when at last they opened the cottage door and stood looking around. Somehow it felt as though Nanny Beale still lived there.

It might have been an old-fashioned English movie set. A big old Windsor rocker stood in front of the fireplace next to a flowered cretonne couch scattered with needlework pillows. There was a cheerful red paisley rug and dozens of silver-framed photographs of small children arranged on the mantelshelf on the oak bureau. Nanny Beale's round tortoiseshell eyeglasses rested on the open pages of a copy of Dickens's *David Copperfield* just as she must have left them. Her gray flannel coat hung in the closet alongside a few simple dresses. Her sensible shoes—black for winter, white for summer—were lined up neatly underneath. On the shelf were her round brimmed hats, the navy and the straw, exactly as Monsieur Marquand had described them.

Bea gave a satisfied little sigh as she stared around. The cottage was simple but certainly adequate. The narrow cherrywood bed with its heavy white quilt, the plain dishes in the kitchen, and the empty crystal vases were good quality, but obviously the choices of a woman who, because of her job, had always lived other people's lives and had little time to form her own taste. Nanny Beale's cottage gave out the message that this was a woman who had what she needed and nothing more. And that was enough for her.

Bea sat tentatively in Nanny's chair. "Nanny Beale, Nanny Beale," she whispered hopefully, rocking gently back and forth. She ran her hand lightly across the pages of her book, fingering the eyeglasses as if touching them brought her nearer. "I feel sure I must know you."

She stared intently at the faces in the photographs on the bureau, hoping to trigger a memory, but they had been taken many years earlier, and were of very English-looking children wearing starched white dresses and stiff little sailor suits and sitting in pony carts outside grand English houses. Or skirts tucked into their bloomers, they were scowling into the sunlight in seaside snapshots that captured them for posterity, paddling in the wind-ruffled ocean at places called Frinton and Margate.

Bea was reluctant to pry further into Flora Beale's private life, but Nick told her not to be so foolish. "If anyone knew anything about *la célibataire* and her husband, it was this woman," he said, rummaging through cupboards and drawers full of plain white linen handkerchiefs and lace collars, starched white aprons and pristine cotton sheets. Nanny Beale had kept everything in its proper place. He smiled as he imagined her bossing her young charges, instilling the virtues of tidiness and cleanliness, exhorting them to brush their teeth and always to carry fresh handkerchiefs in their pockets.

Bea watched hopefully as he searched, but all he found were a few old receipts for groceries and laundry. There was nothing of importance, and he looked everywhere, even in the old tin trunk stored in the loft.

He leaned against the bedroom door, arms folded. "Now just where would an old lady like that keep her secrets?" he asked. Then his eyes met Bea's, and he grinned. He walked into the bedroom and lifted the mattress. He put his hand under and felt around. His fingers closed on something, and he pulled it out.

"Got it," he said to Bea triumphantly.

It was a large manila envelope, stuffed with papers. They took them out and sat at the kitchen table staring at the documents and letters and a small silver key. Several of the letters had English addresses, "Manor"'s and "Hall"'s, and turned out to be glowing references to Miss Flora Beale's excellent temperament, her sobriety, and absolute devotion to the children and to her duty. There were also two letters written in a firm French script. Bea and Nick looked at each other with excitement. They were from Marie-Antoinette Leconte, discussing the employment of Miss Flora Beale.

Flora Beale had written to Madame Leconte applying for the job of nanny to the as yet unborn child.

"I would enjoy the challenge of working in a new country," she wrote, in the careful rounded handwriting of a women whose education, as she told Madame, "was limited to parochial school and ended at the age of thirteen, when I went into service at the local manor house in Oxfordshire.

"But my experience with children covers many years, Madame Leconte," she wrote at the end of her letter. "And I am sure you will agree, there is no better education for looking after children than experience."

Madame Leconte had immediately written back in English, offering her the job. She told her that the child she was expecting meant everything to her. . . . "More than my own life," she wrote.

Bea looked up from those sad words. "Monsieur Marquand was right," she said with a shiver. "Marie Leconte knew she was marked for death."

"I wonder," Nick said, "if even then she thought her husband capable of murdering her. And if so, why she didn't do something about it."

"I'll bet it was feminine pride. Remember, she was *la célibataire,* the dowdy, plain woman always on the edge of the crowd, always alone, despite her money. She was the butt of jokes all those years. Even children in the street mocked her. And here was this handsome young guy, playing the loving husband for everyone to see. Maybe she just hoped she had been wrong about him after all."

"Here's something else," Nick said. He held up a document bound with pink legal tape. "Look, Nanny Beale even went to the trouble to get it notarized."

Their heads were close together as they pored over Flora Beale's words. "I must put this down in writing,"

Nanny Beale said, "so that one day those who need it, will know the truth."

It is simple [she wrote]. I knew it as soon as I saw the husband. He had married poor Marie-Antoinette Leconte for her money. Why else would a handsome, ruthless man like that want a woman like her?

Madame Leconte asked me to come to work for her three months before the child was born—*to get acclimated to my new country and its ways,* she said. But in my heart I suspect it was for companionship. She was without doubt the loneliest woman I ever saw.

I knew Madame only a short while before she died, but I found her to be kind, gentle, and intelligent, though she was not a wellborn woman and did not possess the "good taste" of my previous employers. But there was no doubt in my mind that the child meant everything to her. And no doubt also that Madame did not trust her husband.

Madame gave me a letter she had written to her unborn child. She asked me to keep it safely. It was to be given to the child "if anything should happen and I die before him," she said to me, with that bleak look in her dark eyes, for all the world as if she knew what was to happen just a few weeks later.

Madame Leconte had given me her trust, but she also gave me her most precious possession, the baby that was worth more to her than all her money. She asked me to promise that if anything happened to her, I would care for her child. Of course, I gave her that promise. What woman would not?

And in return she was generous. She told me I would never want for money. She even bought the cottage for me and set up a trust fund that provided me with an annuity for life.

I was in the nursery on the second floor when the accident happened. I heard the sound of raised voices, then a loud bang like a pistol shot. I was afraid, but the baby had awakened at the noise. He began to cry, and it was some minutes before I ran into the upper gallery with him clutched in my arms.

I stared aghast at the terrible scene in the hall below. Madame Leconte was lying facedown on the marble floor, and it seemed to my horrified eyes there was blood everywhere.

Her husband came from the direction of the library. "My God, there has been an accident," he cried, rather theatrically, I thought. All the servants were gathering and staring at the still figure of Madame. "Go. Go away," he screamed at us, and the angry look in his eyes sent us all running.

The "something dreadful" Madame Leconte had feared had finally happened. And though he said it was an accident, I knew in my heart he had killed her.

They buried poor Madame the very next day, and immediately afterward her husband departed for Paris to talk to the lawyers. He did not come back. And so I was left the effective guardian of young Master Jean Leconte, whom I always called with the greatest affection, Johnny.

I had promised Madame I would protect her son. For five years I kept that promise, and we lived in peace at the Villa Mimosa. But when the event I dreaded finally came to pass, I was no match for the enemy.

Bea knew what Nanny Beale had written next, before she even read it. She could see it in the dark recesses of her mind; she could feel it, just the way she had in her dream. . . .

It was seven-thirty on a June morning. The birds had already greeted the sunrise and were quiet, and there was not a ripple of breeze to stir the surface of the ornamental pools. Nothing disturbed the silence as the butler opened the front door, bow-

ing his head deferentially to the little dark-haired boy who raced past him onto the portico, sniffing the air with the eagerness of a released puppy.

He was a small, dark, wizened-looking child, five years old and thin, with sticklike limbs and intelligent dark brown eyes. He bore no resemblance to his blond, blue-eyed, good-looking father, and possessed none of his robustness. Nanny Beale, mindful of her duty to the dead mother, kept him wrapped in cotton, away from other children in case he caught their germs. And mindful of his wealth and his future standing in life, she dressed him in silk from head to toe, like a little Lord Fauntleroy.

Nanny was his friend, and the butler, the chauffeur, the maids and gardeners were his companions. The nursery cupboards were filled with every toy and game imaginable, though he had no young friends with whom to share them. His dearest possession, his truest friend, was a woolly toy dog named Fido because Nanny Beale said a real live dog was too dirty, had too many fleas, bred those frightening "germs."

They had lived this way ever since he could remember, and he was a happy child, content with his life because he knew nothing else. He was the center of his particular little universe.

He sat on the marble steps, feeling the chill through his little blue silk shorts, happily surveying his domain. The morning air was as fresh as the hope in his heart that this day might be more special than the last, because his days were all the same. He stared across the lawns, past the giant cedars, to the azure sea far below. He could hear the peacocks screeching near the rose garden and smell the different scents of the flowers whose names he knew because the gardener had taught him. His favorite was the mimosa, for which the villa was named, but its sweetness belonged only to the springtime.

The twitter of the yellow and blue canaries and the gay parakeets came from the silver aviary that Nanny had told him his grandfather had built as a birthday gift for his mother long ago, and water tinkled prettily in the elaborate courtyard *fountain, mingling with the rush of the fierce little stream from the grotto on the hill above.*

This was his kingdom, his entire world.

There was a new sound, the bronze bell at the gate. The boy lifted his head with interest, scrunching his eyes against the sun.

Footsteps crushed the gravel. A man was walking toward him. A tall, handsome man. The sun glinted on his blond hair. The man stopped at the foot of the steps and stared at him. The boy heard Nanny Beale in the hall behind him, running. That's odd, *he thought, smiling up at the stranger,* Nanny never runs; she thinks it's undignified.

He had been told never to speak to strangers, but he said, "I am Johnny Leconte." He smiled trustingly. "Who are you, m'sieur?"

The man stared coldly at him, taking in his sallow looks, his frail physique, his silk clothes. In a tone of numbing indifference, he said finally, "I am your father." Then to Nanny Beale: "Pack him up. I'm taking him with me." Just as though he were a parcel.

The child turned at Nanny's horrified gasp. "Where are we going, Nanny? Where?"

Her frightened eyes met his anxious ones. "To the land of the heathens," she wailed. "To the very end of the world."

A nameless fear engulfed the boy, and a dark cloud settled over him, cutting off the beautiful morning, the birdsong, the silken air, the sunlight. Cutting him off from his world.

I loved that child [Nanny wrote]. And I intended to keep my promise to Madame, as she had kept hers to me. My heart quailed at the thought, but there was no way in the world that my little boy was going alone with that evil man. Duty is duty. Still, I wondered *why* he wanted his son, after all these years.

There followed the most horrible journey of my life. On the Italian liner out of Marseilles on our way to America, Johnny and I were quartered in a mean little cabin in the very lowest class. His father lorded it in first, never even acknowledging the presence of his son. And when the liner hit a storm in mid-Atlantic, I became so sick I was confined to my bunk, and poor little Johnny had to fend for himself. Then New York and the endless train journey across that big, outlandish country, America. We had to sleep upright in our seats, though I knew his father was sleeping in luxury elsewhere on the train.

We arrived in San Francisco and drove to a grand hotel. Monsieur Leconte quickly got out of the motorcar, but when I moved to follow him, he slammed the door rudely on me and told me other arrangements had been made for us. We were to take the next boat to Honolulu. Alone.

The docks were seething with brawny, evil-looking men, but I could not show my fear to Johnny, who, thank heaven, was too interested in everything around him to be afraid. Our boat was old and rusty, with a villainous-looking crew of heathen Chinese who spoke not a word of English, and the journey seemed endless, with many days of storms when I felt sure the great green waves would engulf us. And what food there was, was foreign, heathen food, and uneatable. Johnny and I were forced to survive on a diet of plain boiled rice.

Then, when we finally arrived in Honolulu, we were put immediately onto another, smaller boat that was to take us to Johnny's father's private island. To his own kingdom.

Flora Beale's document ended abruptly with those words. Bea and Nick looked at each other, longing to know what had happened. They looked carefully through the other papers, but she had written nothing else.

Suddenly Bea began to cry, great silent, desperate sobs. Nick put his arm comfortingly around her. "Poor Bea. But we've made progress. At least now you know what your dream meant." He stroked her hair back from her forehead and said, "Though how you knew it beats me."

"I don't understand," she sobbed. "Nick, it's not just Nanny Beale's words I'm reading. Those words are in my own head; the boy's fear is in my heart. . . . I feel it as though what he went through happened to *me*. And I just can't bear it, Nick. *I'm afraid.*"

~ 18 ~

Millie's yellow curls were freshly done. She was wearing a matching yellow flowered silk dress with a smattering of yellow diamonds pinned across her bosom, and her lips bore a fresh coat of bright pink lipstick. She was sitting at a table on the terrace at the Hôtel du Cap, waiting for Bea and Phyl to arrive from the airport. But she wasn't thinking about her friends. She was thinking about the telephone call she had received in the early hours of that morning, from an attorney in Ohio.

"Who the hell is calling me from Ohio at two-thirty in the morning?" she had demanded groggily, reaching for her eyeglasses and putting them on as though they would help her understand more clearly what he was saying.

The attorney said that he was calling to tell her of the death of a long-unheard-of Renwick third cousin. Tragically the cousin and his wife had been killed, in an automobile accident. Their two young children were now orphans. In his will the cousin said that Millie was their only relative, and he had appointed her their guardian.

Meanwhile, the attorney said, the children had been taken into care. If Millie declined to act as guardian, they would be put in foster homes and he hoped they might eventually be adopted.

"Hell no!" Millie had said, shocked. "Kinfolk is kinfolk, even if I didn't know about them until right this minute.

"Those poor kids need a home," she told him. "Get them anything they need and bill it to me. I just need a little time to work things out. Meantime, tell them their aunt Millie loves them and can't wait to shower them with toys and affection."

She had hung up, astonished but pleased at the idea of suddenly becoming a "mother" at her age. She knew in her heart she had done the right thing.

"Of course, everyone will think it's just another of my whims," she told herself hours later as she was finally drifting back to sleep. "But as always, there is a method in my madness."

She was still sitting on the terrace, staring dreamily out to sea, when she heard her name called. She smiled at her old friend Phyl and her new friend Bea as they walked toward her.

"There you are at last, dearest Phyl," she said, clasping her to her cushiony bosom. "You look wonderful, as always, even if you are still in that everlasting black. Like widow's weeds, dear girl. It's time you made a change."

"You're not the first one to say that." Phyl laughed, remembering Mahoney.

Millie held her at arm's length, inspecting her critically again. "Mmm," she added, "I'm not sure I approve of those dark circles under your eyes, though. Either the shrinks' conference kept you up all night, or someone else did. I hope for your sake it was the someone else. Do you good."

They smiled at each other; they had no secrets. Phyl

knew all there was to know about Millie, and Millie
knew all about her.

"I'm sure Bea has already told you the latest events,"
Millie said, sailing grandly toward "her" table on the
terrace and imperiously waving them after her. "It
seems we're getting somewhere at last, though I'm not
sure I understand *exactly* where. That's your department, Phyl," she said, ordering tea. "Meanwhile, I
have a little surprise of my own." They looked at her
expectantly, and she smiled, enjoying her moment of
suspense. "You'll never guess," she teased.

"Don't tell me you've gone and bought a condo in
Monte Carlo as well?" Bea asked suspiciously.

"Of course I have not. I am already the very proud
owner of the Villa Mimosa. Who could want more?"

"Come on, Millie," Phyl implored. "Don't keep us
dangling."

"I am about to become a mother." She yelped with
laughter as they stared at her with disbelief. Then she
told them about the telephone call from Ohio.

"They are Scott and Julie Renwick. Aged nine and
seven. Now don't you think those are a couple of grand
names? That smug attorney asked when I'd be home so
he could put them on the plane to New York, and I
would have loved to have seen his face when I told him
home was right here, on the Riviera. 'They can come
here and attend the local school,' I told him. 'If it's
good enough for Princess Caroline, it's good enough
for me.' Besides," she added, clutching her hand com-
passionately to her heart, "I thought a change of scenery would be good for the poor little things, after
what happened to them. But I told him they would
have to wait a week or two. Just until the villa is finished."

"*A week or two?*" Bea said faintly, remembering the
villa, reduced to a shell with roofers and carpenters
and painters still crawling all over it. There was just a
huge hole where the new swimming pool was to go,

and landscape gardeners were still busy cutting back the undergrowth and laying new turf.

"Well, maybe a tiny bit longer," Millie admitted. "But I called that stuffy interior designer and told him get his skates on. He has a new deadline. One month, and that's it. After all," she said, glancing appealingly at Phyl, "I can't have the poor kids arrive and have to stay in a hotel. Not after that long journey and all they've been through. They need a proper home, and I am going to provide it for them.

"Imagine *me*, Millie Renwick, *a mother* after all these years." She yelped with laughter again at the very idea. "And that's something none of my useless husbands could achieve. I always said it was their fault."

The fate of Scott and Julie Renwick was the chief subject of discussion over dinner that evening, and it wasn't until later, when they were alone in her room, that Bea was able to show Phyl Nanny Beale's "document" and the letters.

Phyl told her that Mahoney believed someone must have described the villa to her. "It's the only logical answer," she said. "And that same person must have told you the story of the father coming back for the child. That's why you remember it."

"Then, Phyl, *why* do I feel so strongly about it? Why do I have this awful feeling of foreboding, as though it were *me* sitting on that doorstep, waiting for my world to end?"

"Perhaps it was someone close to you?"

"Someone I loved, you mean? But how could I ever forget someone I loved that much?"

Phyl shook her head. "Bea, my advice to you is to look forward instead of looking back. Let the past take care of itself. One day things will pop right into your head again, just the way the scent of mimosa did that first day at the hospital, and you will remember everything. Including who you are."

Bea's copper brown eyes were desperate as she

looked at her. Only Phyl knew the true depth of her
terror at not knowing who she was and why someone
wanted to kill her. But even though she knew Phyl was
right, Bea still needed to find out what happened to
Nanny Beale and little Johnny Leconte, alone on the
island with his wicked father.

Nick had noticed that Marie-Antoinette's husband
was always referred to in the newspaper report of her
death as Monsieur Leconte, and he went to find Marquand, the journalist, in the Café du Marin Bleu to ask
if he knew why he used his wife's name.

"The Foreigner took Marie-Antoinette's name because her father had decreed it in his will," Marquand
said. "Her father said if Marie-Antoinette ever changed
her name, she would lose her inheritance. Of course, it
was just his way of trying to stop her from marrying. He
hated the thought of losing his daughter, even after he
was dead, and he was determined that at least she
would go to her own grave bearing his name. It was all
a matter of inheritance, you see," Monsieur Marquand
added. "And I'm sure the Foreigner came back to
claim his son for the same reason: the inheritance.

"You must understand, my friend, that the old Na-
poleonic code of succession still applies in France. Under its laws a man does not inherit the entire estate of
his spouse. Their children come first. In the Lecontes'
case there was only one child, Johnny, and he automatically inherited half his mother's estate. The Foreigner
inherited the other half, on which he had to pay the
taxes. Then there was the Leconte property. The Villa
Mimosa and the flat in Paris were only a small part of
her property holdings, and a lot of money would have
been tied up in that. By law, the husband could not sell
it immediately. He would have had to wait until the son
was eighteen years old. Then it could be sold and the
money divided.

"So it's my guess that when the Foreigner realized
he couldn't beat the French inheritance laws, he came

back to claim his financial stake in the future: his son. The man was a big spender, you know,'' Marquand added thoughtfully. ''I'd bet that in five years he had gone through most of his share of Marie-Antoinette's fortune and that it had been a lot less than he expected. He must have needed the boy's money.''

Nick called the London bank and arranged to meet with the administrators of the Flora Beale Trust the next morning. ''Maybe now we shall find out what happened to little Johnny Leconte on that far-off island,'' he said hopefully to Bea seeing him off at the airport.

~ 19 ~

A few days later, when Phyl returned to Paris, her hotel room looked as though it had been invaded by a florist. There were fragrant bouquets on every table and even a Hawaiian-style lei of white orchids on her pillow. And there was a message. "I miss you. Please forgive me. Brad."

She stripped off her clothes, took a cool shower, put the orchids around her neck, and called him. "Thanks for the extravagant welcome," she said with a smile in her voice.

"They were also an apology. I didn't dare hope you would call. I don't deserve it. I guess I was just plain jealous."

She shook her head and said with a sigh, "But, Brad, you knew I wasn't going to see another man."

"I'm jealous of anyone who takes you away from me."

She asked, with a sudden flash of her old cool independence, "Isn't that a little unreasonable?"

"It is. But then I'm an unreasonable man . . . where you are concerned."

She laughed, touching his orchids lying against her

breasts, and heard him sigh with relief as she told him to come over.

She opened the door to him half an hour later, naked but for his orchids, her long hair a smoky cloud around her pale shoulders, wondering if she would feel different about him since she had been away and had had time to reassert herself. But he was still as attractive, still as charming, and still as sure of himself as before. He looked her slowly up, then down. He shook his head in disbelief at her beauty and told her he was the luckiest man alive. Then he picked her up in his arms and took her to bed.

The next day Phyl canceled her flight home and all her appointments for the next week in San Francisco. She checked out of her hotel and into Brad's apartment.

They scarcely moved out of it for an entire week. When they did emerge, it was only to stroll around the corner to the bistro or to wander along the boulevards, hands clasped, eyes meeting every now and then to send each other private messages of desire.

Phyl thought of no one else. She knew she was behaving irresponsibly for the first time in her life, but she just couldn't help herself. After years as the "ice maiden" she had become a sensual woman whose body rippled and responded to every nuance of Brad's lovemaking.

Yet there were times when she was aware that even though she knew every inch of his body intimately, she did not really know the man. Brad Kane was a stranger she had known only a few days.

Sometimes she got the feeling that their lovemaking was not enough for him, that he wanted to go further, into dangerous games she did not want to play. The psychiatrist in her became uneasily aware that there were hidden depths and undercurrents in his personality. His unreasonable jealousy about the trip had already shown her that. But she was too infatuated to

care. She told herself she didn't want to analyze her
lover; she only wanted to enjoy the moment.

Then one night, after they had made love and were
finally exhausted and were lying entwined in bed, Brad
began to talk about his family.

He told her his grandfather Archer Kane had been a
Yankee adventurer. He left home at age thirteen and
made his way out west. "My grandfather panned for
gold, dug for coal, picked fruit, worked on a ranch.
You name it, Archer had done it," Brad said, smiling
proudly. "He ended up in San Francisco, and from
there he worked his way to Hawaii on a cargo vessel,
transporting horses and cattle to the Big Island. He was
only nineteen when he met his future bride."

Phyl turned to look at him, her head propped on
her hand, listening with fascination as he told her
about Archer's bride.

Her name was Lahilahi. In Hawaiian it meant "Delicate One," and she was the treasured daughter of no-
ble Hawaiian parents. It was only when the sweet-faced
seventeen-year-old threatened to die of a broken heart
that they reluctantly agreed to allow her to marry the
yellow-haired foreigner.

Brad said, "My grandfather told us they gave them
an elaborate wedding, appropriate for a girl of Lahilahi's position and wealth. There were four days of
feasting and dancing, with luaus and dozens of pigs
baking in the imu, many gallons of poi, lomilomi
salmon, haupia, and much more. The bride wore a sarong of brilliant blue with many leis of imperial feathers, and orchids and maile, with a wreath of fragrant
pakalana flowers crowning her glossy black hair that
my grandfather said fell like a rippling waterfall to below her knees.

"Archer was a very handsome young man, and he
wore a bright flowered shirt, also with many leis, and as
a wedding gift, he gave his lovely young bride a lei of
pearls—small, it's true, but of a beautiful color."

Brad laughed, breaking the spell of the story as he added cynically, "No one could think where Archer got the money for such an expensive gift. They knew he was not one of the rich haoles. But they were just simple Hawaiians; they didn't know the backstreet places Archer knew about, where men could go to pledge their futures—and even their souls—for the loan of a few hundred dollars.

"Archer was smarter than they were: In return for his pearl necklace he gained an island. True, it was small, but it was off the coast of Maui, and it had been owned by the bride's family since the time of King Kamehameha. It was their wedding gift to the young couple. They hoped Archer would grow sugarcane and pineapples there and make his fortune.

"After the four days of festivities were over, the bride and groom set sail for their island in an outrigger canoe. They were accompanied part of the way by hundreds of other gaily decorated canoes, filled with wedding guests singing traditional songs of aloha and farewell. Grandfather said it was a tremendous sight. He truly felt like a king."

"Soon the scent of their maile leis was drowned by the crisp salt smell of the Pacific Ocean. And when the other canoes turned to go back home and his bride waved a final farewell, Archer saw a tear slide down her face. He turned her impatiently around to face their island and their future. He had had enough of Hawaiian weddings, and he was already counting profits on crops yet to be sown."

Brad smiled indulgently. "That was my grandfather Archer. I guess you could call him a pragmatic man."

"I would call him a hard man," Phyl said, thinking of his romantic little bride, so beautiful and so sad to be leaving her loving family behind.

"That's true," Brad agreed. He turned to smile at her. "Am I boring you? I've heard this story so many times. It's part of the Kane family lore, passed down from generation to generation.''

"No, no. Tell me more,'' she said, curling happily into the crook of his arm and burying her face into his neck, loving the smell of him, the feel of his skin, the sound of his mellow voice.

"Then I shall tell you about our island. It's the heart of our family, our soul, you might say. If we have one,'' he added with an abrupt, cynical laugh.

"Can't you just see Lahilahi looking eagerly at her island as its rocky outline emerged from the ocean? She saw that it was small, a mere twelve miles at its widest and maybe seventeen miles long. The northeastern tip was rocky with fierce waves hurling themselves at the precipitous cliffs, and there were dangerous currents that could pull an unwary canoe deep under the ocean within seconds. But the tranquil southeastern shore was rimmed with talc white beaches, fringed by palms, with sea grapes and flowering koalis, morning glories.

"A series of small, cone-shaped mountains, once volcanic, ran like a spine down the center of the island, dividing east from west, catching the incoming storms from the Pacific Ocean and trapping the rainfall on the western side. And the lower slopes had gradually become covered in dense thickets of hau, hibiscus, and their red, yellow, and orange flowers ringed the mountains. Lahilahi said she thought they were like leis around the neck of Pele, the goddess of volcanoes, whose spirit she was certain must live there, waiting to emerge once again.

"Beyond those mountains the western side of the island was a place of deep gulches and tumbling waterfalls. Spanned by rainbows and dense with fiddlehead ferns, it was forested by thick trees and vines and creepers. In between were wide grassy acres interspersed with the gleaming cooled black lava that had flowed years ago from the volcanic peaks to form a river of stone all the way to the ocean.

"The gentler eastern side would have been barren if it were not for the habit of an ancient traveler. He was exploring the island, and as he scrambled over the slopes on his wiry little pony, he scattered the seeds of the pine trees of his native land. The seeds took root, and the trees grew, holding the soil from erosion. And so the valleys were shaded from the fierceness of the sun by tall trees, and grasses and fruits grew readily in the runoff of the rainfall from the mountain slopes.

"As young Lahilahi stepped from the canoe onto her island, she clasped her handsome yellow-haired husband's hand. She gazed around at the curving white beach, at the tall palms and bright flowers ringing the mountain slope and the bare conical volcanic peaks, like the goddess Pele's breasts surmounting her island. And she breathed a sigh of happiness.

" 'Ah, husband,' she said softly, 'we must call it Kalani—"heaven"—for that is surely what it is.' "

There were tears of compassion in Phyl's eyes as she looked at Brad. He was lying on his back, hands clasped behind his head, staring up at the ceiling as though he were seeing the heavenly island. "That's the most romantic story I've ever heard," she whispered.

He threw her a skeptical glance as he got up and poured a glass of brandy. He lifted the decanter, offering her some, but she shook her head.

"I didn't expect a woman of your scientific mind to be thrilled by such soap opera," he said mockingly. "The reality is that the romance was already over. Archer Kane had got what he wanted. He was consumed with pride of possession in his land. The first thing he did was organize the islanders, a mixture of shiftless Hawaiian and Chinese, to help him build a small lodge of koa wood and stones with a palm thatch roof.

"He worked hard that first year, but his crops didn't

do well, and he was impatient and angry. He had thought his island would be the stepping-stone to a fortune, and now it was all going wrong. So he took off for Honolulu, to carouse with whores on the waterfront, trying to forget his problems. And that's where he was, little more than a year later, when they came to tell him about his wife.

"The servants said Lahilahi had dressed herself in her wedding sarong. She had placed maile leis around her neck and threaded fragrant plumeria flowers in her hair. There was a violent storm with huge winds and towering waves. Lahilahi set sail alone in her outrigger canoe into the stormy night."

Brad's pale blue eyes were enigmatic. "She was never seen again," he said quietly.

"Oh, my God," Phyl whispered. "The poor young girl. She killed herself?"

Brad shrugged carelessly. "My grandfather said he didn't know. Of course, Lahilahi's family blamed him. They said he had broken her heart. Archer didn't attend the funeral feast, but he heard that the family cursed him and his offspring into eternity. He just laughed and said what was more important than their curses was that Kalani now belonged to him."

Brad, sipping his brandy, smiled icily at Phyl. "And that's how Kalani became the cornerstone of the Kane family fortune."

A chill ran down Phyl's spine as she watched him prowl the room like a restless cat. She was puzzled that he seemed to see nothing wrong in his grandfather's actions. The only thing that mattered to him, as well as to Archer, was the island and its role in establishing their fortune.

"Don't you pity that poor young girl?" she exclaimed angrily.

He looked at her with surprise. "It was all very unfortunate," he said calmly. "But let's put it this way: If Lahilahi had not died, then my grandfather would not have gone on to achieve what he did. He might have stayed a poor sugarcane farmer all his life."

Brad raised his glass in the air, laughing. "And then what would have become of me?" he demanded. "I might have been eking out a living on a tiny Hawaiian island, hitting the bottle earlier and earlier each evening out of sheer frustration, like a character in a Somerset Maugham story. Oh, come on, Phyl, it was all a long time ago. I can't afford to get emotional about it."

"Nor could your grandfather," Phyl retorted angrily.

"Now you're being silly." She had wrapped the sheet around her and was sitting up in bed, her arms clasped tightly around her knees. "I should never have told you. I thought you would like the story."

Phyl remembered his description of the island, and she realized how much it meant to him. "I did enjoy it," she admitted. "And I know you're just being cynical. You love Kalani, don't you?"

He came to sit beside her, tenderly stroking her hair. "It's the place I'm happiest in the world," he admitted, brushing her lips lightly with his own. "And one day I shall take you there, so you can see if I did it justice."

Phyl smiled again as he put his arms around her. She nestled her face into his neck, dropping tiny butterfly kisses on his skin, feeling the roughness under her tongue. She told herself that everyone had a black sheep in his or her family. In this one it just happened to be Archer Kane.

Then the very next night Brad told her a different family story, one that rocked her back on her heels.

He was talking to her about his childhood, about the holidays he spent running wild on the island. The original lodge his grandfather had built had been expanded into a sprawling, comfortable holiday home, with long lanais cooled by ceiling fans and hammocks strung between the palms. He told her the greenness of the sea was matched by the deep fern-filled gorges and the jeweled intensity of the tiny emerald salamanders. He told her about the flamboyant scarlet birds and the aquamarine undersea world, studded with bright little fishes like Christmas tree ornaments.

Brad's tone was smiling, indulgent as he remembered. Then, with that same quick-as-a-flash mood change, he was suddenly tense.

"My mother hated the island," he said abruptly. "She never went there. She only liked Diamond Head or San Francisco, where she kept an apartment. She loved to shop, and she had closets and closets full of clothes. She rarely allowed me into her room, said I got under her feet. She would shoo me away, half laughing, but I knew that she meant it. Of course, I always wanted to be with her. I loved her. She was my beautiful, bejeweled, adored mother. I was only six years old."

He glanced at Phyl, and his voice became tender again as he said, "She always slept late, and I would creep in in the morning and steal a look at her sleeping face. There would be smudges of mascara under her eyes, traces of lipstick still on her lips, but she always looked peaceful and so innocent when she slept.

"Sometimes I would hide in her closet, amid the tissue-wrapped clothes, waiting for her to wake so I could surprise her. I would sit on the floor gazing up at the fantasy world of rustling color, chiffons and tulles and sequins, thinking of how I would make her laugh.

"One morning I crawled into the closet to hide, looking up at the ruffles of color, the bright blues and greens and reds that she loved. And then I saw the shoes. They were big and made from a chestnut brown leather polished to a fine gleam, and I knew they could not be my mother's shoes. They had pale, shiny soles, and they were dangling above me.

"My eyes traveled upward to the socks. Jazzy red socks. I smiled. I knew only one person who wore socks like that. A man who often visited my mother and whom I had been told to call Uncle Wahoe. I peered at the gray flannel trouser legs and laughed as I emerged from my childish hiding place.

" 'Uncle Wahoe,' I said, 'have you come to play hide-and-seek, too?' "

Brad's voice grew harsher. "I pushed aside the rustling party dresses and stared up at him. There was a rope around his neck. He was hanging from the rail. His head was tilted at a grotesque angle, and his face was purple. His mouth hung open, with the black, swollen tongue sticking out, and his eyes bugged like a toad's."

Brad put his head in his hands. His whole posture was one of despair, and Phyl stared at him with horror. But she did not dare interrupt.

After a while he lifted his head. He lit a cigarette and said quietly, "I stood for a terrified moment, and then I ran to get my mother. She was sitting up in bed with her breakfast tray.

" 'What are you doing in here?' she asked irritably. 'Didn't I tell you never to come in unless I gave you permission?'

"I stared at her. I was frightened, but even then I thought how lovely she was. Tall, dark-haired, and almond-eyed. She had a strong body, and she moved with a deliberate sexiness, every swing of her slender hips calculated to show off her curves.

" 'Why is Uncle Wahoe in your closet?' I demanded, clutching at her hand.

"She shook me away; she was reading a letter and scarcely seemed to hear me. 'In the closet?' she asked indifferently.

"I said, 'He looks so funny hanging from the rail. He scared me.'

"She looked up from the letter. It was from him,

telling her he intended to kill himself because she had finished with him. She had sent him away, and he couldn't bear it. Her face turned white. She screamed, and the servants came running.

" 'You dreadful little boy. Whatever have you done?' she shrieked at me. *It's all your fault.* ' "

Brad looked at Phyl bleakly. "I was six years old. But that is why for most of my life I felt that somehow I was the one responsible for my uncle Wahoe's suicide."

He drew on his cigarette, then stubbed it out viciously. Then he took her in his arms and made love to her. If it could be called "love." Phyl was not even sure at that moment whether he even knew who was in his arms. She closed her eyes; she didn't want to see his face, to witness his pain. It was over in minutes.

"I shouldn't have told you," Brad said harshly later. "But there's something about you, Phyl Forster, that forces a man to reveal his secrets."

~ 20 ~

*M*ahoney folded his arms and leaned against the wall of the inteview room, watching his partner, Benedetti, giving it to a murder suspect. They had brought him in at 4:00 A.M. It was now 10:00 in the morning, and Benedetti was in his element because he was on overtime and they had a guy he knew in his gut had killed a girl by ramming her up against a wall with his automobile.

The suspect, a weaselly little man in his early thirties with thinning hair, a receding chin, and a two-inch forehead that didn't allow much room for brains, claimed he was nowhere near the alley where it happened. He'd been at a club in North Beach with his friends. "Which club?" Benedetti asked again. "What friends? Come on, for chrissakes, man, give yaself a goddamn break. We know it was your car killed her. Your girlfriend was there, your car was there, and you say you were in fuckin' North Beach at some fuckin' club whose name you can't recall, with some fuckin' friends whose names you just don't remember offhand. Some friends, huh? When you don't even know their names?"

The suspect shook his head stubbornly, eyes fixed on the floor at a point to the right of his inquisitor. "I already told ya somebody musta took the car."

Benedetti glanced exasperatedly at Mahoney. He had been at it for two and a half hours and was getting nowhere. The girl had been found squashed up against an alley wall with her guts hanging out, and unless they could get him to confess, this little shit was going to get away with it. Because they had no witnesses and because, despite his pea-size brain, he was street-smart enough to *know* they had no witnesses. He was right: Anyone could have been driving that car. Except they knew he had.

"Why not take a break?" Mahoney suggested. "Let Mr. Zacharias and me have a little talk."

Benedetti nodded. He pushed back his chair wearily. "I'll leave it to you, Mahoney," he said, walking to the door.

It was an old ploy: first the hard-line approach, bludgeoning the suspect verbally, breaking him down until he either confessed or hung himself in a series of lies that got him deeper and deeper into the shit. But this one was a toughie. He hadn't broken. So now it was Mahoney's turn: the buddy routine.

"You look as tired as I feel, Zacharias," Mahoney said. "How about we both have a cup of hot coffee?" Zacharias nodded without looking up. Mahoney went out into the hall and returned with two plastic foam cups of something that passed for coffee. At least it was steaming hot. He put one in front of Zacharias. "Cigarette?" He offered a fresh pack of Marlboros.

Still without eye contact, Zacharias took one, and Mahoney noticed with satisfaction that his hand was shaking. Mahoney was a nonsmoker, but he lit up to keep his suspect company. They sat in silence for a few minutes. "Drink your coffee while it's still hot, Mr. Zacharias," Mahoney said mildly. "It's been a long night, hasn't it?"

Zacharias nodded dully, sipping the coffee. "Listen, fella," Mahoney said a few minutes later, "I've got woman trouble myself. I know how it is. They can fuck you about till ya get crazy." He sighed deeply. "I had this girlfriend, and boy, was she great-looking. Ya know how it is with us cops, we work odd hours, shift work, just like in a factory. Turns out when I'm working nights, so is she. With her best friend's husband. Ya know what I mean? Ya just can't let them get away with a thing like that, can you, Zacharias? I mean it dents a man's pride pretty bad, I can tell ya."

Zacharias said nothing, and they smoked on in silence.

"Tell ya what, Zacharias," Mahoney said easily, "you must be starving by now. Why don't I send out for some Danish? Then you and I can talk. You can tell me all about her." He sighed deeply. "I'll just bet she was a bitch from hell, a looker like that. They just don't know when they've got a good man lookin' after them."

Zacharias glanced warily at him, then nodded. "She was a bitch all right," he said vehemently.

Mahoney smiled sympathetically. "She fuckin' around with someone else, man? Was that it?"

Zacharias nodded. His hands were trembling so much now he could hardly hold the cup. Mahoney sat back in his chair, watching him, waiting for him to crack. He could see it coming; he knew he had him.

The Danish came, and Zacharias wolfed one down without lifting his eyes. "Have another," Mahoney said. "They're almost as good as my Italian mama made."

Zacharias took another, and in between bites he began to spill out his version of the truth: how she was a bitch all right, how he'd looked after her, kept her in style, bought her clothes, food. . . .

"Heroin?" Mahoney suggested, thinking of the festering sores along the girl's arms. He knew the odds were she would have been dead from an overdose or septicemia or AIDS before too long anyway. And she was all of nineteen years old. He hated the bastard in front of him so much he was surprised Zacharias couldn't feel the vibes across the table.

"She was a bad junkie," Zacharias admitted.

"Where'd she get the money for it, friend?" Mahoney asked with a sympathetic smile.

Zacharias shrugged indifferently. "She whored for it, like they all do."

"Man, these women are something else," Mahoney said. "I'll bet she didn't turn the money over to you, the way she should, did she?"

"Yeah. Right. Well, the bitch pulled that once too often, didn't she?" Zacharias exclaimed, erupting with sudden rage.

"Listen, Zacharias," Mahoney said, leaning across the table, putting his face close to the suspect's, and staring into his eyes. "Maybe you had good reason for bouncing her with the auto. You think she deserved it. I'll make a deal with you, fella. You know you did it, and we know you did it. Now, there's no logical way we can get around that fact. But you tell me how it all happened, and I'll do my damnedest to help you. Maybe we can go for a plea bargain. After all, you told me there was provocation, didn't you? I mean, she was working for you and she didn't turn over her earnings. She knew the rules; she just blew it all on heroin instead."

"Yeah," Zacharias agreed wearily. He sat sullenly, and Mahoney could tell he was thinking it over. Out of the corner of his eye he glimpsed Benedetti watching through the window, but he made no sign. He waited for Zacharias to speak.

"Ya promise to get me off?" Zacharias said finally.

Mahoney spread his hands and said quietly, "Zacharias, you know I can't promise that. But if you tell us the truth, I can promise you a fair hearing, and

I'll do what I can for you. See if maybe we can go for a plea bargain, a reduced sentence.''

"Yeah. Well, she asked for it, didn't she?" Zacharias demanded, suddenly belligerent. "She fuckin' asked for it, man. Ya know how it is. . . ."

Mahoney signaled Benedetti, and a couple of minutes later he came in with a stenographer carrying her notepad. Benedetti put another cup of coffee in front of Zacharias and turned on the tape, and Mahoney pushed the package of Marlboros across to him.

"Tell us, man," Mahoney said tiredly, "so we can all go and get some sleep."

Mahoney was due in trial court at two; the case was a typical Saturday night domestic homicide. Several months before the woman had shot her husband through the head as he slept drunkenly in his bed in a sleazy tenement they called home. When Mahoney got there, three kids, all under the age of seven, had been huddled in a corner of the only other room, their heads hidden under a filthy blanket so they couldn't see what had happened. They were covered in bruises, and the mother was just sitting helplessly on a broken rocking chair, crying quietly, with the gun on her lap. The neighbors had called the cops, and Mahoney had been first on the scene.

Her husband had knocked the kids around once too often, she had told him somberly, and then she'd found out he'd been abusing them sexually. Her own face was a mess as she looked bleakly at him: a blackened eye, a bloody mouth, teeth missing. He had been beating her up for years, but when he had started on the kids, that was the end for her. The neighbors confirmed her story, and when he looked at her cowering kids, Mahoney's sympathies were with her. He was sure that the jury's would be also. He just hoped the judge would go easy on her.

He hated the courts, hated hanging about waiting

until it was his turn to be called. After giving his evidence that afternoon, he waited around some more until it was over. Later he paid a visit to the ME at the city morgue to see if he had gotten around to cutting open the bloated body fished out of the bay the previous night and if there were any bullet holes or if the corpse had been drunk and just fallen in. Or if there was any evidence that he had been maybe hit over the head first and been dead before he hit the water.

Afterward he dropped into Hanran's bar and found some of the guys who'd just finished their shift downing a beer and bitching about the day's events. He sat up at the bar and ordered a Bud Light. "D'ya ever wonder why we do this job?" he asked wearily. "Are we masochists or what?"

"The 'or what' is about right," someone replied gloomily. "Who else but a bunch a jerks would do a job like this? My wife complains she hasn't seen me in weeks. I walk in the house, and my kids look at me like they don't know me. I tell 'em, 'Hey, look, I'm your daddy. Ya know, the guy who goes to work and brings home the bucks.' 'Yeah, baby,' my wife says, 'real *big* bucks.' Jeez, Mahoney, I ask ya, is it worth it?"

Mahoney thought of Zacharias, safely behind bars two blocks away and the nineteen-year-old avenged because he and Benedetti had done their job. He thought of the relief on the woman's face that afternoon when the judge had acknowledged the intimidation she had suffered and the fact that she had been protecting her children. He had given her a year suspended, and she had walked free with her children beside her. Mahoney would bet it was the first time she had been able to hold her head up in years without fear of being smacked in the face.

"I guess it's a good job," he said with a pleased grin. "On the good days, that is."

"You look as though it's been a long day, Mahoney.

What ya doin' here anyway? I thought you were on the midnight shift this week."

"Yeah. I guess I just forgot to go home." Fatigue washed over him in a sudden wave as he allowed himself to remember he hadn't slept for twenty-four hours. He said good-bye to his buddies and slowly drove home to snatch a few hours before the next shift began.

He was standing under the power shower, letting first hot, then icy water spray him from every angle in an attempt to revive himself, when he heard the door phone buzz. He stepped from the shower and wrapped a towel around his loins as he walked to the phone.

"Yeah?" he said.

"Mahoney? It's Phyl Forster."

He had completely forgotten she had left a message on his answering machine that said she was back from Paris and was coming around to pick up the cat unless he called her and said it was not convenient.

"Come on up, Doc," he said. "But I warn you, I'm not dressed. Think you can stand it?"

"I'll try, Mahoney," she said acidly.

"I missed you," he said as she stalked through the door, looking as beautiful as he remembered. Maybe even more so. "That new?" he asked admiring the red cashmere blazer she was wearing over a white T-shirt.

"I bought it in Paris."

"I see you took my advice. About the color."

"How do you know it was *your* advice I took? And not someone else's?" She grinned cheekily at him. Coco came running with that loud Siamese yowl that bore no proportion to its size. Phyl picked her up and hugged her.

"Watch out for the cat hairs," he warned. "She's shedding like crazy."

"I don't care. I missed her."

"And me? Ya miss me, Doc?" He grinned, hitching up his towel.

"I see your sartorial sense hasn't improved, Mahoney," she said scathingly. "You still don't know how to dress for a lady."

"You caught me on the hop, Doc. I worked late, and I forgot about your message." He swept her a low bow and waved her into the room. "I'm so sorry, Dr. Forster. Please, make yourself at home while I attempt to make myself more presentable."

Phyl drifted across to the windows. They were wide open, and the night breeze was blowing in. She leaned her elbows on the sill and gazed at the big ship, probably a liner, crossing the dark bay, its lights sparkling like extra stars. Mahoney's two enigmatic Siamese sat like bookends, each one on a corner of the window ledge, sniffing the breeze that ruffled their fur. The fat cushiony tabby snoozed contentedly on the back of a chair, legs dangling like a leopard up a tree after a good meal. Pavarotti's beautiful voice singing the old Italian songs drifted into the night, and something delicious simmered on the big steel stove. Phyl smiled as she turned to look at Mahoney. She liked it here. It felt like home.

He was wearing a pair of blue running shorts, a T-shirt with the name Machonachies Gym, and old sneakers. "At least I chose blue—to match my eyes," he said, catching her amused glance. "Don't complain, Forster. It's hot tonight, and besides, I'm tired." He walked to the stove and checked the pasta. "Speaking of tired, Doc, are those shadows I see under your eyes?"

"They only match those under yours," she said, her chin jutting defensively. "I just got off an eleven-hour flight from Paris. How the hell do you want me to look? At least I have an excuse."

"Me too," he said, "but we won't go into it. Mmm, I thought for a minute there I might have to get jealous. Thought maybe you'd met another guy. . . ."

She sighed, refusing to be goaded. "Thanks for looking after Coco for me, Mahoney. I was wondering if you would mind having her again, just for a few days, this weekend.''

''Sure.'' He didn't ask any questions, just poured her a glass of wine and began serving the pasta. They sat at the table, and he passed her the chunk of Parmesan cheese and the grater.

''Don't you want to know where I'm going?''

''Sure. Where are you going, Doc?''

''Oh never mind,'' she said perversely.

''The pasta's good,'' she admitted after a while.

''Sorry, no gourmet touches tonight. Just garlic and fresh Parmesan.''

''And homemade tagliatelle.''

He shook his head. ''Forneau's deli. It's better than mine. So, tell me about Bea. Sounds like the coincidence of a lifetime, her stumbling across the Villa Mimosa.''

''Don't you believe in fate, Mahoney?'' she asked.

''Yeah. I do. And I also believe in coincidence. I might not catch too many killers if it were not for the coincidences. And you'd be astonished how many 'coincidences' show up on the computer when you run the evidence through it. As Sir Thomas Browne said in *Religio Medici*, 'Surely there are in everyone's life certain connections, twists and turns which pass awhile under the category of Chance, but at the last, well examined, prove to be the very Hand of God.' '' He grinned at her. ''You could say *coincidence* is a way of life with me, Doc.''

''I prefer to think of it as fate. Anyhow, here's another murder for you to think about.'' She told him the story of Marie-Antoinette Leconte, and her husband, and what the old French journalist had seen.

Mahoney finished his pasta and leaned back in his chair, sipping his wine. ''Ya know, you're a very pretty woman,'' he said inconsequentially.

''Mahoney.'' Her sapphire eyes glared at him, and

he grinned back at her. "Goddammit, Mahoney, I'm telling you something *important*. About a *murder*."

"Yeah," he said wearily. "But there's not much I can do about it now. It took place too long ago, and besides, it's outside my area. More important is what happened to the kid. Johnny?"

"The father came back for him five years later. To ensure getting his hands on the inheritance, we think. Though he couldn't get his hands on it until the boy was eighteen."

"Or unless the boy died first."

She looked at him with surprise. "I hadn't thought of that."

"Where did he take him?"

"To Hawaii. I'm not sure which island."

Mahoney shrugged. "That must have been before statehood. They had their own laws then. Anything could have happened. What was the man's name?"

"He took on his wife's name for inheritance purposes. Her father had made it a condition of his will. He was referred to mostly as the Foreigner. No one seems to know his real name."

Mahoney sighed. "Without a name I don't have anything to check. There must be hundreds of islands around Hawaii. He could have disappeared very easily, without any trace, especially in those days. And many did. But tell me, did the Foreigner ever claim the rest of the estate?"

"We don't know yet. Nick is working on it, though."

"Nick?" Mahoney raised his eyebrows, and she laughed.

"I forgot to tell you, Bea has a boyfriend." She described Nick and said how happy Bea was with him, though the mystery of the villa was getting to her.

"He sounds like good news to me," Mahoney said finally. "And at least it seems our killer is not on Bea's trail."

"Do you think the two murders are connected, Franco?" she asked, frowning with worry.

"Doc, I'm not clairvoyant. I don't have a single clue to go on, not even a name. In theory, and with the laws of coincidence, yes, they could be connected. In truth, I don't know. But you had better keep me up-to-date on what else Nick and Bea uncover. Maybe somewhere in all the muddle I can find something that begins to make sense. But I wish it were not all so long ago. I deal in present-day mysteries, Doc. Not the past."

She nodded. "It's odd about Hawaii," she said. "I haven't given the islands a thought in years. Now they've come up in two different connections within a month. I met a guy who lives there," she said, smiling shyly at Mahoney. "That's where I'm going next week. He's invited me over, for a little vacation."

"A guy, huh? Am I gonna have to get jealous after all, Forster?"

She thought quickly of Brad's crazy jealousy; then she laughed as she looked at Mahoney. Mahoney was so straight he would just put all his problems on the table along with the pasta, to be discussed and sorted out. Not like Brad, who had undercurrents even she wasn't sure about.

"You met him in Paris, didn't you?" Mahoney said.

"As a matter of fact, no. I met him on the plane."

"So, some Frenchman has swept you off your cool little feet?" He grinned mockingly at her, and she blushed. "Don't worry, Doc," Mahoney said dryly. "I won't act the cop and ask questions."

"There's nothing to hide," she retorted defensively. "Anyway, he's an American. He has an apartment in Paris. His name is Brad Kane."

"Brad Kane?" Mahoney looked thoughtful. "Now, where have I heard that name before?"

"You've probably heard about the Kanoi Ranch. It's one of the biggest in the States."

"He owns it, huh?"

She nodded. "And I get to see it next week."

"Lucky you," Mahoney said, thinking of blue skies and beaches and sunlight bronzing her beautiful body. "And maybe I am jealous after all."

"I'll send you a postcard," she promised, gathering up her purse and Coco. "Oh, I forgot. I have a present for you." She handed him a bag filled with sacks of herbs de Provence and jars of spices and condiments. "From the Moulin de Mougins boutique," she said. "It was the closest I got to eating there. And don't ask me how I got past the sniffer dogs at the airport. I felt sure they were going to arrest me for illegal substances."

"They can tell the difference," he said, sniffing the sacks of fragrant herbs, pleased that she had thought of him. "Next time I'll take you to the Moulin to eat," he promised. "Treat's on me."

Phyl laughed as he walked her downstairs to her car. "That's a long shot, Mahoney, if ever I heard one."

"Don't you know by now I'm a guy who always plays the long shots?" he said, leaning into the car window, looking at her.

She reached across and kissed him lightly. "Mahoney, you know what? You're sweet," she said.

Mahoney could hear her laughing as she drove away. He heaved a sigh and glanced at his watch. Ten-thirty. So much for sleep. What the hell, he might as well show up early for the midnight shift.

～ 21 ～

$\mathcal{B}$rad's plane, a sleek Gulfstream IV, was waiting on the tarmac at San Francisco International with its engines already warmed up. Phyl was the only passenger, and there was a crew of four to welcome her on board.

"Mr. Kane sends his regrets that he couldn't be here, ma'am," the steward said. "He enjoys piloting the aircraft himself, but today there were just too many business meetings."

The plane was spacious with comfortable chairs set around small tables. There was a smaller cabin at the rear with seats that converted into a full-size bed and a small but perfectly equipped bathroom. The steward presented Phyl with all the latest magazines and a selection of the newest novels. He offered her a glass of champagne and told her their flying time to Honolulu would be five hours. "I hope you will find it a comfortable trip, ma'am," he said, smiling. Phyl was sure she would.

In Honolulu, a Kanoi Ranch helicopter was waiting to take her to Brad's home. They flew low along Waikiki Beach, then soared up over the towering cliffs, giving her a breathtaking view of the black rocks and the pounding foam-flecked emerald ocean. They circled exclusive Diamond Head and came down low over the house. Phyl stared at it in amazement. She was only just starting to realize how seriously rich Brad was. The Kane mansion looked enormous from the sky, sprawling across acres of lush green palm-filled gardens to the very edge of the great cliffs.

Brad was waiting on the lawn. He broke into a run as the helicopter landed. His handsome face lit up with a thankful smile as he swept her into his arms.

"God, I've missed you," he said, crushing her to him.

"This is it," he said with a proud wave of his arm, and she turned to look at the long, low house, a series of Hawaiian-style pavilions linked by lanais and covered walkways. "It's not that much different from Grandfather Archer's day," Brad said, "except I guess it grew a bit."

They walked up the steps to the lanai, out of the hot sun and into the cool, shady rooms. The house was simply decorated in pale shades of cucumber and peppermint with simple floating white drapes and pale marble floors. Dark antique Hawaiian chests and massive tables mingled with the contemporary furnishings and bright abstract paintings.

The servants were Chinese; they wore white jackets and soft black slippers that made no noise on the marble floors, but as Brad escorted her through the house, Phyl noticed they did not smile, and they averted their eyes when they served the drinks.

Brad took her first to see his three Hockneys, his pride and joy, then to the huge Rothkos in the long gallery and the delicate Monet water lilies in the sitting room. There were Edward Hoppers and O'Keeffes and many more modern painters she did not recognize. Finally Brad took her into the formal dining room and showed her the family portraits.

"This is Archer," he said, stopping in front of a portrait of a very handsome man with yellow blond hair and hard blue eyes. He was sitting tall and very straight in a high-backed leather chair with his hands clasped tightly in front of him, and Phyl thought the portrait seemed to crackle with his tension.

"And this is Chantal, my grandmother," he said.

Phyl stared at the portrait. She said, "I haven't heard about her."

"Chantal O'Higgins," Brad said bitterly. "Half French, half Irish. And you will."

Phyl thought Chantal was beautiful, a silver blonde with a sulky mouth and a dissatisfied look in her eyes.

"Here's Jack, my father," Brad said.

Jack's was not a formal portrait like the others. He sat astride a powerful-looking black stallion. With a jaunty smile on his very handsome face, he was the perfect picture of a rich, arrogant young rancher.

"He wouldn't sit for the portrait," Brad explained. "The artist had to catch him on the move. That was his favorite horse, Volcano. The stallion lived up to his name. It killed at least one man I know about."

"*Killed him?*"

"Yeah. Threw him off. There was a party, and the guy was boasting he could ride anything, so Jack put him on Volcano." Brad laughed carelessly. "I guess he learned his lesson the hard way."

Phyl shuddered, wondering what kind of man Jack was to have done such a thing, knowing the horse was dangerous.

"And here's my mother," Brad said softly. "Rebecca."

It was a full-length portrait, and Rebecca was as lovely as he had described: a smooth, oval face, blue almond-shaped eyes, and rippling black hair. She wore a fetching smile and a clinging Nile green chiffon gown with satin ribbons tied, Empire-style, under her generously displayed breasts. She was holding a spray of cream lilies in one hand, and the other rested gracefully on the back of a brocade chair. There was something opulent and overwhelmingly sensual about Rebecca's portrait: the rich textures of chiffon, satin, brocade; the gleam of emeralds and diamonds; the very luster of her skin. It was as though the artist had known her too well, as though he were having a love affair with her.

"She's very beautiful," Phyl said.

Brad shrugged and turned away. "Well, that's it. The whole family."

"What? No brothers and sisters?" she asked, teasing.

He frowned. "None that counted," he said abruptly, walking out into the sunshine.

The temperature was soaring and the humidity was high and Phyl said she thought she was going to melt, so they went for a swim.

The swimming pool was sixty feet long and a deep marine blue, and it seemed to spill into infinity, over the edge of the cliff. She dived in and swam to what seemed the very edge of space, then floated on her back, staring at the clouds puffing up in the blue sky.

"Those are storm clouds," Brad said, frowning. "I hope it's fine tomorrow. I'd planned to take you to see the ranch."

He was right about the storm; by six o'clock lightning was flashing over the sea, and the rain was battering the island. They lay entwined on the huge four-poster bed that had been carved from the magnificent glossy Hawaiian koa wood for his mother more than forty years before. The linen sheets felt sexily smooth against Phyl's cool skin, and Brad's mouth felt even sexier as he began to kiss her. The scent of frangipani and jungly green plants drifted in through the open window, and rain drummed insistently on the roofs. It seemed so peaceful. Yet this time, when they made love, she felt the same crackle of tension she had seen in his father's portrait. And she wondered why.

The next morning they arose with the dawn to

cloudless blue skies. Brad piloted the small Cessna himself on the short flight to the Big Island while Phyl, enthralled by the vista below, sat next to him. The Pacific was a rippling patchwork of emerald and aquamarine with paler turquoise over the sandbanks.

Then they were flying over the peak of the volcano at the center of the island, swooping low over deep forests and canyons and over endless miles of flat plains, where Phyl could see paniolos, cowboys, riding alongside the long, slow-moving columns of prime Hereford cattle—more than sixty thousand of them, Brad told her proudly. They skimmed grassy meadows and the flat shore, ringed with black lava rock and studded with bright green banana trees and lofty coconut palms and sprawling kiawes, on over the emerald golf courses and pink resort hotels.

Phyl thought that it was not gentle scenery: There was a brutality about the foaming sea that hurled itself on the jagged black rocks, then surged and sucked and swirled away again into unknown depths. The rugged peaks and deep, darkly forested ravines looked forbidding, and the miles of flat, empty black volcanic rocks inhospitable. But this was Brad's home, his inheritance, his love.

Brad brought the tiny aircraft in to land, and as they taxied down the short runway, he turned to look at her. "Welcome to the Kanoi Ranch," he said, smiling proudly.

A Jeep drew up alongside the aircraft as they stepped out, and a Hawaiian wearing a large white Stetson called out, "Welcome back, Mr. Kane."

"Thank you, Charlie." Brad shook hands with him. "Dr. Forster, this is Charlie Kalapaani. He runs the ranch. I'm giving Dr. Forster the tour, Charlie," he said, climbing into the Jeep.

They drove from the airstrip along a straight road for ten minutes, then turned into a long avenue lined with huge old banyan trees. "Planted by my grandfather sixty years ago," Brad told her as they sped toward the simple wooden ranch house. It was painted white and surrounded by covered verandas. Inside, it was dark with polished koa wood beams and a treasure trove of the history of the Kanoi Ranch, with the original hand-hewn furnishings and artifacts and dozens of photographs of the ranch and its workers in the early days.

"Archer started out with fifty of the worst acres, full of gulches where his cattle could get lost, and within three years he owned three thousand prime acres," Brad told her proudly. "He increased his acreage every year, and so did my father, until the ranch is now more than three hundred thousand acres. And that's not counting the spreads in Texas and Wyoming."

Phyl studied the map he showed her and said, "No more acres left for you to buy then."

"Oh, I guess I did my share of adding to the Kane heritage, though maybe not in quite the same way. But those hotels and golf courses along the shore are on Kanoi land, and I expect tourism to add a lot of new revenue to the Kane family coffers."

She smiled teasingly at him. "So you're not just a pretty face then."

"You would be a fool if you thought that," he said, suddenly cold. "My work is my life."

He walked outside and stood, shading his eyes, looking out at the fenced corrals. "Can you ride a horse?" he asked.

Phyl laughed at the thought. "Brad, I'm a city girl. There were no horses on the streets of Chicago. Except police horses."

He grinned. "Then we'll take the Jeep."

His good mood returned as they jolted along dusty lanes and he told her there were more than a thousand horses, Morgans and quarter horses and Arabians, in two hundred paddocks and corrals. There were hundreds of miles of pipes feeding water into the many tanks and water troughs, and the lower ranges were planted with special grasses and legumes while the upper, more rainy slopes were naturally lush with clovers and a mixture of nutritious grasses.

They watched the endless line of cattle being driven up the slopes toward fresh pastures while Brad explained how he regularly left land to "rest" and rejuvenate itself and that Kanoi had some of the finest beef cattle in the country because of his system.

Brad introduced her to some of his hundreds of employees, the ranch hands and the cowboys. "But I'm the man in charge," he said firmly. "And I make sure nobody ever forgets that."

Phyl told him it sounded like something his grandfather might have said.

"Of course he did. And my father. 'You are the boss,' my father told me. 'And you had better remind them of it every day. You have to let every man know, from the lowest ranch hand to the highest manager, that this land belongs to you. If a man steps out of line, he is out of a job.' "

It was late afternoon when they took off again, and Brad's spirits seemed to soar with the plane as they skimmed over the beaches and across the ocean.

The sun was setting in a fiery orange glow when Kalani appeared, its twin volcanic peaks silhouetted against the horizon and its shore fringed with tall coconut palms.

A Chinese servant waited in an open-top Jeep, and as they drove to the lodge, Brad proudly showed her his beloved island.

He took her to see the immaculate white-railed paddocks with the fine Arabian horses he bred, and the prize cattle roaming his meadows, and the perfectly tended lush tropical gardens surrounding the lodge. And Phyl marveled at the beauty and perfection of what she saw. She finally understood Brad's passion for Kalani. It was a true paradise.

The lodge itself was a simple sprawling structure that had obviously just grown over the years. The floors were of smooth dark wood; the walls were plain white. It was simply furnished with antiques from the islands and comfortable sofas covered in sand-colored linen.

Brad's room was as plain as a monk's cell, without even a rug on its polished wooden floor. His big bed with the barley-twist posts was made from koa wood and draped with mosquito netting. The only other furniture was a Chinese wooden chair and a low ebony chest, with a framed black-and-white photograph of Rebecca staring haughtily into the camera. Her long, sleek hair was caught up at the back with a flower in it, and she was wearing a black velvet evening dress.

"She was about thirty years old then, I guess," Brad said. "It was before the divorce."

Phyl threw him a surprised glance; he hadn't mentioned a divorce. But just then a houseboy appeared with their bags, and Brad did not elaborate.

An enormous Doberman with burning red-brown eyes and a coat as black and glossy as wet lava rock suddenly ran into the room. Phyl shrank back with a frightened cry, but the dog ignored her, leaping at Brad with yelps of joy. Brad laughed as he caressed the dog, sleeking back its ears and speaking softly to it in Hawaiian. He told Phyl its name was Kanoi, the same as the ranch.

He saw she was apprehensive, and he said reassuringly, "The Doberman's reputation is misleading. It's quite simple: One man, one dog. They pledge their allegiance to no other than their master." He caressed the dog's massive head, and it gazed devotedly up at him. "See how docile he is? Gentle as a lamb."

Phyl shivered as she looked warily at the powerful dog. Brad put his arm around her, and the dog leaped immediately to its feet. It stared balefully at her, tense as a steel spring. She suddenly recalled Bea's terrible scars, and she shivered; she knew a powerful dog like that could rip a man to pieces in minutes if it chose, but thankfully, unless Brad touched her, it just ignored her.

While Brad went to talk to his stable manager, Phyl showered and changed into a simple long black silk jersey shift. She caught up her hair for coolness and tucked a red hibiscus flower into it. Then she added long crystal drop earrings and a splash of Bellodgia and wandered out onto the lanai to wait for him.

The humid evening air clung to her skin, and the ceiling fans wafted welcome patches of coolness over her as she leaned on the lanai rail, breathing in the different tropical scents of jungly greenness and night-blooming flowers, listening to the croak of the tree frogs and the chirruping of the crickets and the whir of unseen wings, high in the treetops. She did not hear Brad coming, didn't know he was there, watching her, until he said, "Do you have any idea how like my mother you look? With your hair up like that, and the flower in it, the way she used to wear it."

His voice had that hard edge, and Phyl turned to look at him, puzzled. "Your mother was lovely. I take that as a compliment."

"I saw it right away when we met on the plane. I noticed you at the airport. You even have Rebecca's walk, the same long, easy stride."

She smiled. "Was that why you wanted to see me again? Because I look like her?"

Brad laughed. He put his arms around her. "God, no. I never wanted to see that woman again. It was *you* I wanted to see again. The oh-so-clever-and-brilliant Dr. Phyl, whose power over men is such I'm sure she could persuade a king to part with his most intimate secrets."

He crushed her to him, breathing in her scent. "What secrets would you like me to tell you tonight?" he murmured between kisses.

"About Rebecca?" she suggested, still curious.

He shook his head. "First I should tell you about my

grandmother, the one and only Chantal." He laughed bitterly. "My God, the Kane men really knew how to choose their women. Every one of them a first-class bitch."

He let go of her and began to pace the tiled floor, tagged by the dog, who never left his side. Phyl leaned against the rail, watching him as he talked.

"It was the nineteen twenties," he said. "Archer was still very young when he met Chantal. And she was even younger *and* with the unlikely but oh-so-impressive name of O'Higgins. The O'Higgins name spelled money—big money—on two continents. Chantal was half Irish, half French, and she was the spoiled, wayward heiress to the O'Higgins cognac fortune." He looked angrily at Phyl. "You saw her portrait. You saw how beautiful she was. Pale blond, with that sullen look in her blue eyes. She had skin like milk and a very tempting mouth, and Archer fell head over heels this time. And I guess so did she. After all, he was a very handsome man, and he wanted her as much as she wanted him.

"Chantal eloped with him to Honolulu, and then Archer brought her back here, to Kalani. *And she hated it*. God, how she hated it. She was shocked when she saw the primitive wooden lodge; she loathed the bugs and lizards and the wind that hurled the Pacific breakers against the rocks on stormy days. She complained that the heat and humidity made her skin feel like blotting paper. She said the servants were sloppy and lazy, and she swore some of the girls had more than just a master/servant relationship with her husband. She was probably right, but despite all her complaints, I guess she loved him, or at least she wanted him enough to stay.

"Archer's crops had never done well. His pineapples had withered, his sugar shriveled, and wild grasses covered most of his uncultivated acres. But he bought a herd of Hereford cattle and shipped in some better horses. They roamed the gulches on the western side of the island, tended by the paniolos. It was difficult, but the cattle thrived, and suddenly Archer was struck by the new possibilities of his land.

"He told Chantal he wanted to expand, to buy more acreage on the main islands, and he would need her money. But Chantal was difficult. She was pregnant; she was bored out of her mind and sulky. Finally she agreed, after many wild arguments, but she doled out the money to him, bit by bit, driving him crazy. Still, he managed to buy his first thousand acres on the Big Island.

"Then Chantal gave birth to a son, Jack, and as soon afterward as she could, she left both of them and took off for San Francisco. She said she didn't want anything to do with either of them, ever again. Not long after, Archer heard she had run off with someone else, and he divorced her."

Brad stopped his pacing and smiled at Phyl. But his icy eyes were not smiling as he said with a shrug, "And that was Chantal, *my dear grandmother.*"

"But what about her son, Jack? Did he ever see her again?"

"He did," Brad said grimly. "Many years later and in circumstances I'd rather not talk about right now."

"So Archer brought Jack up alone, on the island?"

"Almost. He married again a short while later." Brad laughed. "He always said he had been forced into it. He needed the money to buy more acres on the Big Island. He needed a new, sturdier breed of cattle, better horses, good men. He said his island, his ranch, and his son were his three passions. Women came last.

"You see, women were easy for a man like Archer. He never had to look for them; they were always there when he wanted them. And he said he preferred to buy them in Honolulu's brothels or in San Francisco, where they were less trouble and more fun.

"He went to Europe to look for new cattle, but being

Archer, he was also on the lookout for a wife. He was handsome, and he could be charming, but he was a hard man, and he was determined not to let anything stand in the way of what he wanted. And right then he wanted a fortune."

Brad laughed admiringly. "So he married one." He shrugged. "What else could a good-looking young guy with a glowing future but no money do?"

"So what happened to her?" Phyl asked.

"She couldn't last the course either. She took herself back home, and that was that. Until years later, when Archer suddenly presented Jack with a half brother he knew nothing about."

"And?"

He shrugged. "He soon left. I guess the half brother just couldn't stand Kalani either."

"Or maybe he couldn't stand Jack? After all, Jack was there first. And you Kanes are very territorial."

"Jack hated him," he said brusquely. "And rightly so. But that's a long story, and not one I feel like talking about."

He turned away moodily, and later they had a silent dinner, as though he felt he had already said too much. Afterward he left her at the door of her room with just a brief kiss. "You must be tired," he said abruptly. "Get some sleep."

He went off down the hall, and she heard him call the dog to heel and stride down the steps into the night.

Phyl waited a few moments. Then she walked barefoot onto the lanai to look after him, but he had already disappeared. The big moon bathed the island in a silvery light, and it looked even more breathtakingly beautiful than before. But she scarcely noticed. She was thinking that beneath Brad's urbane, charming facade, he was the most complex man she had ever met.

She wandered back through the silent house and

paused outside Brad's room. The door stood open, and a lamp was lit, and she could see it was empty. Suddenly curious, she went in and tiptoed across to the ebony chest. She picked up Rebecca's photograph and stared at it with fascination. Brad was right: She did resemble Rebecca; the big, startled-looking eyes, the same wide mouth, the pale skin and long black hair. "You even have Rebecca's walk," he had said.

Was that the real reason he was attracted to her? she asked herself with a shiver of apprehension. And was that why he felt he could bare his soul to her about the past?

She glanced around nervously. There was nothing else personal in his room, not even a book on the bedside table. The big walk-in closet was as neat and anonymous as his bedroom. Everything was in its place: jackets in rows, shirts stacked in glass-fronted drawers, shoes all in a line. She ran her hand along the row of hangers and buried her face in the soft tweed of his jacket, suddenly longing for him, wanting the feel of him, the scent of him. As she pulled the jacket toward her, she noticed a crumpled green canvas bag pushed into the corner.

It looked old and oddly out of place. It certainly did not look like the sort of bag Brad would ever use. Hesitating, she looked at it. Then curiosity got the better of her, and she pulled it toward her. Inside, she saw a jumble of feminine travel items, cosmetic bag, hairbrush, T-shirts, sweaters. . . .

Hot with guilt, she zipped the bag up and pushed it back into the corner. She quickly told herself that of course Brad invited other women here. Why wouldn't he? He was an attractive man. Plenty of women would be happy to be his guest. Still, the contents of the green canvas bag were not the sophisticated items she might have expected the women in Brad Kane's life to possess. They were the casual, inexpensive sort of things a girl might carry.

It was none of her business, Phyl told herself guiltily, as she hurried back to her room. She was trespassing on Brad's privacy, and she should feel ashamed of herself. And she did. Still, she wondered about the girl who had left her bag there.

She undressed and climbed naked under the sheet, then lay awake for a long time, listening for Brad's return, hoping he would come to her. But he did not, and as she finally drifted into sleep, she wondered again about Rebecca, and the past that troubled him so deeply, and about Jack and the half brother who suddenly arrived out of the blue almost to ruin his life.

~ 22 ~

Nick Lascelles returned to Antibes with the news that he had learned nothing about the Flora Beale Trust, other than it was administered by the London bank, whose instructions were to maintain the cottage exactly as it was, in perpetuity. There were more than sufficient funds to support it, and the bank believed the donor's intention was to preserve the property as a museum or even a sort of shrine. The banker said the names and details were confidential, and he would certainly not reveal them—unless the police were involved and it became official business, of course.

"So now we're back to square one," Nick said gloomily to Bea and Millie over lunch at the hotel. "The only other link we have is the key we found at the cottage."

He took the silver key from his pocket and put it on the table. They all stared at it. It was small, anonymous, just like any other key. "Perhaps it fits a suitcase or a trunk?" Bea suggested.

"The only trunk we found at the cottage was in the loft, and it wasn't even locked."

"Well, what about a cupboard?"

He shook his head slowly. "No locked cupboards.
Nanny Beale kept her only secrets under her mattress.
Unless . . ." He thought for a minute. "You remember how the document finished abruptly, almost in the
middle. She didn't say what happened on the island,
just that they arrived there. And that she was no match
for the enemy—meaning Johnny's father. She hadn't
concluded her story; she hadn't even written 'The
End.' "

"You mean, you think this key opens the door to the
place she kept the rest of her secrets?" Millie asked.

"I'd bet my boots on it." Nick studied the key again.
"Look, there's a number engraved on it." He grinned
cockily at Millie. "Now you tell me where a nice law-
abiding old lady would keep her secrets."

"At her bank," Millie said promptly.

He nodded. "I'll bet this is the key to a safe-deposit
box. Our problem is which bank."

Bea sighed, defeated. "There must be hundreds
here along the coast."

Nick grinned confidently at them. "Then it's up to
me to play detective and find the right one, isn't it?"

Immediately after lunch Nick hurried off on his new
mission, and Bea decided to check on the progress at
the Villa Mimosa. The kitchen and several new bathrooms were in the process of being installed, and the
place was swarming with carpenters and tilers, plaster-
ers and painters. The villa was still hidden under a
mass of scaffolding, but the swimming pool was almost
finished, and a landscape gardener was working with
his team to restore the grounds to their former glory.

Millie's designer had his new deadline, and he intended to meet it, especially in view of the lavish bonus
she had promised, and she was satisfied that though
the house might not be completely finished, at least in
a couple of days some of the furniture would be in
place and it would be habitable.

Millie had intended to go with Bea to the villa, but

then she told her she felt unaccountably weary. "I'll just let you go alone, dear girl," she said, kissing her good-bye. "You can bring me back the progress report."

Millie waved good-bye to Bea and strolled happily along the terrace to her favorite spot overlooking the sea.

She summoned a waiter and ordered a glass of brandy to perk her up. Sighing with satisfaction, she gazed at the pines and olive trees, the pink and purple bougainvillea, and the silvery blue sea. She thought that of all the places in the world she had traveled, this was her favorite.

Silly woman, she told herself, smiling, *you say that about every place you go. You know by now it's not just the place; it's the company you keep. In the old days, when you were young and giddy, it was always a man. And now that you are old, it's that dear girl Bea. You know she reminds you of yourself at her age, though of course, you never let your loneliness and vulnerability show. Always too proud for that, always covered it up under a devil-may-care attitude.*

She laughed, thinking it was too late to care about all that now. The children would be arriving soon, and the Villa Mimosa was almost finished. She had laid her plans, made sure everything was the way she wished it to be.

Millie sipped her brandy happily, gazing out onto the Mediterranean. Seabirds wheeled noisily overhead, the sun was warm on her bare arms, and a gentle breeze rustled the fronds of the palm trees. She heaved a sigh of pure contentment as she put down her glass and leaned comfortably back against the cushions and closed her eyes.

She was fast asleep when the pain gripped her heart as it had done so many times over the past few years. Only this time it was to be the last. She was smiling when she died.

* * *

"I don't believe it," Bea screamed when she was told. "It's just not true. Please, please, tell me it's not true." Her heart felt as though it would burst with the pain as she turned, ashen-faced, to Nick. "Millie was my friend," she whispered. "She was good and kind and generous. When I was lost and frightened, she took me into her life and made me part of it." She began to sob, great, heaving, ugly sobs that almost choked her. "Oh, Nick, why should this happen to her now? Why? It's just not fair."

He held her trembling in his arms. He liked Millie, he had seen the goodness beneath the bluff exterior, and he was shocked and sad that she was gone. But he was desolate for Bea; her fragile persona seemed to be disintegrating under this new blow. He tightened his arms around her, wanting to give her his strength, his support.

She was talking incoherently about Millie, saying she must call Phyl, that Phyl was Millie's friend. He told her gently not to worry, that he would call Phyl; he would call Millie's attorney in New York; he would take care of everything. But first he took Bea to her room and called the doctor to give her a sedative.

The attorney, John Hartley, arranged for the funeral to take place two days later. He told Nick he would be unable to attend, but that he would be arriving to settle Mrs. Renwick's affairs at the end of the week.

It was impossible to get hold of Phyl. Nick left a dozen messages on her answering machine, saying that he was calling about Millie Renwick, that it was urgent, asking her to call him, but she did not reply.

"She must have gone away," said Bea, desolate that Phyl would miss Millie's last big event.

The day of the funeral dawned clear and blue and sunny. "It's perfect," Bea said sadly. "It's just the way Millie would have wanted it."

They were the only mourners apart from a straggle of black-coated waiters and hotel staff keeping discreetly in the background, paying their final respects to Millie Renwick not because she was a generous woman but because, as she had hoped, they were genuinely fond of her.

Bea laid a sheaf of Millie's favorite pink roses and white lilies on the grave. She stood sadly for a moment, her head bowed. She put her fingers to her lips and blew her a farewell kiss, then, with Nick's comforting arm around her, walked away slowly.

Bea could not bear the thought of the hotel without Millie and had decided to move into the Villa Mimosa, even though it still wasn't finished.

She leaned her head on Nick's shoulder as they drove there in the big black funeral car, thinking what a happy day this was meant to be for Millie. And for her. She was going to live in the house of her dreams; only now, without Millie's forceful presence, somehow it all seemed meaningless. The car turned in at the big iron gates, and she opened her eyes as they drove silently up the gravel driveway of the Villa Mimosa.

And there, sitting on the steps, with airline identification tags still around their necks, looking lost and forlorn, were two small, pale, frightened-looking children.

"It's Scott and Julie Renwick," Bea gasped, horrified. She had completely forgotten they were arriving today. In fact, she had forgotten all about them.

Relieved finally to hand over her charges, the distraught Air France representative rushed toward them. She told them that when nobody had met them at the airport, she had been worried. The airline had the address of the Villa Mimosa, so she had brought them here. Her responsibility over, she left hurriedly before they could change their minds.

Bea looked sadly at the children and then at Nick. "What do we do now?" she whispered.

Big-eyed, scared, the two children looked back at them. They were alike as two peas: the same round face and freckles, blue eyes, and ragged fringe of shiny brown hair, hers in a ponytail with the ribbon sliding off it. The boy took his sister's hand, saying nothing, waiting apprehensively for what might happen to them next.

Scotty Renwick again felt the lump sticking in his throat that meant he had to fight not to cry. He swallowed hard, staring back at the woman and the man who were looking at them as though they had never seen two kids before. He felt Julie's small, hot hand grip his even more tightly, and he knew he had to be brave for her sake. Hadn't he been told after Mom and Dad's funeral that he had to be a man now and look after his sister? He knew it was true. It was just the two of them now against the world. But the world was suddenly so much bigger than the small town they had always lived in, where they knew everybody and everybody knew them. These strangers were looking at them as though they had never even heard of them. And this woman couldn't be his aunt Millie. Wasn't she supposed to be old?

He slid his arm protectively around Julie's shoulders, waiting for them to do something. That's all that ever happened now. People did things to them, or for them: sent them places to live, gave them food, smiled a lot at them with that special pitying look in their eyes. "Lucky you," they had said, "having a rich auntie in the sunny south of France. Lucky you going to live in a grand villa." "Oh sure," he had mumbled bitterly, "lucky us."

The red-haired woman was smiling at him now. "Welcome to the Villa Mimosa, Scott and Julie," she said warmly. "Boy, are we glad to see you. Poor kids, you look exhausted. Come on inside, and let me show you your rooms. Millie had them all fixed up specially for you."

Scott glanced down at Julie. Her expression was blank, as it usually was these days. As though she had put her emotions into neutral. Julie hadn't cried once since the funeral, though she had cried buckets before. And so had he, howling like a wolf sometimes, letting out his pain. And his anger, because boy, was he angry. Angry at whoever had caused his mom and dad to die; angry at them for dying; angry at himself for not being big and strong enough to take care of Julie. Angry at not being able to turn the clock back and make everything the way it used to be, the four of them in the little yellow ranch house with the pepper trees surrounding it, dropping endless leaves onto the lawn. He had even promised God he would never complain again about clearing up those leaves if only he would bring Mom and Dad back. But it seemed God wasn't one for bargains.

And now here he was, with Julie, in a foreign country called France where they all spoke stuff he couldn't understand, with two strangers, in an enormous house called the Villa Mimosa that looked like something in the movies. Because even though they smiled at him, they were still strangers. And the truth was he was scared. And homesick.

"Are you my aunt Millie?" Julie said suddenly, looking suspiciously at the woman.

Scott gave her a quick nudge with his elbow; hadn't he warned her not to say anything, not to ask any questions? He had told her to let him take care of it all, that they wouldn't stay here. Leave it to him, he had said, and they would soon be home again. "But, Scotty, where is home?" Julie had asked plaintively, and that awful lump had come back in his throat again. He had no answer; he didn't know. He didn't know anything anymore. He was only nine years old, and he didn't want to be a man yet. He just wanted life to be the way it had always been.

"I'm Bea French," the woman said, hunkering down and giving Julie a kiss on the cheek. She leaned toward him, too, but he drew back. He didn't want any kisses from any more strangers.

"And I'm Nick Lascelles." The man held out his hand, and Scott took it reluctantly. "We're friends of your aunt Millie's," he said. "Come on inside; let's show you around."

Scott took Julie's hand again as they followed them indoors. He stared around the big empty hall, surprised. There was no furniture, no muddy boots kicked into a corner, no coats hanging on a peg like at home.

"This place looks like nobody lives here," he said in his funny gravelly voice that used to make his dad laugh.

"Your aunt Millie was having the villa redone especially for you," Bea said reassuringly. "She wanted it to be finished when you got here, but there's still not much furniture. Just in the kitchen and the bedrooms."

"And there's the swimming pool," Nick said. "Don't forget that."

"There's a pool?" Scott's tired eyes lit with a flash of interest.

"Sure there's a pool," Bea said quickly. "And there's a beach nearby, and lots of boats for fishing."

"Yeah." Scott shrugged his thin shoulders tiredly, glaring at Julie as she ran to Nick and slid her hand trustingly into his.

She looked up at him and lisped plaintively, "Whereth my aunt Millie?"

Bea shot Nick an apprehensive look that said she thought the truth was just too harsh for these poor emotionally battered children right now. "I just told you, sweetie," she said. "Aunt Millie couldn't be here today."

Julie stared at her. "She's dead, ith'nt she?" She turned her sad gaze on Nick. "That's what they told uth when my mommy and daddy died. They thaid they couldn't be with uth anymore."

Oh, God, Scotty thought, fighting that lump in his throat again. *Julie's right. That's what they told us. Oh, God, what will become of us now? They said she was our only relative . . . now we have nobody . . . nobody . . . we are orphans . . . in a foreign country . . . with strangers. . . .*

Nick said gently, "I'm sorry, Julie, but everything's still okay. Bea and I will take care of you."

"*I'll* take care of her," Scotty muttered. "She's *my* sister."

"Bea, my hairth metthy," Julie said, her lisp becoming more pronounced the way it did when she was tired or upset. "And I need to go to the bathroom."

She yawned wearily as they followed Bea upstairs, still holding tightly to Scott's hand. "Remember, don't say anything," he warned as Bea flung open the door and showed them a pink ruffled bower, fit for a princess.

"Millie knew you liked pink, Julie," Bea said as the girl gave a delighted cry and ran toward the menagerie of stuffed animals awaiting her on the window seat. "And that your favorite color is green, Scott," she said, including him in her smile.

"I don't care," Scott muttered, with an indifferent shrug of his shoulders. He turned away, ignoring his sister exclaiming over the beautiful big doll awaiting her in the middle of the brass four-poster.

It was suddenly all too much. He couldn't keep that lump away; tears threatened, and he ran from the room.

He stood in the hallway, his shoulders hunched, his clenched fists thrust into his pockets. Even from the back, Nick knew that he was crying and that he didn't want anyone to see.

He said, "It's all right to cry if you feel like it, Scott. A lot of sad things have happened to you. First your mom and dad, and now your aunt Millie."

"What did *she* care?" he said in a tight, choked little voice. "She didn't even *know* us."

"It's true Millie had never met you, but she knew all about you. And what she knew made her care. She was an old lady, you know, but she told us she had never been a mother and now she could be. She was really looking forward to it, Scott. To being with you and Julie and taking care of you."

He patted Scott's shoulder. "You've had a long journey, son. You're tired, and I'll bet you're hungry. How about you and I going down to the kitchen and rustling up some food, maybe going to check out that pool?"

Scott sniffed back his tears noisily. He still didn't look at Nick, but he followed him downstairs. He sat at the kitchen table, his head lowered, as Nick checked the refrigerator and the freezer.

Nick gave an amazed whistle. He took out a couple of packages. "Good old Aunt Millie," he said with a grin. "She knew what her two American kids would like all right. Hot dogs and french fries."

Scott's eyes lifted with interest, but he didn't say anything. Then Julie ran into the kitchen and climbed onto a chair next to him. She cradled a green plush frog in her arms, watching silently as Nick and Bea prepared the food.

At last they carried their plates out onto the terrace, and everyone sat around the table, trying to force down the food, but they were all choked up. Even Nick ran out of anecdotes. Scott and Julie stared at their plates in silence.

Nick threw Bea a despairing glance and saw there were tears in her eyes. He knew she was on the brink of breaking down. It was all too much: Millie; the funeral; the children.

"Look!" Julie suddenly yelled. She pointed. "Over there."

A big dog crept from the bushes at the edge of the lawn and stood watching them, sniffing the air hopefully.

The dog was long-legged and curly-coated, shaggy, unkempt—and hungry. After a moment hunger got the better of its caution, and it gathered its tattered courage and sidled toward them, crouching low until it was almost on its belly. It lay down at Scott's feet, put its nose carefully between its paws, and raised big, soulful brown eyes to him.

Scotty stared at the dog. He thought the expression in its eyes was like the one he saw in his own eyes in the mirror. He suddenly wanted that dog more than he had ever wanted anything in his life before. *Except to be able to turn the clock back.* But the dog was a stray; he knew these people wouldn't want it in their fancy villa. The dog could never be his, and that's why he couldn't touch it.

Looking at the dog, Bea thought it had a lot in common with her and with Millie's two young orphans. They didn't say a word, but she saw the longing in their blue eyes and knew she had found at least one way to break the ice around their hearts.

"All right, mutt," she said, "you're in."

Scott pushed back his chair with a whoop of delight. He flung his arms around the dog. The lump in his throat was magically gone, and as the dog licked his hand, he caught himself in mid-laugh. *I'm laughing,* he thought, astonished, *I'm laughing again.* And he punched Julie on the arm and said, "He's gonna sleep on my bed."

"No, mine."

"Mine."

"You can share him," Bea said quickly.

"What shall we call him?" Julie demanded excitedly, watching Scott feed him their hot dogs. The dog devoured them and sat, one battered ear askew, happily begging for more.

"He's such a mutt," Bea said, laughing. "How about Poochie?"

They were finally acting like kids again instead of

emotionally exhausted midgets, and she thanked heaven for the dog. She glanced at Nick, and she knew the same thought was going through his mind. *What next? What would happen to Scott and Julie Renwick now that Millie had gone?*

Millie's attorney, John Hartley, arrived from New York two days later. He was an older man, white-haired and stiffly pompous, and he had been Millie's legal adviser for decades.

"Mrs. Renwick had suffered from a heart complaint for several years," he told Bea. "Everything that could be done for her had already been done. She knew she might die at any time. That's why she refused to give up the cigarettes she enjoyed, even though she knew they were bad for her."

Bea suddenly recalled her first meeting with Millie, at the Fifth Avenue apartment that rainy day. ". . . it's not alcohol that will kill me," she had said, "it's these blasted ciggies."

"She wrote this letter for you. It arrived just before she died," Hartley said. He handed her an envelope and sat back with hands patiently folded, while Bea read it.

I know I might not have long to live, and that's why I lived my life to the hilt, dear girl. I thought I was a lucky woman; I had everything I wanted. And then, like a blessing from God, you came into my life, and I cannot tell you how you brightened it. You were the granddaughter I never had, the perfect companion, someone young to laugh with me and be my friend. Someone I could indulge and pamper a little. Someone who listened to my endless silly chatter and laughed along with me at my own foolishness. You made my days complete, and I would have been a lonelier woman without you.

I wanted to help you find yourself again, even

though I knew it would mean you would leave me. I wanted to keep you with me always, but even I am not that selfish, and when you found the Villa Mimosa and its link with the past, I thought I knew how to help you. Then my poor little orphans came along and completed the picture, because I knew then that even if I could not give you back your past, I could give you a future.

I enjoyed my life, dear Bea, so do not mourn me too long. Now I want you to enjoy yours. My attorney will take care of everything for you.

Your dear friend and surrogate grandmother,

Millie Renwick

Bea looked sadly at the attorney. "She was so good," she said quietly. "A true friend."

"She was indeed a good woman," Hartley agreed. "Most people saw only her frivolous facade. They never knew how many charities benefited from her generosity—and always anonymously. But now, Miss French, to the contents of Mrs. Renwick's newly drawn will."

He cleared his throat, looking at her over the top of his half glasses. "Mrs. Renwick wanted you to have the Villa Mimosa. She did not leave it to you in her will; she had already purchased it in your name. She made it clear from the very beginning that she wanted this house to be yours and yours alone. She says here that she hopes it will bring you everything you ever hoped it would, including happiness."

Bea's eyes widened with astonishment.

"Mrs. Renwick also left you the sum of five million dollars because, as she said, she wants you to have a future, since you have no past."

"Five million dollars."

"Exactly. But there is a condition: Mrs. Renwick wants you to take responsibility for the children. She asked that you bring them up as if they were your own. She felt that by doing so, she was *ensuring* that you had

a future. You would have a home, a family, and sufficient money to provide for your lifestyle. After further
substantial bequests to universities and hospitals and
various charities, and of items of jewelry, both to you
and to Dr. Forster, the remainder of Mrs. Renwick's
fortune, amounting to around two hundred and fifty
million dollars, is to be placed in trust for the children,
Scott and Julie Renwick."

Later that day, after the attorney had left, Bea told
Nick her news. "Millie was sorry for me, not having a
past," she said tearfully. "So she wanted to give me a
future. And now look at me, the chatelaine of the Villa
Mimosa, and 'mother' of two kids who barely know
me."

"And a *millionaire*," Nick said, stunned. "*And* you
are the 'mother' of two *extremely rich* little kids."

"My God, Nick, what shall I do?"

Nick put his hand under her chin. He lifted her face,
smiling encouragingly at her. "Do what you always
do," he said. "Call Phyl. She's probably at her office by
now. After that," he continued, "I suggest we crack
open a bottle of champagne and drink a toast to your
dear good friend and surrogate grandmother, Millie
Renwick."

Bea tried calling Phyl's work and home numbers endlessly but still only got the answering machines. Worried, she placed a call to the San Francisco Police Department and asked to speak to Detective Mahoney.

Mahoney picked up his phone on the first ring.
"Yeah?" he said, sipping his third cup of coffee in half
an hour. He propped his feet on his cluttered desk and
tilted his chair, teetering back and forth lazily. "Jesus,
Bea French. How the hell are ya? And *where* the hell are
ya? This line's so good I swear you're down the hall."

"I'm still in France," she said. "At the Villa Mimosa.
Oh, Detective Mahoney," she wailed, "Millie's dead

and she's left me all this money and two children and I don't know what to do. . . . I've been calling Phyl and she's not there and I'm so concerned—''

Mahoney sat up suddenly alert. "Okay, honey, take it easy. You just tell me all about it, and then we'll see what to do.''

She spilled out her story and said finally, "Then I couldn't get hold of Phyl to tell her and she missed the funeral, and now I still can't reach her, and oh, Detective Mahoney—''

"Fine. Okay, Bea. First thing is don't worry about Phyl. I happen to know she's with some guy she's crazy about. I guess she forgot to tell you about Mr. Hawaii, huh? This little vacation was a spur-of-the-moment thing, and she just stayed on a bit longer than she'd planned. She's going to be heartbroken about Millie and about missing the funeral. That's a tough break, and Phyl's not being there made it harder for you.''

"Nick was with me," Bea said, sounding calmer now. "He helped.''

"Yeah. Good for Nick. You like him, huh, Bea?''

"He's a nice guy," she said a touch defensively.

"Now where have I heard that before? Listen to me, young Bea French. Millie must have loved you a lot to do what she did. Trusting you with those two orphaned kids. She figured it was three of you against the world now, instead of just one. And from the vibes I'm catching about Nick, maybe it's even four. Those sound like pretty good numbers to me. So keep your chin up, babe. Be glad you had Millie's friendship and love.'' He grinned. "And after those words of wisdom, I'd better give you the doc's number in Hawaii.''

"Thanks, Detective Mahoney," she said, sounding relieved.

"Franco, please," he said, smiling. "I thought we were friends now. After all we've been through together?''

"Best friends," she said fervently.

"Call me if you need me, babe," he said. "And maybe I'll get over there to see you all one of these days."

Mahoney put down the phone and glanced at the clock. It was exactly seven. He picked up the receiver again and dialed the Hawaiian number.

"Kalani. Good evening." An Asian-accented voice responded immediately.

"Yeah, good evening to you. I'd like to speak to Dr. Phyl Forster."

"Yes, sir. And who shall I say is calling her?"

"Tell her it's Franco Mahoney."

He propped his feet on the desk again and leaned back, anticipating her surprised voice.

"Who is this?" a man's voice demanded crisply.

He guessed it was Mr. Hawaii in person, and he jerked into an upright position. "My name is Franco Mahoney. I wish to speak with Dr. Forster."

"The doctor cannot come to the phone. Do you want to leave a message?"

"Yes, I do." Franco raised a quizzical eyebrow. Mr. Hawaii sounded like an arrogant bastard. "Tell her Mahoney called. That's M-A-H-O-N-E-Y," he spelled slowly.

"It's a common name, Mr. Mahoney. I know how to spell it."

There was acid in his smooth voice, and Franco frowned. He was more than an arrogant bastard; he sounded like a first-class jerk. "Great," he said abruptly. "Then if you would just ask the lady to call me, any time, day or night. It's urgent. And she has my number. Okay?"

"I'll give her the message," the man said coldly, and the line went dead.

Mahoney slammed down the receiver. "Jesus," he said, astonished. "The doc certainly knows how to choose 'em."

He stalked down the hall to the coffee machine,

hands thrust in his pockets, staring at the floor, puzzling over the exchange of icy words. *That is some jealous guy,* he concluded, grabbing his fourth cup of coffee since six-fifteen. And it was only seven-ten. He had the feeling it would be a long night.

He was right. The first call came almost immediately: an arson attack in the Tenderloin. The fire was still raging out of control, and so far two bodies had been recovered.

He and Benedetti got down there fast, with Benedetti at the wheel of the Chevy from the police pool, lights flashing and siren blazing. "I dunno"— Benedetti grinned, satisfied, as the traffic parted for them—"sometimes it's okay being a cop."

Mahoney winced as they ran yet another red light and swung around a corner with a screech of brakes. "Yeah. Except maybe ya should consider going back to driving school. Jesus, man, look out, will ya!"

Benedetti's grin grew even wider as he glanced at his partner. "What's the matter? You scared, Detective?"

"You betcha. With a maniac like you at the wheel! Remind me to ask for a different partner when I get back to the squad room. That way I might live longer."

They saw the flames four blocks away and came to a stop just as the roof, in a flurry of sparks and glowing debris, caved in. "God help them, I hope all the fire department's out of there," Mahoney muttered.

"It's all over but the shouting," the fire chief told him. "Two dead so far, and all my men are accounted for. There's no doubt it's arson; there are gasoline-soaked rags all over the place." He held out a piece of cloth for Mahoney to see.

Mahoney said, "Put it in the plastic, Benedetti. We'll have it checked." He scanned the crowd of watchers with narrowed eyes; arsonists almost invariably came to watch their own fires. That was their high. He didn't know what they might be thinking about the people they had just killed, and he didn't care. He just wanted to put them away for as long as possible. But tonight he was unlucky. His famous sixth sense seemed to have deserted him. No one in the crowd of bystanders seemed to have even had the faintest guilty whiff of gasoline on him.

"Strike one," he said to Benedetti. They started to head back just as the next call crackled over the car radio: a stabbing outside a bar. "Hey, any messages for me?" Mahoney demanded as they careened off again.

"Nah, nothing," the duty officer said over the radio.

"Just let me know if a Dr. Phyl Forster calls, okay," Mahoney said. "It's important."

"Will do. Ten-four." The duty officer signed off.

"You got a new girlfriend?" Benedetti asked curiously. "I thought it was serious with the Italian chick—what's her name?"

Mahoney sighed. "For your information women have not been called chicks for at least a decade. And the young lady you are referring to still deigns to see me occasionally. When I have the free time."

"Yeah, you're right, that's the problem. Time. They get tired of waiting for ya, find themselves a guy with more sociable hours. Still, some of the guys manage it to the altar. You going to Connors's nuptials Saturday?"

"Wouldn't miss it," Mahoney said as they screeched to a halt again outside the Hot Trash Bar.

Lying facedown in the alley, the body was surrounded by a crowd of ghoulish onlookers, held back by a couple of uniformed cops. The victim had been mugged coming out of the bar and dragged into the alley, where he had been stabbed and his wallet removed. Several witnesses had seen the culprit take off out of the alley, and they had a description, but no one was willing to say he had seen the killing. Nobody wanted to get involved.

"Par for the course." Mahoney sighed. And it was. By midnight the body count from the arson attack, the stabbing, and assorted other homicides totaled four, plus one "critical" hovering between here and eternity in intensive care in the SF General. And the total of suspects behind bars amounted to zero.

He was morosely typing up his reports on the IBM, sipping coffee and munching a cinnamon Danish when the phone rang. "Yeah?" he snarled tiredly.

"Mahoney? Is that you?"

"Doc." He dropped the Danish and tucked the receiver under his chin. He leaned back, smiling. "Sure it's me. Who else were you expecting?"

"You sound so . . . tired."

"You don't sound too great yourself, for a lady on a vacation." He thought she sounded subdued, and he wondered if the arrogant Mr. Hawaii was in the room, listening to her conversation.

"I'm fine," she said a little too briskly. "I got your message."

"I'm surprised. The boyfriend didn't seem to like the idea of another guy calling you. A tad possessive, huh?"

"You said it was urgent," she replied, ignoring his jibe.

"It is. Look, you had better sit down for this one, Doc. It's about your friend Millie." He told her about Bea's calling and about Millie and what had happened.

He thought Phyl sounded tearful as she said she would never forgive herself for not being there. She told him she would return to San Francisco the following day and would call him when she got back.

Mahoney put the phone down thoughtfully. For a cool, collected lady, she sure sounded uptight. Just like Mr. Hawaii.

~ 23 ~

$\mathscr{P}$hyl put down the phone and looked at Brad sitting across the room from her. He was smoking a cigarette and drinking brandy. The Doberman, still tense as a coiled spring, was sprawled, as always, at his feet.

"Trouble?" he asked lightly, meeting her accusing blue eyes.

"Why didn't you give me the message that Mahoney had called? If I hadn't seen his name written on the pad, I would never have known."

He shrugged. "I guess it slipped my mind."

"I know you better than that. Nothing ever slips your mind. You remember every detail of your family's history."

"That's different," he said curtly. "That's important."

"And telling me that someone wanted to speak to me urgently was not important?"

"Well, was it?"

"You didn't tell me because it was a man calling."

"I don't like *anyone* calling you here. You should have respected my privacy. You should not have given him this number."

She stared at him in disbelief. "I can't just disappear. I have patients; things happen—"

Brad suddenly stabbed out the cigarette and leaped to his feet. The dog followed, bristling. He grabbed her by the shoulders, thrusting his face into hers. "I told you before, *nothing* is more important than you and me. *You just don't listen.*" She heard the dog growl softly. "When you are with *me,* Phyl, I expect total devotion. *No one else matters.* Why don't you understand that?"

"You're crazy," she retorted, pushing him away.

He grabbed her by the arm and spun her around to face him. "Is that what you think? You think I'm *crazy.*" His laugh was bitter. "I'm probably the most *rational* person you know, Doctor. At least I know what I want from life, and I go all out to get it." His expression changed, and he smiled, suddenly gentle, running his hand along her cheek. "And I want you, my beautiful Phyl," he murmured, "my muse, my confessor. Only you."

Phyl glanced at him warily. This was more than a lover's tiff; Brad was crazy with jealousy. "I have to leave first thing in the morning," she said coldly, pulling away from him.

"But, Phyl, why?" He looked boyishly bewildered. "We're so happy here together. Please don't spoil it. Don't leave me. You see," he added, almost pathetically, *"I need you."*

Phyl hesitated; he had done one of those sudden about-faces, and he was his old charming self again. Then she remembered Millie. "A friend of mine died suddenly," she said in a shaky voice. "I have to go back."

"Phyl. I'm so sorry. I didn't realize."

"Well, now you do."

She left him and walked to her room. She heard him following her, trailed by the Doberman.

He stood in the doorway with the dog crouched next

to him, watching her pack. Tears for Millie were spilling down her face. "I'll fly you back myself," he said penitently. "I'll go to the funeral with you. You can come back here afterward."

"It's too late, Brad. The funeral is already over."

"Then why do you need to go?"

She sighed, exasperated. "It's complicated. There is a patient involved. I have to talk to her. She needs me."

"I told you, so do I. *Need you*."

Phyl stopped folding clothes into the suitcase and looked at him standing in the doorway. There was a desperate look in Brad's eyes, and she knew he meant it. She guessed a little jealousy was acceptable, but his bordered on the unreasonable. She went over to him and put her hands on his shoulders. "You're a fool to be so jealous," she said softly. "You know I would stay if I could."

"I guess so," he said reluctantly. He pulled her to him. "Who is this Mahoney whose number you know so well?"

"Just a friend," she replied.

Brad clamped his arms around her. "I don't want you to have any friends," he whispered in her ear. "I don't want you to have anyone but me in your life." His icy tone sent a foreboding shiver up her spine.

In bed later she watched Brad sleeping. He lay on his back, his arms and legs flung wide. She thought with his bronzed, firm-muscled body and silky blond hair, he looked like a statue of a young Greek god. Beautiful but somehow defenseless. She remembered their fight and his menacing face close to hers; he had looked so different then from the man innocently sleeping beside her. Thinking about it now made her frightened. For the first time in their relationship, she began to wonder in a professional way about his instability.

* * *

Phyl unlocked the door of her apartment and kicked it shut behind her. She threw her bags on the floor, then hurled herself on the sofa, where she stretched wearily.

Only a few months ago this apartment had seemed like her fortress, her refuge against the world. It had been tranquil, silent, orderly. Her life had a calm routine that she enjoyed. Well, maybe *enjoyed* was not exactly true, but at least she had been in charge of her own emotions, even if she hadn't allowed them to surface much.

Then she had let down her guard, and now she was involved with a crazily jealous man whose troubles she suspected ran even deeper than mere jealousy. Her good friend had died, and she hadn't even made it to the funeral. And her patient/protégée had been forced to face a crisis alone when she had given her word she would be there for her.

Phyl sighed angrily. Her carefully controlled world was crumbling at the edges, and she knew it. It was time she pulled herself together.

She picked up the phone and called Bea. To her surprise she sounded cheerful and relaxed.

"I called you in Hawaii, but I couldn't get through," Bea said. "I spoke with Detective Mahoney though, and he was a great help. He's such a nice guy, Phyl, so straightforward. He helped me sort out my priorities."

"I'm just sorry I let you down," Phyl said. "And I'm desperately sorry that I missed saying good-bye to Millie. How could I have been so stupid as to not let you know where I was—"

"It's okay, I understand, and I'm sure Millie would, too. Besides, Nick helped me. He's been a rock, Phyl. Someone to lean on. I don't know how I would have coped without him. He's here now, helping me with the kids. Scott and Julie," she added.

They talked about the inheritance and the children, and Phyl said it was typical of Millie. She offered to fly

out to be with her, but Bea said she had Nick and for
the moment she was okay.

"Just don't forget my promise," Phyl told her as they
said good-bye. "When you need me, I'll be there. You
can count on it."

Feeling a little better, she wandered into the bedroom, stripping off her clothes as she went. She stood
under the shower, letting the hot water wash away her
fatigue—*and her sins*. She wondered what she was going
to do about Brad.

Silent and grim-faced, he had flown her from Kalani
to Honolulu, but she had insisted on taking a commercial flight to San Francisco.

"Why?" he had demanded angrily. She had not told
him, but she knew the reason: it was that she had to
start picking up the threads of her independence again
before things went too far and she lost all control. She
could not allow Brad Kane to dominate her life.

At the airport she reached up to kiss him, but he
stepped back angrily. She turned quickly away and hurried through the gate. She felt his eyes burning into
her, but she would not look back. If that was the way
Brad wanted things, then she wasn't playing.

She stepped from the shower and wrapped herself in
her oversize white terry robe, then wandered into the
kitchen, wondering why the apartment seemed so
empty. She smiled. How could she have forgotten? Of
course. The cat.

She dialed Mahoney's home number, but there was
no reply, so she called him at work. "I'm back," she
said, unexpectedly eager for the sound of his reassuring voice.

"So you are," he agreed.

"I spoke to Bea," she said. "I think I straightened
things out about not being there for her when I said I
would."

"Right," he said coolly.

Phyl held the receiver away from her, staring at it,

frowning. What the hell was wrong with Mahoney? "Are you okay?" she asked.

"Sure. It's just been one of those weeks. You want me to drop off Coco? Or maybe you're planning another vacation?"

"Hey, Mahoney," she said, startled, "what's wrong? I thought we were friends."

There was a long silence. Then he said, "I thought Mr. Hawaii might be there with you, that's all."

She laughed, relieved. "Well, he's not. He's home. Alone. On his island."

"Great. So what are you doing tonight? You got a hot date with someone else?"

"No, I do not have a hot date. And I'm not doing anything. Unless of course, you were intending to invite me somewhere?" She suddenly wanted to see him. "Mahoney," she said into the strained silence, "the treat's on me. All you have to do is name the time and place."

"My place," he said. "Eight o'clock. And wear something fancy. It's a wedding."

"You're not getting married?"

"Not unless you're asking me, Doc. No, it's a colleague. I couldn't make the ceremony, but this is an Irish-Italian wedding, and there's going to be dancing and carousing and a hell of a lot of drinking all night long. See you at eight."

She wore a new red lace dress, short and clinging, with a wide neckline that left her shoulders bare. She swept up her hair, and since she had no fresh flowers, she tucked a big red silk rose into it. She thrust her suntanned feet into high-heeled red sandals and flung a black silk shawl around her shoulders. She looked at herself in the mirror with satisfaction. Her spirits suddenly soared. She didn't know what she felt about Brad and his crazy jealousy anymore. All she knew was that she was glad it was Mahoney she was dressing up for tonight.

"Well, look at you," Mahoney said, opening the door to her. "You look like my high school prom date."

"I should have known better than to bother." Phyl sighed resignedly, walking up the stairs.

"I see you took my advice about color," he added mockingly. "On you red looks good. In fact," he said, eyeing her long suntanned legs and smooth shoulders appreciatively as she slipped off her shawl, "on you it looks terrific."

She twirled for him, smiling. "Am I really okay? You said dressy, but I wasn't sure."

He shook his head admiringly. "Doc, let me tell you Connors just got married today. But when that hot Irishman sets eyes on my scarlet woman, you may find you've caused the quickest divorce in history."

She laughed. "You look pretty fancy yourself tonight, Mahoney." She fingered the satin lapels of his tuxedo. "Like a late-night talk show host. Or maybe a political candidate? Or perhaps the next mayor?"

"Not this week, babe. It's been a toughie. It must be the summer madness. It happens every year about this time. There's a mini heat wave and people go crazy and start killing each other. There are more bodies stacked in the city morgue than you or I would care to think about. And not one of them in the 'solved' account."

He took a couple of glasses from the cupboard and a bottle of champagne out of the refrigerator. She watched him.

"Talking of butts," she said, with a cheeky grin, "yours is looking pretty good, Mahoney."

"So I've been told," he said coolly, pouring the wine.

She caught sight of the champagne label and said, impressed, "You went to all this expense just for me?"

"Nothing but the best," he replied, lifting his glass in a mock toast. "Oh, by the way, Coco is asleep on my bed. You've been away so long she's almost forgotten you."

"Well, I haven't forgotten her," she said, rattled.

"So? What's with Mr. Hawaii?"

Embarrassed, she lowered her eyes. "I haven't come here to discuss my private life."

"Why not? You got something to hide?"

"Mahoney!" She glared at him with exasperation.

"You want *me* to talk about him then? I thought he was cold—*icy*, in fact. I also thought he was rude, arrogant, and possessive. I thought he was just too fuckin' jealous for his own good." He looked at her and added, "Or yours."

"Mahoney!" she exclaimed again, her blue eyes blazing.

He shrugged. "Well, you asked me—"

"No, I did not!" Their eyes met, and she began to laugh. "Oh, hell, you're right about him," she admitted finally. "He is possessive, and he is jealous." Her smile was replaced by a worried look. "In fact, Mahoney, sometimes he scares me, he's so jealous."

"Does he have any reason to be?"

She shook her head. "You know what's really worrying me? He thinks I look like his mother. *And I do.*"

Mahoney shrugged, not understanding. "So what's wrong with that?"

"It's a bit creepy, that's all. He hated her. He told me all these horror stories, about how promiscuous she was, how she flaunted her affairs. He said everyone knew about her. She even drove one guy to kill himself. . . ."

Mahoney whistled, impressed. "It doesn't take a top psychiatrist to figure that one out, Doc."

"It's not like that," she said defensively. "Most of the time he's charming, warm, and sensitive. He's handsome, urbane, a respected businessman. His ranch is his life."

"He just hates his mother, that's all." Mahoney

wasn't smiling now. "Look, Phyl, if you *feel* there is something wrong, then believe me there *is*. Trust that old gut instinct."

"You mean, he's really thinking about his mother when he's in bed with me?" she asked in a small, frightened voice.

"Why didn't you ask *him* that?"

"I did, almost. I asked if he wanted me because I looked like Rebecca, and he just laughed. He said it wasn't true. I have to believe that, Mahoney."

He nodded. Phyl was a woman who did not give her favors lightly. Even though she was a psychiatrist, she was a woman and unable to accept the possibility that Brad might have some perverted reason for wanting her in his bed.

"Anyway, I left him. At the airport." She shrugged. "He was mad because I wouldn't let him fly me home. So I guess it's good-bye."

Mahoney grinned. "Then there's no need to worry." She was still frowning. "Okay, tell me your next problem," he said.

"Oh, Mahoney, I wasn't there for Bea."

"True. But she has come to terms with that. It was just circumstances."

"It was *unforgivable*. Besides being my friend, she's my patient. I behaved irresponsibly."

"Hey, we're all human."

"*I'm a doctor!*" she yelled, still angry with herself. "*I should have been there.*"

"Listen, it worked out," he said soothingly. "Everything's okay. No more breast-beating, all right?"

Phyl raised tearful blue eyes to him. "I missed Millie's funeral."

He sat beside her and put his arm around her shoulders. She nestled her head in the crook of his arm, and he heard her sniffing back the tears. "Go ahead, babe," he said, sighing exaggeratedly. "Let it all out. You'll feel better."

He heard her giggle through the tears, and she said, "Oh, stop it, Mahoney."

"Your mascara's running," he said, looking at her critically.

"Oh. Oh, damn."

"A good curseword like 'damn' can surely relieve your feelings," he said mockingly.

"Prick," she retorted, pushing him away.

He laughed. "That's my girl. Come on, Doc. Fix your face. We've got a wedding to go to."

The celebrations had begun at four-thirty that afternoon at the Hibernian Banqueting Rooms, and by the time Mahoney and Phyl arrived, around nine, the place was jumping. The band, augmented by several members of the SFPD, was blasting Beach Boys' hits, and half the room was singing along. The dance floor was crowded, and the bar was five deep, and fresh supplies of Italian goodies were being ferried across to the buffet that ran the length of one wall. Irish and Italian flags celebrating the union hung like banners from the ceiling, and swags of red roses were intertwined with shamrocks. The bride, gorgeous in white silk and lace and ten yards of sequin-studded veil, was sitting with her new husband and their families at the head table. Mahoney pulled Phyl through the crowd to pay their respects.

"Connors, you old bastard, she finally made you an honest man," he said, hugging his colleague. He looked admiringly at the bride. "I always told Connors you were too good for an old mick like him. You look wonderful, baby. A beautiful bride."

They laughed, and he took Phyl's hand and introduced her. "This is Phyllida Forster, known as Phyl," he said. She threw him an amazed glance, wondering how he knew her proper name, and suddenly found herself engulfed in a bear hug from the bridegroom.

"Jeez, Mahoney," he said admiringly. "Where'd you

find her? I tell ya, she's too classy for an old mick like yourself.''

"But you're *Dr.* Phyl," the bride, Sandra, exclaimed.

"Not tonight," Phyl assured her. "Tonight I'm just this old mick's date."

They laughed, and Connors said, "Save me a dance for later, Dr. Phyl. I'll let you analyze me anytime."

Most of the men on Mahoney's shift were propping up the bar. Benedetti saw them coming. He nudged the guy next to him and said, "Look what Mahoney has caught himself." They turned as one man to look, and appreciative grins appeared on their faces.

"Whaddid ya have to do to get her here, Mahoney?" somebody yelled. "Put the cuffs on her?"

"Okay, wise-ass," Mahoney said, "we all understand you don't know how to behave in front of a lady, but we'd appreciate it if you would try. Allow me to introduce Phyl Forster."

"The doc," Benedetti said reverently. "Can I ask ya one question, ma'am? What the hell are you doin' with a jerk like Mahoney? There's half the SFPD here tonight be happy to take over from him, anytime you say."

"Thank you, guys," Phyl said demurely, accepting a barstool and a host of compliments and banter from Mahoney's colleagues.

"She's one of us tonight," somebody said, pinning one of the mock SFPD detective badges that decorated the tables on her. "Clinton," he yelled to the barman, "a drink for Detective Forster."

"So," Benedetti said, moving closer, his beer belly bulging over a turquoise cummerbund, "tell us how you happened to meet Mahoney."

"It's a long story," Mahoney said, "and too racy for your delicate ears."

"How about a dance, Doc?" someone said. He whirled her onto the floor to the beat of "La Bamba" and danced with her until someone else tapped him on the shoulder and took over.

Half an hour later Phyl finally made it back to the bar. She sipped a glass of water, fanning her hot face with her hand.

"All right, you guys, enough is enough," Mahoney warned. "The lady needs food."

He took her hand and led her through the crowd, stopping every couple of minutes to introduce her to his friends.

The buffet tables were laden with every kind of seafood, as well as enormous platters of lasagna, cheese gnocchi, pâté-stuffed ravioli, eggplant parmigiana, stuffed tomatoes, salads, half a dozen different breads, and bottles of red wine. That was on the Italian side. The Irish were represented by poached salmon and Galway oysters, Colcannon and soda bread, and Guinness and Paddy's. The tables were decorated with flags and shamrocks and roses, and the hospitality seemed never-ending.

Mahoney piled Phyl's plate with goodies, grabbed a bottle of wine, and led her to a quiet corner. "I'll bet you haven't eaten today," he said, sliding an oyster into his mouth.

"You're right," she said, contentedly doing the same.

They ate hungrily for a few minutes, and then she said, "I like your friends."

"Yeah, they're good guys." He grinned at her. "I guess they're right, though. What is a girl like you doing with a beat-up old cop like me?"

Her eyes met his, and she said, "First, you're not old. Or if you are, then that makes me old, too, and I refuse to accept that. Second, you're certainly not beat-up, Mahoney." She reached out and ran her fingers lightly over his face. "You must be the department pinup."

"Yeah, well, anything seems good after Benedetti and his beer belly."

"And third, you are a good cop, Mahoney. I know that."

"Thanks for the compliments, lady." Their eyes locked. "Just hold on there for a sec," he said finally. He stood up and threaded his way through the crowd to the bandstand.

When he got back minutes later, the band swung into "The Lady in Red."

"They're playing our song," he said, holding out his hand to her.

The lights dimmed, and couples began moving under the flickering old-fashioned mirrored ball in the center of the ceiling. Mahoney wrapped his arms tighter around her, and Phyl gave a happy little sigh. "You're right," she murmured in his ear, "this is like the high school prom. I haven't slow-danced like this for years."

"Then you don't know what you're missing," he whispered back.

"Your friends are watching us," she said.

"Let's give the lecherous old buzzards something to talk about." He pulled her even closer. She tilted her head back to look at him.

"Mahoney . . ."

"*Franco,* please. After all, this is an intimate moment. . . ."

"That's just what I was going to mention . . . I mean, I was wondering if the old Mae West saying was right: 'Is that a bunch of keys in your pocket or are you just pleased to see me?' "

Mahoney unclamped one arm from around her. He grinned as he removed the handcuffs from his pants pocket. "Sorry to disappoint you, Doc. But if that's what you want, I'd be happy to oblige."

"Oh, Mahoney," she said, laughing, wrapping her arms around his neck. "I haven't had this kind of silly fun since—well, it's so long ago I don't even remember."

"Me too," he said tenderly, looking down at her smooth dark head. "Has anyone ever told you you're a damn pretty woman, Phyllida Forster?"

"How did you ever find out my name?" she demanded. "I never tell anyone."

"You forget I'm a cop. I have access to such things as names and dates and addresses and telephone numbers." He grinned. "It's on your driver's license."

They danced for a long time until there was a tap on Mahoney's shoulder and the bridegroom, Connors, took over. Mahoney whirled away with the bride, and Phyl didn't see him again for another hour while she danced her feet off with young Irish cops and tarantellaed with old Italian pappas. Back at the bar again she laughed at the jokes and banter and stories, queening it from her barstool surrounded by her admirers. She was having such a good time she didn't even think of Brad Kane.

Just before midnight the detectives decided to shift base to Hanran's, their local hangout. Phyl swept into Hanran's flanked by San Francisco's finest, and the outgoing shift, propping up the bar, turned to whistle and stare. "Here, babe, sit by me." "Come on, honey, you don't know what you're missing." "Drop Mahoney, lady, I can do it better," they yelled, making way for her.

"Normally," Phyl said, cocking her chin mockingly at them, "normally, fellas, I would say you are the biggest bunch of sexist pigs I have ever met." They yelled and stomped, and she held up her hand for silence. "But," she said with a smile in her voice, "tonight I think you're paying me the greatest compliment a man can pay a woman. And I want you to know I appreciate it."

"Yea, Doc," they yelled, applauding and signaling the bartender to put up more of whatever she was drinking.

It was three in the morning when Mahoney finally

drove her home. Her head was on his shoulder, and she was grumbling contentedly about the discomfort of such a position in a Mustang. "For crissake, Mahoney, can't you get a proper car?" she asked sleepily.

"You are talking about my pride and joy," he said in a hurt tone.

"I know all about your pride and joy," she murmured. "Don't try and pretend those were really the handcuffs, Mahoney."

He laughed as he parked outside her apartment building. "I should never have let you near those guys," he said. "They're coarsening you."

"Maybe that's what I need." She sighed, straightening up. "A little coarseness."

"Just for flavor," he agreed.

"Like oregano or rosemary . . ." she said as he held the door open. She swung her legs out and wriggled forward, holding up her hands. "Help?" she said, smiling at him.

He took her hands, then slid his arm around her waist as they walked up the steps. She turned her face up to him, eyes closed, and said dreamily. "A good-night kiss, Mahoney?" He laughed and put his lips lingeringly on hers. "Mmm," she said, "very, very nice."

"I'd better see you to your apartment, Doc," he said as she yawned and leaned against him. "It's been a long night."

"So it has," she agreed. And then with a sunny smile: "And such a fun one. I haven't had such a good time in years."

"I'm glad," he said, taking her keys and unlocking the door.

Brad Kane's Porsche was parked half a block up the street. He leaned forward, his eyes boring into them as they walked together into the building.

He took a Gitane from the almost empty pack and lit it, dragging deeply. He knew which apartment was hers, and he watched her windows, groaning with despair as the lights finally came on. He stubbed the cigarette out viciously. He had seen Rebecca behave just that way so many times: giddy, flirtatious, leading men on. She was just like his mother after all.

His eyes fixed on her window, he leaned forward, tensely, watching, waiting.

Phyl kicked off her shoes and walked toward the kitchen. "Coffee?"

Mahoney shook his head. "Why not just have a glass of water, Doc, and then go to bed? You'll feel like a new woman in the morning."

She heaved a happy sigh. "I kind of like the woman I am right now, Mahoney."

"Good." He walked over and dropped a kiss on her cheek. "You know what?" he said seriously.

"What?" Her eyes were very blue and innocent.

"You really are a very pretty woman," he said, smiling as he turned and walked to the door.

"Thanks, Mahoney," she called after him. "For tonight." He waved as he closed the door behind him.

She was smiling as she sauntered into her bedroom, shedding her clothes as she went. And she was still smiling as she instantly fell asleep. With her makeup on. Something she hadn't done in years.

Mahoney had noticed the black Porsche 938 parked half a block away when he drove past earlier. The cop reflex had noted that it was the only car on the no-parking street and there was a man in it, and he had wondered automatically what he was up to. It was still there, and as he climbed into the Mustang and switched on the ignition, he saw the Porsche's lights go on. He waited for the guy to take off and pass him so he could grab his number and run a check on him, just in case he was up to mischief, but instead the Porsche backed up a half block and made a quick right down a side street.

Mahoney shrugged; he was off duty, and besides, he wasn't really up to tackling villains in expensive

Porsches tonight. The guy was probably some pricey private detective making a bundle staking out an erring wife or husband. What the hell, it was none of his business anyway.

~ 24 ~

Julie hurled herself into the swimming pool after Scott, sending an avalanche of water over Poochie, who pranced along the edge, barking warnings at them.

"Silly old dog," she yelled, scooping more water over him, shrieking with delight as he shook himself in a wild flurry of droplets. She shrieked again as Scotty hauled himself out of the pool and then jumped back in almost on top of her.

She went under and came up laughing and choking, searching for Scotty to get her revenge. She waved eagerly at Bea, who was sitting by the pool, watching them. She thought Bea was the prettiest woman ever, and she had already decided she wanted to be just like her when she grew up.

Bea had laughed when she'd told her. "I'm not sure that's possible, sweetheart," she had said. She always called her sweetheart, and Julie liked that. Nick called her Jules, and she liked that, too. "I think from the photographs I've seen you are going to look just like your mom. And that's a compliment, Miss Julie, if ever there was one, because your mommy was a very pretty lady."

Oh, she was, Julie thought fervently, leaning her chin on the curved edge of the pool and letting her legs float out behind her. Mom was just the prettiest of all. She thought how much her mommy would have liked the blue skies and sunshine. Her mother had hated those cold gray Ohio winters. Julie loved it here, and she knew Scotty did, too. The only thing was he kept reminding her that it was only temporary, "like a vacation," he said. "One day they'll send us back to Ohio and we'll end up in foster homes after all."

"No, they won't," Julie said stubbornly, but she was still scared.

Scotty said, "Course they will. They are not our relatives. We are nothing to them, Julie. Just a couple of kids they are looking after. Guardians, that's all they are."

But she still didn't want to believe it. And she didn't want to go back home because there was no home anymore. Besides, she didn't want to leave Bea.

Something told her Bea was different. She was hurting, too; Julie sensed it. And she liked that little sneaky feeling of warmth creeping into her own heart again, into her life. Sometimes hours went by without her thinking of what had happened.

Julie fastened her eyes on Bea. She didn't ever want to let go of her.

Bea thought Millie must have known her better than she knew herself, she had fallen so neatly into her new role. She was watching the children hurling themselves tirelessly in and out of the water. They had been doing it for hours. Every now and then they turned and splashed Poochie, making him bark and dance on his hind legs with excitement.

The whine of a lawn mower came from somewhere in the front of the villa, and the new Portuguese housekeeper's shrill voice fought with the squawk of the green African parrot Scotty had begged Nick to buy last week when they went to the pet store to look for a couple of parakeets. The man in the store had said that it was a talker and that it knew half a dozen songs, but it had remained stubbornly silent for the first five days until the dog barked at it and it suddenly cursed in fluent French.

The Villa Mimosa had come back to life, and Bea only wished Millie could be there to see it. The old brooding feeling had disappeared, and now it was filled with light and the sound of children's laughter and squabbles, with music, squawking parrots, and barking dogs. There were Rollerblades on the terraces and bicycles in the hall and a scatter of toys and T-shirts and beach towels, as well as the aroma of something good cooking in the kitchen.

Scotty and Julie Renwick were behaving more like normal kids again, though there were nights when she went in to tuck them up and found them huddled together in Scott's bed, with the tracks of tears on their innocent sleeping faces. She would carry Julie back to her own bed, and the exhausted child would lift her heavy eyelids and give her a direct searching gaze that struck to her very soul. She knew Julie was looking to see if it was her mother kissing her good-night.

"It's only me," she would whisper, and the little girl would sigh deeply, half choking on a sob, as she stuck her thumb comfortingly in her mouth. She gripped Bea's hand tightly, and Bea would stroke back her damp hair and sit quietly until the child finally fell into the deep sleep of exhaustion.

Scott never cried in front of Bea, but sometimes she would watch him disappearing up the hill toward the grotto. She would see his small, crouched figure, perched on the rocks, staring out to sea, and she'd guess he had sought solitude to cry away his pain.

She and Nick were doing their best to make life normal for them. They had established a routine with a French tutor for an hour each morning. Then they went to the market in Cannes or Nice or Antibes and maybe had lunch in one of the cafés. Later, after a rest, they went to the beach, or swam in the pool, or Nick would take them out in the little boat he had bought for putt-putting around the harbor.

In the fall they would begin school, and by then Bea hoped they would be better able to put the past behind them and be ordinary kids again. Meanwhile, they were still fragile and unsure of their new way of life.

Bea felt a world away from sudden death in a ravine, from murder and a lost past, from no-person to some-one with an identity. And she thanked Millie every day for her new life. But the terror of not knowing who she was and why someone had wanted her dead still haunted her. She would wake from some troubled dream that she was falling down into that neverending dark tunnel and almost think she had the answer. But when she blinked herself awake, sweating with fright, it was gone.

Poochie pranced over to her, backside and tail wiggling enthusiastically. Poochie had been a godsend. The kids adored him. The dog looked at her, its intelligent brown eyes shining with joy at the surprise of still being alive. "We're survivors, you and me, old boy," she said, rubbing its curly head affectionately.

She thought of Nick, out searching for the elusive bank vault with Nanny Beale's secrets, and she almost hoped he wouldn't find it. At this peaceful moment, life seemed perfect just as it was. She had her home, the children, and Nick. She was afraid of the past. She did not want to know about that other young woman who was her. She felt safe as Bea French. Her attacker could never find her here and finish the job he had failed at before. It was only on those long, restless, lonely nights she wasn't so sure.

The children called for her to come on in the pool, yelling with delight when Poochie leaped in after her, paddling around with a bewildered grin on his funny face.

They were playing a wild game of water volleyball, shrieking with laughter, when the telephone rang. Bea climbed from the pool to answer it.

"Nick?" she said, smiling.

"How did you know it was me?"

"It's simple. Nobody else calls. At least not at this time of day. Are you coming over for supper?"

"I'll be there about seven. Can we have dinner alone tonight? Without the kids, I mean. I need to talk to you."

"Sure. They eat at six anyway. They're always starving by then. But what do you want to talk about?"

"I found it, Bea. Nanny Beale's safe deposit. We were right. There were other documents. I'm bringing them with me. I want you to read them."

As she put down the phone, Bea thought he had sounded ominously quiet, not the least bit triumphant at his find. She wondered what was wrong.

When Nick arrived, the children swarmed all over him, begging him to go for a bike ride or Rollerblade with them along the terraces or run down the hill to the sea.

"Let's go fishing," Scotty yelled excitedly.

"No, let's ride our bikes to the very top of the hill and then coast all the way down," Julie shouted louder.

"Not tonight, guys." Nick ruffled Scott's shaggy hair and gave Julie a bear hug and shooed them affectionately from the room. "I've got to talk to Bea about something."

They ran off to chat with Jacinta in the kitchen. Nick looked at Bea.

"It wasn't easy to get hold of this," he said, taking several manila envelopes from his briefcase. "I must have conned my way through fifty banks, pretending I'd made a mistake every time they looked suspiciously at me because the key didn't belong to them. I gave them this phony laugh and said, 'Silly old me, I've got so many of these, I always forget where I've put things.' "

Bea smiled. "Until the final one."

"Until I finally have what we were searching for." He put the papers in front of her. "This is Marie-Antoinette's letter to her son, Johnny. And I can tell you it makes harrowing reading."

Bea looked doubtfully at him, "Do you really think we should be doing this?" She felt as though they were intruding into a dead woman's secrets, into private things she might never have wanted other eyes to see.

"I certainly do. For your sake and mine. You believe there is a link somewhere here with your past. And I want to solve this mystery for my book. It all happened long ago, Bea. We're not hurting anyone reading this."

"I suppose you're right," she agreed, but she was scared. "Only, Nick, I don't really want to know about my past anymore. Let's forget about the past. Let's leave it alone. I'm happy the way things are."

Nick gripped her hand comfortingly. "You must have a family somewhere, Bea. Relatives who are looking for you, wondering about you. You had a life before this, and you have to find it, even if you decide never to go back to it. You have a responsibility to yourself and to your family."

Bea sighed as she reluctantly began to read Marie-Antoinette Leconte's letter. She knew he was right.

My beloved son, Jean,

It is my dearest wish that you will never read this letter, because then it means I will never know you, I will not be there to hold my baby in my arms, to watch you grow, to count your birthdays and help you climb the rocky path of life. But if I cannot be there, then when you are old enough, I want you to know the truth, about myself and about your father, Archer Kane.

First I will tell you about myself, so you may know

your mother a little better. Gossip will tell you that I was not a pretty woman. I know their mocking name for me—*la célibataire*—and though I always pretended not to care, I was hurt. I yearned to be pretty and glamorous, like the smart beauties I used to see at dinner and at the casinos and in the cafés, but they never even spoke to me. How can I explain that inside I felt beautiful? But to them I was just the plain, rich woman who never belonged. And I was lonely.

Archer Kane recognized my loneliness. He was a handsome man, as fair and golden as I was dark and sallow. He looked like a young Greek god to me, the lonely *célibataire*.

He was a man who felt completely at home in the new laissez-faire atmosphere of the Riviera; there was a *loucheness* that suited him; plenty of easy women, drink, and money. But even I knew there were as many fortune hunters looking for women as there are women looking for lovers, and to capture a rich good-looking woman was often difficult. These women were older and worldly-wise, and they knew a fortune hunter when they saw one. For them an affair meant fun, a few gifts, a whiff of passion, and on to the next.

I noticed him, of course. How could I not? He was the handsome young American, always at the center of the crowd lunching on the terrace of the Hôtel de Paris, or in the cafés, or at the casino. I saw him watching me, I caught his eye every now and then, and he would always smile politely and bow his head, acknowledging my presence.

I know now that he was stalking me, that I was already marked as his victim. He was twenty-seven years old, and I was forty-one. I was uneasy with people, shy and plain. He was handsome and in with the social set, and he was said to have a big cattle ranch in Hawaii.

I knew all about him, but I had never met him, or
any of his acquaintances, until he spoke to me that
day. I was sitting at a café table in Cannes, alone as
always. I was wearing a wide-brimmed hat to keep the
sun from my face, but also to hide my plainnesss.
How can I make you understand how ashamed I was
of the way I looked? The Riviera was thronged with
beautiful people, all so young and slender and chic,
wearing the fashionable new styles that on me
looked merely clumsy and stupid.

I remember wondering how Archer had even recognized me, I was so hidden behind my big hat, but I
confess I was pleased that he had. More, I was
thrilled when he introduced himself and asked if he
could sit with me for a while. We drank lemonade
while he told me about his ranch, chatting sociably. I
noticed people glance at us, and I blushed with
pride that he had singled me out for his attention.

I think he knew from that first blush that I was his,
but nevertheless he courted me assiduously. He invited me to dinners at the best hotels, to lunches at
the beach, and to dancing at the Hôtel de Paris.
Though I already owned the silver Rolls, he encouraged me to buy the very latest automobile, an open-
topped scarlet Bugatti with a dove gray leather interior that I knew everyone envied as I drove by.

He escorted me to the fashionable shops and salons I had always been too shy to enter, afraid they
would make fun of my stocky, full-bosomed figure
because all the other women were reed-slim and
fashionably breastless. He took me to have my hair
bobbed in the new style, encouraged me to try
makeup, massages, perfume. Archer Kane made me
feel good about myself for the first time in my life.
He knew how to seduce a woman.

He was charming, sociable, handsome. The perfect suitor. When we got married a few weeks later, it
was a nine-day scandal. I knew what the gossips said

—that he was just another fortune hunter who got lucky, "but at what a price, because Lord knows *la célibataire* has been around a long time"—but I didn't care. I was in love, and I thought he loved me.

I was prepared to be happy anywhere with him, even on the primitive island where he took me. And even when I saw the famous ranch was nothing much more than a few wild acres. But this was to be my new home, my new life with my handsome, adoring husband, and I willingly gave him money so that he could buy more acres and more cattle and expand the lodge on Kalani. And also—unknown to me then—to indulge his male lust in Honolulu. Because, as he told me cruelly when I found out and confronted him, he found his wife old and ugly and unappealing.

The blue eyes that had once gazed so adoringly at me now raked me with contempt; the caresses had become cruel blows, and I soon realized that when he was "nice" to me, it was only because he wanted money. Then I found out I was pregnant.

It was like a miracle for me, a woman of forty-one, having her first child, and it brought me the first true happiness I had felt since I had come to Kalani. I did not tell Archer. I waited to see what would happen next.

He finally came to me with some legal documents that he wanted me to sign. He said they gave me an equal share in his ranch, but I saw that they really gave him control over my fortune. I refused to sign them, and I was finally forced to face the truth.

Sick and disillusioned and heavy with child, I left him. I returned here, to my old home, the Villa Mimosa, that my beloved father had built for me when I was still his "little princess," long ago, when I still believed—because he told me so often—that I was a pretty girl and that the world was mine. He had built the silver aviary so that I would always hear the sound of the songbirds I loved, and the grotto on the hill with the stream, and the fountains so I would hear the music of the water. And he had filled the exquisite gardens with my favorite mimosas whose scent marked my birthday every spring. It was my home, and now it became my refuge. I would have my baby there and bring him up in its peace and security. I never wanted to see Archer Kane again.

Then suddenly he arrived. He told me that because of me, he was deeply in debt and would be forced to mortgage his lands. He stood to lose everything—his cattle, his ranch, even his island—unless I gave him money. He promised to go away, so I gave it to him, but by now it was obvious I was pregnant. He said he had decided to stay after all. He wanted to be with me, to help me. After all, he said, it was his child, too.

I'm ashamed to confess that at first a part of me wanted to believe him. But I could not allow myself to trust him. I wanted nothing to do with him, but he was my husband, and there was nothing I could do. I refused to let him near me, I would not go out with him, though he tried to cajole me because, I know now, he wanted us to appear together as the happy couple. At the Villa Mimosa he was always the perfect gentleman, the adoring young husband with the older pregnant wife. He played his cards well; he never even looked at another woman the whole time. And then you were born, my dear son.

You look so fragile and small, lying there in the crib I arranged myself, purchasing the soft voile and the lace and ribbons to make it beautiful for you. I longed for you so much, and now here you are. And I love you with a mother's devotion.

It was not an easy birth, remember I was older, and I was still shaken and quite ill when your father came to see you the next day. He looked at you in your crib, and I allowed myself to think for one fleeting moment that maybe he would love his son and that there was some hope for our happiness. But then I saw from his face that he feels nothing for you. He said you did not even look like him. You were a Leconte, not a Kane.

And now, my son, as I write this letter, you are one week old. Today I think you smiled at me, even though Nanny Beale said it was not a real smile yet. You mean everything to me, and Archer knows it. There is something in the air here, a crackle of tension permeating the house, though he is still playing the role of the charming husband. I do not trust him, and next week, when I am stronger and can go downstairs, I intend to confront him. I shall tell him that I mean to divorce him on the grounds of his numerous adulteries. I will tell him that he will not receive another cent from me. And that you, dear little Jean, will inherit everything.

And that is the reason I am writing this letter, which I hope Nanny Beale will never have to give to you.

Archer is a dangerous man. He is ruthless and uncaring. I want you to understand that if anything bad happens to me, no matter what he claims or says, it will not have been an accident. Nor would I ever kill myself. You are too important to me for that. I am hoping, always hoping, my dear son, that I will be here to watch you grow up and to share your life. And I want you to know that I love you.
Your devoted mother

"So the Foreigner really did kill her," Bea said, looking at Nick with shock.

"And he got away with it. At least now we know his name. Archer Kane. Still, it all happened too long ago for retribution." Nick shuffled the other papers, looking at her. "I want you to read this later. It's written by Johnny Leconte. It's his own story, telling what happened." He hesitated. "I thought you might prefer to read it when you are alone, without all the distractions of the children, and dogs and parrots and supper."

He put the papers back into the envelope and took her hand. "Let's take the kids for a walk," he said, smiling, trying to cheer her up. "Buy them some ice cream."

"Ice cream." The children hurtled through the door, and Bea laughed at them.

"You must have invisible antennas turned to words like 'ice cream' and 'french fries' and 'Nintendo'—"

"Can Poochie come, too?" Julie said.

"Sure he can." Bea looked at the pair of them, in their grubby T-shirts and shorts with the new shine of happiness on their faces, and she felt sorry for Marie-Antoinette Leconte, who never had the chance to give her son, Johnny, a dog and take him for ice cream. "Wash your hands and faces and put on clean shirts," she said, smiling as she envisaged the clean shirts soon to be liberally daubed with ice cream.

"You know what?" Nick said with a grin. "You make a great mom."

Bea looked at him, at his almost good-looking face, at his nice gray eyes that always held a hint of a smile, and his good, lean body. Nick had shared all her problems about her mysterious past, he had shared her sorrow over Millie's death, and he had helped her with the children. Their friendship had grown deeper, and she was aware that was the other reason he wanted her to find the truth about her past: he needed to know if there was somebody else in her life, a lover, or a husband, someone who mattered to the person she used to be.

She smiled as she kissed him. "That's to say thank you," she said as he slid his arm around her, "for everything."

"Hey, no smooching," Scotty yelled from the doorway, and they turned, laughing, to chase him down the marble steps where little Johnny Leconte had had his fatal meeting with his father so many years before.

~ 25 ~

 Phyl opened the package that had been delivered by special Brinks van and stared at its contents with amazement. There was a necklace of pearls the size of quail's eggs with a pavé diamond clasp, a pair of pearl and diamond drop earrings, and a matching ring. The card read in Millie's handwriting, "To remember me by."

She held the card against her cheek, smiling as she thought of Millie resplendent in shocking pink and the very same pearls at the opera last year. How could she ever forget her?

The phone rang, and she answered it absently.

"I have to see you," Brad said.

His voice sounded tense, and she bit her lip, hesitating. "Brad, I think it's better if we don't see each other again," she said finally.

"Please, Phyl. Please. It can't just end like this because of a silly quarrel. At least let's discuss it. Give me a chance to apologize."

"Where are you?"

"Here in San Francisco."

Phyl debated with herself. She knew it was more than

just a silly quarrel, but she still felt that old allure. Brad could be so sweet, so charming; maybe she was being a bit hard on him after all. She sighed as she caught a glimpse of herself in the mirror. She looked like a wreck after last night's partying with Mahoney and his colleagues. But she guessed Brad was right; she owed him a chance to explain himself.

"Give me an hour," she said. "You had better come over here."

"I know where you live. I'll be there." He sounded elated.

Phyl smiled as she showered, remembering Mahoney and the wedding celebration. It had been years since she had had that kind of careless fun, without strings, without responsibilities. Just nice people having a good time. Somehow it helped put her problems with Brad in proportion. She could handle it now, she thought confidently. She dressed quickly in black jeans and a white linen shirt, cinching them together with the silver and turquoise belt from Santa Fe. She brushed back her hair and tied it firmly into a knot, smoothed on her signature red lipstick, and then in memory of Millie, put on the extravagant pearls.

She paced the room nervously, waiting for Brad. Her footsteps seemed to echo in the silence, and she wished she had the cat to keep her company, but it was still with Mahoney. She would call him later and arrange to pick it up.

She was remembering slow-dancing with Mahoney the previous night when the doorbell rang. When she answered it, Brad held out an armload of calla lilies.

"For you," he said, looking penitent.

She smiled at him ruefully. "You're not a man who does things by halves, are you, Brad?" she said, taking the enormous sheaf of flowers into the kitchen.

He glanced around curiously. "So this is your lair," he said. "I wondered what it would be like."

"And?" She faced him, arms folded defensively across her chest.

"It's exactly you. Cool, clever, cultured. And beautiful."

"Thanks." She watched him prowl her home. He was wearing jeans and a blue work shirt. With his outdoors tan and rangy stride, he looked as out of place in her glossy urban apartment as a Thoroughbred racehorse at the local horse show.

"Today you look like a cowboy," she said.

"After all, that's what I am," he said, studying the paintings. "A rancher."

"And proud of it. Maybe too proud, Brad."

"What do you mean?" He looked genuinely puzzled. "Don't I have a right to be proud of my family and their achievements?"

Phyl thought about that; after all, hadn't most of America's great fortunes been made by the robber barons, and weren't they all American legends now? "I guess you're right," she admitted. "In a way."

"I like this," he said, standing in front of a small oil by David Oxtoby of a green English lawn and a clipped yew hedge. "And this." He was looking at a tempera by Tindle of a wooden chair standing by an open window, the muslin curtain blowing in a breeze. It had a bleached, otherworldly look, and it was one of her favorites.

He turned to face her. "I'm not used to saying sorry," he said stiffly. "I find it very difficult." She looked at him, saying nothing. "Do you want me to go on my knees to you?" he demanded. "Weren't the flowers enough?"

"The flowers are beautiful, Brad. It was a nice thought. But do you really expect me to forgive you for the way you behaved? Without an apology?"

"You are right. It was unforgivable." He gripped her shoulders and pulled her toward him. "The truth is, Phyl, I did it because I'm in love with you. I'm so damned crazy about you I just can't bear the idea of anyone taking you away from me."

"But no one was taking me away from you. It was an urgent call from a friend—"

"Was that the same friend you were out with last night?"

She pushed away, staring at him with astonishment. "How do *you* know who I was with last night?"

"I called you for hours and you weren't here. I just guessed you were with someone else. . . ."

"It's none of your goddamn business who I was with, Brad Kane. Not anymore."

"Don't say that. Please."

"Oh, Brad," she said wearily, "it was all so beautiful, so special. . . ."

"It can be again." He caught her in his arms, holding her so close she could feel the muscles of his chest hard against her breasts and the strong, wiry length of his body against hers. "I'm sorry, Phyl. I'm really sorry." He sounded desperate. "There, I've said it. Now *please*, tell me you forgive me."

She felt herself capitulating, falling under his sexual spell. "I'm a busy woman," she said quickly. "My work takes up most of my time. I've been irresponsible, playing when I should have been working. I have to get back to my own life, Brad."

"Don't abandon me." It was a cry from his heart, and she recognized it. Mahoney's handsome, smiling face suddenly came into her mind. Her body remembered the feel of his arms around her, their steps fitting perfectly as they slow-danced. Mahoney, the joker, the tease, the good friend. Mahoney, the dedicated cop, the poet, the opera buff. And rich, handsome, overly proud Brad Kane with all his problems somehow seemed less enticing.

She breathed a sigh of relief. She was finally free of Brad Kane's dangerous spell. But looking at his despairing face, she knew she had to let him down gently.

"I promise I'll see you when I have time. But on my terms."

"I'll take anything I can get," he murmured, "the crumbs from your plate, a kiss on the hem of your garment, a glance from your jeweled eyes. . . ." He dropped a gentle kiss on her forehead, and she laughed, remembering how much she had enjoyed him. Perhaps it would be all right after all; perhaps they could be friends.

"In that case you can take me to lunch," she said briskly.

"Anywhere," he said eagerly, his anxious look disappearing. "The moon, Mars, Venus."

"Il Fornaio, around the corner," she said, laughing with him despite herself. "For pizza. I'm starving."

They had a corner table by the long windows. After they had ordered, Brad eyed her necklace and said coldly, "Who gave you the pearls?"

She heard the warning note of jealousy in his voice again. "Brad, these were left to me by my friend, the one whose funeral I missed."

He played with the cutlery, not looking at her. "She must have thought a lot of you to leave you such an expensive necklace."

"Millie also left me the matching earrings and ring. They're really too fancy for daytime, but I felt like wearing her pearls. Somehow it makes me feel closer to her. I can remember the last time I saw her wearing them. It was last year at the opera. We saw *Carmen*, and Millie even dressed for the part, in shocking pink flounces."

"They must be worth a small fortune," Brad persisted.

"Millie was a very rich woman, though perhaps not quite as rich as you," she said with a coaxing smile. "And she was free with her money. She spread it around. She alway wanted to help other people, and she was a sucker for any sob story. That's why she took on my patient as her social secretary—the one I told you about with the lost memory. Anyway, Millie left her millions in her will, as well as two orphaned children that she has to take care of. She said she was giving a future to the girl with no past. And I guess she was right because Bea seems happy enough now."

"The woman sounds like a typical misguided philanthropist. I would say that girl got very lucky," Brad said savagely.

"Millie Renwick was not misguided," Phyl said angrily. "She knew exactly what she wanted to do, and she had the means to do it."

He looked up from the pizza, his eyes suddenly alert. "Renwick?"

"Yes, Millicent Renwick."

"I've heard that name somewhere else recently."

"You've probably read about her in the society columns. Or maybe in the obits. Anyway, she bought this villa in the south of France, and she gave it to Bea. The Villa Mimosa."

"The Villa Mimosa?"

"Yes. It's a beautiful place, although Bea is convinced it has a mysterious past. Anyway, now it's hers, and she's living there with the two children, Scott and Julie Renwick, aged nine and seven. So I guess she has her hands full."

"You said Bea was your patient? What exactly is wrong with her?" Brad took a gulp of his red wine and glanced at her with hooded blue eyes.

"I told you, she had an accident and lost her memory. She doesn't remember anything about it. It's just one of those strange things."

"And will her memory ever return?"

Phyl sighed regretfully. "Who knows? I hope so, for her sake."

"You are too involved with your patients," Brad said with some tenderness. "You take on all their problems."

She smiled. "Including yours."

"Do you mind my talking to you about my family?"

"I think it's probably very good for you."

He leaned across the table and gripped her hand. "Phyl, come back with me to Hawaii. Please, just for the weekend. I need you there. *I need to talk to you.*"

There was total despair in his voice. Panicked, she wondered what he might do to himself if she said no. But it still wasn't right for him to put her in this position. "I don't know if I can . . . there's so much to do. . . ." She hesitated.

"It's easy," he said pleadingly. "I'll fly you to Honolulu myself. *Please,* Phyl. I need you." He gripped her hands tightly. "I've never said those words to anyone else in my life. But I'm saying them to you now. Come with me, Phyl. I promise faithfully to have you back in San Francisco on Monday morning."

How could she resist such a cry for help? She knew only too well how it felt to be alone. "Oh . . . all right, but no strings," she said, hoping she was doing the right thing.

She could tell Mahoney didn't like it when she called and told him she would be returning to Hawaii the following weekend. "Are you sure about this?" he asked worriedly. "After what you told me about him?"

"He says he's a reformed character, Mahoney. What can I do? I really feel he needs to talk, and that's the only reason I'm going. Brad needs me."

Mahoney sighed. "Sounds like a ploy to me."

"I had such a great time last night, Franco," she said softly. "You're a terrific dancer."

"It's only one of my talents," he replied morosely. "I didn't get to show you the rest."

She laughed. "Don't tell me you'll miss me."

"Who the hell said I would?" he demanded, grinning. Then, suddenly serious, he added, "Look, Phyl, take care, will you? This guy sounds a bit unstable to me."

"Don't worry. He's as sane as you and I, whatever that means. Will you hang on to Coco for me? I'll call you when I get back on Monday."

"Sure." He was about to hang up when he thought of something. "Doc," he said, "what kind of auto does Mr. Hawaii drive?"

"A Porsche nine-thirty-eight. Black. Why do you want to know?"

"Just wondered," he replied.

Well, well, he said to himself, heading down the hall to the coffee machine, *the hunch paid off. Mr. Hawaii was spying on her last night.* He remembered Phyl's leaning affectionately against him as they walked up the steps into her building and his putting his arm around her, kissing her. He gave a dismayed whistle as he thought about Mr. Hawaii's unreasonable jealousy. He hoped Phyl knew what she was doing. And maybe in the meantime he would do a little quiet checking on Mr. Brad Kane.

~ 26 ~

$\mathcal{T}$he children were bathed and in bed. There had
been no sound from them for the past half hour, and
Bea assumed, as thankfully as any birth mother, that
they were finally asleep.

It was ten o'clock, and she was alone. She covered
the parrot's cage with a blanket, listening to its mutter-
ing as it settled sleepily on its perch. She then took the
ominous manila envelope containing the Leconte family secrets with her into the kitchen, fixed herself a cup
of tea, and sat at the big pine table. She stared at the
envelope. For some reason, she was reluctant to face
the answers it contained.

Poochie lapped noisily at his bowl, then flopped at
her feet. The kitchen clock ticked the slow minutes
away. The soft night breeze filtered in through the
open window, and somewhere in the distance she
heard the faint sweet sound of birdsong. Was it a
blackbird? she wondered. Or perhaps a nightingale?
She listened to the usual summer night sounds of
crickets and frogs as the villa settled deeper into its
own silence.

When she could put it off no longer, she removed

the sheaf of papers from the envelope. They had been
written by Jean Leconte himself. Johnny, Nanny Beale
had called him.

Unwillingly she began to read.

I am writing about events which are better forgotten, and I am writing them only because Flora Beale
has urged me to. "For posterity," she says, meaning
for any future Lecontes who will come after me and
wish to claim their inheritance.

For myself I no longer care, but Nanny Beale in-
sists it is their right. Since I am twenty-seven years old
and unmarried, it seems a remote possibility, but I
have to admit she has a point. And in that case, so
that my mythical future descendants should know
the truth, I shall do as she asks. I shall begin, therefore, at the beginning, which for me meant the Villa
Mimosa and Nanny Beale.

Bea shivered with foreboding. It was just like before.
She knew she had heard the same story in her head,
someone was telling it to her, so vividly that it seemed
engraved there. It only needed Johnny Leconte's own
words to unlock her memories.

When you are a small child, it is not always the
faces of people that you remember; it is the way they
sound, or walk, or the smell of them. Nanny Beale
was the first person I really knew, the first woman I
ever loved. She was my mother and my friend, my
helper and my fierce guardian all rolled into one.
And the fresh, starchy smell of her white apron is my
first memory.

She was small and round with a ramrod-straight
back, and I remember watching her prepare for our
daily walks. She would put on her hat, navy felt in
the winter, pale straw in the summer, and she would
say solemnly, "Remember, Johnny, a lady always

wears a hat." Then she would skewer it fiercely with
a terrifying sharp steel pin surmounted by a blue
glass ball. I would wait for her to yell because she
had stuck it in her head, but Nanny was an expert,
and that never happened.

In the summer she wore sturdy lace-up shoes with
"sensible" heels. She had a chalky paste to keep
them white, and sometimes she let me help her
clean them. I remember that when the shoes dried,
they threw off small puffs of white dust with every
step she took.

I suppose she must have been in her fifties then,
but to me she seemed ageless. Of course, I had little
to compare her with except the maids, and they
seemed closer to my age than hers. She was a sweet-
faced woman, but she could act very aloof when we
were out on our drives in our big silver Rolls, nodding like a countess to the hoi polloi along the
Croisette or the Promenade des Anglais. I suspect
the truth was she never recognized anybody because
she was so nearsighted she couldn't see two feet in
front of her nose, and she refused to wear her eyeglasses in the street. What mysterious creatures
women are; even Nanny Beale had her small vanities.

But she was an Englishwoman to the core, and she
never let her standards slip. I was dressed like a
prince, in silk and lace. No animals were allowed for
fear that they might get fleas and spread germs. So
woolly old black and white Fido was my pretend dog,
and I can still remember how I loved him and how I
later mourned his loss.

I remember the nursery with Nanny's old Windsor
rocker, always planted firmly in front of the fireplace
in winter because when the mistral blew, she complained its chill got into her bones. And her little
round tortoiseshell eyeglasses always marking the
open page of the book she was reading. I remember
the smell of the toast we made over the glowing red

coals, and tea with honey and ginger cookies. For a French child, it was a very English upbringing, but I knew no other children, so I never knew I was missing anything. I was happy at the Villa Mimosa, with Nanny Beale and my dog, Fido, and the gardeners who taught me all about the plants, and the parakeets and canaries in the silver aviary. I wanted nothing else. My world was complete.

Until the day my father returned for me and sent me into exile to Kalani.

He was a frightening man, though now I understand that he was handsome in a hard way. And I was a puny, disappointing child, small and thin and as sallow as a beeswax candle. I had no idea what a "father" meant, since I had never had one. I had never even met one. But I could tell from Nanny's terrified voice and his harsh one that his return was not a welcome event.

I was quite relieved when we did not see much of him on our long journey to Kalani, and I thought travel a fascinating occupation and a lot more interesting than the daily sameness of life at the Villa Mimosa. Little did I know how I would later long for that safe daily routine.

When Nanny got sick on the liner in the middle of the Atlantic, I roamed the big ship alone. We were in a stifling little hole of a cabin on the very lowest level, and it was filled with fumes from the boilers and smells from the kitchens. I didn't even know that my father was aboard. I certainly never saw him, and he never came inquiring, from his first-class stateroom, about the small son he had banished to the bowels of the ship. But I enjoyed my freedom, and I made many new friends among the sailors, something I had never done before. I confess I was enjoying myself, and I thought that if this was what life with a father was like, it wasn't bad.

Standing on the lower deck, clinging to Nanny's

hand, I gaped at New York's famous skyline, and then, almost before I knew it, we were on an enormous steam train, heading west. To San Francisco, Nanny said, but it might as well have been Timbuktu for all I knew about the world and geography.

At first the train journey was fine. We changed at Chicago into another steaming monster, and my father disappeared into his smart comfortable private carriage, while I spent many hours running up and down long swaying corridors, making a nuisance of myself, as Nanny said. But it was a long and tedious journey with no sleeping cars for us, and she was willing to let me run off my energy so I could sleep stretched out along the hard plush seat.

We were heartily sick of that train by the time we arrived in San Francisco and drove to a big hotel. I remember staring up at the blond silent stranger who called himself my father and had changed my life so drastically, as he glanced scornfully at us from the sidewalk.

"Stay in the car," he commanded in the tone I used to Fido when he was bad. "You are going to take the boat immediately to Honolulu."

And so we were sent off to the docks, to the motor vessel *Hyperion II*. Even a child like me could see this boat had seen better days. Flakes of paint clung like scabs to its rusting hull, and small, wiry foreign-looking men that Nanny called Orientals were swarming all over it, making ready for departure.

"Heathen Chinese," Nanny breathed in my ear as we walked up the gangplank as if to our doom. I didn't know what she meant, but my heart sank at her ominous tone. I clutched her hand, watching them warily. Her fears were groundless, of course, though she refused to eat their "heathen" food, and we ate only plain boiled rice.

A day or two into the voyage we were almost drowned in a storm. I had never seen waves like that in the Mediterranean, huge, glassy, and green, racing at us and hurling gallons of icy water into our miserable cabin until everything was awash. It was a relief when we finally made it safely into Honolulu harbor. Almost immediately we were off again, in another rust bucket, this time to Maui.

I remember looking back at Honolulu's busy waterfront and the long white strand of Waikiki, wishing I could stay, but it was not to be. Two days later, when we arrived at Maui, there was a small motor launch waiting to take us to our final destination: Kalani.

The stretch of water between Maui and Kalani was a glassy green swell that pushed the little motorboat up one side and down the other with a stomach-churning lurch. Nanny's back was firmly straight, and she held a black umbrella aloft to keep off the sun. Her face was as yellow as her straw hat, but there was a determined look in her eyes. "We shall not be sick," she told me firmly, gritting her teeth together, and I nodded in agreement because in truth, I did not feel ill. I was quite enjoying my boat ride.

The rocky outline of Kalani appeared on the horizon, and as we drew nearer, I saw the tall coconut palms and the tangled jungly vegetation fringing a strip of white sand. I remembered my daily routine at the Villa Mimosa and the uneventful days, and I thought Kalani looked different, exciting. I thought maybe the man who was my father was waiting there for me, to show me around my new home. I stared eagerly at the island, clutching Fido to my heart.

As the motor launch with the silent Chinese at the helm approached, the wind brought the scent of the island: spicy, rich, pungent. Quite different from the fresh rosemary-clean perfume of the Riviera. Nanny clutched my hand tightly in hers. "Remember your home is the Villa Mimosa," she said grimly. "Never forget it, Johnny. And one day you will go home again."

I was an obedient child, and I looked solemnly at her, sealing those memories in my brain for future comfort. Suddenly I was infected with her fear. We were approaching the unknown. "Pray, Master Johnny, pray for us," she whispered as we glided closer.

I narrowed my eyes against the setting sun and saw a short sun-bleached wooden dock. And on it, dripping water, his blond hair sleeked back to his finely shaped skull, his narrow loins wrapped in a skimpy piece of cotton that clung to him like a second skin, stood an older boy. Waiting for us.

Nanny Beale's face turned an outraged scarlet as the boat slid alongside the dock. "Naked as the day he was born, or near enough as makes no difference," she exclaimed loudly, glaring at him. "Have you no shame, young man?"

The boy threw her a contemptuous glance. Then he looked at me. I flinched as his narrow blue eyes flicked over me. His jaw set angrily, and his well-shaped mouth turned down in a sneer as he took in my silken finery.

"A monkey," he exclaimed contemptuously. "You're nothing but a wizened, fancy-dressed little monkey."

And forever after that was how I was known on the island of Kalani. *The Monkey*. It was my half brother, Jack, who gave me that name, and he never let me forget that I was the lowest creature on God's earth.

~ 27 ~

$\mathcal{P}$hyl was sitting under a shade tree by the pool at the Diamond Head mansion. Brad was behaving perfectly. Why then, she asked herself, did she feel this tension between them?

She stared around, lazily admiring the avenue of blazing red royal poincianas, fragrant pink plumerias, and vivid yellow blossoms of the leafless gold tree that more than lived up to its name. Nature had made no mistakes in Hawaii. It mixed and matched colors with tropical abandon to create a chromatic harmony that mere man could never achieve.

She watched Brad, swimming long, easy laps in the marine blue pool that stretched to the very edge of the cliff. The sun was dipping into the blue horizon, and the silent Chinese servants were already setting the table on the terrace for dinner.

It was a scene of perfect beauty, peace, and contentment. Then why, Phyl asked herself again, did she feel so uneasy?

They had arrived at Diamond Head last night, and Brad had kept his word; he had looked after her, and he had not attempted to make love to her. Her room was filled with white orchids, the fine linen sheets were delicately scented with lavender from Provence, and her bathroom was stocked with expensive soaps and lotions.

He had taken her for dinner to Michel's, an elegant restaurant overlooking the ocean, and he had talked entertainingly about the ranch and Paris and about flying and horse breeding, and he had not asked a single question about her life. She knew he was making an effort, and she began to relax, enjoying his company. But she was glad when he said a brief good-night at her door and walked quickly away, without kissing her.

In the middle of the night she had awakened with the uneasy feeling that something was wrong. Then she saw Brad's shadowy figure by the window and the glow of his cigarette. She watched him silently, afraid to move. After a while he crushed out the cigarette and walked to the bed. Without thinking, she closed her eyes and lay perfectly still, pretending to be asleep, but even so, she could feel his gaze burning into her. Then she heard him groan. She peeked under her lashes as he strode quickly onto the terrace. The dog ran to his side, and the two of them disappeared into the night.

She sat up, shivering with fright. She thought of locking her door but told herself she was being ridiculous. Brad meant her no harm. He loved her and wanted her, and she was denying him that. And Brad was not a man used to rejection.

This morning he had been sunny and smiling, and he had not mentioned his secret visit to her room. He had suggested an excursion to the volcano crater or a drive around the island. "All I want is for you to be happy," he'd said warmly, and she could have sworn he meant it.

But she felt a new element in their relationship. She was still attracted to him, but there were undercurrents that made her apprehensive. She was sure they had to do with the past and his childhood.

Brad climbed from the pool and came toward her, shaking water from his blond head, sleeking it back, smiling at her with his father's hard blue eyes. Phyl wondered for the first time if the resemblance was more than skin deep.

"Tell me about Jack," she suggested after dinner. They were in the sitting room. It was a sultry night with flashes of silvery blue lightning over the ocean and an occasional faint crackle of thunder. The night air moved sluggishly under the ceiling fans, fluttering her long hair and flattening her chiffon shirt coolly against her breasts. A Bach cantata played softly on the stereo, and there was a distant roar of surf from the rocks at the foot of the cliffs.

She kicked off her sandals and stretched out on the pale mint linen sofa, looking at Brad. He leaned forward, his hands linked in front of him. She thought she had never seen a more handsome man, but it was an abstract thought, lacking in passion. "Handsome" was not the right adjective for Brad. He was beautiful, like a perfect animal—lithe, sleek-muscled, bronzed. He was a man in the peak of physical condition, and he was also a man with a troubled past. And that was why she had come to help him.

"Jack was just like Archer," he said. "For them the old saying 'Like father, like son' was true. Archer taught Jack about life and that the best man always won. Regardless of what it took to do it. Archer had no morals, and neither did Jack."

"And is that what Jack taught you?" Phyl asked carefully.

He laughed. "I'm my own man, Dr. Phyl. And what I am has nothing to do with Jack and Archer."

"Don't you believe it," she replied coolly. "Parents and families are at the root of most psychological problems today."

"Are you planning on analyzing me then?"

His tone was suddenly cold.

"No, I am not going to analyze you," she said
smoothly. "I'm not here on business, Brad. But I am
here to help you. Besides, I'm curious about your family. It's not often one gets to hear firsthand about the
rise of a dynasty such as yours."

"They were no angels, it's true. They just did what
they felt they had to do. It all seemed logical to them,
and of course, it was. Or there would be no Kane ranch
today. And the one person who could have taken it
away from us became Jack's mortal enemy.

"Jack was nine years old when his father told him he
had a half brother. Archer had never even mentioned
another son before. Jack had simply not known. He
went wild with jealousy and rage. He said he would kill
his half brother, but Archer just laughed. He ruffled
his hair and said indulgently, 'Not yet, Jack. Not until
Johnny's eighteen and comes into his inheritance. It's
a fortune, young Jack. And make no mistake, we shall
need it.'

"Jack said he brooded all night about what his father
had said, and he realized there was nothing he could
do about the half brother. Archer's French wife had
died and left him a lot of money, and he had spent it.
Now he was broke. True, he had spent some of it on
things that mattered: he had bought thousands of
acres of ranchland on the Big Island and the best
breeds of imported cattle, the finest horses. He had
bought the Diamond Head mansion, expanded the
lodge on Kalani, and started breeding Thoroughbred
Arabians. He also had a retinue of forty servants here
at the mansion and more at the lodge. He bought
speedboats, a hundred-foot yacht, and a fleet of cars.
He threw lavish parties and filled his swimming pool
with French champagne. He bestowed diamond bracelets on beautiful and willing women, and he lived life
to the hilt. Archer King's reputation for high living and
wild women spread as far as San Francisco and beyond.

"Jack had seen it all: the drinking, the women, the

lavish lifestyle. Archer never bothered to hide anything from him. Jack was a wild, outdoorsy boy who liked nothing more than riding the range with the paniolos, but when he was seven, his father decided to send him away to school in San Francisco. 'We've got to civilize you, boy,' he told him. But no school could hold Jack O'Higgins Kane for long. After he had run away a few times, Archer brought him home again.

" 'Like father, like son,' he said proudly. 'There's no institution strong enough to hold down my boy.' Then he asked Jack what he wanted from life.

" 'I'm like you, Dad,' Jack said. 'I want Kalani and the Kanoi Ranch. And one day it will all be mine.' "

Brad lifted his head and smiled at Phyl. "Even at that young age Jack had his priorities straight, though he did manage to get an education, of sorts, later. There were a series of unsuitable tutors here at Diamond Head, but they never seemed to work out, and for a few years Jack was allowed to run wild on 'his' island. At other times, he spent weeks at the ranch, living with the paniolos, roping cattle and riding the range with them.

"Jack had always been king of his castle on Kalani. He was his father's only son and heir. There was no mother to boss him around, no one to tell him what to do. And he was a wild, turbulent, headstrong nine-year-old when the half brother arrived to live with them on 'his' island."

"Trouble?" Phyl asked, smiling.

Brad shrugged carelessly. "It was just a boyish feud. Sure, Jack hated the half brother. He was the interloper. Jack was used to total authority on his island.

"Archer told him not to worry. He said the boy was a bit 'soft in the head.' He would stay on the island. He would never set foot on Diamond Head or the ranch or Honolulu. And that's what happened. Of course, people knew about him, but over the years he was forgotten, and those who did recall would just say, 'Oh, yes, I believe there was another son. A bit crazy,' they said. 'Archer Kane kept him on Kalani for his own good.' "

A shiver ran down Phyl's spine as she listened to the heartless story. She thought Archer Kane was a monster. "What happened to the boy?" she asked.

"Oh, Jack said he was a weird little kid, only five years old, undersize and thin and sort of wizened-looking. He said he looked just like a monkey. And that's what he called him." Brad laughed, enjoying the joke. "The Monkey. Jack said he made his life hell for a few years, and then there was some trouble on the island and the kid just disappeared. No one knew where. They thought he'd taken a boat out and drowned in a storm."

"Like Lahilahi," Phyl said, shocked.

"That's a ridiculous connection," Brad said angrily. "The boy did something stupid. The Pacific is a big ocean and treacherous. He should have known better."

"What if he didn't drown? What if he were still alive? What would you do, Brad, if he suddenly appeared to claim his half share of the Kane ranch?"

"You are talking nonsense," Brad said distantly. "He will not reappear, I can assure you of that."

"How can you be so sure?" she persisted.

"There are strong currents around Kalani. Many boats have come to grief in those waters. The bodies are usually swept out to sea."

But Phyl thought there was something in his eyes, a wariness, as though he were hiding something. He poured himself his nightly brandy, then walked to the window, the faithful Doberman, Kanoi, at his heels. He stared at the flickering stormy sky and said moodily, "It's all so long ago. The past is the past. What does it matter now? Archer and Jack were what they were. They knew what they wanted, and they took it."

"And do you know what you want, Brad?" Phyl asked, suddenly curious.

His hooded gaze met hers. "Yes," he said. "I want you."

~ 28 ~

The lodge on Kalani was made of wood, raised on posts from the ground—a barrier against the voracious termites, I learned later. A wooden veranda called a lanai encircled it, and the roof was made from palm thatch. To me it looked like a house from a fairy tale. But it was soon the scene of my worst nightmares.

My half brother, Jack O'Higgins Kane, was nine years old and much bigger and stronger than I. He was tall and very good-looking, with his shaggy mane of yellow blond hair and hard blue eyes, like his father's. He was a natural athlete, and he could do all the things I had never learned. He could swim like a porpoise and ride a horse bareback. He could climb the tallest palm trees, scaling them like the monkey he called me, deliberately sending the iron-hard fruits crashing down where I was standing so I had to jump out of the way to avoid being killed. He could shoot a hunting rifle and knock tin cans off a wall fifty yards away. He strode barefoot around the island, never heeding the stones in his path. He shouted at the servants, and they were forced to jump to his bidding. Whatever Jack wanted he got.

It took me only one day and one night to realize that Jack Kane, my half brother, was my rival and my mortal enemy. He frightened me with his shouting, his contempt, his showing off. But I had Nanny Beale, and I knew I was safe with her. Then, a few days later, the motorboat returned, and with it, my father, Archer Kane.

We watched him come ashore, Nanny and I, standing back a little way from the dock. Jack rushed past us. He jumped up and down, waving excitedly. Then he dived smoothly into the water, and we could see him swimming to the boat, sleek as a seal, to meet his father. As the boat slowed, he clambered agilely aboard. We saw him gesture angrily toward us, and my stomach clenched in sudden fear because I knew he was telling his father bad things about Nanny and me.

The boat docked, and Jack leaped out first. He waited for Archer, and then the two of them walked past us toward the lodge without so much as a glance our way.

"Mr. Kane," Nanny Beale called after them, angrily, "I need to speak to you about conditions here. They are not suitable for a young child."

My father turned and looked at us, and for the first time I understood what "cold" eyes meant. His froze me on the spot. "The conditions here are good enough for my other son, Miss Beale," he said in an equally icy voice. "I do not see any reason to make any changes." He thought for a moment and then said, "I will speak to you in my office in half an hour."

Nanny clutched my hand even tighter as we approached the office at the appointed time. I could hear her breath coming quickly, as it always did when she was agitated, and I clutched Fido to my chest, wishing I could think of something to say to comfort her. I said, "Nanny, why don't we just go home? Back to the Villa Mimosa. I don't like it here."

"That's just what I intend to tell Mr. Archer Kane," she declared firmly.

But Archer had beaten her to it. "Miss Beale," he said, lifting his eyes indifferently from a newspaper he was reading, "you will pack your things immediately. The motor launch will take you to the Big Island, and from there you will take the regular cattle boat to Honolulu. Your passage has been booked to San Francisco, and your return ticket to France will be waiting for you."

I heard her gasp with relief as he turned back to his newspaper. "Then we are going home," she said, and my heart rose hopefully along with hers.

"You are going home, Miss Beale," my father said from behind the paper. "The boy stays."

"I will not leave without Johnny," Nanny cried heatedly. "He cannot live here. He is not used to such wildness. His mother wanted him brought up at the Villa Mimosa; she trusted me to take care of him. I *insist* he comes with me." Astonishingly, she banged her fist on his desk.

"I think you forget, Miss Beale, that his mother is dead," Archer said, suddenly angry, "and that he is *my* son. Go pack your things, and be down at the dock in an hour." He glanced at me and said decisively, "There will be no lingering good-byes. The boy will stay here until you have gone."

"Nanny," I wailed, clinging to her. But she was beaten, and she knew it.

"Be a brave boy, Johnny," she whispered tearfully. "Eat all your meals and grow big and strong. When things seem bad, remember I am thinking about you and that the Lord is on the side of the good. Don't forget me, Johnny," she said finally, kissing my cheek. "I shall be there, at the Villa Mimosa, waiting for you, when you come home again."

But my heart sank as I watched her go. I knew it would be a long time, if ever, before I saw her again.

Jack Kane set out to make my life hell. But it wasn't until later that I learned why he hated me so much. My jealous half brother knew more about me than I knew myself.

He started in a modest way, putting huge, hairy spiders in my bed and forcing me to eat wriggling mealy grubs and daubing me with red paint, like an Indian. He grinned wickedly at me because there was nothing on the island to remove the paint, and he knew I would have to live with my red face until it finally wore off with ferocious scrubbing.

He fed my dinner to the pigs, so I was half starved; he set trip lines across the paths and sent me innocently running up them and laughed as I fell. He took me into the forest, where he had dug a trap and shrieked with joy as I tumbled into it. He kept me a terrified prisoner there until dusk, when a servant came looking for me. He crept into my room at night, and I opened my eyes and found him grinning at me, holding a knife at my throat. "I'll kill you one day, Monkey," he whispered menacingly, sticking the point in, nicking my flesh. I felt the hot trickle of blood, and I believed him.

I grew impervious to his taunts about my thinness and my looks, but I lived in dread of the new tortures he might dream up for me. He was consumed with a jealous rage. He was king of his castle, and he intended to keep it that way.

When Nanny Beale left, I thought I was alone, that there was no one who would even care about me. But there was a servant girl on the island, Maluhia, whom my father, Archer, favored. She was a beautiful mix of Chinese and Polynesian, exotic, gentle,

soft-spoken, and kind. Her name, Maluhia, meant
"peaceful," and she told me it had been given to her
by her mother, a poor woman already burdened with
too many girl children, in the hope that this child's
life might live up to her name. Sadly it had not.
Through various family disasters she ended up alone
and homeless at age thirteen.

Maluhia's skin had a warm golden sheen to it, and
she walked with the fluid grace of a Hawaiian
woman. She wore creamy plumeria blossoms in her
long, glossy black hair, and she smelled of lilies and
sweet fresh air. She was twenty years old, and Archer
had bought her when she was fourteen from the Honolulu waterfront brothel where he had discovered
her. Now she was his "personal servant," and she
was grateful to him for being rescued from the
squalid life she had led. She had a sweet oval face
and luminous almond eyes of a light brown color
and a soft rosebud mouth. She was uneducated,
beautiful, and kind. And too good for a man like
Archer Kane.

I knew that like me, she was afraid of him, though
he did not treat her badly, only indifferently. She
was there for his use when he wanted her. In Honolulu Archer lived the life of a rich society gentleman
with his fleet of cars and his yacht and his speedboats, his Diamond Head mansion, and his grand
parties. But on Kalani he was the old-fashioned
"master" with a master's rights.

Maluhia was witness to Jack's daily cruelties. She
overheard when he told me that his father despised
me, that no one cared whether I lived or died. Jack
said I was an interloper and this was his territory,
that I was sponging on his father, taking things that
didn't belong to me. "Even the food you eat belongs
to *me*, Monkey," he snarled, and though Maluhia
glanced sympathetically at me, she dared not say any-

thing. But late at night, when she heard my stifled sobs, she came and sat on my bed and held me close.

"Poor Johnny," she whispered in her lilting island voice. "Poor, poor little Johnny. It is not true. You know I care about you. And Nanny Beale still cares about you. And look, Fido cares about you, too." She put the little toy dog in my arms and tucked the white sheet tightly around me and whispered, "Do not be afraid, Johnny. I will not let anything bad happen to you."

Maluhia took me under her wing, a mother bird to a wounded sparrow. But alas, she, too, was an endangered species. I heard her telling my father that Jack was taunting me and leading me into dangerous games where I got hurt. "Johnny is only a little boy," she pleaded.

I peeked through the door and saw Archer push her roughly aside. He would not hear a word against Jack, and she saw that he did not care, that Jack had the freedom to torture me as and when he wished.

Jack dared me on, knowing I could not compete. And poor, foolish child that I was, I fell for every one of his ploys. "Be brave," Nanny Beale had said when she left me, and "brave" was what I was going to be.

Jack dared me to climb the forty-foot coconut palm, not even explaining the special way it is done, laughing when I ripped my hands and skinned my shins, skidding down from the meager height I had managed to achieve. He dared me to jump from high rocks that were easy for a nine-year-old but impossible for a small boy like me, and when I closed my eyes and hurled myself from the top, his mocking laughter rang in my ears. And he laughed even harder as I lay on my bed later, moaning with the pain of the sprains I had suffered.

One morning I awoke in my usual haze of misery, dully anticipating the day's tortures. I reached out, as I always did, for my old friend Fido. I sat up and felt under the sheet for him. I leaned over and searched under the bed.

I heard Jack outside on the lanai, laughing, and I guessed he had taken my dog. Fear mingled with anger as I ran out, still in my nightshirt, to confront him. He was sitting on the lanai rail, tossing Fido high into the air, catching him casually by a foot or an ear, grinning mockingly at me. "Want him back?" he demanded. "Then come and get him."

I charged madly at him, but he vaulted over the lanai rail and started walking backward, away from me. I clambered over the rail after him, and he began to run. "If you can catch me, Monkey, you can have him back," he yelled, waving Fido teasingly aloft.

I stumbled after him, too distraught even to be aware of where I was going, tripping over stones and scratching my face on the bushes. The dog was the only thing from the past I possessed. To me, he symbolized the security of the Villa Mimosa, of Nanny Beale and my sweet, ordered existence. Fido belonged to the time before I knew about fear and evil. Before I had had to learn to be "brave" and live by my wits. And I loved Fido desperately.

When I finally caught up to Jack, he was standing on the rocks at the edge of the ocean, still holding Fido over his head.

"You are nothing, Monkey," he yelled triumphantly. "They wouldn't even give you a real dog because you were too stupid to know how to look after one. So Nanny gave her goddamn namby-pamby pissy-pants little pansyboy a stuffed one. And you were dumb enough to think it was the real thing."

I lunged at him, and he kicked out at me, catching me in the chest and sending me sprawling back onto the rocks, where I smacked my head. Crazy with pain and anger, I jumped to my feet and at him again, to pummel him while I reached desperately for the dog.

He leaped nimbly away from me onto another rock. His blue eyes raked me mockingly up and down as he held Fido out over the water. "Okay, let's see how brave you are now, Monkey," he yelled, laughing at me. "If you love your stupid little woolly dog so much, go get him." And he tossed Fido into the ocean.

And poor sap that I was, I jumped in after Fido.

Jack knew that I could not swim and that Fido was lost. A few minutes later he fished me from the surf, choking and retching seawater. Because you see, my lithe, strong, murderous half brother had remembered, just in time, that he could not let me die. Not yet.

He knew that he could not let me die for another thirteen years, when he and his father would have their hands on my inheritance. Those thirteen years yawned in front of me, a terrifying chasm.

Suddenly there came an unexpected reprieve. Archer decided that Jack must return to school. "There's more to running Kanoi Ranch than riding a range," I heard him snarl angrily to a sullen Jack. "We employ paniolos to do that. How the hell do you expect to be able to run this place, after I'm gone, if you don't learn? You'll go back to school, Jack, and then to college, and you'll be a credit to me." And when Jack said stubbornly he was damned if he'd go back to school, he yelled, "You'll do as I say, son, or I'll give the goddamn ranch to the Monkey."

There were no more protests after that. Jack knew his father was capable of anything, especially after he had been drinking, and I guess he knew he was right about running the ranch. And if anything in the world ever meant anything to Jack Kane, it was the

Kanoi Ranch. I knew he ached to possess it with every fiber in his body. I would have said "with all his heart," but by then I knew Jack had no heart. He went off to school in Honolulu, and I was left in peace with Maluhia and the servants.

I was almost six years old now and still puny when Maluhia took me to meet Kahanu, the young Hawaiian in charge of the Thoroughbred horses. He also oversaw the prize herd of pedigree Herefords kept specially on the island for breeding.

Kahanu was around thirty years old and solidly muscular, with a broad Hawaiian face, shiny copper brown skin, a shock of thick black hair, and narrow amber eyes. Maluhia told me she thought he was the handsomest man she had ever met. She had no one else to confide in on the island, so she told me her secret: She was in love with Kahanu, but she was afraid to say so because of Archer. I, too, was afraid of Archer, so I did not question this, but I understand now that she was afraid because she was Archer's concubine, his possession.

Maluhia begged Kahanu to help me. "Make Johnny strong, like you, Kahanu," she pleaded. "Teach him all that you know because if you do not, I am sure he will die." She looked at me sadly, because she recognized a broken heart when she saw one.

Kahanu put me on a piebald pony, bareback. I clung desperately to its mane, not knowing what to do. "Sit up straight," he yelled at me. "Grip with your knees." I gripped and straightened up as the pony paced slowly around the corral. After a while I stopped being so afraid and began to look around me, enjoying myself. Sitting straight-backed, I waved to Kahanu and Maluhia, and they laughed and waved back. And for the first time, on the back of that little dappled pony, I felt a thrill of achievement.

Kahanu let me help around the stables, and every morning, when the sun woke me, I rushed there. I worked shirtless alongside him, currying the horses, mucking out the stables, hosing down the yards. I adored my new friend, and I hung breathless with admiration over the corral fence, watching as he broke a new colt.

I followed him everywhere. He let me eat with the men, squatting on the ground, scooping poi and sweet baked meats from a banana leaf with my fingers the way they did. Later, exhausted, I would fall asleep in my own secret place in the hayloft.

Months passed, and Jack still did not return to the island. Maluhia told me that Archer had sent him to boarding school in America. He was behind in his studies, and he would not be allowed back on Kalani until he had done better. I cheered when she told me, whooping and hollering like a normal little kid as I danced over to Kahanu's room in the stables to tell him the good news.

"Then you are not gonna waste your time neither, Johnny," he told me. "Don't think you're just gonna loaf away your days doing nothing but currycomb a horse and ride a little pony around the island. No, sir, I'm gonna teach you to be a man, so when that little bastard, Jack, comes home again, you can take him on. And win."

So I began my crash course in bodybuilding and physical skills. Kahanu taught me to climb trees, to chop wood, to box, to paddle a canoe, to fish. The Chinese cook taught me the martial arts, and Maluhia taught me to swim. And gliding naked with her under the crystal green water with tiny jeweled fish darting around us, I was happy again.

Many months passed in this fashion, and I was beginning to believe that life would always be as serene and beautiful as this. Kahanu had even given me a

Hawaiian name—Ikaikakukane, meaning "One of Manly Strength," to commemorate my new prowess.

And then, when I was eight, Jack returned, and the torture began all over again.

The Hawaiians had given me a new name, but they also had one for Jack. Lauohomelemele, the Yellow-haired One. He took it as a compliment to his superior "white man" status, but the Hawaiians knew better, and it was always said with a subtle contempt.

Everyone on the island, the stable hands, the paniolos, the Chinese servants, hated the Yellow-haired One. He treated them all like dirt, throwing orders around and kicking the servants out of his way when they didn't move fast enough. He threw dishes at the Chinese cook when he didn't like the food, and he even had grown men fired and banished from the island when he complained to his father about their work or their slowness or their "bad attitude." Archer gave him full power. "It's good training for when you run the ranch," he said approvingly.

Jack was arrogant with Kahanu, but secretly he was afraid of him. Archer said Kahanu was the best man on the island; he was clever and a good worker, and he was brilliant with the Thoroughbred horses. Kahanu was valuable, and therefore, Jack did not have power over him, and Kahanu knew it. The Hawaiian ignored him and went about his work, whistling carelessly, while Jack hung around, hoping he would ask him to help, and when he did not, he would ride angrily off in search of another prey. Usually me.

He was twelve when he came home again for the school vacation, and I was eight. We eyed each other warily, and I saw his eyes widen as he looked me up and down. I was no longer the small, wizened little Monkey. I had shot up five inches, and my thin arms and legs were filling out with new muscles. But he had grown, too; he was always a good athlete, and now his body had bulked out. He was becoming a man, and he was ready to follow in his father's masculine footsteps.

Jack had always treated Maluhia with the scorn he felt she deserved. But now he began to look differently at her.

Whenever Archer was home, Maluhia served at the dinner table. She put on a colorful sarong and fastened her black hair into a fat, glossy braid, and she walked barefoot so as to make no noise as she carried the dishes of rice and pork and shrimp to the table and offered them to her master.

That first night they came home, Archer and Jack were seated at the table and Maluhia was serving them, as usual. I, of course, was supposed to take my food in the kitchen, but mostly I ate with Kahanu and the paniolos in the stables. I lay on my stomach in the jungly garden, hidden from sight, watching the quick green lizards dart up and down the wall and keeping a wary eye on Jack and his father at the dining table on the lanai. Ours was a war of surprise attacks, and I needed to know where Jack was at all times so I could prepare my defenses. Only this time I was not the one on Jack's mind.

I watched Maluhia serve Archer and then offer the dish to Jack, bending forward politely. Jack glanced at her and then said something to his father that I didn't catch, but they both laughed coarsely. And then Jack reached suddenly forward and put his hands on Maluhia's breasts.

She leaped back, dropping the dish, clutching her sarong to her breasts as she stepped quickly away from him. Jack said something to Archer, and they both roared with laughter. I saw Maluhia's head droop in shame, and I wanted to run to defend her. But I was no match for the two of them.

In the days after that Jack became even bolder, slapping Maluhia's behind as she walked by him and cupping his hand slyly over her breasts. Maluhia said nothing, but I seethed helplessly with the shame and anger I knew she was feeling.

"Come here, let's have a look at you, Monkey," Archer called a few days later. I had been keeping out of their sight as much as I could, spending my days with Kahanu. I hoped they had forgotten me, but I was wrong. I walked reluctantly out of the stable toward them. Archer pushed back his Stetson and put his hands on his hips, assessing me like a prize steer.

"Well, damn me, if the Monkey isn't growing up," he finally said, astonished. "He's bigger and stronger. Maybe there's some Kane genes in there after all. How old are you now, boy?"

"I am eight years old, sir."

"Eight, huh?" He glanced at Jack and said with a grin, "How many years does that leave us, Jack?" Then, laughing uproariously, he turned away. "Kahanu," he yelled over his shoulder, "put this boy to work. If we have to put up with him for ten more years, he might as well earn his keep."

"Yes, sir, Mr. Archer." Kahanu saluted respectfully.

I kept my distance from them, sticking close to Kahanu, riding the canyons looking for lost cattle. Sometimes we would take his little boat out fishing for grouper, and afterward we would bake the fish over a driftwood fire, miles away from that evil lodge. So it wasn't until Archer had left for Honolulu and Jack was at loose ends that he came looking for me.

"Hey, Monkey," he called, striding toward me and slapping me on the shoulder. "Why don't you and I go fishing?"

"I have work to do," I replied, stiff with fright despite myself.

"Aw, come on, Monkey," he said cajolingly. "Let's

forget our differences. You're older now, and stronger. We're more like equals now, I'd say."

I looked into his smiling face, and warning signals flickered up my spine. I did not trust him.

"I'm busy," I replied curtly, turning away.

"Come on, Monkey." He followed me, throwing a friendly arm across my shoulders. I froze and turned my head to look to him. The only other times Jack had ever touched me was to punch me or kick me. "Come on, fella," he said tauntingly. "Don't tell me you're afraid."

I never learned. I rose to his taunt, just as he knew I would. My expeditions with Kahanu had taught me how to handle a boat.

"Okay," I agreed cockily.

I followed Jack along the sun-bleached wooden jetty, and we climbed into his little boat. He untied the painter and jerked the outboard into action, and we chugged off, heading to a place where he said he knew shoals of grouper were to be found. It seemed a long way to me, and after a while Jack's jolly, bantering tone dissolved into silence.

After about half an hour I was becoming uneasy. "Why do we have to go this far to find grouper?" I asked him. "There's plenty to be found right off Keeper's Point."

"These are better," he said curtly, shading his eyes with his hand and staring at the small island we were approaching.

I stared at it with interest. It was the only other place I had seen since I came to Kalani more than three years before. Archer had made sure I never left the island, and I didn't even know what a town or a school was. I was as ignorant of the world and its ways and of culture and education as I had been when I was five years old. I was excited to see this new place, and when the little boat crunched onto the sand, I leaped out and pulled it into the shallows while Jack held the anchor ready.

I waded confidently onto the shore and turned to look for him. He was in the water, pushing the little boat back out to sea. I ran after him, but he jumped quickly into the boat and bent down, frantically jerking the outboard motor. It growled into life, and I stood chest-deep in the water, watching as the boat sped away from me. Good swimmer though I was, I knew I could never catch it.

Jack was standing in the center of the boat. I saw him punch his fist triumphantly in the air and heard him laughing. "Now let's see how much you've learned, Monkey," he yelled as he sped away, leaving me alone on the deserted island.

He would come back, I told myself confidently. He couldn't just leave me there. Alone.

I looked at the dense mangroves behind me and sniffed their fetid, swampy smell. They looked dark and dangerous, and I walked quickly away down the beach, searching for shade. A stunted bush was all I found, and I crouched in its meager shadow, waiting.

Hours passed. I watched the sun dip lower in the sky until finally the glowing red ball touched the horizon, and then, with tropical suddenness, it was gone, leaving an otherworldly greenish afterglow. It was then I knew for certain Jack was not coming back to get me. I was alone on a deserted island, and I was afraid.

I had thought I would die of the heat, but now I was cold. And thirsty. There was no water anywhere near the beach, and I had not dared roam farther away in case Jack returned and I missed him. I paced around in the half-light but found nothing. I crouched on my rock again, clasping my arms around my hunched knees, staring vainly out to sea. The greenish afterglow slid gently into midnight blue and then almost imperceptibly into darkness. There was no moon. It was just black.

I told myself it would be all right. Jack would return in the morning. Maluhia would miss me, and Kahanu. But morning was a long way off, and from the blackness behind me I heard fearsome rustling sounds, like animals on the prowl. I imagined alligators crawling toward me, ready to rip me limb from limb and crunch me up. In my head I heard tigers and lions breathing close to me and the hissing of snakes ready to strike. In the blackness, I thought I saw scorpions and giant toads and venomous spiders. My new courage disappeared beneath a thousand imaginary fears as I huddled on the cold beach, waiting for Jack to return and get me.

I breathed a huge sigh of relief when the fearful night ended, planning how, when Jack arrived, I would swagger toward him, pretending I didn't care about spending a night alone on a deserted island. I would tell him of the fruit I had found to eat, and the crystal spring of water behind the mangroves, and how I had seen a twenty-foot alligator back there and not been the least bit scared. I would pretend I was a regular little Robinson Crusoe, whose story I knew because it had been one of Nanny's favorite books.

The sun lifted higher in the sky, and still Jack did not come. I was dying from hunger and thirst and was finally forced to search around for a stream or fruit, all the things I had planned so confidently to tell Jack I had done. But I was no Robinson Crusoe, and there was no fresh water, only the brackish, evil-smelling swamp, and no fresh fruits hanging conveniently from a tree.

I finally found a coconut washed up by the tide into a rock pool, and I pounced thankfully on it. Then I realized I had no machete to open it. I smashed it onto the rocks, again and again. I could almost taste its cool juices trickling down my parched throat. But when it finally cracked, most of the milk spilled out before I could catch it. Sobbing with fear and frustration, I licked up what was left of the precious juices.

I sought the shade of the scrubby little bush again and sat somberly watching the sun's burning passage through the sky. Every now and again I dipped into the ocean to cool myself, but the salt water crusted on my skin as it dried, and the sun burned me even more.

As the sun began to set again, I stumbled along the beach, dizzy from the heat and weak from hunger and dehydration. Surely Jack would come now, before darkness. But when the green afterglow filled the sky again and then turned gradually to midnight blue, I realized that he was not coming. Jack was never coming back. He had left me here to die.

I knew that by now he must have made up some story about my falling overboard and how he hadn't noticed until it was too late. "Poor Monkey's drowned," I imagined him saying with a triumphant gleam in his eyes and a mock-sorrowful look on his face.

I lay spread-eagled on the beach, too weak to care anymore about alligators and snakes and lions. I closed my eyes, and a feeling of tranquillity came over me. It would be so easy just to fall asleep and, as Maluhia would have said, "let the Lord take me."

I was unconscious when Kahanu arrived with the dawn and carried me tenderly back to his boat. Back in Kalani, Maluhia bathed my sun-blistered flesh with cold cloths and made potions from aromatic leaves to bring down my raging fever.

"The Yellow-haired One is the true son of the father," Kahanu said ominously. "Evil passes from one generation to another. . . ."

Later Maluhia told me that when she had told

Kahanu I was missing, he had gone straight to Jack and asked him where I was. Jack had denied ever seeing me, so they had searched the island.

"He must have fallen off the cliff and drowned," Jack said casually, but Kahanu knew by then he was lying, and he exploded with anger. I had been gone a long time. He knew they were talking life and death now.

He grabbed Jack's arm and twisted it behind his back. "Where is he, you little yellow-haired bastard?" he demanded, and Jack screamed and said he would tell his father, that Kahanu would be whipped, he would lose his job and be sent from the island.

Kahanu inched his arm up even farther, and Jack screamed louder. Then Maluhia whispered in Kahanu's ear the secret reason Archer wanted me alive. "If the Monkey dies," Kahanu said softly to Jack, "it is you who will get the whipping. Mr. Archer will whip you until you are dead, too, and you know it."

Jack sobbed into the silence, but he knew that Kahanu was right. Archer would kill him if he had ruined their chance of getting at my fortune. So he told them where I was; he said I had leaped off the boat and swum to the island and refused to come back. He said I had told him I never wanted to see Kalani again, I would manage on my own. . . .

"Evil, lying little bastard," Kahanu snarled, jerking Jack's arm upward until it snapped with a sound like a pistol shot. He screamed in agony. "Murderer," Kahanu whispered in his ear. "You fell from a tree and broke your arm. Remember? Just the way the Monkey never left Kalani."

Despite his pain, Jack recognized that a deal had been made and that Kahanu would not tell his father. He nodded his acceptance. The next day he was taken by boat to the doctor in Maui to get his

broken arm set. He then returned to Honolulu for
the rest of his vacation, before going back to school.

I had won, and Kalani was mine again. For the
time being.

The years drifted slowly past, and I was happy in a
fashion, though my restless dreams were still filled
with images of the villa. I longed to see Nanny Beale
again, to smell the mimosa blossoms in springtime
and hear the songbirds in their silver aviary. But
Kalani was my reality.

Every now and then Archer would send a lazy,
half-baked "tutor" over to the island, to keep up the
pretense to his social friends that he was doing the
right thing, and poor Johnny was being educated,
despite being "soft in the head." Somehow they
managed to teach me to read, and I devoured all the
books in the house, even those whose pages were
half eaten by termites. One of the tutors, a gaunt
young English alcoholic, brought watercolors and oil
paints and an easel. Whiskey was his tipple, but when
that was not available, rum made a good enough
substitute, or beer or wine or, in extremity, turpen-
tine or rubbing alcohol.

He was usually too hung-over to do much teach-
ing, but when his hand was steady enough, he
painted well. I would stand on the rocks next to him,
watching him magically re-create the seascape and
the great swoop of the cliff, and my own hand itched
to emulate him.

He showed me the paints, explaining the different
textured papers for the watercolors, and how to treat
them first with a clear wash and then how to apply
the colors. He showed me how to go about mixing
pigments to make my own oils, and he gave me char-
coal and taught me to sketch.

I was transported into a new world. I stopped riding the gulches with Kahanu and instead began to

draw and paint. I was obsessed by it. It took me over completely. And again I was happy.

Jack never returned to Kalani in those years before he went to college. I don't know whether Archer got wind of his murderous intentions toward me before my allotted time was up, but he was kept out of the way, and life was peaceful. When my drunken art tutor had to be deported back to Honolulu with a severe attack of delirium tremens, Archer made sure that I had a stock of art supplies. He wanted me kept quiet and happy enough not to cause trouble.

In that peaceful period, before I was fifteen, I painted my memories of the Villa Mimosa. I painted Nanny Beale as I remembered her, and the nursery with Fido on my bed and Nanny's rocking chair by the fire. I painted Kalani's lush green gorges spanned by rainbows, and the showy red cardinal that came to sit on the lanai rail every evening, hoping for tidbits. I painted Maluhia combing her long, silken black hair, and the beauty of a broken hibiscus blossom; I painted Kahanu on a galloping mare. Everything I saw offered a new perspective, a new detail, a new way to use color.

"You have a special way of seeing things," Maluhia told me, because when she looked at her portrait, it was not exactly the young woman she saw in the mirror. She knew that instead, I had captured something of the girl she was in her heart.

I was left pretty much to my own devices during those years. Kahanu had taught me well, and though I was still thin, I possessed a deceptive, wiry strength. I could ride any horse and rope cattle as well as any paniolo, but, after being kept a virtual prisoner on the island for ten years, I was a rough country boy, unused to life in a normal society. I ate peasant meals from banana leaves and wore ragged shorts and slept mostly in the stable loft. Maluhia saw to it that I kept myself clean and that such clothes as I had were laundered. And she insisted that I not use the island patois but speak "properly" and without the sweet Hawaiian lilt. Still, I was an island boy. I was a young savage.

Then Archer came to the island, and this time he brought Jack with him. Jack was nineteen, and I was fifteen. There were ten long years of hatred between us as we looked at each other. Lauohomelemele and Ikaikakukane—the "Yellow-haired One" and the "One of Manly Strength."

Archer was drinking heavily by then. He ordered dinner to be served and insisted that I sit with them. He was always smart in his custom-tailored white sharkskin suits, his panama hats, and handmade shirts, and even though the night was hot, he was wearing an elegant dark blue flowered shirt of Chinese silk. And Jack was the perfect suave young college man in an immaculate white linen shirt and linen pants.

Archer was still a handsome man, though the liquor was beginning to show in the puffiness under his eyes and the tremor that afflicted his right hand after he had downed a few shots of his favorite scotch whiskey. And Jack was handsome all right. Tall, blond, and strong-jawed.

His hard blue eyes simmered with hate as he looked at me in my old shirt, faded by the sun and many washings from blue to a soft gray, and the rough denim shorts that had once been his and were now worn to a smooth and I thought pleasing pale blue. Thanks to Maluhia, they were immaculate, and I was freshly showered and saw nothing wrong in my appearance—until I looked at the two of them in their finery.

Archer was on his fourth or fifth scotch. His hand shook with a fine, insistent tremor as he pointed at me and guffawed. "Put that wild boy in a roomful of civilized folk in Honolulu or San Francisco," he yelled, "and they'll say, 'You know what? Archer Kane was right. That boy is a savage. He *must* be soft in the head.' "

"For chrissake, get out of here," Jack snarled, looking at me as though I were a leper. "You're not fit to be in our company."

"No, no. Sit down, boy." Archer grinned genially at me. "Tell me, what are you up to these days?"

"I help Kahanu with the Thoroughbreds. I ride with the paniolos. I fish for food for the table," I said.

Archer erupted in laughter. "There, what did I tell you? Wasn't I right about him? Well, kid, I guess you had better go back to the stables and the paniolos where you're comfortable. They say every man seeks his own level in life, and I see that you have found yours."

With that, he turned his back on me and snapped his fingers for Maluhia to bring his food.

I glared resentfully at him over my shoulder as I made my way back to the stables. I hated the disparaging way he treated Maluhia almost more than I hated his cruel attitude toward me. But I could do nothing about either. "Get out of here, you hick," Jack yelled viciously after me. "You're an ignorant pig, an eyesore in your hand-me-down shorts. You're not fit to sit at the table with civilized men."

I knew Archer and Jack sat late on the lanai, discussing business and drinking. Nevertheless, early the next morning they were at the stables, where Kahanu had their horses saddled up and waiting. I lurked inside the stalls, hoping not to be noticed, and they soon went off with Kahanu to inspect the cattle.

For the next few days I managed to keep out of their way, and they did not ask for me. I rode out early with the paniolos and often slept out with them, under the stars on a grassy hillside. Life was simple and sweet away from the plotting and sophisticated corruption of the Kanes, and I thought that if I had no more than this, I could be happy.

Then Archer went back to Honolulu, and Jack was alone again. So, of course, he came looking for me.

It was late evening as I rode back with the men, sweat-soaked and smelling like a steer from a long, hot day spent branding the new cattle. There were only a dozen paniolos on Kalani, and they were older men who had been sent over from the Kanoi Ranch on the Big Island and given the easier job of caring for Archer Kane's prize herd. Archer's philosophy was that it was no use wasting the cowboys' lifetime-earned skills by putting them out to pasture themselves and wasting money on pensions. He figured they were still able to work, and Archer got his money's worth instead of paying them retirement pensions.

I'll say this for Archer Kane: He was a good rancher. He understood his business, and he understood his men. Those old guys would have withered and died without their jobs to go to, and Archer understood they would rather work and make an honest week's pay doing the only thing they knew than be turfed off the ranch, living in some broken-down shanty village, talking about the old days. They hated him all right, everybody did, but he gave them what they wanted, and in return they worked hard and kept their mouths shut.

Now, when they saw Jack waiting for me, they turned their eyes away, concentrating on their horses, giving them buckets of freshwater and throwing blankets over them, allowing them to cool off before feeding them.

Jack was leaning back with his elbows hooked over the corral fence, one foot propped on the rail, smiling a sinister little smile. "Hey, Monkey," he called. "Come over here. I want to talk to you."

I walked slowly toward him. Out of the corner of my eye I saw the paniolos sidling away into the stables. Jack and I were alone. Then, with a sudden thrill, I realized that for the first time I was not afraid of him.

"What's all this I hear about you painting?" he said coldly.

I came a step closer. I stood with my legs apart, my arms folded. "What about it?" I demanded, looking him squarely in the eye.

"You are here to work, not to paint," he snarled. He tilted his arrogant chin, pushing his cowboy hat to a better angle, looking down his nose at me. I measured him up: He was six-one to my five-seven and around 190 pounds of solid muscle to my thin, wiry 130. His jaw jutted aggressively, and the urge to hit him almost overwhelmed me. I hid my bunched fists and said instead, "Archer knows about the painting. Who do you think supplies the paints?"

"Well, no longer," he said. He pointed triumphantly to a pile of rubble lying in the corner of the yard. "There'll be no more 'painting' on this island, you fuckin' little pansyboy. You'll earn your keep just like the rest of the paniolos." His nostrils flared as he sniffed the air. "You smell just like a half-breed anyway; you might as well be one of them."

He strode across to the pile of rubble, and I stared after him as he pulled a box of matches from his pocket. "Watch this, Monkey," he called, striking a match and setting light to the rubble. "That's all your fuckin' pansy paintings going up in smoke."

He jumped back as the oil paints and the turps exploded in a sudden whoosh of flames. I watched numbly as my memories went up in a pall of noxious blue smoke. They were my images of the times I had felt happy on Kalani. Jack was burning Maluhia and

Kahanu and Fido; he was burning the fish freshly caught from the crystal ocean, the paniolos sitting around their fires, the numb-eyed cattle as they were seared by the branding iron. He was burning the red cardinal and the green lizards and the dappled pony on which I first rode proudly around the paddock.

Jack Kane was burning my life, and I launched myself at him like a hot-branded steer exploding from the pen. "I'll kill you, you bastard," I heard myself screaming. "I'll kill you."

My speed took him by surprise. I had him on his back. My hands were on his throat as he rolled over, kicking out at me. I had learned the martial arts from the Chinese cook, and I knew how to kill a man. I raised my rigid hand and brought it sideways across his windpipe. He gagged, unable even to scream, searching desperately for breath.

"I'll kill you," I said, and even as I said it, I realized I was enjoying myself. The thought of killing him was so pleasurable that it shocked me back to my senses. I was frightened by the depths of my hatred and by the power of my anger.

I straddled his chest, staring down at his purple face. And then I glanced up and saw Maluhia standing at the edge of the yard, watching us. Her hands flew to her face in horror as our eyes met, and I knew I could not do it. If I killed Jack Kane, I would be a murderer. And he was not worth it.

I climbed off him and waited as he struggled to regain his breath. After a while he sat up, rubbing his throat. He stared malevolently at me through bruised, puffy eyes.

"You're soft in the brain all right," he called hoarsely after me as I turned and strode away. "A mental retard like your fuckin' mother. Nobody wants to know you. Nobody cares if you live or die." He clambered to his feet and stood arrogantly with his hands on his hips. "Coward," he yelled mockingly. "Afraid to finish the job?"

I stopped in my tracks, my fists balled in readiness. For a moment he almost had me, just as in the old days. But this time I ignored his taunt and stalked back to the corral, climbed on my horse bareback, and galloped away.

I rode to the northeastern tip of the island, pushing the horse to go faster, all the way to the very edge where the cliff fell two hundred sheer feet, into the rocky Pacific.

The horse dug in its hooves, whinnying with fear. I leaped off and gazed down at the powerful ocean hurling itself in a solid wall over the jagged rocks, then dissolving into a curtain of foam and spray, surging and roiling, sucking bits of driftwood and flotsam into its infinite depths. I was beyond caring. I told myself there was nothing to live for, that anything, even the nothingness of death, was better than this.

I stood for a long time, until the sun began to set and I finally lifted my eyes from the rocks and the boiling sea and looked at the beauty around me, illuminated in a golden red glow. And I sank to my knees and howled like an animal. For the first time since I was seven years old I was crying.

I slept under the stars that night, on my windy clifftop, communing with myself, asking myself what I would do next. There was only one answer: I had to leave Kalani. But how? Kahanu was in charge of the motor launch—the only boat big enough to safely make the crossing to Maui. I could not ask him to help me because Archer would surely find out, and then Kahanu would lose his job. And I knew Archer's vengeance was such he would make sure Kahanu never got employment again on the islands. The supply boats made their way to Kalani once a month, and occasionally a cattle barge came to transport the animals to the ranch on the Big Island, but the crews were in Archer's pay, and they would no more think of helping me escape than they would of cutting their own throats.

The only answer was Jack's little outboard motorboat. It was small, a mere seven feet in length with a shallow centerboard. It was meant for put-putting in the shallows and for fishing, not for crossing the twenty miles of treacherous channel between Kalani and Maui. The channel had notorious currents, and the winds could blow up the weather in less than an hour, bringing fierce squalls and thunderstorms. It was a risk, but one I knew I would have to take.

I lay on my back, watching the passage of the stars across the tropical night sky. Venus glittered as brightly as a diamond and looked so close I felt I could reach out and grab it. And as shooting stars catapulted across the heavens like celebratory fireworks, I planned my escape and wondered what I would do with my new freedom.

I rode back slowly before dawn, looking for the last time at the landscape I knew so well. The long grass was pearled with dew, the birds were beginning their morning chorus, and my country boy's alert ears heard the rustle of a thousand small creatures. I loved Kalani and knew its beauty, like the knowledge of its evil heart, would always be part of me.

I planned to steal cans of fuel from the storeroom and stash them in the undergrowth behind the dock. Jack's boat was beached nearby, and it would be easy under cover of darkness to load on the fuel and some food and glide silently out into the darkness, letting the current take the boat until I was far enough away to start the little motor. After that, steering by the stars, I would have to put my trust in my own skills and in God.

I wiped the sweat from my horse. Then, with a

final affectionate slap on her hindquarters, I set her galloping across the paddock. I watched the mare wistfully for a while, savoring my last sight of her, kicking up her heels and whinnying with the sheer delight of being free. I hoped I would soon feel the same way.

I skulked back to the lodge, keeping an eye out for Jack, but it was barely dawn, and no one was around. Except Maluhia.

She was on the veranda outside the kitchen. She was crouched in a fetal ball with her knees hunched under her chin. She stared at me dully with blank golden eyes, and I noted with shock her swollen mouth and bruised face.

"Maluhia," I gasped, sinking to my knees beside her. "What happened?" But even then I knew. I had observed Jack often enough sitting at the table, sipping whiskey with his father, coveting her supple body, the firm upward thrust of her breasts under the sarong. Jack had gone to her room, and Maluhia had rejected his advances. When she screamed, he'd beaten her into silence and submission.

This time I knew I would kill him. Livid with rage, I stalked toward his room, but Maluhia cried out. "He is not worth it, Johnny," she sobbed. "After all, I am only a bought woman. What else can I expect?"

But my anger only grew as I listened to her tell me how worthless she was. I knew she had more integrity and dignity than the man who had bought her. I grabbed a knife and went looking for Jack, while Maluhia ran to get Kahanu.

I found Jack snoozing in a hammock slung between two palms where the lawns sloped down to the sea. I took the knife from my belt and slashed the rope, spilling him onto the grass. Jack scrambled quickly to his feet, then crouched low in a boxing stance. He raised his fists, grinning.

"I guess you found out I took what you've always

wanted." He taunted me as he circled me. "Funny, I thought Maluhia was a mother figure to you. But then, you're not beyond a little motherfucking, are you, brother? Just for the record, she wasn't worth it. It's a myth what they say about Chinese women. Maluhia's not woman enough for a man of my appetites and dimensions, though I'm sure she would suit a little monkey like you just fine. As for me, I'll take a good warm-blooded white woman any day—"

I lunged at him with the knife, catching him on the shoulder. As he dodged backward, I stumbled and almost fell. I saw him put his hand to his shoulder, then look at his bloody fingers. And in that moment he forgot all about the inheritance and needing to keep me alive for three more years.

I was desperately trying to regain my balance when he jumped me. He grabbed my hand and twisted it behind my back until I let go of the knife. He bent to get it and I drop-kicked him, but his rage had given him lightning speed. He took hold of the knife and slashed out at me. I heard a faint hiss as the flesh of my cheek opened to the bone, and I tasted the warm, metallic flavor of my own blood.

I kicked and fought in my Oriental style, but I was no match for his extra height and weight and the sheer power of his rage. He lunged at my neck, at my chest, my groin. I put up my arms to protect myself, screaming not with fear but with an anger that matched his. I did not care whether I lived or died. I loved gentle Maluhia, and I wanted to see Jack dead for what he had done to her.

Strong arms finally forced Jack off me. Kahanu punched him to the ground. He snatched the knife and towered murderously over him.

"No no, Kahanu," I heard Maluhia scream. "I am not worthy of such an act of retribution. I am only a *kawahine*, a concubine."

A tremor ran through Kahanu's massive torso as

he looked from her to Jack. Then he strode to the water's edge and tossed the bloody knife into the ocean.

Jack sat up, rubbing his jaw, wiping the blood from his face. He was laughing. "I hope you die, you motherfucking little Monkey," he yelled, clambering to his feet. "I'll get you yet—when you're not hiding behind Maluhia's skirts and Kahanu is not around to protect you." He was still laughing as he walked away.

Kahanu picked me up and carried me back to the stables. He laid me down on the sweet fresh straw and Maluhia bathed my wounds, but I was bleeding badly, and she could not staunch the flow.

Kahanu looked worriedly at Maluhia. He knew I needed medical help. He said that when it was dark, he would take me by boat to Maui, where his family lived. The doctor would stitch me up, and his family would hide me and look after me until I was better.

Maluhia was the eyes and ears of the household, she knew everything, and now she told me that Archer was planning to kill me when I was eighteen and to take "my inheritance."

I didn't know what she was talking about. "What inheritance?" I asked because as far as I knew I was penniless. She shook her head; she didn't know. But she knew Jack could no longer be trusted; he wanted me dead. *Now*.

"I won't go away without you," I said stubbornly, realizing that I was leaving her at Jack's mercy.

She said, "You are only a boy. You must go at once to Maui. When you are strong enough, you must go far away, where they will never find you." And then she pressed her life savings, forty dollars, into my hand.

"Never come back, Johnny," she whispered, bending to kiss me good-bye.

I told myself I would remember her sweet, chaste

kiss forever, and the scent of the plumeria blossom
in her hair, the cool smoothness of her lips, and her
soft dark eyes shining with love and unshed tears. I
knew I would never see Maluhia again, and the
wrench in my heart was more painful than my
wounds. As the boat slipped away from the dock into
the darkness, I sat in the bow, staring sadly back at
the now-invisible island, holding her in my memory.

"Go back where you came from," Kahanu urged
me as the boat lifted over the waves. "Tell no one
who you are, or they will surely find you. Make a new
life for yourself. You are being thrust into manhood,
my friend. The gods are telling you to take the opportunity of a new life."

I watched the handsome bronze giant guide his
boat across the channel, and I thought how strange
it was that Jack Kane should be the one who had
finally given me my boat ride to freedom.

I wondered what I would do with such a prize. I
had not left Kalani for ten years. I had never seen a
town or a city. I had never even been to Honolulu or
Maui. I thought with a sinking heart that Archer had
been right. I was a savage, and I did not know how to
behave in a civilized society.

I stared across the waves at Maui. I had Maluhia's
forty dollars in my pocket and the bundle of clean
clothes she had sent with me. And I was free.

~ 29 ~

$\mathcal{I}$ knew Kahanu planned to tell Archer I had made my escape on Jack's little boat, as I had originally intended. He said he would scuttle the boat and tell them that I must have been lost at sea. I don't know whether they believed him or not, but no one came looking for me. Kahanu's family cared for me as they would their own son, and I envied their slow island way of life, the gentleness of it, each day blending sweetly into the next.

They were happy people, and I still remember them gathering on the lanai of their small frame house on the long, warm evenings, greeting friends and neighbors who always stopped by for a chat or to share a meal. Someone would be strumming a ukulele, and they would sing the lovely old chants and songs, and the women would dance; even the old ones were still caught up in the rhythms and the joy of their island life. I envied it, but I was apprehensive and anxious to move on.

Five weeks later, with many farewell leis and alohas, I was on a slow boat heading for Honolulu.

The island of Maui and Kahanu's family had been

an easy transition for me; I understood them and
their way of life. After all, I was more like them than
like my so-called family. But Honolulu was a sprawling, crowded city, hard-edged and fast-paced for an
island boy like myself. And when I saw the famous
Kane name emblazoned on the wharves and ships
and even on a street sign, I knew I was in enemy
territory. I wasted no time: I gave myself a new
name, John Jones, and got a job on the first cattle
boat I came across that was plying between Honolulu
and San Francisco. Ironically, it turned out to be a
Kanoi Ranch boat, but no one knew me. After all, no
one had ever seen Johnny Leconte. I could handle
cattle, and that was all anyone was interested in.

I had been awed by Honolulu, but I was terrified
by San Francisco. I had never seen such tall buildings, so many automobiles, such throngs of people,
such shouting and bustle and noise. I hesitated to
cross the roads, not knowing which way to look. I did
not know what to order in the cheap café I went to
or how to pay. People looked strangely at me in the
street, staring over their shoulders at my ragamuffin
clothes. Ashamed, I went into a store and bought
two shirts and the first pair of real pants I had ever
owned. I also had my hair cut by a barber, and when
I saw myself in the mirror, I saw a different person.
But I knew I was still a raw country lad in the big city.

I counted my money and found that I had only
five dollars left. I would have to get a job, but the
only thing I knew was cattle. I was wondering what to
do when a young fellow, standing in line at a hot dog
stand on Market Street, spoke to me. He was wearing
a smart uniform with a short red jacket and black
pants, and he told me he worked as a bellhop at one
of the big hotels. He looked me up and down in a
friendly style, and I guess I looked needy all right, so
he told me there was a job available if I was interested. Now, I had kept to myself on the cattle boat,

barely exchanging more than a few words with the other men, and this fellow was the first real person I had encountered outside the islands.

His name was Augustus Stevens. "Call me Gus," he said cheerfully as we walked back together to the hotel. He was smaller than I, and just as thin. He said he was from the East Coast and had come out west to seek his fortune. He was sixteen years old at the time, and many years later I was to see his name again, as the president of a famous oil company, so I guess he finally made that fortune. But then he was struggling to hold it all together, just as I was, and we formed an instant bond.

That afternoon I became a bellhop with my name, Johnny, written on a badge pinned to my smart red jacket, running errands, opening doors, and hefting baggage at one of the city's deluxe hotels. The basic pay was poor, but Gus had said that the tips helped even it up, and he was right. I found myself a small cheap unfurnished room in the Chinese quarter and by eating mainly rice and bean sprouts in the local restaurants, I found I could just manage.

I had gravitated to the Chinese quarter because I felt safe there. I understood the customs of the Chinese better than those of the brash, hard-eyed men I worked with. But there was still not enough distance between me and the islands. I knew Archer and Jack often came over to San Francisco, and I was constantly on the alert, looking over my shoulder in the streets and keeping a watchful eye out at the hotel. I needed to put many thousands of miles between the Kanes and me before I could feel that I had really escaped them.

I hoarded what few dollars I could with the vague notion of somehow making my way back to France and the Villa Mimosa. I wondered if Nanny Beale was still there. And if she would remember the boy she had left on Kalani all those years ago. But when I read in the newspapers about the war raging in Europe and that France had been occupied by the Germans, I knew that Nanny and the villa were just a dream.

The year was 1941. I had settled into my job at the hotel, taking pride in my quick service, smiling my thanks for the tips I received. On my days off I explored the city with the eyes of a man seeing the pyramids for the first time. I traveled on the clanging cable cars, and on the ferries that took me across the bay to the woods and hills. Occasionally I visited a movie theater with Gus. Mostly we went to westerns. I enjoyed the horses and the action.

And then, on December 7, the Japanese attacked Pearl Harbor, and the United States was at war. I thought with horror of Oahu—that peaceful island and the waterfront and all the wonderful ships I had seen, now devoured by flames—and of the many lives lost. Filled with anger, I immediately went with Gus to enlist in the Navy.

"How old are ya, kid?" the recruiting sergeant asked me, with a twinkle in his eye.

"Eighteen, sir," I replied confidently, just the way Gus had told me to.

"You've got the right sentiments, son," he said kindly, "but you need a few more years' growing before you can stand up for your country."

I was bitterly disappointed. In the back of my mind had been the hope that I might be sent to Europe. Gus was luckier. Somehow his streetwise confidence got him through, and he walked from that storefront recruiting office a full-fledged member of the U.S. Navy.

Gus wasn't the only one to leave the hotel. Men were drafted and sent immediately for training, and with help at the hotel in short supply, I suddenly was transferred and promoted to waiter. I was observant, I learned quickly, watching the others to see how they behaved, but underneath I still did not know the rules of life. I was still the wild boy from the islands.

Two years passed. San Francisco bristled with Navy personnel; they occupied all the hotels, and their girlfriends and wives flocked into the city to be near them. I was seventeen. One more year, I told myself; then I could legitimately enlist in the Navy. I followed the war news, still with the vague hope that I would be sent to the Mediterranean. Meanwhile, I got myself a new job.

The St. Francis was a grand hotel with a smart clientele: The men were officers; the women classy, chic, rich. One of them whom I served regularly kept a suite there on a permanent basis. She said her husband, an officer, was "down in the sticks" at Camp Pendleton, the Marine base near San Diego, and she refused to go anywhere near it.

"It's the back of beyond," I overheard her complain to her friends as they drank their usual six o'clock cocktails and assessed the evening's amusements.

She was fortyish, attractive and flirtatious, with blue eyes and a pale, almost translucent skin. Her hair was a natural silvery blond worn in a fashionable pageboy, and her wide, predatory mouth was the color of the cardinal that used to sit on the lanai rail on Kalani in the evenings.

I noticed her because she was pretty and always gay, always laughing and joking with her friends and the officers they went out with. But there was a restless quality about her. I noticed her eyes searching the room all the while she was talking, and I wondered what she was looking for. Sometimes I would feel her eyes rest speculatively on me.

I blushed as I felt her look me up and down from across the room. I was young and innocent; I had hardly even spoken to a girl. I was tall now, and wiry and muscular, and I thought she was mocking the way I looked in my tight black pants and short red brass-buttoned jacket.

She watched my face as I put the martini carefully on the table in front of her, and I turned away from her smiling gaze because I knew I was not exactly handsome. My face was too thin, my features were too strong, and thanks to Jack, a scar ran in a deep groove from beneath my left eye almost to my chin. But Mrs. DeSoto seemed to find me interesting.

"I can see you are a good waiter, Johnny," she said. "I shall have to make sure I get you when I call room service. They are always so slow, and then there's always a mistake, somebody always forgets something." She sighed. "It's bad enough there's a war going on without the room service waiters making our lives hell."

She smiled at me again, her cardinal red lips stretching over her beautiful even white teeth. *Like pearls,* I thought, dazzled.

"Thank you, Johnny," she said, giving me a generous tip along with an intimate glance that made me blush again.

After that I often served her in the bar, and she always tipped me well, always gave me that smile, and let her hand touch mine as she slipped a dollar into my palm, making me feel hot and uncomfortable.

A few weeks later I was on room service duty. It was after midnight. No one liked the graveyard shift because you got all the drunks, but somehow as the youngest I always ended up with it. Mrs. DeSoto called down: She wanted a bottle of gin, a bottle of vermouth, and ice sent up right away.

"I'm glad it's you, Johnny," she said, flinging open the door and smiling at me.

I walked past her into the room and placed the tray on the side table. I looked at her. She was wearing a long, slinky red evening dress, gathered at the hip, and a diamond and ruby pendant nestled in the low V neckline, just above the white curve of her breasts.

"Open the bottles for me, Johnny, would you?" she said, sinking onto the sofa. "And then pour me a drink. Wait, I'd better show you exactly how I like it." She glanced up at me through her lashes and gave me that smile again. "So you'll know for next time."

The room was lamplit and smelled of her perfume, rich and musky. I handed her the drink with a trembling hand, and she leaned toward me and put the glass to my lips. "Taste it, Johnny," she murmured. "Then you'll know *exactly* how I like it."

I took a discreet swallow, and the alcohol caught at the back of my throat. I began to cough, and she stood with her hands on her hips, laughing at me. "I bet you've never even taken a drink before," she said. She sat on the sofa again and patted the cushion next to her. "Come sit here beside me, Johnny, and tell me what else you have never done before. So I know what else to teach you."

I sat next to her, hypnotized by her knowing blue eyes and her sexy red mouth. "Look at you," she said, running a finger down the length of the scar on my face, "You're like a young buck, on the way to becoming a stag." She gave me that special smile again, and I wanted to grab hold of her, to kiss her. "Such an attractive young innocent," she said thoughtfully, holding the drink to my lips again.

She stood up and put a dance record on the Victrola. It was Glenn Miller playing "Moonlight Serenade." I gulped down the martini, watching as she drifted around the room in time with the music.

"It's my favorite," she said as it finished. She shook her hair free from the net snood she was wearing and stretched her arms luxuriously above her head. "Don't you like it, Johnny?" she asked, fixing two more martinis.

"Sure," I mumbled, watching her swaying hips as she glided across the floor and put the record on again. She turned and looked at me. Then she drank the martini down and tossed the glass into the fireplace. And she began to dance again. Only this time she also began unbuttoning her dress, swaying closer until she stood before me. And then she let it slide to the floor.

She was a blond vision in a red satin slip and high heels, and I was lost. She sat next to me and began slowly to remove my clothes, everything except my tie. "Now what shall we do with this? I wonder," she asked, playfully pulling me toward her. She smelled of rich perfume and gin and her own flesh, and I was drowning in the scent of her, the softness of her, the sheer lavish femaleness of her. I couldn't wait.

The first time I was too quick, but then she taught me control, how to make love to a woman. "You're a good learner, Johnny," she told me. "I shall remember you. Except I still don't know your name."

And my senses blurred with alcohol and perfume and sex, I blurted out my real name. "Johnny Leconte."

She stared wide-eyed at me for a long moment. Then she threw back her head and laughed, her long white throat rippling. I looked at her, puzzled.

"Isn't that amusing!" she gasped at last. "It's just too good to be mere coincidence. I mean, how often do you hear the name Leconte? I knew Archer Kane had changed his name when he married the Frenchwoman and that he had a son. It is you, isn't it? Johnny Leconte?"

My heart sank as I stared at her, still not comprehending. "Of course," she exclaimed, still laughing, "you don't know who I am. Why, my dear young buck, I am Chantal O'Higgins. I was Archer's second wife. The mother of his goddamn son Jack.''

I threw on my clothes as fast as I could and ran for the door, not daring to look at her. She was still laughing as though it were the best joke in the world.

I left the hotel that same night, and the next morning I faked my age and successfully enlisted in the Navy. But somehow I knew that one day that fateful encounter with Chantal O'Higgins DeSoto would come back to haunt me.

~ 30 ~

$\mathscr{I}$ learned a lot in the U.S. Navy, but my education was more about men and war, and life and death, than book learning. I did two and a half years' service on a destroyer, mostly in the South Pacific. Regretfully I had to let go of my dream of ending up in the Mediterranean.

It wasn't difficult for me to adjust to war conditions. After all, I had spent most of my life in a state of siege. I already had that extra sixth sense that warned of danger, and my formative years in Hawaii had also made a sailor out of me. I was used to the ocean and its ways.

That does not mean I was never afraid. I would have been a fool not to be. Whenever I manned my turret gun and faced the enemy across a few hundred yards of gray water, that old metallic taste of fear was in my mouth. War was a bitter and thankless business, but as recompense I had the camaraderie of my fellow sailors, my colleagues in arms. I learned at last how to live with my fellowmen, how to accept friendship and offer it in return. I finally became civilized, if not quite a man of the world. I doubted that I would ever become that. The psychologists say that one's personality is formed in the years before puberty, and mine was battle-scarred.

Still, despite living on the knife-edge of war, dodging torpedoes, and suicidal aircraft on bombing raids, I was almost happy. At last there was the right number of miles between me and the Kanes. My eighteenth birthday had come and gone, and I knew, had I still been on Kalani, I would have already suffered the planned "fatal accident." Death in the service of my country was preferable; at least that would be honorable.

I was tempted to stay on and pursue a naval career when the war ended in 1945, but I lacked the education to become an officer, and my prospects were limited. Besides, I had the old urge to paint again. I had taken to sketching the sailors, playing cards in their undershirts and steel helmets, or sprawling in exhaustion on their bunks after a long night on watch, or reading mail from home, and I captured the longing expression in their eyes as they thought of their wives and children. From memory I sketched battle scenes of warships blasting the hell out of each other, of fire and mayhem and bloody, broken bodies. And of convoys slipping silently across the horizon while we, the vigilantes of the South Pacific, kept watch.

The captain saw my sketches. He praised them and hung them in the wardroom. When the long war finally ended, he submitted some to the chief of naval operations. A few were framed and displayed in lofty corridors in Washington.

I felt sad the day I became a free man for the second time in my life. The U.S. Navy had taken me in as a rough boy and molded me into a man. I also missed the camaraderie and the discipline. I would have to think for myself again now.

I was sure of only one thing: I wanted to paint. I

had the bit of money I had managed to save, plus the financial sweetener we got to ease us back into civilian life, but I knew it would not last long, and I also knew I could not go back to the West Coast or to Hawaii.

My life became a series of odd jobs. I worked the summer season as a waiter in mountain resorts in the East to make enough money so I could spend the winters painting. I had no idea if my art was "good." It was just something I felt compelled to do, the single driving force in my life.

There were girlfriends in those days, sweet young things, mostly models who fell for the romantic young artist in his icy "garret"—actually a loft over a hardware store in a little seaside town in Maine. I fell in and out of love along with the seasons, but my only true loves were the sea and my art.

The years drifted past slowly as they do when one is young. Occasionally I sold a painting, but it was always a terrible wrench when I had to let it go. I wanted to keep them all because they were my memories of the people I met and the places I had been and the girls I had loved. I was, as usual, painting my life. But I never painted Kalani or anything to do with my childhood. They lurked in the back of my mind, like an unexploded torpedo.

By the early 1950s my paintings were beginning to be noticed. I was offered an exhibition at a small exclusive New York gallery, and I sorted through my canvases carefully, reluctantly parting with those I considered my best. I bought myself a new suit for the occasion and shaved off my winter beard. I felt foolish and out of place as I stood in the gallery, clutching a glass of champagne and eavesdropping on the comments of the viewers. To my surprise they were mostly complimentary, and soon a row of little red stickers adorned my works. I was a minor success, but at least now I was an artist who had sold at an exhibition. On the strength of that I received a commission from a man of power and high finance to paint a portrait of his wife.

My subject was plain but with dramatic bones that lent her great dignity. She had married her husband when she was eighteen and had stuck with him through all the hardships, living in garden apartments on Long Island and tenement apartments in New Jersey, until he had finally struck it big in the life insurance business. Mergers were followed by acquisitions, and over the years he had become a renowned, if shady financier as well as a multimillionaire. And now he lived like a lord. He was seen at every charity function and every fancy dinner, and he was a close friend of those in high places in Washington.

The only thing was his wife was never seen with him. Sometimes his daughter accompanied him, but more often it was a stunning blonde less than half his age, ablaze with diamonds and high couture.

I knew the portrait was a ploy on his part to make his wife feel he still cared. *And to keep her quiet,* I thought as I looked at her the first time we met. I also knew the reason he had chosen me as the artist was that I was cheaper than the better-known ones, and he thought his wife wouldn't know the difference.

She was a sweet woman with a gentle kind of charm, a genuine goodness of heart that refused, against all odds, to see bad in anyone. I liked her, and I gave that portrait everything I had.

I dressed her in bronze green velvet, like a medieval princess, with her hair upswept, showing off those dramatic cheekbones and her Nefertiti nose. I hung her with gold and emeralds, and she lifted her chin proudly, standing tall and straight as a woman who values herself should. Shining through this arro-

gant pose were her wonderful dark eyes, filled with a
warmth and innocence that we rarely see.

That portrait became the cornerstone of my success, even though I was never in essence a portrait
painter. It went on loan to various museums and the
name John L. Jones began to be heard. I even read
about myself in the newspapers and in *Time* magazine. I received more commissions, but I put them
all on hold because I finally had enough money for
that trip to Europe.

I traveled across the Atlantic by ship, the way I had
come; only this time I had a decent cabin in second
class. I could not yet afford first, but it was of no
account. I was going home. I lingered awhile in
Paris, stretching out the blissful moment of my return, and drinking in the sights that the war had not
destroyed. I saw the museums and the paintings, and
I sipped red wine in boulevard cafés and watched
the world go by.

When I finally boarded the sleeper train to the
south, I was like a lover held too long at arm's length
by his *amoureux*.

Though I could not remember it exactly, the Côte
d'Azur was somehow, magically, how I had always
imagined it: the way the light fell on the green hills,
the sandy white lanes, the umbrella pines, and the
tall cedars pointing like needles into a vivid blue sky.
But it wasn't until I saw the Mediterranean that I
knew the true meaning of "azure." I was trembling
with delight. It was an artist's dream, the light an
inspiration.

I checked into a small auberge on the coast run by
a couple of sturdy peasants, mother and daughter.
The father was a fisherman who went out with his
nets at night and returned at dawn with samples of
the catch that later adorned our dinner table. They
were a charming family, simple and courteous to the
stranger in their midst, and they were intrigued

when they saw my easel and realized I was an artist and that I wanted to paint them. I was delirious with the way of life, the freshness and the still-unsullied beauty of it, the quality of the food and the wine, and the slow pace that belonged to a Mediterranean climate.

But having arrived, I nervously put off my search for the past. I told myself it was because I wanted to paint, but the truth was that now that I was there, I was afraid of what I would find. I was afraid that Nanny Beale was dead, perhaps killed in the war, or maybe that she had gone back to England. I was afraid that the Villa Mimosa belonged to someone else and that I would be forbidden entry to it, and my dreams would have to stay mere dreams. Most of all, I was afraid I would find Jack and Archer Kane there, lording it over my old home.

But I had to do it. I had to find out about my past. About Nanny Beale and the truth about my mother.

I found the Villa Mimosa right away, of course, the way a cat taken and dropped hundreds of miles away can find its way home. I cycled along the sandy road leading up the hill and past the crumbling pink stucco wall, half hidden under its burden of bougainvillea and roses. My heart was pounding like a rider in the Tour de France as I leaned my bike against the wall and rang the bell, peering through the rusting iron gates up the gravel drive.

The *gardien,* a pleasant fellow in blue work overalls who said he was also the gardener, answered my ring and told me no one was there.

"I used to know someone who lived here," I told him, fishing for a response. "The Leconte family."

His face lit up, and I could see he was pleased to hear the name mentioned again.

"They are long gone, m'sieur," he told me. "Madame is dead, and her husband, the Foreigner, and the son live far away on some tropical island. I heard they returned once, after the war, to claim the boy's fortune, but they never came here to see the villa. The boy's old home, m'sieur. The very place he was born. It would have broken Madame Leconte's heart to know her son cared so little for the place she loved best.''

I realized that Maluhia had been right. There was an inheritance, and the Kanes had got their hands on it after all. I guessed that Jack had posed as me, pretending he was Jean Leconte and claiming my fortune. I shrugged. I didn't give a damn about the money. I was alive and free, and I was happy in my own way. I wanted nothing more.

The *gardien* saw my interest in the house and offered to show me around. As we crunched up the gravel path and the beautiful pink-washed villa came into sight, I remembered with total recall the day my father came to get me. I remembered myself as a small boy sitting on the marble step, so cool against my bare legs, with the morning sun on my face and my beloved Fido clutched in my arms. And I felt again the terror when my father's eyes met mine with such blank indifference and he said, "Pack him up. I'm taking him with me." And then I recalled the black cloud that settled over me, blotting the sunshine out of my life forever.

I knew the villa. I remembered every detail, the marble floors, the great curving staircase with the koa wood banister that Archer had installed, as a present to my mother when they married. I hesitated at the door of my old nursery, looking at the empty room that had been Nanny's domain.

The old fire grate still had the big brass club fender with the leather seat, but her high-backed rocking chair was gone, and the big toy cupboards were empty. I opened the door to my bedroom and saw my little cherrywood bed, my initials, JL, that I'd scratched on with a pin, were still there. I ran my

fingers over the place, smiling as I recalled how furi-
ous Nanny had been when she had seen what I had
done.

I walked slowly through my mother's empty
rooms, imagining her looking out at the view of the
sloping lawns and the fountain sparkling in the sun,
past the cypresses to the sea. I thought of her being
awakened by the melodious chirping of her gay little
canaries and songbirds in the silver aviary that the
gardien told me had been destroyed in a storm long
ago.

I stood by her window, wishing I had known her,
thinking that the Villa Mimosa was my rightful inheritance. I could legitimately claim my fortune; I could
live here in this wonderful house, be free to paint,
knowing I would never have to spend another summer season as a waiter in the Catskill Mountains
again. But I knew I would not.

I thanked the *gardien* for his courtesy and asked
hesitantly about Nanny Beale. I feared the worst, remembering how old she must be and expecting to
hear him say he knew nothing or that she had gone
home to England to die. Instead he told me she was
living in a little cottage, just down the hill.

"She stayed here right through the war," he told
me proudly, "though many times the Germans
threatened to intern her because she was English
and they suspected her of being a spy." He gave an
insouciant Gallic shrug and said, "We were all involved in the Resistance in some way around here,
channeling the escaped prisoners and the English
airmen along the coast to Spain and then Portugal.
Our little boats played host to more than just fishes
in those awful years, m'sieur," he added with a sly
grin.

I cycled at top speed to the bottom of the hill and
down a sandy white lane curving around the little
peninsula to where there were a few scattered

houses. I knew which one must be hers: It was tiny and whitewashed, with a plume of smoke curling up from the chimney, even though the day was warm. The garden was a riot of English roses and delphiniums and big white daisies and lavender. And there, bending over her herbaceous border, wearing a large straw hat and sensible white lace-up shoes, was an old lady.

My heart jumped as I leaned on the gate watching her. She was totally absorbed with her task of snipping the finest blooms, placing them in the wooden garden basket beside her. Her back was stooped, and I noticed that arthritis had twisted her hands into grotesque shapes. I was shocked to see how tiny she was when in my childish memories she had been tall and stately.

She lifted her head, suddenly aware of my presence. Our eyes met, and it was as though time had stood still. Each saw before us the person that now existed and the one that used to be. I saw the strong-boned face that was indelibly imprinted on my memory, crumpled now and crisscrossed by a network of fine lines and the marks of pain of her crippling arthritis, and the faded patient eyes that told me she bore it with all her old fortitude.

And she saw the boy she used to know in the tall young man, his frailness gone, his sticklike limbs sleeked out with muscle, and a face that had finally grown into its features. She told me proudly afterward, it was the face of an interesting-looking man. Not handsome, but a face no one would forget. Especially with the evil-looking scar running along the cheekbone.

"You haven't changed that much, Johnny," she said quietly, her eyes smiling at me. "I still recognize you."

"And I you, Nanny Beale."

I jumped over the garden gate and clasped her to

me. Tears were running down both our faces, but I felt her frailness and knew that I was now the strong one.

"I thought you were dead," she murmured, her voice trembling with emotion. "Then they told me you had returned and claimed your inheritance. I said that it couldn't be you, that you would have come here to the Villa Mimosa, that you would have found me. All these years I've thought about you, and every night I said a prayer for your safety. And every birthday that passed I wondered if you were still there to enjoy it, because I knew the man who took you was evil and capable of anything."

I took her arm and we went inside, and she smiled at me through her tears. "I'll bet you never thought you would see your old Nanny cry," she said, "but these are tears of joy."

She bustled about fixing tea, and we sat by the fire, she in her rocker and I on a straight-back wooden chair, balancing plates properly on our laps. We had starched white damask napkins and old-fashioned ginger cake taken from the special red tin she kept in the larder, but we were too busy talking and rekindling our love for each other to eat it. She poured tea from an old brown pot, though I noticed she was forced to use both hands to lift it and the cup trembled noisily on its saucer as she passed it to me.

I had come home again, and I sighed with the sheer glorious happiness of it. I looked around her room, seeing her things just the way I remembered, and I said, "I shall never leave you again, Nanny. I'm here now, and I shall look after you."

I told her briefly about my years on Kalani and my life after. I did not want to distress her, and I said I was happy with my life.

"But you must fight for what is yours, Johnny," she said, looking with concern at me over the tops of her round tortoiseshell eyeglasses. "When I heard that Archer Kane had been here with his supposed 'son,' I went to the *notaires* and said it could not be you. They described the man who claimed he was Jean Leconte; they said he was tall, blond, blue-eyed, a young giant. I told them you were dark-haired and dark-eyed, like your mother, but they said time changes a person. Of course, I knew they were wrong. I guessed it was Jack Kane. And all my hopes for you disappeared, Johnny. I felt sure they had killed you, too."

"Too?" I asked, puzzled.

And then she told me about my mother.

The teacup shuddered noisily in its saucer again, only this time it was caused by my trembling hand. Nanny handed me the letter written to me by my mother before she died, and I read it numbly. I thought about the pain my unknown mother had gone through: the plain little rich girl growing up and finally being forced to acknowledge her lack of beauty; the solitude imposed on her by her father deepening into isolation after he died; and finally the poor *la célibataire* living in lonely splendor at the Villa Mimosa, falling head over heels for a man she thought saw her as she really was, with the inner beauty she knew she possessed.

But Archer Kane never saw the beauty of my mother's nature; he never cared about her soul. All he wanted was her money, and now he had it.

"You must fight for what is rightfully yours," Nanny said firmly again. "Go tell them what has happened, claim your inheritance."

I shook my head miserably. My mother's fortune had blighted my life. I would rather be poor and free and happy.

"But when you marry," Nanny urged, "what then? You cannot deny your children the right to claim their grandmother's fortune. It is what she wanted. The Kanes have stolen it, just the way they stole your childhood from you.''

I remained adamant about not wanting the money. I told her that all I wanted to do was to paint and that now I felt I had found my spiritual home. When she finally saw I would not change my mind, she persuaded me to write my story down "for the next generation.'' She said she would take it, with my birth certificate and her own "document'' telling the story as she knew it, along with my mother's tragic letter, and place them all in a safety-deposit box at the bank. She would put the key to the box in her bureau drawer and a copy of the document under her mattress for safekeeping, just in case she wished to add anything to it. And then, she said, she would finally be content.

Flora Beale had kept her promise to Marie-Antoinette Leconte. She had done what she could to protect her son and also her future grandchildren. "When they are old enough,'' she told me, satisfied, "they will make their own choice.''

As for me? I too have made my choice, and I am happier for it. I have no wish to possess the Villa Mimosa, with all its sad memories, though it is probably the place I love best in the world. I have no need of my dear mother's fortune because I have seen how money and greed can destroy a man. And I have learned how to live on my own terms. I have my painting, and I am back in my homeland, and I have found my old mentor and friend Flora Beale, and a man could wish for no more. I am finally happy.

~ 31 ~

$\mathscr{B}$ea was still curled up on the green wicker sofa on the terrace when the sun came up the next morning. She clutched the papers telling Johnny Leconte's story to her chest, watching the glow of rising sun spread over the sky and turn the Mediterranean into a lake of gleaming gold.

She stretched the weariness from her bones and walked back along the terrace into the hall. She stood looking at the place at the foot of the stairs where Marie-Antoinette Leconte's body had been found and ran her hand along the smooth koa wood banister, as Marie-Antoinette must have done so many times before.

"I'm so sorry," she whispered. "I'm sorry for what happened, and I'm sorry I never knew you."

She went to her room and called Nick. She told him that she had read Johnny Leconte's story and asked him to come over right away.

She was waiting on the steps when he drove up half an hour later.

They sat together, hand in hand, on the marble steps. "Just as Johnny used to sit," she said with a sad half-smile. "Of course, it was he who told me the story I now remember so well. I can't think how I ever forgot. He was such a vivid raconteur, and the way he wrote it was exactly the way he told it to me. Now I remember everything, and I'll continue where he left off.

"He told me that in 1954 he rented a little stone house in St.-Paul-de-Vence, a tiny village up in the hills behind the coast. He said it was an enclave of artists, writers, and musicians, like-minded souls who gathered in the cafés in the square of an evening to share a meal and a glass of wine and sometimes afterward a game of pétanque. The hill villages then were still the way they had been for centuries, with the same families, the same simple way of life. He said it was like stepping back in time to a more innocent era.

"He told me he had finally rid himself of the past, and he painted with a new freedom. He painted a hundred pictures of Nanny Beale, bending over her roses in her garden, pouring tea from her old brown pot, dozing on the vine-shaded terrace. I remember his showing them to me and explaining that they were not portraits as such; they were never photographic reproductions of a set of features. They had a subtle dreamlike quality, and as Maluhia once said, they captured the person she was in her own heart.

"He showed me the paintings he did of the village women with their lined, weather-burned faces, their sharp eyes crinkled against the strong light, with black scarves covering their hair and white aprons over their black dresses, and their large peasant feet thrust into clumsy black shoes. Somehow, with the magic of his brush, he captured the gentle bovine innocence of their children and the stooped backs of the men who had worked half a century in the fields. He painted the owner of the café, his bulk propped against his zinc bar, his sharp eyes forever scanning the little saucers on each table, assessing who had paid and who had not. He painted the priest sitting on an old wooden upright chair outside his little white church. His arms were folded across his ample stomach, his legs out-stretched, his hat tilted over his eyes, and his black soutane blowing in the mistral, as he dozed.

"And he had painted a dozen pictures of Maluhia. His color palette changed from the clear, sunbaked Riviera tones, and his paintings became more dream-like, more exotic; outlines of shape and form half hid-den beneath a veil of color: Maluhia combing her long black hair, like a silken screen hiding her face, the plumeria lei around her neck covering her breasts, a mere hint of an image. He painted the slender naked girl swimming under a crystal green ocean, as at home in her watery environment as the jewel-colored fish he remembered so well."

She looked at Nick, and he nodded. He knew those paintings; everyone did. They hung in some of the most famous museums and galleries in the world.

"He put his heart into those paintings of Maluhia," Bea said softly. "He told me he would never forget her. He said that her love had made his life on Kalani toler-able and that he had wondered if he would ever love anyone like that again.

"Then one day he met Séverine Jadot. She was visit-ing from Paris, where she lived with her mother. He was sketching the village men at their evening game of pétanque, and she stopped to admire his work. She was as tall as he was, and she had fiery red hair and a piquant face with a dusting of freckles and expressive green eyes. He followed her into the café, and they began to talk."

Bea smiled as she thought of their meeting for the first time, imagining them when they were young and passionate. "They fell in love," she said softly to Nick, "and instead of going back to Paris, Séverine moved in with him. He was crazy about her, and of course, he took her to meet Nanny Beale.

"He said the old lady put on her hoity-toity countess expression because in her opinion, no woman was good enough for her Johnny. She served them tea and ginger cake, and he could tell she was watching Sévérine's manners and assessing her upbringing, but Sévérine was the model of French politeness, *de bon genre*. Even Nanny Beale couldn't fault her.

" 'Marry her,' she whispered to him as they left. 'It will be the best thing you have ever done.'

"He said he just laughed, but he knew she was right, and anyway, he had already asked Sévérine to marry him. Nanny was a witness at their wedding a month later. The ceremony was conducted by the same village priest whose portrait he had painted in the same simple village church. The wedding party was held at the café, and all the locals came, and all the other artists and the writers and the musicians. He said there was music and dancing until late into the night, and it was the best party they ever had.

"It was the early 1960s then. He was in his forties, I guess, and Sévérine would have been in her late twenties. They lived a simple life in their little stone house in St.-Paul-de-Vence, but things were changing on the Riviera. It was taking on a new kind of sophistication and tourists were beginning to penetrate their little stronghold.

"Nanny Beale didn't live to see the changes, though. One spring evening she was reading a passage from her favorite Charles Dickens. She put her eyeglasses down on the open page as she always did, to mark it. Then she just fell aleep and passed peacefully into another world.

"That's why her cottage looks the way it does. Johnny said it shouldn't only be the rich and famous who are remembered. He wanted it kept exactly as she left it. He said it was to be like a museum commemorating Flora Beale's unselfish life of service to others, her dignity and simplicity, and her goodness.

"After she died, he and Séverine moved farther away into the hills of Provence. They bought an old farm near Bonnieux, overlooking the fields of lavender and poppies, and they were happy there. He wanted only to paint; he had no business head and no time for art dealers. If it had been up to him, he would never have wandered farther from home than Avignon or Aix. So it was Séverine who took his paintings to Paris and arranged an exhibition at a major gallery. It had been a long time since his first portrait had caused such a stir, but he had not been forgotten. And those years of seclusion had given him the time to develop his talent. The paintings of Maluhia and Nanny Beale caused a sensation.

"After the success he was restless. He said he couldn't paint; he needed a change of scenery. There was to be an exhibition in New York, and they went there and stayed awhile and found they liked it. But he could never live in a city, so they bought an old mill in the Berkshires."

Bea's golden velvet eyes were filled with the warmth of her memories as she looked at Nick. "That's where I was born," she said softly. "On the twenty-eighth of July, 1968.

"They named me Marie for my grandmother Leconte and Laure because it was pretty. I was like my dad, a skinny waif of a child, with my mother's red hair and his dreamy brown eyes. We spent every summer at Les Cerisiers, the farm in Provence, and I grew up speaking French as easily as English.

"And then, when I was fourteen and he knew I was old enough to understand what he had to say, my father took me to see Nanny Beale's cottage. And the Villa Mimosa."

She dropped Nick's hand as she said, "My father and I sat on these very steps, gazing at this same magical view, while he told me the terrible story of his life. We were so close, so in tune with each other's emotions

I was devastated by the pain of what he had gone through. I felt it so deeply it was almost as if it had happened to me, as if I were the innocent happy child on the cool marble steps, listening to the songbirds and clutching Fido to my heart. As if I were the one whose small safe world ended that day, with the great black cloud shutting out the sun forever."

Tears coursed down her cheeks, and Nick put his arms around her. "It's all right, Bea," he said. "It's all right now, love."

She nodded, letting her tears fall. "He said he was telling me because Nanny had been right. He said one day, when I was older, I would have the right to claim my grandmother's fortune. If that was what I wished.

"I told him I didn't want anything to do with it. I didn't care about the money. But I thought he should have the villa. 'It should be yours,' I said to him. 'It's the place you loved, where you were happy. And Grandmère Marie-Antoinette would have wanted us to be here.'

"He just smiled and said it wasn't possible. 'Let sleeping dogs lie,' he told me, 'in case they turn around and bite you again.' "

Bea wiped away her tears and said wearily, "So that was that. He never lived at the Villa Mimosa again. Life went on happily. I was the child of an artist, but it was a normal sort of life, and I was a normal sort of kid. You know, I did all the usual things, sleep-overs, and high school, and then college." She smiled thinking about it. "They never sent me away to a smart prep school because Dad said he couldn't bear to part with me. 'The only day you're going to leave home is the day you marry,' he said laughingly. And Maman really had to work on him to let me go to college. I went to Vassar —not too far away, so I could come home weekends. And how I loved coming home; it was the best place in the world. My father loved his solitude, he needed it in order to paint, and our house was a sort of haven of tranquillity. It always seemed miles away from the harsher realities of life.

"I guess they didn't have any really close friends; there was just never time for them. They were complete, you see; the perfect couple. They didn't need anyone else.

"It was just a normal loving childhood," Bea said. "I didn't even realize my father was famous until my teacher in high school told me. I remember being surprised. After all, he was just my dad."

She fell silent. She took her hand from Nick's and hugged her knees under her chin. Her eyes were closed, and her face was tight with emotion. "I can't talk about the rest," she said in a strangled voice.

Nick put his arms around her and held her, stroking her short, springy hair, waiting for the trembling to stop.

He knew the story. It had been in all the papers. Johnny and Séverine Jones were on their way to the opening of an exhibition of his latest works at a gallery in Washington when their car had skidded in the rain and gone off the road. It was four hours before the police emergency services had been able to cut them from the wreck. They both were dead.

"I wish I could help," he said quietly.

"Not even you can bring them back."

"What did you do? Afterward?" Nick asked.

"I came here for a while, to the farm in Provence. Then I went home again."

"And?" he prompted.

"I don't know," she said. *"I still don't know what happened at Mitchell's Ravine."*

The children came running into the room, their bare feet pattering on the tiles, the dog skittering behind them. They stopped with a jolt, staring at Bea's tearful face with big, frightened eyes.

"What's the matter?" Scotty said gruffly, fear catching in his throat. It couldn't be happening again, he thought panicked. Bea wasn't leaving them, was she?

Julie ran to her. She flung her arms around Bea's neck. "Don't cry, please don't cry, Bea," she wailed, tears spurting from her own eyes. "I'll do anything, I'll be good, I'll tidy my room, I'll clean up after Poochie. Only please, please don't cry. I love you, Bea," she sobbed, all her fears surfacing. "Don't cry, don't leave me. I want to stay with you forever. . . ."

Scotty ran to join her, entwining his thin brown arms tightly around Bea's. The two of them clung like limpets, and Bea managed a smile. "I love you, too," she whispered. "But now I want to tell you about my own mother and father, about why I'm crying. And why I understand so well what happened to you."

Holding them close, she whispered the story in their ears, of how her own mother and father had been killed in an automobile accident, just the way their parents had.

"I was grown up, of course," she said quietly, looking at Nick as she spoke. "I was supposed to be able to cope with grief. But I just couldn't face seeing anybody. I wanted to be in the place where we had all been so happy together, the home my parents loved best: their farm in Provence, Les Cerisiers. I needed to do my crying alone."

"We cried, too," Scotty said, sniffing back his tears. "We cried and cried, Bea, but it didn't bring them back."

She ran her hand through his rough hair. "No, darling, crying doesn't bring them back," she said. "It's just our way of saying we loved them and we shall always miss them. Crying is a good thing, Scotty, remember that."

"It made me feel better," Julie volunteered, gazing up at Bea. "But I still wanted my mom and dad."

"Me too, baby," Bea said, kissing her upturned face. "But now look at us. How lucky we are to have found each other. Now we are a whole new family. Of course, I know I'll never take the place of your real mother and father; that's only right. But now we have each other, and that makes me very happy.''

"Then you won't cry anymore?" Scotty asked anxiously.

"Oh, I don't know, maybe I will cry now and then. Just as you do," she added, smiling at him. "But remember, that's a good thing to do. It makes us feel a bit better, a bit closer to them. One day, as time passes, we shall be able to remember them without crying, we'll remember all the good things and the happy times we spent with them."

"How long will it take, Bea?" Julie asked wistfully, wiping a tear away with a grubby finger.

"A little while, baby, a little while. You'll see, one day you will smile as you remember something your mommy said to you."

"I can tell you that's true," Nick said from the background. He looked at Bea, and she thought his glance was almost as wistful as Scotty's. She smiled, including him in the new family.

"Whatever would I do without you?" she said.

Still wistful, he shook his head. "I was hoping you would never have to try."

Scotty darted a quick glance at him, then at Bea. His blue eyes narrowed as he looked shrewdly at them. "Are you two going to get married?" he asked with a grin.

"Oh, yes, yes." Julie danced over to Nick, her tears blending into a sunny smile. "Please, please, Nick. Then we'll have a real mommy and daddy again."

"This is the damnedest proposal of marriage I've ever heard," Nick said, looking intently into Bea's eyes.

"You mean I should wait for you to go down on your knees?" she said, smiling.

He grinned as Scotty tugged at him. "On your knees, quick," Scotty said urgently.

Nick knelt, and the two children knelt down next to him.

"Darling Bea French, Marie-Laure Leconte. Will you do me the honor of becoming my wife?" Nick said as humbly as he could manage.

"Oh, please become his wife. Say yes, say yes, yes, yes . . ." the children chanted.

Bea's eyes brimmed with love as she looked at them. "How could I possibly say no?" she said.

Julie threw her a worried glance. "Does that mean yes?" she asked suspiciously.

"It means yes," Bea said.

"With all your heart?" Scotty asked, making sure.

"With all my heart."

"Are we yours forever now?" Julie asked, still anxious.

"Forever."

"It's forever, Julie," Scotty said, solemnly catching her hands in his.

"Forever, Scotty."

"Yea, yea," they yelled, suddenly cavorting around the room, turning cartwheels and leapfrogging over chairs as the dog danced madly after them, barking its head off.

"I wasn't joking," Nick said seriously, taking her hand.

"Nor was I."

"I love you, Bea Marie-Laure," he said, bending to kiss her lips.

"And I love you," she whispered back.

"They're kissing, they are kissing . . . uugggh," Julie yelled, laughing with joy.

"That's our new mom and pop," Scotty yelled back, skidding across the polished floor, heading for the kitchen to tell Jacinta.

~ 32 ~

The sky was black and moonless without even the suggestion of a breeze. Phyl sat on the sofa in the beautiful summer room at Brad's Diamond Head mansion, watching him as he prowled the floor, still talking. It was four in the morning, and she was tired but fascinated by what he was telling her. *"I want you,"* he said, looking broodingly at her, but instead of being thrilled as she would have just a few weeks ago, she felt a shiver of fear.

She asked herself why. He was the same good-looking, sexy, more than eligible man she had fallen for in Paris. The difference was that she was now seeing him with professional eyes. He was revealing a dark, troubled streak in his character that was interesting, but at the same time repelling.

As she listened to him, she knew she had never been in love with Brad. She didn't even know him. It had been one of those heated all-consuming affairs that were doomed to self-combust. She wished she had never come to Hawaii, now that she saw how disturbed he was. But the man was searching his soul, baring his emotions and his life to her. She owed it to him to listen, to try to help him.

"I lied to you about the Monkey," he said. "The reason he ran away from the island was that he was responsible for the death of a servant. Her name was Maluhia. She was young and pretty. He raped her, and so she threw herself over a cliff. But somehow the Monkey escaped in Jack's little boat. My father never believed he had drowned. He always said one day he would come back to haunt him.

"Archer was drinking heavily by then, and the responsibility for Kanoi was falling on Jack's shoulders. He found out that their financial affairs were in chaos, and the ranch was in dire need of an influx of capital. Archer spent money like there was no tomorrow. But Jack was different."

Brad's eyes met Phyl's. The quiet desperation that she saw in them touched her.

"You see, to Jack the Kanoi Ranch was his identity, his reason for being. He valued it above everything. Above morals, above his own life. Even above his father's life.

"Jack was in Honolulu the day the Japanese bombed Pearl Harbor. He said when he saw what they had done, he was filled with murderous rage. He just wanted to get in there and kill the bastards with his bare hands. America was at war, and supplies were at a priority. The ranch got a financial reprieve thanks to the government, and Jack joined the Marines."

Brad laughed, his mood changing as he said, "God, he was a tough fighter," he said proudly. "He earned himself a couple of medals for valor, won, he told me, because of his total uncompromising hatred of the enemy. 'No one hates quite like Jack Kane,' his fellow marines used to say. 'All he wants to do is kill.'

"Archer had been given the rank of major in the Army and a desk job supervising the Japanese interned on the island, which allowed him plenty of time to run the ranch.

"Then the war was over, and the need for money raised its ugly head again. Archer figured out a plan. Europe was in chaos; many years had passed since his French wife's death, and by now the Monkey would have been of an age to inherit. But he had no proof that the Monkey was dead, and anyway, he knew it would have been too difficult to take his claim through the French courts. So he took Jack to France and passed him off as Marie's son.

"He said it was easy. The old lawyers and bankers who knew about *la célebataire* were all dead, and the legal papers had been lost. He just gave them the birth certificate, Jack signed his half brother's name, and they handed over the inheritance.

"You see," he said, spreading his hands wide and looking appealingly at Phyl, "to them the ranch had to come first. It may not have been strictly legal, but Jack said it was the right thing to do."

"And do you agree with that?" Phyl asked quietly.

"Of course I do. I would have done the same myself." He shrugged her question impatiently away as though it scarcely mattered. "The money should have been Archer's by rights anyway if it were not for the French legal system."

He began pacing the floor nervously again. The dog crouched near the door, watching him, waiting for a command, but for once Brad was not aware of it.

"They were in Paris," he said abruptly, "and Jack told me Archer was drunk with triumph.

" '*La célibataire*'s fortune is finally ours,' he said. 'No one can ever take it away from us. Now we have enough for everything, Jack. For Diamond Head, the ranch. Whatever you want it's yours.'

"Jack was around twenty-four years old then, I guess, but he knew he had to take control of the ranch before

Archer threw all that money away on booze and women and high living, just the way he had before.

"They were in the Ritz bar, drinking champagne and congratulating themselves, when Jack noticed a blond, expensively dressed woman across the room, staring at them. She was smiling, an odd, knowing little smile. She was older, but still very attractive and smart-looking, and there was something eerily familiar about her. She caught his eye, and then she got up from her table and walked over to them.

" 'Surprise, surprise,' she said, kissing Archer on the cheek. He just stared at her, with a stunned look on his face. She turned to Jack and said, 'The last time I saw you, you were a squalling, red-faced infant. I have to admit you have improved since then.' She blew him a kiss, throwing back her head and laughing.

" 'Don't you know me?' she asked, still laughing. 'I'm your mother, Chantal O'Higgins.'

"Jack said he felt the same sudden rush of hatred toward Chantal as he had toward the Japanese after Pearl Harbor. He could have killed her with his bare hands right there in the Ritz bar. He had never seen her before, but he'd read plenty of dirt about her in the gossip columns."

Brad glared at Phyl and said bitterly, "Didn't I tell you the Kane men really knew how to pick their women? Well, Chantal was a true bitch.

"She told them she was in France to check her properties in the Charante. 'Fortunately,' she said, 'the Germans liked cognac and they left them in good shape. Lucky for me the family trust is in Switzerland, huh? I get to keep it all.'

"She stood mocking them with her eyes and her smile. Then she said, 'I heard your third wife left millions, and most of it went to your son. By the way,' she added casually, throwing out her bombshell, 'did I tell you I met Johnny? Of course, he's not nearly as handsome as you, Jack. But I want to tell you, *he is something else in bed.'* Her peals of mocking laughter rang in their ears as she turned and walked away.

"Jack leaped up to go after her, but Archer held him back. 'Sit down, you fool,' he said angrily. 'Don't give her the satisfaction of thinking you believe her.'

"But Jack did believe her. He knew it wasn't the kind of thing Chantal could have invented on the spur of the moment just to rile them. *His goddamn half brother was still alive. And he had screwed his mother.* He burned with humiliation, and he said to Archer, 'One day I'll find that little bastard Monkey. And then I'll kill him.'

" 'You'd better,' Archer replied, ordering a scotch. 'Or else he'll be back to claim the money. And where will the Kanoi Ranch be then?' "

Brad poured himself a brandy. He swirled the amber liquid, staring blankly down into the glass. Phyl thought it was almost as if he had forgotten she was there, he was so caught up in the story of the past.

Finally he tossed back the drink and said, "Jack knew Archer was capable of running through the second fortune even faster than he had the first. But this time the money was in Jack's name. All Jack wanted was the ranch. He gave Archer enough money to live out his rich man's life, and then he began to build up the business again.

"He put everything he had into the ranch; it consumed his life. And he did anything he had to to make it a success again. But he told me that he never forgot that the Monkey was out there somewhere and that one day he might return to claim back his fortune.

"Jack worked hard those years, and he played hard. There were plenty of women in his life; they liked him all right. They always had. Then he met Rebecca Bradley at a party in San Francisco. Even afterward, when he hated her, he always said she was the most beautiful woman he had ever seen.

"Rebecca was rich and spoiled and very social, and

she looked down her nose at the young rancher. 'A wild man' she called him mockingly when they were introduced, and Jack said he laughed, remembering the Monkey and thinking how ironic it was that he was now the one being called wild.

"He said Rebecca was elegant and proper, but underneath he sensed a like spirit. She was just as wild and wicked as he was, and he loved it. He told me the first time she let him make love to her was in the back of her father's chauffeured limousine.

"They were driving home from a party out in the hills somewhere, and it was dark. The chauffeur kept his back discreetly turned, but Rebecca knew he was aware of what was going on, and she liked it. She always liked that sense of danger, Jack told me. She enjoyed the feeling that she might be caught. She wanted to do it in hotel elevators, in bathrooms at crowded parties, up against an alley wall, like a cheap hooker."

Brad turned his pale, ravaged eyes on Phyl. "That was Rebecca," he said bitterly. "And she never changed."

His hand shook as he poured another brandy. "But Jack was giving her what she wanted, and Rebecca decided she couldn't live without him, so they got married a couple of months later. It was the wedding of the year in San Francisco. Her father was a Hawaiian sugar baron, and there was mixed blood in there somewhere, you could see it in her long black hair and the shape of her eyes, but her mother was an old guard socialite, and the cream of the society crop attended their nuptials."

Brad stopped his pacing and looked at Phyl. "Wait here," he suddenly commanded, holding up his hand. He strode off into the hall, and the dog trotted quickly after him, its claws clicking on the wooden floor.

Phyl shuddered, thinking about what he had just told her. She knew she was finally getting to the truth about Brad, and she was afraid of what he was going to say. She wished they were in her office, that Brad was just a patient and she his doctor. She looked nervously at him as he came back in the room, clutching a silver-framed photograph.

"Here," he said, pointing with a trembling finger at the couple standing outside a church in their wedding finery, smiling for the cameras. "That's my father. And that, god damn her, is Rebecca." He groaned like a man in pain, then suddenly hurled the photograph across the room.

Phyl gasped as it hit the wall and the glass shattered onto the floor. The dog ran toward it, sniffing and growling softly.

"Oh, God," Brad cried with anguish. He knelt in the debris and picked up the scarred photograph

"Why did I do that?" he demanded, flourishing the photograph under Phyl's nose. She drew back in alarm. "I know why," he cried angrily. "My mother was no good. She was a cheap lay. She was insatiable. Anyone was fair game to her: her husband's friends, her own friends, a casual acquaintance. Even after I was born, she just kept on doing it, taking what she wanted."

He sank into a chair and put his head in his hands. "I was the decoy for her assignations," he whispered through his fingers. "She used to take me along with her. After all, who would suspect a woman of screwing around when her child was with her? But she did. She made me a witness, an accomplice to her dirty little game.

"My father was away at the ranch a lot of the time, and she would take me to San Francisco. We would set off, and I would think, *Maybe this time it will be fun, just the two of us together. Maybe this time it will be all right.* But I hardly saw her, except when she dragged me along to her 'social events,' as she called them. She would give me toys and books and tell me to be a good boy. She said she and her friend were going into the other room, and I was not to disturb them; they had a lot to talk about."

Brad lifted his head and looked bleakly at Phyl. "And I never did," he said. "I was the good boy, the model son. I wanted to please her, and I did as she asked. Until the day she kept me waiting so long—two hours, three, four even—that I got frightened. I put my ear to the door of the room, but there was no sound. I was afraid that she had forgotten me, that she had gone off and left me. I thought maybe she had died . . . I pushed open the door and peeked inside. The curtains were drawn, and a lamp was lit on her side of the bed. I saw her clothes scattered on the floor, and I breathed a sigh of relief. I knew she could not have gone away and left me without her clothes.

"I slid through the door, peering into the darkness. And then I saw them. She was lying there naked, her black hair flung across the pillows. His head was on her breast, and he was sleeping. She turned and looked at me. Our eyes met. Then, still looking at me, with a smile of terrible complicity, she took his genitals in her hand and began stroking them.

"I heard him groan and he began to stir and I ran, terrified, from the room. Her mocking laugh followed me as I closed the door."

Brad was looking at Phyl, but she doubted he saw her. "Her laughter has haunted me ever since. I hear it in my dreams, waking and sleeping. And that smile. It was not the smile of a mother for her son." He shook his head despairingly. "She was so beautiful.

"Afterward we went shopping, and she bought herself a new hat, red with little feathers in it. And then we went to tea at some grand hotel she liked. She met her friends there. 'Look at me, what a good mother I am,' she said, laughing with them, 'taking my son out to tea.' And she gave me that knowing smile again. 'He's a boy who knows how to keep a woman's secrets,' she said, and they all laughed."

Brad lapsed into a deep silence, his head in his hands. Phyl waited, almost afraid to breathe in case she triggered another dangerous memory.

He sighed deeply. "Years later, after they were divorced, I asked my father why he had put up with her. He just shrugged his shoulders and said he took his own pleasures where he could. Besides, she was part of the great Kane image: the beautiful society heiress, the glamorous wife and mother. In an odd sort of way I guess they suited each other. She took what she wanted, and so did he. And he told me that women meant nothing to him. He reminded me that the only thing that mattered in our lives was the Kanoi Ranch. 'Never forget that, son,' he said. And I never have.

"My father told me the history of the ranch, how Archer had started it and about their financial difficulties over the years, trying to hold it together. And about the fortune that should have been theirs years ago if it were not for that half brother.

" 'That goddamn wizened little Monkey tried to steal our birthright from us, Brad,' my father said. 'If it hadn't been for your grandfather Archer's cleverness, he would have done it, and you and I would not be sitting here, on one of the biggest cattle ranches in America. I know I should have killed the Monkey when I had the chance because I know in my bones he is still out there somewhere, liked a coiled rattlesnake waiting to strike. He will try to take that fortune from us one day, son. He will want to take everything the Kane family has worked for all these years: our sweat and toil, our land, our heritage. *Our name.* Make no mistake, he will come to claim his fortune, and when he does, we must be ready to act. Quickly and without mercy.' "

Brad looked calmly at Phyl and said quietly, "I have been waiting for that moment all my life."

Phyl perched warily on the edge of her chair. Brad's mood swings from anger and violence to icy calm presaged trouble; she was sure of it. "And do you think it will ever come?" she asked softly.

He stood up, poured himself more brandy, and gulped it down. "Not now," he said coldly. "Not anymore."

The icy shiver ran down Phyl's spine again. Did he mean that the Monkey had returned? And that he had killed him? She was afraid to ask. Suddenly she was afraid even to be here alone with him.

"Jack almost killed Rebecca, you know, before she left," Brad said, casually. "He said she had flaunted her affairs once too often and something in him just snapped. He grabbed a rifle and threatened to shoot her, but she just laughed and walked away. She knew all about him and all about the Kane family. 'Like father, like son,' she said contemptuously, daring him on."

"Oh, God," Phyl whispered, afraid to ask what happened.

"He should have, but he didn't," Brad said moodily. "He just beat her up a bit. It was what she deserved. I was watching from the doorway, and I was glad. I was glad when she went away and it was just my father and me, alone. They got divorced, and we got on with our lives, running the ranch. He sent me away to school and college, but I couldn't wait to get back."

He began pacing again, backward and forward, his hands in his pockets, his head down. "I never saw my mother again. Archer had died several years before, and then we heard that Rebecca had had a stroke. She lingered for a while, but nobody ever saw her. They said that one side of her face was paralyzed, grotesque, but that the other half was almost normal, still beautiful. But she couldn't speak, and she couldn't walk. She died a couple of years later.

"Jack was drowned in a boating accident the year after I got out of college. They said he was drunk, but I didn't believe them. He was a good sailor, and he was just caught in one of those sudden storms. I knew he would have made it through if he could. He wouldn't have left me alone.

"I inherited everything. The ranch, the houses, the island." He laughed bitterly. "And the ever-present threat of the Monkey. The rattlesnake at the heart of the Kane family, waiting to strike."

Phyl looked at him, debating whether to ask the fateful question. But she had to know. "What did you do about it?" she whispered.

Brad came to stand in front of her. He looked deep into her eyes. He leaned forward and tenderly stroked her cloudy black hair away from her frightened face. "Why, I took care of it, of course," he said gently.

Phyl stared up into his handsome, gently smiling face, into his beautiful, mad eyes. She thought of Mahoney saying, "You get so you can feel who the villains are, even when they are cloaked in normality. Straight, decent-seeming folks, just like you and me. But the famous Dr. Forster must know better than anyone what goes on in people's minds. In those deep, dark recesses. Things that are hidden behind good looks and charm and expensive clothes. The wife beaters, the child abusers, the murderers. They are just folks, like you and me."

He had been describing the man she was looking at. Brad was a textbook sociopath, and she, the clever psychiatrist, had failed to see it.

Phyl flinched as she felt his hands on her shoulders. Afraid he would see the panic in her eyes, she dropped her head quickly. She had to stay calm, humor him. She had to get out of here. . . .

He said in that gentle, concerned voice she knew so well, "My poor Phyl, I've kept you talking all night. Look, the sun is already up. Go to bed, my love. Get some rest." He glanced at his watch and added lightly, as if the long soul-searching confessional night had never happened, "I almost forgot. I'm due at a meeting at the ranch first thing tomorrow morning. I'll fly over there now."

She closed her eyes, trying not to cringe as he dropped a quick kiss on her forehead. "I'll be back later," he promised, sounding just like his old self. "I want you to wait here for me. Don't go out. Don't leave this house. Promise me?"

She nodded numbly. "I promise."

"Good." He smiled, satisfied. "I shall trust you this once then."

Phyl watched him walk to the door. He whistled for the dog. The long night and the drinking had left no marks on him. His face was smooth, smiling. In his expensive shirt and well-pressed jeans he looked every inch the rich, urbane man of the world.

He turned to smile good-bye at her. "Wait for me, Rebecca," he said as he closed the door.

~ 33 ~

*P*hyl listened for the sound of his car leaving before she ran to her room and began frantically throwing her things into her bag. She telephoned the airport and booked a seat on the next flight out. Then she called a cab and paced the floor nervously until it arrived. A silent Chinese servant appeared from nowhere to carry the bag for her, and she wondered, surprised, how he had known. He must have overheard, she decided, wondering what else the servants overheard in this house of secrets.

She hesitated at the door, thinking what Brad would do when he found her gone without an explanation. She decided to write him a note: "Brad, it's better if we do not see each other again. There is nothing I can do to help you."

She gave it to the servant and climbed quickly into the cab, looking over her shoulder through the rear window, half expecting to see him come tearing down the road after her with that vicious Doberman at his heels.

The flight was already boarding, and she took her seat. She breathed a sigh of relief when the doors were finally closed. She almost wept, realizing how frightened she had been. She didn't even want to think about the implications of Brad's confusing her with Rebecca. All she wanted was to sleep and wake up five hours later in San Francisco. And then she wanted to see Mahoney. She shivered with fright. *Oh, God,* she thought, *I really need Mahoney.*

It was a slow Sunday on the 8:00 A.M. to 4:00 A.M. shift. Mahoney figured the clock must have gotten stuck a couple of hours ago. He guessed he should be glad the drug dealers and the armed robbers and the domestics were giving him a break, but time was dragging.

He fiddled with the computer until Brad Kane's name came up again. He had replayed the details endlessly because there was still something about Mr. Hawaii that bothered him. And here he had confirmation that the man was violent.

The first incident had taken place in college. Brad had attacked another guy in a bar. Nothing unusual, you might say, for college kids with too much beer inside them. Except this had been a particularly vicious attack: a broken glass shoved in the other guy's face. Mr. Hawaii had gotten reprieved on that one because his father had hired him a smart lawyer. An undisclosed amount of damages had been paid to the victim, and Brad Kane had gotten a two months' suspended sentence.

A couple of years later he had been arrested for possession of an offensive weapon, a knife. He hadn't used it, but the victim said he had threatened to, and this time the victim was a woman. A hooker, in fact. In Honolulu. Again money changed hands and a warning was issued, and nothing more was said.

The third episode was more recent. A few months ago a servant in the Kane household had been killed. The report said that one of Brad Kane's dogs, a Doberman, had suddenly gone wild and attacked him. Brad

Kane had shot the dog himself, then had called the police. He told them he was devastated. The victim was an old man who had been employed by the family for more than fifty years. He said he had to leave on urgent business, but he would answer any questions on his return. And he had—a month later, when he came back from Paris. By then the old man had been buried, at Kane's expense, and the inquest was a mere formality. A sworn statement, an expression of regret, and that was it.

Mahoney sighed as he shut down the computer. One incidence of youthful violence after drinking might be dismissed. Two certainly were not. A third, inexplicable one was just too much in any man's life.

He considered calling Phyl in Hawaii and telling her what he had found, that he didn't like it, and to get the hell out of there. Just then the phone rang.

It was Phyl. There was a booming sound. "I'm calling from the plane," she said. "I need to see you, Mahoney."

"What's wrong?" he asked quickly. "Did he harm you?"

"No. I'm okay. My flight gets in around three."

"Why don't you come around to my place? I'll leave a message on your machine if I get hung up here."

"I need you, Mahoney."

"Glad to hear it, Doc. After all, we are here to serve." He could tell she meant it.

The phone rang again almost immediately. When he picked it up, an English voice said, "This is Nick Lascelles. I'm a friend of Bea French and Phyl Forster."

"How ya doin', Nick?" Mahoney replied breezily. "I've heard a lot about you from Bea. And I want to tell you all of it was complimentary."

"I can't get hold of Phyl," Nick said, "so I thought I'd better call you. We were doing some research, finding out about the villa. I guess Bea told you about it. Well, we found out the connection. She remembered the little boy in her dream was her father. He lived in that house until he was five years old. He took her back there when she was fourteen and told her the whole story. She's really upset, Detective Mahoney, because she also remembered her parents were killed in a car crash last year. He was the artist John Jones."

Mahoney gave a whistle of amazement. He knew and admired Jones's work. "I remember reading about it in the newspapers," he said. "It's a tough break. But what about the rest of her family?"

"There is none. She was left alone."

Mahoney wondered if that was one of the reasons she had lost her memory. It was surely a big enough trauma. "What about Mitchell's Ravine?"

"That's just it. She still doesn't know who tried to kill her. Or why. It's driving her crazy. She was terribly upset, but the children helped her, and she seems better now. Still, I thought I had better call you and let you know. Bea says you're a friend."

"Yeah. We're good buddies. Bea didn't seem to have too many friends when this happened, though. And it sounds as though they are a bit thin on the ground even now. What the hell, the girl is the daughter of a famous artist. Surely somebody would have missed her."

"She said she had just dropped out for a while after the funeral. She came back here to their farm in Provence. She wanted to be alone. I guess people respected that, so no one bothered her. Eventually she went back to the States, to their house in the Berkshires, and she doesn't remember anything else after that."

"Right. Give me her full name, Nick, and I'll get to work on it."

"It's Marie-Laure Leconte Jones. She was born in 1968, and the family's main home was the Old Mill, Faversham, Massachusetts. They spent their summers at their farm, Les Cerisiers, near Bonnieux in Provence.''

Mahoney nodded. ''Thanks for being there for her, Nick. Stick with her; she needs all the help she can get.''

He put down the receiver, switched on the computer, and drummed up the long list of names of women flying from warm countries into San Francisco International the week that Bea had been attacked. He scanned them quickly. They all were accounted for. He glanced through the long list again. That's when he caught it. The name had been marked checked off. Goddamn computers were not infallible. They made mistakes just as people did.

''M. L. L. Jones,'' it said. ''United Flight 511 from Honolulu. Dep.: 1800 hr. Arr. 2300 hr.''

Hawaii! Again. He whistled in surprise. Maybe lightning did strike twice in the same place after all. As he placed a call to the Honolulu Police Department, he wondered what the young recently bereaved Marie-Laure had been doing in Hawaii. He told himself it was probably just that she had needed a vacation. Still, it was worth following up, and he asked his colleagues in Honolulu to find out when she had arrived, what hotel she had stayed at, and anything else they considered relevant. Then he shrugged on his jacket, signed out, and went home to meet Phyl.

She was waiting for him outside his building. She had on no makeup, and there were deep shadows beneath her blue eyes.

''You look like hell,'' Mahoney greeted her.

''That's the way I feel.''

She fell into his arms, and he held her. ''Hey, Doc, what's going on?'' he asked gently. ''I know I'm a great-looking guy, but I didn't think I rated anywhere near as high as Mr. Hawaii.''

Her arms tightened around his neck. ''Don't even

mention his name," she said in a muffled voice, her face buried in his chest.

"That bad, huh?"

"That bad."

"I don't want to be the one to say I told you so. I already gave you my opinion."

"I know. And you told me not to see him again. I should have believed you," she said, following him up the stairs to his apartment.

"You should have believed yourself. Your gut and your head told you something was wrong. You just didn't want to acknowledge it."

She sank into a chair. "I admit it," she said, looking up at him repentantly. "How could I, of all people, have been so stupid, Mahoney?"

He shrugged. "It's easy. You just believed what Brad wanted you to believe. That's the art of a con man."

"He's more than that. He's very seriously mentally disturbed."

"Is that right?" He walked into the kitchen and began fixing coffee. "It might interest you to know that I've been doing a little research on Brad Kane myself. I can't say I was totally surprised to find he had a record." She looked at him with alarm. "Oh, nothing too serious," he said. "Just cutting up a kid with a broken beer glass in college and threatening a hooker with a knife. Nothing really truly bad. Yet."

"He scared me, Mahoney," she said.

"What happened?" He poured thick rich espresso into small cups and put them on a tray with a bowl of brown sugar.

"He called me Rebecca."

He glanced sharply at her. Then he grinned. "The mother?"

"It's not funny," she said defensively.

"You're damn right it's not. It's sicko, baby, that's what it is."

"He terrified me. He talked right through the night,

pacing the floor like . . . like a caged animal. He told me everything about his wicked grandfather and Jack and Rebecca.

"Oh, God, Mahoney," she wailed, "I think he's killed someone."

He handed her the cup of espresso. "Sugar?" he asked politely. She spooned some in, looking numbly at him. "Okay," he said, "first drink the coffee. Then tell me everything. From the beginning."

Phyl did as she was told, and for once Mahoney listened in silence. "So you think he killed this guy Monkey?" he asked.

She nodded. "What else could I think?"

"And you thought maybe he was going to kill you?"

"I don't know," she said helplessly. "He veered between rage and gentleness. I was afraid. You know, that gut feeling, the one you tell me I should listen to. I couldn't believe it. I looked at him, so nice-looking, so successful and—oh, I don't know. He's a man who has it all, I guess. And then I remembered what you'd told me. About murderers and the child abusers looking like regular folks, hiding their sins behind expensive clothes and a facade of normality.

"As a psychiatrist I understood what had damaged him. I understood about Rebecca. And I knew Jack was a bullying father, a man without a scrap of moral sense. I felt almost sorry for him, for a while. And then I realized it was too late. He had gone over the edge into his fantasy. Oh, he was able to keep up a perfect facade. No one would have ever guessed. And that's when I was afraid, because I knew he was capable of anything."

"You think he has confused you in his mind with Rebecca?"

"He has," she agreed quietly. "He swings between love and hate for her. But I know that the hate is winning."

"We've got ourselves a problem," Mahoney said. "Where is Mr. Hawaii right now?"

"After this night of madness," she said, with astonishment, "after letting it all out—something I swear he has never done before—he calmly says he has a meeting at the ranch. He'll fly there and be back later. The ranch comes first, whatever else is happening!" She shuddered. "Thank God he remembered, or I—I don't know what he might have done. . . ."

"So he's still in Hawaii?"

"Yes."

Mahoney grinned. "Pity. I thought I could ask you to stay the night here. For safety purposes, of course, just in case he showed up."

She laughed, despite herself. "Even you can't pull that one off."

Mahoney headed for the kitchen again. He took a chicken out of the refrigerator and began hacking it up with a cleaver. Phyl grimaced, and he grinned at her. "Don't worry. I'm just fixing us some soup. Meanwhile, just so you don't think things are all bad, here's a bit of good news. Bea has got her memory back."

Phyl's jaw dropped. "Oh, God," she cried. "And I wasn't there to help her. Again."

"She didn't need you," Mahoney said, searing the chicken in a copper-bottomed sauté pan and throwing in a fistful of chopped vegetables. "Nick was there." He told her what Nick had said.

"So there it is," he said finally. "Bea is Marie-Laure Leconte Jones. And by some strange stroke of fate, she flew from Honolulu to San Francisco the night she was attacked."

Phyl's eyes widened. "Of course it's a coincidence," she said.

"You know I'm a great believer in coincidence. Especially where crime is concerned." He handed her a glass of red wine.

"Poor Bea. Marie-Laure, I mean," she said sadly.

"She loses her parents, and then she's attacked by some madman. No wonder she blocked it all out of her memory."

"No wonder," he agreed, adding chicken stock.

"I'm going to France," Phyl said, heading determinedly for the phone. "I'm calling the airlines and getting the first flight out to Paris tomorrow."

"Of course you are, Doc," he said calmly. "But first you eat, then you call the airlines. The soup will be ready in ten minutes, and I bet you haven't eaten in twenty-four hours."

He was right. Mahoney booked her on a flight to Washington with a connecting flight to Nice. She realized with relief that the trip to see Bea would put thousands of miles between her and Brad.

Phyl looked at Mahoney. He was leaning against the window frame. Behind him was a panorama of brightly lit vessels skimming across the bay and the twinkling lights of the bridges hung like garlands in the sky. His arms were folded, and he was humming along with a Mozart aria playing in the background. He looked relaxed, at ease with himself and his surroundings, and Phyl thought of the contrast with Brad, pacing in her apartment like an enraged animal.

"What are we going to do about him?" Mahoney asked, reading her mind.

"Tomorrow I'll be gone," she said firmly. "I'll send him a letter and tell him I can't see him anymore. I'll recommend a therapist in Hawaii. Perhaps by the time I get back he will have come to terms with it."

Mahoney glanced at her skeptically. "You really think so?"

Wearily she reached for her jacket. "Let's hope."

He drove her home in tired silence. "I wish I were coming with you tomorrow," he said as he dropped her off.

"Me too." She looked at him wistfully.

"Remember to take care of yourself as well as Marie-

Laure. I'm not sure which of you needs looking after more." He kissed her lightly on each cheek and watched until she disappeared through the doors. Then he gunned the Mustang down the empty street.

Riding up in the elevator, Phyl wished she had the cat with her. She hated the idea of the empty apartment, but Coco was staying at Mahoney's until she got back from France. As she unlocked the door, she remembered how she used to treasure her privacy. Now she recognized it as loneliness.

The apartment was in darkness, and she hesitated. She could have sworn she'd left a lamp on. She always did. She felt a prickle on her neck as she peered into the darkened foyer, sliding her hand along the wall to the light switch. And then her hand connected with someone else's warm flesh.

His arms were around her, and one hand was clamped across her mouth as he kicked the door shut. "You left me again, Rebecca," Brad whispered harshly. "Why did you do that? When you know how much I love you?"

He switched on the light. She spun around, staring at him in horror. "How did you get in here?" she demanded.

He smiled coolly, holding up a key. "I had yours copied when you were in Hawaii," he said calmly. "I wanted to make sure I could reach you anytime. Day or night."

His eyes held hers like a stoat mesmerizing a rabbit. He was immaculate in a blue cashmere blazer and chinos and tasseled loafers—the perfectly turned-out gentleman. But behind the gold-rimmed glasses, his pale eyes were not smiling. They were icy and withdrawn, and she knew he was living out the fantasy in his head.

"I'm sorry if I startled you," he said. "God, look at you, you're shaking." He stepped toward her, arms outstretched. Instinctively she backed away. "Oh, come on, Rebecca. You know I'm no good at saying I'm sorry. I came here to take you home, that's all. You know you're always happiest at Diamond Head. And I want you with me. I don't ever want you to leave me again.''

Phyl edged toward the bedroom. Her terrified eyes were fixed on his. "Don't walk away from me," he said with a puzzled smile. "You know you love me. I just want to hear you say it."

She was almost at the bedroom door now. Her heart was pounding like a marathon runner's. If she were quick enough, she could shut the door and lock him out. She thought longingly of the bedside telephone and Mahoney. . . .

"Say it, Rebecca," Brad said, walking toward her. "Say it, my darling. Say you love me. Tell me you will never leave me."

Her limbs had turned to stone. She was frozen with fear as he came closer. The smile had gone, and his eyes were cold.

"Brad," she said desperately, "this is no good. Of course, I care about you. You are my friend." She took a quick step backward, holding up her hands to ward him off. He was as tense as the Doberman, and she was afraid to say the wrong thing, afraid to trigger his madness.

"More than friends," he said as she took another cautious backward step toward the bedroom. "A love like ours is forever, Rebecca. You know that."

She could see the door handle from the corner of her eye. *One more step*, she thought, *just one and I'm safe. Then I'll call Mahoney.* She leaped suddenly for the door and slammed it behind her, sobbing with fear. But it would not close. She looked down and saw his foot in its expensive tasseled loafer, and she heard him laugh as his hand, then his shoulder came through the gap.

The door flew open, and she crumpled to the floor. She put her head in her hands, sobbing great gasps.

She could feel his eyes on her, but he said nothing.

Finally she peeked through her fingers at him. He was looking at her; his arms were folded, and his face was expressionless. Suddenly he knelt on one knee next to her and took her hand. "I can't let you reject me again, Rebecca," he said gently. "Not again."

He pulled her to her feet, looking sadly at her. "Poor girl," he said softly, "poor beautiful girl." He smoothed her wild hair gently back from her face, gazing intently at her. Then he took both her hands in his.

"Brad," she said desperately, "you mustn't call me Rebecca. I'm Phyl. Remember? I'm the doctor. The one you like to talk to."

"The witch doctor," he said. "I remember."

"Rebecca was your mother, Brad. You told me everything about her."

"Not *everything*," he said levelly, and his voice sent shivers down her spine.

He was still holding on to her hands. His grip was like a vise, and she imagined his hands on her throat, squeezing the life out of her. *Killing Rebecca.* She fought back the wave of terror, fighting to keep her wits about her. The only way she could win was to try to talk him out of it.

"We have to talk about this, Brad," she said, speaking slowly, trying to keep the tremor out of her voice. She had to let him know that she was in control, that she was the one who called the shots. It was her only chance.

"You told me I was your confessor, and now I want you to tell me everything about Rebecca. I am here to help you, Brad, you know that."

"You betrayed me," he said, gripping her tighter. "You promised you would stay. You know you should not have done that, Rebecca." He bent his head and kissed her on the lips, drawing her passionately to him.

Phyl went limp in his arms; she trembled with the urge to scream, to push him away. He lifted his face from hers and stared into her eyes.

"Brad, please, I have to talk to you," she said quickly. "I'm just so tired . . . I feel so awful. . . ."

He swung her into his arms and carried her to the bed. He gently laid her down and sat beside her. There was a puzzled frown between his brows as he picked up the pillow and turned to her.

She stared at the pillow in his hands and knew what he meant to do. Her eyes were dark with terror.

"Why do you look so frightened, Phyl?"

She gasped as she realized he had called her by her own name; he had remembered who she was. She cast around frantically for a way to get him out of the apartment. "I'm so hungry, Brad," she said quickly. "Why don't we go out for a bite? You must be starving, too. We could go to Il Fornaio. You know you like their tiramisu. We could talk this over sensibly. I want to help you, Brad. I promise I'll do everything I can."

She saw the doubt in his eyes. "You promise you won't leave me again?" he said, stroking her arm rhythmically.

"Yes, yes. I promise." She stared breathlessly at him, waiting, praying for him to say yes.

The telephone suddenly shrilled, shattering the silence. Phyl's eyes fastened on the phone. Her lifeline. "I'd better answer it," she lied quickly. "I was expecting someone to call. My—my colleague. If I don't answer, he'll wonder why."

Brad held up his hand. He shook his head as he looked at the telephone, still ringing on her bedside table. She was overcome with frustration and fear. She'd almost had him convinced, almost got him out of there. . . . Oh, God, who the hell was calling her?

The ringing stopped, and they sat motionless in the deepening silence. Brad was still staring at the night table, and she wondered if he was going to pull the phone from the wall. Instead he picked up the photograph of Marie-Laure. It was the one Phyl had taken before she left for New York, looking sweet and pretty, with her cropped head and wide, scared eyes.

Brad held the photograph under the light, studying it for a long time. "How do you know her?" he asked in that "other" voice.

"She's my patient. The one I told you about, with the lost memory. I told you she had become a friend."

"What is her name?"

His eyes were hooded, and she saw the tremor in his hand holding the picture. She said, puzzled, "Her name is Bea French."

"French?" He glanced at the girl in the picture and then back at her. "Are you sure?"

"Well . . . no. I forgot she just got her memory back. She's Marie-Laure Leconte Jones." Phyl began to laugh hysterically. She knew she wasn't making sense. . . .

Brad stood up. He put the photograph in his pocket, and then he looked at her, lying on the bed, sobbing and laughing at the same time.

That remote look was back in his eyes. "Poor darling. You are overwrought and tired. Why don't you get some sleep now?"

She lay, frozen with fear, as he strode to the door. He looked back at her and smiled his old, confident smile. "There's something I have to do. Then I promise you everything will be all right. I'll be back in a couple of days. Why don't you plan on coming to Kalani with me this weekend? We can continue our discussion there. After all, Kalani is the center of my life, the soul of the Kane family. And I want to share it with you, Phyl. I want to share my whole life with you."

He was still smiling as he walked away. She heard his purposeful footsteps and then the click of the door latch. And then nothing.

Phyl lay still, too afraid to move. She strained her ears. Maybe he was trying to trick her. Maybe he was waiting for her behind the door, ready to grab her by the throat as she emerged. . . . She swung her feet cautiously to the floor. She listened again.

She tiptoed barefoot across the room, then flattened herself against the wall and peered around the door. She slid through, looking nervously around. He might still be hiding, waiting to grab her, waiting to kill her, finally. Her nerve suddenly cracked, and she screamed, running like a madwoman from room to room, flinging open doors. "You crazy bastard," she yelled, "come out, come out. . . ."

Finally she slid the bolts on the front door and sank, sobbing, to the floor. "Oh, dear God," she sobbed, "help me, help me. . . ." She dialed Mahoney's number, clutching the phone to her ear. It rang and rang. "Answer it goddammit, Mahoney," she groaned, "answer, please, please answer. . . ."

Mahoney swung the Mustang around the corner onto Phyl's street in a squeal of rubber, cursing as he saw the black Porsche speeding down the middle of the road toward him. He threw the Mustang quickly right, mounting the sidewalk and narrowly missing a fire hydrant.

"Jesus Christ, man," he snarled, staring angrily over his shoulder at the Porsche's disappearing taillights. Then he groaned as he realized he was looking at Brad Kane's car.

He leaped from the Mustang and ran across the road to Phyl's building. He put his thumb on the bell and left it there until the doorman, red-faced with anger, confronted him.

He flipped him his badge and said, "Dr. Forster. Is she home?"

"She is," the doorman retorted. "And one ring would have done."

"Not tonight," Mahoney said, striding across the soft carpet to the elevator.

"Wait, I have to tell her you're here," the doorman yelled. "It's the rules."

"No rules tonight, fella," Mahoney said. "Don't you dare pick up that phone."

He pushed the elevator button and then waited impatiently for the doors to slide shut. When he had called Phyl and she had not answered, he had been worried. He knew she was home, and he let it ring. When she still didn't answer, he wondered uneasily what was up. Something was wrong, he knew it. He wondered if Brad Kane had shown up, but Phyl had said he had been on his way to the ranch. He should have been back on Diamond Head. Then he had remembered. Brad Kane had a Gulfstream IV. He could be anywhere he wanted before anyone else had time to buy a ticket.

He strode from the elevator and rang Phyl's bell. He put his head to the door, listening. There was no sound, and he banged on the door. "Phyl," he yelled. "It's me, Mahoney. Open up."

She flung it open and hurled herself, sobbing, into his arms. "Mahoney, oh, thank God. Oh, Franco," she cried.

"Okay, okay. Take it easy, baby." He led her gently inside. "Was it Brad? Did he hurt you?"

Her shocked blue eyes met his. *"He was going to kill Rebecca,"* she said.

"What stopped him?"

"The phone rang. It sort of broke the spell, I think it brought him to his senses." Phyl's legs suddenly turned to jelly, and she sank helplessly onto the sofa. He looked at her white face. Then he inspected her meager stock of liquor and poured her a stiff bourbon.

"You look as though you need it," he said. "And I want you to answer some questions." She nodded, sipping the bourbon, looking trustingly at him.

"Did he assault you?"

She shook her head. "I mean, he grabbed my arms

and put his hand over my mouth, but he didn't hit me.''

"Did you let him into the apartment?"

"He was here when I got back. He took me by surprise.''

"Then how the hell did he get in?"

"He had my keys copied. He said he had taken them when I was in Hawaii.''

"What about the doorman?"

She shrugged. "I don't know. Yes, I do. You know the way Brad is. He looks as though he owns the place. He had been here before, and I guess the doorman knew he was a friend. He probably told him that I'd asked him to wait for me, that I had given him the keys. . . . I guess.''

She looked pleadingly at him. "What are we going to do?''

"Nothing much we can do. He gained illegal entry to your apartment, but he can always claim you gave him the keys. After all, you were friends. He can say it was just a lovers' tiff. We see them all the time, though not usually in apartments as fancy as this.''

"But he's *crazy*, Mahoney. He thinks I am his mother. He's in love with *her*—not me!''

Mahoney knew it, and that was what was worrying him. Crazy men were unpredictable. There was no way to know what Brad Kane's next move might be. "You said he left when the phone rang? Do you mean he just got up and split?''

She shook her head. "He had me on the bed. He took the pillow, I thought he was going to suffocate me. . . . I was trying to talk to him, to calm him. Suddenly he seemed to come to his senses; he remembered who I was. I wanted to get him out of here. I suggested we go and have something to eat, talk it over. Then the phone rang, and we both jumped. We just looked at it, listening to it ring and ring . . . and then it stopped. Brad was staring at the night table and I thought he was going to rip the phone out of the wall. But instead he picked up Bea's photograph.''

Phyl looked at Mahoney with bewilderment. "He asked me who it was. I had mentioned her to him once before and told him about her lost memory. I said her name was Bea French, and then I got confused because she's not Bea French anymore.

"And then Brad did something really strange. He put the photo in his pocket. He said there was something he had to do, and he would be back later. He said I should plan to go to Kalani with him this weekend and we could talk some more. Then he left."

"But why would he take Bea's photograph? Had he ever met her here?"

"Never. He never met Bea, I swear it."

Mahoney prowled the floor, his hands clasped behind his back, asking himself what Bea French or Marie-Laure had got to do with a crazy guy who had been in love with his own mother and had transferred that fixation to Phyl. He sighed, looking at her, sitting on the edge of the sofa, clutching the empty bourbon glass, with her knees together and her ankles buckled like a kid. He thought she looked terrible. Her face was totally drained of color, unless you counted the shadows under her eyes.

"Come on, sweetheart," he said, taking the glass from her. "You're coming home with me."

She smiled tremulously at him. "For safekeeping?" she asked, remembering how they had laughed earlier about the idea.

"Damn right, baby," he said, throwing her jacket over her shoulders. "You can have my bed. Coco will curl up behind your knees for company, and I'll be in the next room, making sure nobody disturbs you."

"Oh, Mahoney," she said, leaning against him as they went down in the elevator. "Whatever would I do without you?"

* * *

Four hours later Mahoney was still up. He was in his favorite place, leaning against the window frame, watching the fog rolling in great soft waves across the horizon until it finally blotted out the bridges and the landscape. The tabby's yellow eyes followed him as he began to pace the floor again. He wished he could put on some music, something sad and haunting and a bit kitsch, an aria by Puccini or Verdi. But Phyl was sleeping the sleep of the dead. Or *almost* dead, he amended. Thanks to his opportune telephone call.

The thing he didn't get was the Marie-Laure Leconte connection. Why would Brad want her picture? Maybe he had another fixation. Maybe he had multiple fixations. They were not dealing with a "normal" man here. Yet it was a fact that Marie-Laure had flown in from Hawaii that night. But that was the only link.

He decided to put Marie-Laure on the back burner. The important thing was, what was he going to do to protect Phyl? Brad Kane would be back, and then he was not going to take no for an answer.

He sighed as he finally threw himself onto the sofa and closed his eyes. It had been a long night. He would think about it later, when his brain was functioning again. In a few hours, he would put Phyl on the plane to France. At least there she would be safe, and it would give him time to find out more about Mr. Hawaii.

~ 34 ~

It was a beautiful morning in Cannes. A soft breeze rustled the palms, fluttering Marie-Laure's short hair as Nick drove the red Alfa convertible along the Croisette and then up through a maze of one-way streets.

"Where are we going?" she asked.

He just grinned and said, "It's a surprise."

He parked outside the City Art Gallery. "I think I know what the surprise is," she said.

"Bet you don't," he said.

He took her hand and they ran up the steps to the entrance. He walked her quickly through the galleries. "Close your eyes," he ordered finally.

"It's going to be one of my father's paintings, isn't it?" She smiled. "Of Nanny Beale, I'll bet."

"I told you, it's a surprise. Okay, now you can open them," he said quietly.

Marie-Laure stared at the full-length portrait of the plain, dark-haired woman in an unsuitable yellow silk dress. Her features were large, but she had a pleasant expression, and her long hair was caught girlishly back with a ribbon, though she was no longer young. Unsoftened by the artist's brush, all her uncertainty about herself was revealed in her somber deep-set brown eyes.

"Marie-Antoinette Leconte," she said quietly. "My grandmother."

"I found it quite by chance," Nick said. "I was hunting down pictures in the newspaper archives when I read about it. Isn't she exactly the way you imagined her? It was painted a few years before she met Archer Kane. Before he tried to make her over into his version of a twenties flapper with bobbed hair and short skirts."

"The saddest thing must have been that he took her dignity away." Marie-Laure sighed. "I'm glad she was painted like this, the way she really was."

They walked from the gallery back to the car with their arms around each other, still thinking about Marie-Antoinette Leconte. Then they drove to a favorite café near the marketplace for lunch and afterward to the jeweler's to buy an engagement ring.

"I want Phyl to be the first to know," she said happily surveying the diamond in its antique setting. "Let's keep it our secret until she gets here."

Brad Kane drove the sleek black Ferrari up the curving gravel drive of the Villa Mimosa. He knew Marie-Laure or Bea, as she was known, was out; he had seen her leave. And shortly afterward he had telephoned the housekeeper.

"My name is Johnny Leconte," he lied. "I am an old friend of Miss French from the States. I'm meeting her for lunch in Antibes. She asked me to pick up the children and bring them with me." The housekeeper hesitated, but he laughed with reassuring charm. "She said it will be a special treat, their first taste of the famous bouillabaisse."

He felt her relax as she agreed to have the children ready in ten minutes.

They were waiting on the steps for him, and he saw the boy's eyes widen as he looked at the car.

"Wow," Scotty yelled, "oh, wow, a real Ferrari! Oh, man!" He almost fell down the steps in his hurry to inspect the gleaming black monster. He ran his hand along the paintwork, peering at the sleek leather and wood interior and the glittering instrument panel.

Brad grinned at him. "Hop in, my friend," he said easily. "I'll show you how well she drives."

Jacinta came toward him, holding Julie by the hand.

"Hi," Brad said genially. "I'm Johnny. And I know you are Julie because Bea told me all about you."

Unsmiling, she stared at him. "Where is Bea?" she asked suspiciously.

"Didn't I tell you? She's waiting for you at the restaurant," Jacinta said, eyeing Brad and his expensive car approvingly. "Now you just go with Mr. Johnny, and have a good time."

Scott clambered excitedly into the Ferrari with Julie after him.

"Don't worry, I won't speed," Brad said, throwing Jacinta an easy smile. "I'll take good care of them," he promised as he revved the powerful engine and drove off in a spurt of gravel.

After a leisurely lunch Nick dropped Marie-Laure off at the villa. He knew she was still afraid of what she might remember about the night at Mitchell's Ravine, and he hated to leave her alone, but he had things to do. He told her that he would be back in an hour and that they would go together to meet Phyl at the Nice airport.

"I'm glad I found you, Nick Lascelles," she called after him as he drove off. He beeped his horn cheerfully as he rounded the bend in the drive and disappeared.

Marie-Laure felt good as she walked up the steps into the villa. Into *her* villa, she reminded herself with a

smile as she thought of Millie. There wasn't a single
day that went by that she did not think of her. The
Villa Mimosa was the best memorial Millie could ever
have had.

"Julie," she called, walking through the silent hall,
"Scott." But no one came running to welcome her.
She went out onto the back terrace. Shading her eyes,
she looked across the lawn at the pool, but that, too,
was empty. She circled back to the kitchen and asked
Jacinta where they were.

"But your friend picked them up, the way you asked
him to," Jacinta said.

Marie-Laure stared at her. "But Nick was with *me*."

"Not Mr. Nick. Your friend Monsieur Leconte came
for them in his big black Ferrari." Jacinta smiled. "The
children loved it. He told me you had sent him to collect them and they were meeting you for lunch at a
café in Antibes."

"Monsieur *Leconte*?" Marie-Laure's knees gave way,
and she sank weakly onto a chair.

"He said his name was Johnny Leconte," Jacinta
said, looking worried. "Is something wrong,
mam'selle?"

"It's him," Marie-Laure whispered to herself. *"He finally came to get me."* Panicked images flashed into her
mind as she remembered with sudden awful clarity the
man who called himself Johnny Leconte and what had
happened. Her heart lurched as she realized the past
had finally caught up to her. Brad Kane wanted her
dead, and now he had taken Scott and Julie. She knew
only too well that he was capable of murder and he was
using the children to get her.

The telephone rang, and she ran to answer it, praying it was Nick. She would tell him everything. He
would know what to do. He would help her. Jacinta
watched anxiously as she picked up the phone.

"The children want to say hello to you, Marie-

Laure," Brad said in that easy voice of his. "Or do you prefer to be called Bea now?"

A violent rage swept through her as she realized what he had done.

"Where are they?" she screamed. "Why have you taken them?" She heard him laugh. Then Scotty came on the phone.

"Hi, Bea," he yelled. "Your friend has a terrific car, and he even let me start it. When are you coming to meet us?"

"Soon, Scotty," she replied, her voice trembling with relief because he sounded so normal.

Then Brad said, "Here's Julie," and she could almost see him smiling. But she heard the edge of uncertainty in Julie's sweet little voice as she said, "Bea, why didn't you meet us for lunch like you said?"

"I . . . Julie, Nick and I got held up. I'll see you soon, though."

Brad got on the phone again. "I told her you would be here for dinner, for certain." He laughed lightly, easily. "Though, of course, I did not mention what might happen if you were not."

His voice had that remote freezing edge that she recognized, and Marie-Laure suddenly knew without a shadow of a doubt that this was the real Brad Kane she was talking to. The man with the mad obsession. A man crazy enough to kill.

Her heart felt like solid rock in her chest. "Where are you?" she asked.

"I'll give you directions. Get a pen and write them down," he said briskly. "Take the A-seven Autoroute du Soleil west, past Salon de Provence. Exit at Cavaillon and pick up the D-two, then the N-one hundred to Apt. Stop at the Café Saintons, three kilometers after the Gordes turnoff. Be there at six o'clock. Wait for my call."

She wrote it down. "What are you going to do with the children?" she asked shakily.

"My dear Marie-Laure, you know I have no interest in the children. They mean nothing to me. They are not part of this. Obviously you will tell no one about them—or us. You will not go to the police. That is part of our bargain. Otherwise I agree it would be a pity for such nice little children not to enjoy a long and happy life." He laughed softly. "The decision is yours, Marie-Laure."

"I'll be there," she said quickly.

"Wait at the café for my call. And make no mistake, if you have told anyone or brought anyone with you, I shall know."

The phone went dead, and she sat helplessly cradling it, wondering what to do. She thought of Nick's coming back to get her and of Phyl's arrival at the airport in a couple of hours. She remembered Scott's happily telling her about the beautiful black Ferrari and the wavering edge of uncertainty in Julie's voice. And she knew she could not tell anybody. She had to do as Brad said. And she had no time to lose.

She leaped to her feet, then realized she was going to meet a madman, a killer and had no weapon. There was no gun in the house, not even a hunting rifle. She saw the rack of sharp kitchen knives and quickly took one. *Not too big*, she thought, so she could hide it in her pocket. Then she realized with shock that she was thinking like a criminal. *Like a murderer.*

She read the scribbled directions again and realized she didn't need them. She knew exactly where Brad was. She crumpled the paper and threw it at the basket just as Poochie came gamboling in from the garden. He jumped enthusiastically at her, but she pushed him away. She put the knife in her purse, then ran outside and got in the Mercedes. Poochie's claws skidded on the marble hall floor as he ran after her. He stood at the top of the steps, his big, shaggy head cocked to one side, staring pleadingly at her. Marie-Laure hesitated. The thought of his company was comforting, and maybe it would be a good idea to have the dog there for the children. Because she had no idea what might happen to her. Or them.

She opened the door, and the dog bounded in beside her, barking joyously as they sped off down the gravel driveway. She wondered briefly how Brad had known about Les Cerisiers, then remembered the newspaper reports of her father's death had been full of details about the house in Provence where he did most of his work. It would have been easy for Brad to get directions. And she knew the roads of Provence as well as she knew her own face. It was Marie-Laure Leconte, not Bea French, who was setting off to meet her destiny for the second time.

At the San Francisco Police Department, Mahoney grabbed his first cup of coffee of the day. He paced the corridors, thinking about Bea—aka Marie-Laure Leconte Jones—still troubled by the idea that there was something he had missed. He poured another cup, then checked the files once again: the flight manifestos, the private planes. And there it was: the Gulfstream IV from Hawaii to San Francisco, piloted by Brad Kane on the night of the attack.

Mahoney sat back in his chair, thinking about coincidences and telling himself that in this case one plus one surely added up to two. It proved Brad had been in San Francisco at the time of the crime. And the man was crazy enough to kill. There *had* to be a connection; he felt it in his bones.

He put through a call to the Villa Mimosa. Nick Lascelles answered. "I'm glad I got you, Nick, instead of Bea," Mahoney said. "I wanted to ask her some questions, but it's tough over the phone because they are likely to upset her. I wanted to ask if she knows a man called Brad Kane."

"Brad Kane? I don't know if she knows him personally, but she certainly knows about the Kane family."

He quickly filled Mahoney in on the story of Johnny Leconte and Archer Kane and the Kanoi Ranch on Hawaii.

Mahoney tilted his chair back and breathed a sigh of satisfaction; he finally had his motive. And his man.

Then Nick said, "The thing is, though, I just arrived at the villa. I arranged to meet Bea, but she's not here. Nor are the children. The housekeeper said a friend of Bea's picked the children up earlier in a black Ferrari. And the weird thing is he told her his name was Johnny Leconte. She said when Bea got home, the man calling himself Johnny Leconte telephoned her. Jacinta heard Bea speaking to the children on the phone and arranging to meet them somewhere.

"Detective Mahoney, we're supposed to be picking up Phyl at the Nice airport right around now. Bea wouldn't just forget that. Phyl's coming here was important to her. She couldn't wait to see her. And who is this guy calling himself by Bea's father's name? I'm worried, sir, and I don't know what to do."

"Don't do anything," Mahoney yelled. "Don't make a move. Especially do not call the police. Let me take care of it. Go and meet Phyl and warn her. Tell her the guy is Brad Kane. Tell her I'm on my way."

Mahoney slammed down the phone. He contacted Interpol and alerted them to the situation. Then he called the FBI. International kidnapping came under its jurisdiction. He didn't even want to think about murder. Within the hour he was on a special flight heading for Washington. He would then take the Concorde to Paris, where another plane would be waiting to fly him to Nice. He prayed to God he would make it in time.

Phyl paced the terrace of the Villa Mimosa distractedly. Nick had filled her in on what had happened on the way back from the airport. Fear and guilt weighed on her heart as she thought of Bea and the children, alone with Brad Kane.

Nick was leaning against a pillar, staring blankly across the lawns. He finally threw his hands up in the air. "I can't stand just *waiting*," he said with frustration.

Phyl stopped her pacing and looked at him. Their eyes met, and she knew the same terrible thoughts were going around in his head.

"Why didn't Bea leave a note?" she cried. "At least give herself a chance?"

"Because Brad Kane had the children and he told her not to. That's the power of the kidnapper: the threat of what he might do." Nick didn't say it, but they both knew that Brad Kane was not an ordinary kidnapper; the ransom he was demanding was Bea's life.

"But she knew it was dangerous. She must have remembered what happened to her at Mitchell's Ravine. Oh, God, Nick, what can we do?"

"I'll ask Jacinta again, see if she remembers anything else," he said, heading for the kitchen.

"Tell me again *exactly* what happened, Jacinta," Nick said, keeping his voice gentle because the housekeeper was obviously distraught.

"I know now I should not have let the children go," Jacinta wailed. "But he was such a nice man, so friendly and so—so smart, and kind to the children. He did not look like a kidnapper—"

"Yes, Jacinta, I know that," he said. "Look, the police will be here soon to ask you some questions. But first I want you to tell me again *exactly* what happened."

"He telephoned," she said. "Mam'selle Bea answered. She spoke nicely to the children; it sounded normal to me. I heard her arrange to meet him. She wrote down some directions, and I went back to my cooking because I thought now everything is all right

. . . and then she left in the car. The dog jumped in beside her—"

"The directions, Jacinta," Nick said quickly. "Where did she write them?"

"On the pad, sir. By the telephone, here in the kitchen."

Nick grabbed the pad. The top page had been ripped off. Of course, Bea would have taken the directions with her . . . unless— He looked at the wastebasket, but it was empty. Then, on the floor behind it, he spotted a crumpled ball of paper. He pounced on it. "Autoroute du Soleil," he read, "exit at Cavaillon, D2 to N100. . . . 3kls G. exit . . . Café Saintons. . . ."

"My God, Phyl," he yelled, "I think we've got it."

"We must tell the police at once," she said quickly.

"No, Mahoney said not to. He said to do nothing. Just wait for him."

"At least let's leave a note for him," she said. "He has to know where we've gone."

They wrote the note with the directions and told Jacinta to give it to the first policeman to arrive. Then they took off in the red Alfa, following Bea's directions to the café in the village in Provence.

~ 35 ~

The Café Saintons was a typical roadside stop, set back a pace or two and up a couple of steps. There was a tiny iron-railed terrace with a couple of plastic tables and chairs and faded umbrellas emblazoned with the Kronenbourg logo. Inside was the usual cheap gray-speckled floor and zinc bar with a glass-covered plate of wilting commercial pastries and a couple of browning bananas.

The patron was leaning on the counter, reading a newspaper. He glanced up briefly as Bea walked in. She looked quickly at the few customers, but none of them was Brad Kane.

Bea ordered a brandy and asked for a bowl of water for the dog. The surly patron served her without a word and without bothering to remove the ash-laden cigarette from his lower lip.

Poochie slurped the water noisily, then settled himself under the table, behaving for once like a well-brought-up French dog. Bea gulped the brandy, her eye on the telephone by the counter, willing it to ring. When it did, noisily, a minute later, she almost jumped out of her skin. The patron dropped ash over the wilting bananas as he answered it.

Bea got up from her chair, gazing anxiously at him, but he was talking animatedly, obviously to a friend. She sank back down and checked her watch. It was five minutes to six. She eyed the patron nervously; he was throwing his arms about and talking about the Marseilles football team. He looked as though he might talk forever, and the six o'clock deadline was fast approaching. She stared at him, silently willing him to get off the phone.

He finally finished his conversation and began to serve another customer. Her eyes were riveted to the phone. She heard the minutes tick by on the big wall clock: six-one, six-two, three, four. On five it rang. And this time she got there first. *"Excusez-moi, monsieur,"* she said quickly to the patron, snatching the receiver, *"mais j'attends un coup de téléphone."*

He shrugged, watching her as he wiped the zinc with an old rag, then lit another Gauloise from the butt of the one in the yellow Ricard ashtray.

"You were on time," Brad said evenly. "And alone. I'm pleased to see you accepted my terms."

She sank onto a barstool, clutching the phone with both hands. "Where are the children?"

"They are here, with me." There was that smile in his voice again as he said, "I don't have to tell you where to meet me, do I? It's a place you know well."

She knew he meant the Leconte farm. "Les Cerisiers," she said.

"Wait for me there. If you are alone, the children will be released unharmed. You have half an hour."

Bea slammed down the phone. She flung money for the brandy on the counter and, without waiting for her change, ran down the steps and hurled herself into the car. Poochie barked excitedly as he jumped in beside her. She gunned the Mercedes and squealed onto the main highway almost under the wheels of a giant nine-

wheeler truck. She scarcely even heard the long blast
of its horn as she sped toward the Bonnieux turnoff.

Nick ignored the speed limits. It would normally take
him a couple of hours to Cavaillon, but tonight he cut
thirty minutes off that. It was a silent drive; both he
and Phyl were too worried to talk.

Besides, Phyl thought, staring out at the countryside,
they had discussed it endlessly. What more was there to
say?

They were cruising along the N100, searching for
the Café Saintons. In the deepening dusk they almost
drove past it. It was, after all, just an anonymous little
roadside stop like a hundred others along the route.
There were a couple of pickup trucks parked outside
and a blue Opel Rekord with German plates, but Bea's
white Mercedes was not there. Nor was the black Ferrari.

The patron lifted his eyes from the sports section of
his newspaper and looked at them sourly. *"Bon soir,
m'sieur, 'dame,"* he said, folding the paper and lighting
another cigarette. The other customers flicked interested glances in their direction as Nick ordered two
Kronenbourgs and asked the owner if he had seen a
red-haired young woman earlier.

The patron removed the beers from the refrigerator
and slapped them onto the zinc with a couple of damp
glasses. He shrugged indifferently. "It's possible,
m'sieur. Many people come in here; it is a popular
café."

Nick stared at him with exasperation. "A pretty
young woman, short red hair. She had a large brown
dog—"

"Ah, the dog. Of course, m'sieur, why did you not
say so?" He ground out his cigarette and wiped the
damp circles slowly off the bar with a wet rag. "She was
here," he said. "She was waiting for a telephone call.
After it came, pfff, she was off like a rocket. 'Out of

here,' as they say in the movies," he added in a terrible approximation of an American accent.

"Do you know where she went?"

"How would I know? I'm no mind reader."

Nick looked at Phyl. "There's only one place we can try. The family's summer home was near Bonnieux." He threw some money on the counter and grabbed Phyl's hand as they ran from the café.

The patron stared after them. He looked at the two untouched beers and the money. He glanced at the other customers and shrugged in disbelief. "Mad foreigners," he said, taking a swallow of the Kronenbourg and returning to the sports page.

They almost missed the Bonnieux turnoff, a narrow little road leading through flat fields of vineyards, then snaking steeply up to the village perched on top of the hill. It was dark when they finally got there. The steep cobblestoned streets were empty, and the medieval stone houses already shuttered for the night, but they found a couple of cafés open, and a gallery selling the works of local artists and craftsmen. And the proprietor knew where Johnny Leconte Jones lived.

"Everyone does, of course," he told Nick, regarding him suspiciously. "But he was a very private man. He needed his solitude for his art, and we respected that privacy. No one around here would tell you where Monsieur Jones lived."

"But it's urgent," Phyl said desperately. "His daughter, Marie-Laure, is a friend of mine. In fact, she is my patient. She needs help, I've come all the way from San Francisco to help her . . . please, m'sieur. . . ."

Bea sat on the terrace waiting for Brad. She had been there an hour, and there was still no sign of him. Now it was almost dark. Her stomach was tied in a thousand knots, and her heart thumped rapidly as a dozen different scenarios passed through her mind: the children bleeding, abandoned, shot . . . or maybe pushed over a cliff, like her. . . . "Dear God," she prayed, "just let him free the children, I'll do anything, just let them go unharmed . . . I promise."

She remembered the first time Brad had called her all those months ago. She had just returned home from France, where she had gone after her parents' funeral. She hadn't yet contacted any friends to let them know she was back, and she was in the middle of unpacking in the sad, silent house when he called.

"Hi, I'm Brad Kane," he said. "I don't know if you've heard about me, but I think I have some explaining to do. Some amends to make for the things my grandfather Archer Kane did."

She had recognized the name instantly, of course, from her father's story, and she had been on her guard. "How did you know about me?" she asked warily.

"I read your father's obituary in *The New York Times*, and I saw a photograph taken at the funeral in a magazine. I can't tell you how sorry I am."

He sounded so warm, so sincere she felt herself wanting to believe him. Still, she asked herself why he was calling now, after all these years. Her father had never wanted anything to do with the Kanes. "Let sleeping dogs lie," he had warned.

"Look, maybe this is a bad time," Brad said hesitantly. "I don't want to upset you. In fact, quite the opposite. I've been learning a bit about my own family history. *Our* history, Marie-Laure. After all, we are related. In fact you may be my only living relative."

And you may be mine, she thought with surprise.

"I need to get things off my mind, expiate my grandfather's sins. That's why I need to talk to you. Marie-Laure, the Kanoi Ranch is one of the largest in America. And half of it legitimately belongs to you. I'd like you to come out here to Hawaii and see it. See for yourself what your grandmother's money helped create. I think, I hope, she would be proud of it, despite everything. And I'd like to think Johnny Leconte's daughter would be, too."

"My father didn't want any part of the ranch. He didn't want to know anything about the past," she said passionately. "He hated Jack Kane."

"I know," Brad said sadly. "And with good reason. But I am not Jack. I am his son, and I have to live with the guilt. Please, for my sake as well as yours, Marie-Laure, won't you allow me to make amends? Don't let me go on feeling all this guilt. At least come and see the ranch. Maybe you'll even fall in love with it."

He sounded so nice, as though he really wanted to see her. In her loneliness the thought of Hawaii and the ranch was tempting. It would be fascinating to see the place where her father had grown up. Perhaps Brad was right; perhaps they could finally make up for all the past evil. She forgot her father's warning and went.

A sleek Gulfstream IV was waiting in San Francisco to fly her to Honolulu, and then a small two-engine Cessna took her the short last hop to the ranch. Brad was waiting for her at the airstrip, and she was surprised to see how handsome he was. She hadn't known what to expect, but she remembered her father had said the Kane men were blond and good-looking, and she thought Brad must look like them. He was wearing jeans and a denim work shirt and boots, and as she shook his hand, she told him that he looked like a real working rancher.

"Of course I am," he said, looking deep into her eyes. "Your photograph did not do you justice," he added. "I didn't expect anyone as pretty as you."

He was so relaxed she felt instantly at home. They drove up the long avenue of banyans to the little ranch house built by Archer Kane. He showed her the flower gardens and the sprawling acreage with the pedigree herds of the finest cattle. He took her to see the little town built by the Kanes for the paniolos and their families and the school and the medical facility and the church that Kane money had built.

"Just so you don't go on thinking we were all bad," he said lightly, smiling at her. "And so you'll know that your grandmother's money was put to good use."

At the end of the long day they drove back to the airstrip. As they climbed back into the Cessna, he said casually "And now I'm taking you to Kalani."

Kalani. The beautiful, terrible island where her father had been kept prisoner for ten long years. Brad saw what she was thinking, and he leaned over and took her hand. "Marie-Laure," he said gently, "let's both go and exorcise our ghosts."

Brad piloted the Cessna himself. He circled the island, pointing out the twin volcanic peaks, the great cliffs on the northeastern tip, and the forested gulches, and the meadows with the contentedly grazing prize Herefords. In the Jeep on the way to the lodge, Marie-Laure tried to imagine the skinny little "Monkey" and his lonely life here. There had been happy times, her father had told her, when Jack and Archer were away and he was left alone with Maluhia and Kahanu. And then he had discovered painting, and that had given new meaning to his life.

The lodge was a long, low white house with a palm thatch roof. "It doesn't look much different from when your father lived here," Brad said easily as a Chinese servant came running down the steps to collect her bag. "In fact, I've put you in his old room. I thought you would like that."

She threw him a grateful glance; he seemed to think of everything.

Her father's old room was small; there was just enough space for a narrow brass bed and a night table. A braided blue rug covered the dark wood floor, and some old black-and-white photographs of Kalani hung on the walls. French doors led out onto the lanai and the glorious view of the gardens and the ocean.

Marie-Laure lay down on the bed. She put her hands behind her head, staring out at the lawns and the palm trees and the ocean. Her father must have lain here, just this way, looking at the very same view, and praying that Jack Kane would not come back. How many mornings, she wondered, had the little five-year-old boy woken in that familiar haze of misery, wondering what fresh torture Jack would have in store for him that day? How many nights had he lain here wondering how he could escape. *Wondering if he would ever escape.*

Yet from all that madness, all that violence, Brad Kane had emerged unscathed. He was gentle, and good, and sympathetic. He understood that what Archer and Jack had done was wrong. She was smiling as she showered, anticipating the evening ahead, and it occurred to her that she hadn't felt like smiling since her parents died. Perhaps it was good that she had come to Kalani after all. She put on a simple cream silk shirt and long black skirt and the new red sandals she had bought on an impulse in Avignon just last week. She hesitated at the door, looking back at her father's old house with a sudden flash of doubt, remembering his words of warning. She was looking forward to seeing Kalani, but she still did not want anything from Brad Kane.

He was standing on the lanai, leaning against the rail with a drink in his hand, watching a pair of red cardinals greedily pecking scraps from a dish. Two enormous black Dobermans crouched on either side of him, their burning eyes fixed on the birds.

"Don't worry," he said, seeing her look of horror. "The dogs are well trained. They won't go near the cardinals. Unless I give them the word, of course."

"But you won't," she said anxiously.

"Of course I won't. The birds come every night to be fed, just as they have done for decades. Your father would have known them well."

He poured her a glass of champagne and said, "I

think this merits a toast. To the reunion, finally, of the Lecontes and the Kanes." He raised his glass and touched it to hers. "To us, my dear Marie-Laure. The survivors."

"To us," she repeated, wondering uneasily what her father would have thought.

Brad was the perfect host. The dogs sat docilely behind his chair as they ate the simple meal of freshly caught mahimahi and he talked to her about the history of the ranch and about Kalani. He told her the story of Archer's Hawaiian first wife and how the island she had named Kalani—Heaven—was their wedding gift and became the cornerstone of the ranch and the Kane family fortune.

"And half of that fortune is now yours," he said, holding her eyes with his own.

She could see he meant it, and she was touched. She reached out and took his hand across the table. "I don't need it, Brad," she said. "I don't want it. The past is the past. Kanoi Ranch belongs to you. Besides, I can see how much you love it, and it means nothing to me."

"You are very generous, Marie-Laure," he said, with an odd little smile.

"It's not generosity. My father felt that his inheritance blighted his life. It was the cause of his unhappiness, and he wanted nothing to do with it. Nor do I." She hesitated. "Except perhaps for the Villa Mimosa."

Brad threw back his head and laughed. "I offer you half the Kanoi Ranch and you tell me all you want is the Villa Mimosa. Do you know, I've never even seen it?"

"I have. Just once," she said. "It's beautiful. Kalani is your place, but the villa belongs to my family. It was my grandmother's house; my father was born there. He was happy there, for a while, until . . ." She didn't want to say any more. Brad Kane knew the story of

Johnny Leconte's abduction from the Villa Mimosa just as well as she did.

"Then of course, it is yours," he said abruptly. "And now I'll say good-night, Marie-Laure. I have some paperwork to do."

"Good night, Brad," she called after him, puzzled as he strode away. The two huge black dogs followed silently at his heels, like shadows.

She slept soundly that night in her father's old room. The soft slap of the waves hurling themselves onto the shore lulled her dreams. And when she woke and saw the pearly dawn sky and the flocks of brightly colored birds chirruping outside her window, she smiled and thought that Lahilahi had named her island well. It was truly "heaven."

A Chinese servant brought a tray with hot coffee and rolls. The tropical colors of the sliced fresh fruits looked like a jeweled mosaic on a plate.

Curiously she asked the servant how he had known she was awake.

He smiled mysteriously. "We always know, missy," he said, busily setting out the dishes on the table on the lanai.

He looked frail and thin as a reed in his white cotton mandarin jacket and black trousers, and though his delicately boned face had almost no lines, Marie-Laure knew he must be very old. She asked him how long he had worked for the family.

"For many years, missy, since I was a young man," he said clasping his hands and bowing his head courteously. "First I worked a long time for Mr. Jack at Diamond Head. Then, after he died, for Mr. Brad. And now, when I am an old man, I stay here mostly on Kalani. Mr. Brad says it is easier here for me." He smiled mischievously at her. "He want me to retire, but I say no. No retire. Like your father, I work till I die."

Marie-Laure laughed and asked him his name. He told her it was Wong. "Is not my real Chinese name, missy. Mr. Jack gave it to me. He said he could not pronounce my real name. So now I am Wong.''

Marie-Laure suddenly realized that she was with someone who had actually known Jack Kane personally. Someone other than his son, that is. Didn't people say servants always knew everything? If anybody did, this old Chinese man would know the truth about her father's torturer.

She said, "What was Mr. Jack like, Wong? Was he a bad man?''

The old Chinese hesitated, his head bowed. "Mr. Jack was proud man, missy,'' he said finally. "He very proud of the Kane name. Sometimes he good man, sometimes bad.'' He sighed. "Sometimes very bad. But I am only his servant. I see everything, but I say nothing.'' He looked up at her and said, "I no speak bad of a dead man.''

He bowed again, and she watched him walk slowly away. "Wong,'' she called after him. He turned and looked at her, his hands folded patiently. "Did you ever know the boy they called the Monkey?''

He shook his head. "No, missy. I never did.''

Brad came toward them, the dogs, as always, following at his heels. "Marie-Laure, good morning,'' he called cheerfully. "I hope you slept well.''

The dogs crouched obediently on their haunches as he smiled down at her. "I'm sorry but something has come up. I have to return to Honolulu. I had hoped we could spend a couple of days here, but I'm afraid it means we have to leave this morning.''

He shrugged irritatedly. "It's business. Otherwise I wouldn't do this to you. After all, you've only just arrived on Kalani. Never mind. At least you got to see it. And perhaps you'll find Diamond Head even more to your liking.''

Wong and one of the dogs, Makana, flew with them to Honolulu. The dog lay quietly at Wong's feet until

the plane began its descent into Honolulu; then it began to howl loudly.

"Quiet, Makana," Brad yelled from the cockpit.
"Wong, shut that dog up."

Wong patted its big head and said something in Chinese, and the dog stopped its howling though it still
trembled nervously.

"No matter how many times that animal flies with
me he always howls when we're landing," Brad said
impatiently. "Wong has spent as much time with the
Dobermans as I have. He practically brought them up.
He is the only other person they answer to besides
me."

Marie-Laure thought that the tiny Chinese must
weigh half what the Doberman did. One leap and he
would have been flattened on the ground.

"You don't control a dog like that by force," Brad
told her, reading her mind. "The secret is in their
training. They are ruled by commands."

Marie-Laure thought of the exuberant joyous retriev-
ers that had been her own family pets, and she felt a
pang of sympathy for Makana.

The Kane helicopter was waiting in Honolulu to take
them to Diamond Head, while Brad went downtown to
his meeting. "Wong will make sure you have everything you need," he assured her, waving good-bye.
"Just make yourself at home."

Marie-Laure stared down, amazed, as the helicopter
hovered over the Diamond Head house. It was a dream
mansion enfolded in tropical greenery, with fountains
and flamboyant blossoms and a cobalt blue pool that
seemed to slide over the edge of the great black cliffs
into the huge green foam-flecked breakers combing
the Pacific.

Wong escorted her to her room, but he looked so
old and tired she would not allow him to carry her
shabby green canvas bag. She followed him, glancing

admiringly at the paintings and other works of art they passed.

"This was Mrs. Kane's room," Wong told her, flinging open a door. It was a big, beautiful, light-filled room with a view across the tree-studded lawns to the sea. Wong took her bag and put it in the biggest closet Marie-Laure had ever seen.

"Madame must have liked clothes," she said with awe. "Wong, do you mean Brad's mother?"

"Yes, missy. Her name was Rebecca. She was very beautiful. There is a portrait of her in the dining room. And all the others. Mr. Archer and his second wife, and Mr. Jack."

Marie-Laure couldn't wait to see them. Wong showed her around, proudly pointing out the family portraits, but he didn't need to tell her who they were. Her father had described that cruel, arrogant face and that look of icy indifference so well she would have known Archer Kane anywhere. She could understand why poor, vulnerable *la célibataire* had fallen for him, though; he was certainly a handsome, virile-looking bastard.

Jack Kane's blue eyes stared mockingly at her, just the way he must have looked at her father. "You thought because you were a Kane, you were king of everything," she whispered to him. "But you didn't win in the end, Jack. All you got was the money."

Rebecca was even more beautiful than she had imagined, glamorous and glittering with emeralds and arrogance. It must have been a family trait, she thought, amazed; even the wives had it. Chantal did, too. The artist had caught the curl of her lip, the impatient hauteur in her eyes, though Marie-Laure thought there was a hint of self-mockery in there somewhere.

Marie-Laure felt better as she turned away from those long-dead faces. It was good that she had come here and confronted the ghosts of her father's life. She believed he would have approved of that.

She went back to her room and found a maid unpacking her bag, and she was forced to smile when she
saw her T-shirts, a dress, a skirt, and a couple of shirts,
hanging forlornly in the vast closet. Her simple things
were just not up to the grandeur of their surroundings.
Rebecca's closet needed haute couture and hatboxes
and Vuitton steamer trunks, not an old green canvas
duffel from L.L. Bean.

She put on a bathing suit and swam laps in the magnificent pool. Then she lay on a beautiful bamboo
chaise under a shady umbrella, sipping iced tea
brought by another slippered Chinese servant, and
thinking about Brad.

He was behaving very well toward her, she told herself. He couldn't be more hospitable, more sympathetic, more generous, offering her half the Kane
ranch. Then why did she still have this sneaking feeling
that something was wrong? *Why* was he being so nice?
She kept remembering what her father had told her
about all the Kanes: that the only thing that mattered
in their lives was the Kanoi Ranch and their name.
Nothing else counted. They had even killed to keep it.

Then *why* would Brad Kane suddenly offer to give
her half the Kane ranch? It was like offering her a half
share in his heart.

Suddenly uneasy, she sipped the iced tea. Brad Kane
was a hardheaded businessman. He was not a philanthropist or a born-again Christian or a madman. It just
wasn't in character. He knew exactly what he was doing. If he wanted to give her back part of the ranch, he
must want something in return.

Her father's words of warning repeated themselves
endlessly in her head, she could hear his voice telling
her, "Let sleeping dogs lie, in case they turn around
and bite you . . . again." Something was wrong. And
she suddenly didn't want to stay around and find out
what it was. She had to get out of there.

She ran back through the paradise gardens to Rebecca's room. She repacked her bag, took a shower, then put on a white T-shirt and jeans and her red sandals and went out onto the terrace to wait for Brad.

It was twelve-thirty when he returned. "It's good to see a pretty girl waiting for me when I get home," he said breezily, pouring himself a whiskey.

He offered her one, and she shook her head, wondering if she could be wrong after all. He looked so cool and handsome and suntanned and . . . rich. He looked as though he owned the world. *Then why,* that nagging little voice asked again, *does he want to give half of it to you?*

"You're very quiet, Marie-Laure," he said, watching her.

"I'm tired. I did a lot of swimming . . . laps," she replied evasively.

"I thought we would have lunch at the gazebo," he said. She could see a pretty white wooden folly at the edge of the cliff. He took her hand and pulled her to her feet, sliding a friendly arm around her shoulders as they strolled toward it with the Doberman at their heels.

The gazebo was built like a Hawaiian pavilion, a white wooden octagon, open on all sides, with a curved thatched roof that came to a point at the top. Heavy canvas curtains were swagged back between the posts ready to shut out the wind, and the view was tremendous: straight down the steep black cliffs to the rocks and the great, high-crested Pacific rollers gliding majestically toward them.

Wong was arranging dishes on a buffet, but Brad dismissed him, saying they would serve themselves.

For a moment, looking at the beauty all around her, Marie-Laure was tempted to believe his offer. These lovely gardens filled with heavy-scented tropical blossoms, the emerald lawns, the rolling ocean view. All she had to do was say the word, and half of this could be hers. But when she glanced at Brad, she caught a strange expression on his face, a distance and coldness that sent warning prickles up her spine.

"Come, let's eat," he said, with a quick smile. His expression was neutral again, and she told herself that she was just being silly, that she had just imagined that icy look.

She nibbled at a salad, and Brad did not seem to be hungry. He sat silently, drinking his whiskey, watching her.

Black clouds appeared over the sea, blocking out the sun, and a sudden strong wind whipped the waves into dark, foam-speckled mountains. She shivered, looking nervously at him in the deepening stormy dusk, wondering why he was so quiet. "Brad, I think I should leave in the morning," she said quickly. "You have been a wonderful host. Thank you for showing me the Kanoi Ranch and Kalani and for your generous offer. But I cannot accept. I just don't want any part of it."

He looked at her expressionlessly. Still, he said nothing, and Marie-Laure felt those warning prickles again. She thought apprehensively that even though Brad was looking at her, he didn't seem to be seeing her.

She got up and walked nervously to the edge of the gazebo. She leaned against the rail, looking out at the ocean, wishing she could think of something to say to break his strange silence. She turned to speak to him, to apologize again for her sudden departure. And then she saw the shotgun, lying on the chair behind him. It was a handsome weapon with a polished wooden stock ornamented with silver.

"That's a beautiful gun," she said, surprised she hadn't noticed it before. "But what do you shoot here?"

"Predators," he said viciously. "Sit down, Marie-Laure Leconte."

There was a sudden whiff of danger in the air, as tangible as the aroma of the whiskey. She froze, staring at him.

"I said, sit down."

There was an edge to his voice that made her obey. Her knees buckled, and she sank into the chair opposite him. "I'm sorry I can't stay any longer," she said, frightened, "but it's better this way. My father was right. I should not have come—"

"Be quiet," he snapped impatiently, "and listen to me, you silly girl." Her brown eyes widened with shock. "Of course you are right," he said in a remote voice. "You should not have come here. And your father should not have come here. Archer Kane should have killed him at the Villa Mimosa when he killed his mother. It would have been the best thing for all of us." He smiled coldly as he took another gulp of his drink. "And it would have saved me a lot of trouble."

"What do you mean?" Marie-Laure pushed back her chair. She got to her feet and edged nervously away from him. The Doberman gave a low growl and it glowered menacingly.

"You were stupid and silly to think I would give you even the smallest fraction of the Kanoi Ranch. You have seen it. You know that it belongs to the Kane family. That it was our hard work, our intelligence, our dedication, *our superiority* that made this place. All Marie-Antoinette Leconte and her son contributed was money. Not another goddamn thing. They didn't build this house; they didn't create Kalani; they didn't plant the avenue of banyans and build that little ranch house and the medical facility and the church and the houses for the workers. They did nothing, Marie-Laure."

He fell silent again, and she looked appeasingly at him. "I know that, Brad," she said quickly. "You have done wonders—"

"Jack was right," he said, as though she had never spoken. "He said he should have killed the Monkey that night on the island when they had the fight. He should have stuck that knife into his heart and been done with it. He regretted it all his life. He said to me,

'I know in my bones he is still out there somewhere, like a coiled rattlesnake waiting to strike. He will try to take that fortune from us one day, son. He will want to take everything the Kane family has worked for all these years: our sweat and toil, our land, our heritage. *Our name.* Make no mistake, he will come to claim his fortune, and when he does, we must be ready to act. Quickly and without mercy.' ''

Marie-Laure drew a sharp frightened breath as Brad slammed down the empty glass. He stood up, towering over her.

"My father is dead," she cried. "He never wanted anything to do with Kalani and the Kanoi Ranch. He never wanted to come back here. He didn't want anything from the Kane family."

"But *you* are not dead, Marie-Laure. And one day *you* will get to thinking about things. About this rich ranch and this beautiful house and Kalani and all that money. And you will go to a smart attorney with your story and your claim. You'll want more than half then, Marie-Laure. You will want it all. And you see, I cannot let that happen."

"You're crazy," she cried, stepping backward away from him. "I told you I don't want anything from you. I don't want the Leconte name ever to be associated with the Kanes. My father was right about you. You live above the law; you have no morals; your grandfather killed his wife to get his hands on her money, and he would have killed Johnny, too, when he was eighteen. I should never have come here. I should not have listened to you. I should have trusted my father."

Purple lightning zigzagged suddenly across the midnight dark sky. "It's too late now," Brad said. He leaned against the rail with his arms folded, watching her under hooded lids.

"I was going to leave tomorrow," she said, edging toward the steps. "But I think it's better if I go now."

His cold, bitter laugh followed her as she hurried

down the steps, freezing the blood in her veins. She
started to run. She heard Brad shout a command, and
she glanced over her shoulder. "Kill," he cried again.
And then she saw the Doberman, a fleet black arrow in
the stormy darkness, racing toward her. She screamed
and flung up her arms as the powerful dog launched
itself at her. She felt a searing pain as its jaws clamped
down on her arm. Then she heard Wong shout.

"Down, Makana," he yelled at the dog, and ran
toward her. "Drop it. Down, you bastard dog."

The dog let go on command, and Wong flung himself between her and the animal.

"Kill," Brad yelled again, running toward them
through the dark and rain with the shotgun in his
hands.

The Doberman grabbed the old Chinese man by the
throat and sank its teeth deep into him.

"Oh, God, oh, God," Marie-Laure screamed. The
old man was on the ground, and the dog was tearing
his face to pieces. There was blood everywhere, spurting from the big artery in his neck. A shot rang out,
and the dog lifted its bloody mouth from the old man.
It stared for a moment at her, then gave a thin, un-
earthly wail. Its burning red-brown eyes glazed over, its
legs crumpled, and it slid in slow motion to the
ground, beside Wong's body.

Fear lent wings to Marie-Laure's feet, and she took
off down the slippery path, waiting for the shot that
she knew would send her into eternity, too. Nothing
happened, and she glanced back over her shoulder.
Brad was standing in the pouring rain over the two
bodies. She saw him throw the shotgun aside and kneel
beside them. "Oh, God," she heard his anguished cry,
"look what they have done now." He raised his head to
the sky, howling his agony.

She fled down the path toward the house. She had
to get out of here as fast as she could . . . she would
go to the police . . . tell them her story . . . tell

them he was a madman. . . . Even as she thought it, she knew it would not work. They would look at Brad Kane, the gentleman rancher who owned a good part of the islands, whose family had lived here for generations. And they would look at her, a hysterical young woman with some wild story about an attack, and she knew whose side they would take.

She started running down the drive to the gates; then she remembered that her money and her credit cards were in her room. She dithered helplessly; she could not get far without them.

She looked back toward the house and saw the servants running, heard their cries of distress and guessed she had a few minutes' grace. She ran to her room, grabbed her pocketbook, and fled back through the gardens down to the gates. The guard had heard the shot. He had run to see what the trouble was, leaving the gates unguarded. She pressed the electronic device that opened them and slid through. Then she began to run down the hill, jogging steadily in the rain, her heart thudding in her throat.

It seemed ages before she saw a gas station, and she began to slow down. She checked her watch. She had been running for twenty minutes. He wouldn't dare come after her in a public place, she thought, fumbling in her bag for a coin.

She went to the pay phone and called a cab. Then she went into the washroom and cleaned herself up. Her arm was bleeding, and she washed it, then took off her T-shirt and wrapped it around the wound. She put on a light sweater to hold the improvised bandage in place. She rinsed her face with cold water and combed her wet hair and then went back outside to wait for the cab.

Her throat was parched from running, and she got a Coke from the machine and sipped it, still trembling inside. She thought of Brad's grieving face as he looked down at Wong and his wild, agonized howl.

And she remembered the dying dog, its eyes glazing over, sliding in slow motion to the ground. She knew that Wong had saved her life, and because of him, Brad would not be coming after her. Not yet.

The cab circled into the court, and she ran toward it. She climbed in thankfully and leaned back against the cushions.

The next United flight left in two hours. Two hours! It stretched in front of her like eternity. She bought a ticket and hurried from the counter, hiding herself in the crowd, watching, waiting. But there was still no sign of Brad Kane when at last her flight was called.

She breathed a sigh of relief when she finally boarded the plane and took her seat. Now she was safe.

And then she arrived in San Francisco. And Brad was there, waiting for her.

Now, sitting on the terrace of her family's beautiful old farm in Provence, Bea wondered how she could have ever thought she would be safe again. Brad Kane was obsessed with the Lecontes. He was crazy. She had not realized how fast he would act. And how silently. She had not known that he was in the Gulfstream and on his way to San Francisco before she had even boarded her United flight. She could not have known that he was a man who could buy anything he wanted and that he would know where to go to get what he needed— the syringe with the fast-acting anesthetic that would safely put her out for hours, for instance—so he could kill her and make it look like an accident. And then the Kanoi Ranch would finally be only his.

She felt his presence before she saw him. There had been no sound; he was just suddenly there, a deeper shadow against the blackness. She saw the glow of his cigarette as he put it to his lips.

"So, Marie-Laure," he said in that quiet, flat tone, "we meet again."

Poochie bristled and lurched to his feet. He growled and showed his teeth warningly.

Brad laughed. "I hope you haven't brought that mutt here to defend you. Somehow I don't think he's the right breed."

"Where are the children?" Bea asked quickly. She was amazed that her voice sounded so calm. Now that she was seeing her killer face-to-face, she felt a hatred so intense it shocked her. But she had to keep a veneer of calm if she was to win. She had to know he had kept his word and they were all right.

"I kept my promise," he said. "They are in a taxi en route to the Villa Mimosa."

She peered warily into the dark, tracking his hand with the cigarette. "How do I know that's true?"

He shrugged indifferently. "I guess you will just have to trust me, Marie-Laure."

She saw him crush out the cigarette, and then he walked toward her. She put her hand in her pocket, gripping the sharp little kitchen knife. The sweat of fear stuck her hair to her head, and she trembled with hate for him and for Jack and Archer. They had gotten away with their crimes, but she wasn't going to allow Brad to get away with his. Not again. She would kill him first. She sobbed as she realized what she was thinking. Brad Kane was turning her into a killer, a murderer. No better than all the Kanes.

Then she saw the gun in his hand. Poochie gave another deeper growl. She could see his bared fangs gleaming, and she gripped his collar more tightly.

"We are going for a short ride, Marie-Laure," Brad said, ignoring the dog. "A little sight-seeing. Pity it's so dark, but then you must know these roads like the back of your hand." He took her arm and marched her to her car. He held the door open and indicated with the gun for her to get into the driver's seat. Poochie got in next to her, whining, not understanding.

Brad climbed into the back and said, "Okay, start

driving. Make a left at the T junction. You remember, where it begins to climb steeply."

Marie-Laure sensed the gun leveled at her head. She started the car and did as he said. Of course, she knew the place he meant. It was a lookout point where she had spent many a lazy afternoon, scanning the peaceful valley hundreds of feet below, watching the cars crawling like ants up the steep roads to the beautiful *village perché* on the opposite side; listening to the summer sounds of the birds and the crickets; feeling the sun-warmed rocks beneath her as she lay there, admiring the poppy fields spread like a red carpet that changed with the months to acres of lavender or sunflowers, and vines ripening under the hot sun, readying for the fall harvest. The lookout point was an even more precipitous drop than Mitchell's Ravine.

Her hands shook as she drove slowly up the hill, casting around wildly for a way to escape. She still had the knife, but it was no match for his gun. Goddammit, she told herself savagely, she wasn't drugged this time; she would fight for her life. . . . She was not just going to let him push her over the edge again. . . . He would have to shoot her first. . . .

It suddenly occurred to her that Brad could have shot her just now on the terrace, if he had wanted to. She had been a sitting duck. He could have saved himself all this trouble. But he had not. He didn't want to shoot her. That's why he'd had the Doberman attack her and why he had pushed her over Mitchell's Ravine. Because he didn't want it to look like murder. He still wanted it to look like an accident.

She stopped the car at the top of the road. "Drive to the edge," he commanded. She did as he said, then switched off the engine, waiting. Brad did not make a move, did not say a word. The silence was deafening. She imagined the gun pointing at her head, but now she was sure he did not want to use it. The familiar night sounds began to penetrate her consciousness:

the croak of tree frogs; the scurrying of nocturnal animals; the startled whir of disturbed birds. Somewhere, in the valley far below, she saw a car's headlights. She watched hopefully as they flickered, then disappeared. And then nothing. She was alone with Brad Kane.

She heard Poochie whine as Brad got out of the car. In the glimmering darkness she could just make out the outline of the gun, pointed at her.

"Why are you doing this?" she screamed, suddenly needing to understand. "I told you I don't want the ranch. I don't want the money. I don't want anything you've got—"

"You still don't see it, do you?" he said. "All his life Jack was waiting for the Monkey to come back and steal his land, to take his birthright from him. I'm only protecting my interests, keeping Kanoi for the Kanes. I cannot allow you or any future Lecontes to jeopardize that. It is, my dear Marie-Laure, time to redress the balance of things.

"I think this is the best way," he said, and she could see he was smiling at her. "We have to make sure this time, don't we?"

He opened the car door. He reached in and released the hand brake, started the engine, and put it in gear. Brad held her back with one arm as he reached for the accelerator. With a terrified scream Marie-Laure suddenly wrenched herself free. She hurled herself out the other door and Poochie leaped out after her, barking frantically. She lay stunned on the rough stony grass as the car lurched toward the precipice. It teetered for a few seconds on the edge, then slid over gently. She heard the terrible shattering of glass and the great rending of steel as it bounced from rock to rock down the steep slope—and then the huge explosion as it burst into flames. She would have been in that inferno if Brad had had his way.

Fear brought her to her feet, but Brad grabbed her from behind. He locked his arms around her and forced her toward the edge of the precipice. She screamed, endless throat-tearing screams, digging in her heels, clinging to the thorny branches in their path, scrabbling for a foothold on the loose stones. She had to get the knife, it was her only chance. She had to kill him before he could kill her. She heard Poochie's wild snarl and saw his black silhouette against the red glow of the inferno as the big dog hurled himself at her attacker, taking Brad by surprise and knocking both of them to the ground.

Marie-Laure rolled away and scrambled quickly to her feet. She saw Brad put the gun to the dog's side, and she kicked it out of his hand. She reached down to grab it, but he was too quick for her. He snatched it, then smashed it savagely down on the dog's head. Poochie gave a high-pitched yelp and fell back. Marie-Laure cried out with fear and anger as Brad grabbed her foot and dragged her once more toward the edge.

She kicked out at him and rolled away, but he was on top of her in a second. Then he was banging her head against the stones. The pain was intense, and she knew it was never going to stop. She was slipping away into unconsciousness, and she fought it. She couldn't let him win; she *would not*. . . . Somewhere in the back of her brain, over the noise of her own screams, she became aware of a new sound. Then suddenly there were lights and other people.

Brad was up on his feet in a minute, pulling her with him, holding her in front of him as a shield. Groggily she made out the half circle of gendarmes. Their guns were aimed at them, and dimly she heard Nick's voice shouting to her to "hold on." And then she slid backward down the familiar black tunnel into unconsciousness.

"Brad," Phyl called softly. "Brad, it's me."

He peered into the lights, puzzled. "Rebecca," he said in a harsh whisper. "What are you doing here? I thought you were waiting for me in San Francisco. We were going to Kalani. Remember?''

Phyl's numb heart felt as though it were no longer part of her body as she looked at him. This was not the charming lover she had known. It was not the urbane man of the world, the rich, handsome rancher, who had it all. She was looking at a stranger.

Taking a deep breath, she walked into the circle of light created by the cars' headlights. Brad was still holding Bea's limp body, and she could not tell if she was dead or alive.

"Let her go, Brad," she said softly, close to him.

His pale eyes searched hers as he said, "I had to do it. You know that, don't you? You, of all people, must understand."

"I do, Brad. I understand. But I think I know a better way."

She was shaking with terror. All it would take was one quick thrust and Bea would be over the edge.

Brad looked at the surrounding gendarmes. He seemed suddenly to come to reality. "It's too late now, isn't it?" he asked, looking at her searchingly.

She nodded, unable to speak. He was changing in front of her eyes, from the cold-blooded, mad hunter with his prey back to the easy, charming man she had known.

"And too late for us," he added softly. "If I hurt you, I'm sorry, Phyl. You were the only woman I might have loved."

He pushed Marie-Laure toward her. Then he put the gun to his head. His wild, mad eyes met Phyl's for a split second. "You traitor, Rebecca," he said viciously as he pulled the trigger.

Her own screams echoed in her ears as Brad's handsome blond head exploded into a thousand bloody fragments and he spun over the edge into the abyss.

~ 36 ~

Mahoney arrived at the Villa Mimosa early the next morning. They were sitting on the terrace, sipping lemonade, looking out over the sloping lawns, at the towering cedars and the needle cypresses pointing into the clear blue sky, out to the tranquil view of the Mediterranean whose color had once made Johnny Leconte redefine the word "azure."

Scott and Julie had been found frightened but unharmed, locked in the trunk of Brad's car, though Mahoney had no doubt he would have killed them, too. Brad would have wanted no witnesses.

Bea—or Marie-Laure, as they must now learn to call her—had her head wrapped once more in bandages, and she said wryly she was beginning to like the shaved-head look. She was badly cut and bruised, but it was nothing compared with the relief in her heart, now that she knew who she was and the fear was finally gone.

She was just glad she didn't have the stiff white plastic collar that Poochie had to wear to stop him from scratching the row of stitches on the back of his own poor shaved head. He was lying happily at her feet, sated with as much steak as a dog could eat. And Nick was holding her hand as she told them the story of what happened to her that day at Diamond Head and how Brad had caught up with her at the San Francisco airport.

"It's all over now," Phyl said comfortingly as they watched the children racing joyously across the lawn to the pool. "You have to learn to forget, to get on with your life."

Marie-Laure smiled at her affectionately. "It's thanks to all of you I'm still alive. And I intend to stay that way." She glanced around at her home, at her children, her man, her friends. "After all," she said, "I've got a lot to live for."

Phyl leaned back against the cushions. Her eyes were still swollen from the tears she had shed, and she looked pale and exhausted.

"You could use a touch of that red lipstick," Mahoney said with a grin, pulling a chair companionably next to her and pouring himself a glass of lemonade.

She glared at him, but he thought it was a weak glare, none of her usual flashing-blue-eyed stuff.

"The U.S. cavalry to the rescue," she said sarcastically. "Just a bit too late."

"Yeah. Even the Concorde wasn't fast enough. And they haven't yet found a way to beam us over, like Captain Kirk. But the FBI and Interpol have those magic computers that keep us all in touch. So the cavalry did get there in time after all." He threw her a serious glance and added softly, "Thank God."

"But how did you find out it was Brad?"

"Two and two. I should have caught it earlier, when I heard Hawaii mentioned. A private plane piloted by Brad Kane came in from Hawaii that night." He shrugged. "I should have known."

"No man is infallible," Phyl said gently, not wanting him to feel guilty.

"And no woman," he replied, meeting her eyes. "Maybe you should remember that."

He held her eyes for a long moment. She knew he meant what had happened to her baby, to Marie-Laure, to Brad. She could not be all things to all people anymore. She was not perfect. She just had to be Phyl Forster, a woman doing the best job she could. And getting on with her own life.

Mahoney leaned over and whispered in her ear, "Guess what?"

She leaned back and looked at him. "What?"

"I've made a reservation tonight at the Moulin de Mougins. Remember, I promised one day I'd take you there—see if their chicken is as good as mine?"

She put her head back and laughed, and then she kissed him. It was a happy kiss. "Mr. Long Shot," she said, remembering.

His eyes crinkled at the corners as he gave her that wide, mocking grin.

"That's me," he agreed, taking her hand and kissing her back.